Praise for Heather Skyler's
The Perfect Age

"Skillful, sensitive . . . traces the twin trajectories of a mother aching for change and her budding teenage daughter."

—*Elle*

"Effortlessly graceful . . . astute."

—Marisa Silver, *New York Times* bestselling author
of *Mary Coin*

"A gorgeous debut."

—Ann Hood, bestselling author of *The Obituary Writer*
and *The Red Thread*

"A lovely, winning novel, full of moments of startling emotional truth."

—Jessica Shattuck, author of *The Hazards of Good Breeding*

"Sultry, reflective . . . perfectly captures the languid heat of long Las Vegas summers and the irresistible temptations of love at any age."

—*Publishers Weekly*

"[A] beautifully wrought coming-of-age story . . . rich, smart, and nuanced . . . brutally realistic and starkly honest."

—*Library Journal*

VEGAS

GIRLS

Also by Heather Skyler
The Perfect Age

VEGAS GIRLS

A novel

heather skyler

Skyhorse Publishing

First Edition

This is a work of fiction. Names, places, characters, and incidents are either the products of the author's imagination or used fictitiously.

Skyhorse Publishing books may be purchased in bulk at special discounts for sales promotion, corporate gifts, fund-raising, or educational purposes. Special editions can also be created to specifications. For details, contact the Special Sales Department, Skyhorse Publishing, 307 West 36th Street, 11th Floor, New York, NY 10018 or info@skyhorsepublishing.com.

Skyhorse® and Skyhorse Publishing® are registered trademarks of Skyhorse Publishing, Inc.®, a Delaware corporation.

Visit our website at www.skyhorsepublishing.com.

10 9 8 7 6 5 4 3 2 1

Library of Congress Cataloging-in-Publication Data

Names: Skyler, Heather, author.
Title: Vegas girls : a novel / Heather Skyler.
Description: First edition. | New York : Skyhorse Publishing, 2016.
Identifiers: LCCN 2016015717 (print) | LCCN 2016029530 (ebook) | ISBN 9781510710832 (hardback) | ISBN 9781510710856 (ebook)
Subjects: LCSH: Female friendship--Fiction. | Secrets--Fiction. | Families--Fiction. | BISAC: FICTION / Literary. | FICTION / Contemporary Women. | FICTION / Family Life. | GSAFD: Bildungsromans.
Classification: LCC PS3619.K95 V44 2016 (print) | LCC PS3619.K95 (ebook) | DDC 813/.6--dc23
LC record available at https://lccn.loc.gov/2016015717

Cover design by Laura Klynstra

Printed in the United States of America

For the three most important women in my life: my mother, Juliet; my sister, Jennifer; and my daughter, Lux.

The past beats inside me like a second heart.
　　　　　　　　　　　　—*The Sea*, John Banville

MONDAY

IVY

Her first instinct was to try and hide. She was at one end of the frozen foods aisle, right by the ice cream, and Jeremy was down at the other end, peering into a freezer with a washed-out blonde in a long, flowing skirt clinging to his arm.

Ivy's son, Lucas, was sitting in the front of her cart, chewing on a piece of torn-off French bread, happy for the moment, but who knew how long that would last. She pulled a gallon of chocolate out of the freezer, plunked it into the cart, then began to make her escape when she heard his voice behind her.

"Holy shit. Is that Ivy Jacobsen?"

She turned, and Jeremy and the blonde were standing in front of her. He was smiling, but the blonde looked out of it, her eyes watery and slightly bloodshot, stoned. He hadn't changed that much since she'd seen him last, over ten years ago now at least. His black hair was still spiky from his days of trying to be a punk rocker, and while she was happy to note that he no longer wore his customary black eyeliner, his eyes still gleamed a bright, cracked-glass green. His body was as lean and wiry as it had always been, and he wore his same uniform of black T-shirt and skinny black jeans. A silver chain around his neck held a green pendant partially covered by his shirt, and Ivy couldn't decide whether it was a marijuana leaf or a turtle.

"Hey Jeremy," she said, trying to sound surprised and pleased. "Wow, what are you doing here?"

"Um, I live here. Remember?" He laughed. "You're the one who moved away."

"Right, of course. I meant on this side of town."

"Slumming," he said, then both he and the woman beside him laughed. "Taking in the lame part of town."

"That's for sure," the woman added in a low, smoky voice.

It's all lame, Ivy thought, but said, "We moved back to Las Vegas a year ago. Frank's mom was dying." She nodded grimly, then added, "She's dead now." Her words floated out and hung over the head of her child, making her feel like a crass, terrible mother. This was her son's grandmother she was talking about. The good one.

"Sorry to hear that, about Frank's mom," Jeremy said.

His tone was sincere, gentle, and Ivy recalled with sudden clarity the kindness he had often shown her, the tender way he'd cradled her in the old blue chair after her mother ran away. The peanut butter cookies he made for her with a chocolate kiss pressed into each one's center.

"So who is this little pudgeball?" he asked, leaning to peer into Lucas's face. He straightened up, then added, "This is Gretchen."

The woman nodded. "Pleasure," she said, in a mildly sarcastic tone.

Ivy introduced Lucas, who would be one this weekend, then tickled his chin to make him smile. "We call him Lucky," Ivy added, then immediately wished she hadn't. The revelation of her son's pet name struck her as too intimate.

"Lucky," Jeremy seemed to roll the name around in his mouth, tasting the flavor. "That's a really cool nickname." He smiled the crooked, flirtatious half-smile he'd cultivated in high school. "Though that sort of seems like something you should name a cat."

"Our cat's name is Ferdinand," she told him, hearing for the first time how ridiculous that sounded. A cat named after a bull from a children's book. A baby named after a cat.

"Still married to old what's his name?"

"Yep," Ivy said. "I guess my dad was wrong. It was smart of me to marry my high school sweetheart after all."

"I thought *I* was your high school sweetheart," Jeremy said, leaning closer.

She laughed again and glanced at Lucky, then Gretchen. Neither one appeared to be paying attention to this conversation. "Yeah," she agreed. "I guess you were."

He held her gaze for a moment, then said, "I heard you were working for a big drug company or something."

"Oh, I was in sales at Elysian for about five years or so. I just quit to stay home with Lucky."

"Selling drugs." He smiled again. "Did I make it on your resume as a mentor or something?"

She frowned. "Very funny."

"Hey," Gretchen said as she tugged at Jeremy's arm. "Let's get out of here. I'm starved."

"Okay," he said, glancing down at her as if he'd forgotten she was there. "Motherhood suits you," he told Ivy. "You look great." He reached into his back pocket, then pressed a card into her hand. "Keep in touch," he said.

"Thanks," she said, sliding the card into her back pocket without a look, and watched as they turned and walked away, back down the frozen foods aisle, Jeremy swinging the empty red basket beside him.

Back home, Ivy warmed up some brown rice mush for Lucky, then made a cheese sandwich for herself, feeling jangled and off-kilter from her run-in with Jeremy. Every day, something here reminded her of her old life, the one she'd left almost twenty years ago when she moved to Wisconsin to go to school. Usually it was only something small: the sight of a bright pink oleander bush, the dry smell of creosote, a locust shell clinging to the mulberry tree out front. She realized that despite having been back in Las Vegas for a year now, this was the first time she'd run into an actual person from her old life.

She had agreed to move back here only if they could live as far away from her former neighborhood as possible. She never wanted to see that old apartment building again, never wanted to drive past the Charleston Mall, now called something else, never wanted to eat at El Burrito, never wanted to hang out in Jaycee Park, never wanted to risk running into her mother, though who knew where she was living now—maybe as far away as Paris.

Despite the fact that they were only renting this house, the move now felt permanent. Frank had been offered a job he loved, principal of Grant Elementary School, and now that Frank's mother was dead, Frank's father would be bereft without them.

This was how Ivy found herself in a part of Las Vegas called Anthem where every house was new and looked exactly the same: stucco, red tile roof, swimming pool, cactus garden, palm trees. Frank loved all of it: the warm weather, the pool, the nearby mountains, the lizards and snakes and wide streets. It was definitely a "nice" neighborhood for Lucky, Ivy had to agree, but it was sterile, lifeless.

Through the window over the sink she could see a mourning dove sitting on the branch of the acacia tree. She considered picking up Lucky and carrying him to the window to see the bird—this is something she would typically do—but she couldn't summon the energy.

After lunch and cleaning up the dishes in the sink, Ivy remembered the card Jeremy had given her and took it out of her back pocket, staining it with warm water and soap. Black gothic letters in the center of the sky blue card read: JEREMY BURNHAM, CATERER. Beneath that there was a phone number, email, and website.

Frank had tried to convince her to hire a caterer for Lucky's birthday party since the guest list—mostly adults with a few toddlers and infants thrown in—was nearing fifty already. She had argued against the expense, pointing to her own skills in the kitchen plus the fact that people mostly just want cake and booze at parties.

But now, holding the card in her damp hands, she considered the idea.

She imagined Jeremy walking through the sliding glass doors carrying a tray of food, sitting down in the hot sun to pass out his peanut butter chocolate kiss cookies. He would look out of place in his black outfit. She would feel uncomfortable around him in her bathing suit. Frank would interject some sort of snide comment about the food, or Jeremy's clothes or demeanor, anything that offered the opportunity for mild, sideways ridicule.

No, it would be a bad idea to invite an ex-boyfriend back into her life, to invite a person who'd caused her so much trouble and heartache. Jeremy had always been able to persuade her to do things against her essential nature, and she could feel his tug now, even from the small blue rectangle in her hands. She shook her head and set the card on the small shelf above the kitchen sink, unwilling to put it in the garbage can where it belonged. She could show it to Jane later; that was reason enough to keep it. They could laugh together about the idea of him catering a kid's birthday party. What would he make? Mini pot brownies? Tiny shot glasses of rum?

JANE

It began to snow. Bluish-white flakes as big as moths landed on the new grass of the backyard, then disappeared. Jane watched through the kitchen window with disbelief. She'd been planning to wear sandals on the plane.

In the living room she could hear Rocky and Fern trying to wake Adam to say good-bye. She should go and say her good-byes too, but the snow held her, its strangeness this late in the year unsettling, somehow sinister. A robin hopped out from beneath the redbud tree and looked up at the sky, then spread its wings and lifted into the air.

In the living room, Jane found her children hovering over their father's sleeping form. The two of them looked like urchins with their straggly hair and smudged, puffy coats. Fern's purple tights held in her chunky, child's legs like sausage casings. Jane thought she had combed their hair, and she had definitely washed their coats just last week, but their grubbiness persisted.

Adam stirred beneath their gaze but didn't wake, so Jane moved to shake his shoulder. His skin was pale from the long winter, and the shadow of beard on his chin only served to emphasize his handsomeness, which annoyed her.

This morning in the mirror her own face had been drawn and tired, the pink stripe she'd added to her blonde hair after getting fired last week an obvious mistake. Its brightness broadcast her neediness, her desire to live another life.

"Adam," she said in her normal voice, shaking his shoulder again. "The kids want to kiss you good-bye."

He stirred then and opened his eyes, which were blue and surprisingly clear despite his bad habits, namely, drinking too much and sleeping too little. He smiled and reached for Fern, who was closer, then pulled her against him in a hug. Rocky perched on the futon beside him, and was given the second hug. "Your turn, Mom," Rocky said, when the kids were both standing again.

She bent to kiss her husband on the cheek, but he reeked of beer, and she could only bring herself to kiss the air beside him. He gave her a wry smile, and she shrugged, then said, "See you in a week, I guess."

Jane worried that the flight would be canceled, but it wasn't even delayed, and she wondered if she'd imagined the snow, but there it was when she leaned to push up the rigid shade, still moving past the plane's window as they waited for takeoff.

Their seats were near the back of the plane. Jane had an aisle, Rocky was beside her in the middle seat, and Fern was flying free of charge on Jane's lap. The cutoff for flying on a grown-up's lap was age two, but Jane had lied about Fern, who had turned three several months ago but was small for her age, in order to save money. It looked as if they might luck out and the window seat would be vacant, but right before the doors closed, a tall, middle-aged man with thinning gold hair scooted in beside them.

Jane nodded hello and the man nodded back, then looked at Rocky who was making soft explosion sounds. Up close she saw the man was younger than she'd thought, perhaps closer to her own age, thirty-six.

"I didn't expect to see any kids on this flight," the man said in a jovial way.

"Why is that?" Jane asked.

"Well, Las Vegas," he shrugged and raised his palms. "Not much of a family destination, is it?" His voice was crisp, with the jauntiness of a Brit's but he didn't have a trace of accent as far as she could tell.

"I'm from there," she said, trying to sound conversational rather than irritated. "Don't worry, you won't run into us at the craps tables."

He smiled slightly, and she saw that he had terrible teeth. For some reason this cheered her. "Craps isn't my game either," he said. "Just going for a friend's bachelor party. Which isn't really my thing either. But he's a friend." The man shrugged again, then buckled himself in and pulled a magazine out of his briefcase. Jane tried to see the cover, wanting to know what he was reading, thinking it would tell her something essential about his personality, but he held it on his lap in such a way that it was impossible.

As the plane rose into the air at last, Jane felt a lessening of the pressure in her chest: they'd made it. The plane lifted, floating past the snow, tunneling through the heavy clouds, until finally they emerged into yellow sunshine. It came through the window, warm and reassuring as a hand on her shoulder. It occurred to her that she hadn't felt the sun on her face like this in many days, and she looked forward to the week ahead. She would spend as much time as possible lying beside Ivy's pool, absorbing enough heat and light into her skin to slough away this past winter, which still clung to her like a living creature, something damp and cold with a haze of gray fur.

"I'm hungry," Fern told her, so Jane retrieved a bag of goldfish crackers from her bag and handed them over. Fern pushed it away with a frown, so Jane dug out the chocolate chip cookies and handed her two, hoping the rush of sugar would put her to sleep in an hour.

An elderly woman wearing giant glasses sat across the aisle, and she leaned close to Fern now and said, "Isn't that a yummy breakfast?"

Jane nodded, offering the old woman a wan smile. Her voice was sugary, but Jane could tell her words were meant to judge. That was a Wisconsin specialty, saying things to kids that were meant to be a jab at the parents. Jane could still remember carrying Rocky in the Baby Bjorn around the Art Fair on the Square on a humid summer day, and the older woman who had leaned into his face and said, "Oh, you look so hot in there." The woman never met Jane's gaze, just talked to the baby on her chest, then walked away.

Maybe she was being unfair, calling it a Wisconsin specialty. Perhaps old women everywhere offered up criticism in this way. She suspected, however, that if she still lived in Las Vegas no one would ever speak directly to her babies. And would this be any better?

She could hear the couple in the row in front of her talking softly. "Wait until we get to the hotel," a woman's voice said.

"I *can't.*"

"Yes, you can," she said firmly, though her words were followed by a laugh.

Jane imagined they might be on their honeymoon, and an image of her own honeymoon, spent in a top floor of the Flamingo hotel flashed through her: She stood undressed in front of the floor-to-ceiling window, Adam behind her, holding on to her hips. Las Vegas had been a dusky pink in the early morning light, soft and lovely in a way it never was from a regular vantage point during an ordinary time of day. Her life, in that moment, had felt uncomplicated, gauzy with love.

Yesterday afternoon she and Adam had fought while the children were downstairs, most likely listening to their parents' tense voices. Adam had promised the kids a trip to the children's museum downtown, then changed his mind in the morning, explaining he was tired from such a long week.

"You can't do that to the kids," Jane said, calmly at first. "You got them all excited, then pulled the plug."

"People change their minds. They need to learn that."

"Then don't promise them anything!" Her voice rose. "It makes you look like an asshole."

"Well, maybe I am an asshole and they need to learn that, too!"

"I think they already have!"

In the end, Jane had driven the kids to the museum, her body tight with anger, and pulled them through the exhibits. Adam showed up half an hour later when they were in the room with the giant set of teeth and slipped his arms around Jane from behind, startling her. They hadn't touched in weeks.

Jane was drifting toward sleep now, the plane riding smoothly through blue sky, when an abrupt dip in the air jolted her. She opened her eyes and quickly touched Rocky's shoulder, Fern's knee. The plane bumped again and Rocky said, "Fun," and looked up at her with a grin, his single dimple denting a cheek. Fern started to cry.

Jane pulled her close and closed the tray table. She stroked her hair and murmured soothing words into the top of her warm head. "This is just called turbulence, sweetie. No big deal. Everything's fine."

Fern howled louder, and Jane instinctively covered her daughter's mouth with her hand, then realized that looked a bit brutish on her part and took it away.

The man beside them sighed loudly, with obvious disgust.

"Sorry," Jane said to him, then turned back to Fern and whispered fiercely, "Stop crying. Everything's fine."

The fasten seat belt sign dinged on and Jane told Rocky to put up his tray table, but he was right in the middle of a drawing and started to protest loudly. "I'm not done yet, Mom. One more minute!" He leaned over and began to draw furiously, pressing the crayon so hard against the paper that it snapped. He looked at the broken crayon in his hand, then began to cry too.

"Rocky, honey, it's fine. There are more crayons."

"No more black ones," he sobbed.

The plane dipped again, causing Fern's cries to grow in intensity. Rocky threw his crayon on the ground, crossed his arms, and continued his heartbreaking boy's wail.

"For God's sake," huffed the man.

"Sorry," Jane said again but gave him a look of pure hatred.

He absorbed the look, then pushed the button for the steward-ess. "I think I'll tell her that I need to move so you can purchase this seat for your daughter."

"My daughter is fine right here."

"She should have her own seat, don't you think? She's awfully big to sit on your lap for the entire flight." He smiled meanly. "I have kids, you know. I understand the airline's rules."

"Look," Jane said, trying to make her voice softer and appealing, but hearing the hardness that she couldn't shake from her words. "I just lost my job. Please, don't do this to me."

There was a tap on her shoulder and Jane turned, preparing herself for the bland face of the stewardess. But it was the old lady reaching over from across the aisle. "Let me take her for you, dear," she said. "I have a little practice with this."

Without a moment of consideration, Jane handed her daughter across the aisle. Jane expected Fern to resist this stranger, almost hoped she would, but her daughter snuggled into the larger wom-an's lap right away and within five seconds had calmed down and stopped crying.

Rocky was slowing down now, too. Jane handed him another cookie, and that stopped the tears as quickly as if she had turned off a faucet.

The stewardess appeared then at Jane's elbow and asked the man if he needed something. "I'm not supposed to be up right now," she added. "Because of the turbulence." As if to prove her point, the plane dipped again and she fell against Jane's seat, then righted herself.

"Sorry," the man told her, looking sternly at Jane. "The problem has been solved."

Jane returned his gaze, feeling a mixture of relief and hatred. She would not smile or thank him, no matter what, she told herself.

After a few long minutes of silence, the man cleared his throat and said, "I am actually sorry to hear about your job. What's your line of work?"

She couldn't believe he was trying to appease her now after having been so cruel, but she couldn't bring herself to give a stranger the silent treatment, so she shrugged with as much nonchalance as she could muster, then said, "I was a reporter. At the *Wisconsin Times.*"

He nodded. "Lots of layoffs there I hear."

"Yep," Jane said, wanting suddenly to tell him that she had not merely been laid off, but fired for a single, ridiculous mistake, but this was a secret she'd kept from everyone, even Ivy, so she said nothing.

He nodded again, then picked up his magazine, which Jane now saw was *Psychology Today*. She couldn't decide if this made him interesting or creepy.

The fasten seat belt light blinked off and the captain announced that they were free to move about the cabin. The crisis had passed; still, Jane felt a thread of unease run through her.

She looked over at Fern and saw she had fallen sound asleep against the woman's chest. Jane felt a pulse of jealousy. That was one of her favorite parts of being a parent: holding a sleeping child on her lap. "Thank you," Jane said to the woman.

"My pleasure, dear," she said.

She looked across the woman toward the window, a brilliant pane of blue sky. They were likely close to Denver by now, where they would stop for an hour but not change planes. Jane wished she had booked the window seat. She wanted to see the silvery grid of the city beneath her, the white tops of the Rockies. Later, she would watch for the first signs of desert below the plane, recalling the bare mountains near Nevada that looked like the bumpy knuckles of a giant. Then the blue surprise of Lake Mead and the pale, reddish sand. Finally, the white and aluminum glimmer of casinos lined up in a row.

Rocky had finished his picture and leaned against her, asleep in an instant. Jane freed her arm and put it around his shoulder, pulling him closer. She smoothed his shaggy blond hair out of his eyes and rubbed his back through his sweatshirt.

"So what was it like," the man beside her asked, "growing up in Las Vegas?"

She shrugged. "Ordinary." This was a question she'd been asked hundreds of times, and she always answered that it was ordinary.

He shook his head. "I don't buy it. C'mon, I really want to know."

"It was hot," she told him, as if reading from a script. "The days it rained—about four a year—were the ones we looked forward to."

"I can see that," he nodded. "What else?"

"I don't know. It was normal to me." She tried to think of things an outsider would like to hear. "I ate a lot of ninety-nine-cent breakfasts in high school with my friends. I saw a lot of people walking around in wedding gowns. I pulled my first slot machine when I was twelve, on a dare."

He smiled, appearing satisfied, and turned back to his magazine. She, however, was now dissatisfied. I learned about disappointment there, she could have told him. I learned to live outside of my life, as if I were watching a movie.

But she could have also said that she learned about joy. About love and friendship and sex—the same things people learned growing up anywhere.

The drink cart pulled up beside her, and Jane ordered two glasses of orange juice for the kids when they woke up, then quickly asked for a glass of red wine for herself, despite the fact that she shouldn't spend the extra money. She expected the man beside her to make a snide comment since it was still morning after all, but he said nothing, just ordered a Diet Coke and went back to reading.

Jane sipped her wine, feeling the warmth of it slide through her. The price of the wine was worth it, she decided, for this pocket of calm. Her children continued to sleep, and she thought about how strange it was that she'd arrived at this moment: she was a grown woman with two kids of her own, leaving her husband, flying home.

JEREMY

He had been trying to casually bump into Ivy for weeks, lurking around the new part of town where he heard she'd moved, but now that it had actually happened, he felt disappointed. He had imagined a long embrace, a shared look, a promise of future meet-ups. There had not been enough time, he decided, to get under her skin and remind her why she should want to be with him again, after all these years apart.

In the car beside him, Gretchen smoked a cigarette and fiddled with the radio, stopping on a commercial for dog food, then honing in on a classic rock station playing the Stones. Jeremy punched the button to shut off the sound and Gretchen gave him a wounded look. "What the fuck?" she said.

The curse word hit him in the gut. He couldn't recall Ivy ever uttering a swear word. "I need some peace and quiet," he told her. "My head hurts."

"Oh," she said, and crossed her legs beneath the long skirt. "Sorry."

His head did hurt, he realized, and his stomach was churning with regret, though this regret was useless, he knew. Ivy had married Frank a long time ago, and now she had a baby, too, and she would never be his again. He thought he might be able to accept that if they could be friends.

At Gretchen's apartment on Charleston, he fixed a goat cheese and red pepper frittata, then sautéed a side of asparagus, and they sat eating lunch together on the floor beside the coffee table. When the plates were cleared and washed, Jeremy reached under Gretchen's long skirt and pulled off her black underwear, then they had sex on the green couch, her skirt billowing around their legs like a flowered sail. With his eyes closed, Jeremy tried to pretend the woman beneath him was Ivy, but it was no good. It had been too long for him to remember what Ivy felt like, though he did recall the slightly peppery scent of her skin in summer.

Gretchen's neck smelled of coconuts, and he bit her shoulder to see what she would do, wanting her to get angry with him. Instead, she yelped, then laughed. The laugh reminded him a little bit of why he liked her, and they finished, then lay together on the scratchy couch, listening to the traffic outside without speaking.

After Gretchen left for work, Jeremy drove home and prepped for his party at six. It was for a small group out in Henderson, a book club celebrating a two-year anniversary, which struck him as odd, but he was happy for the work. He made a pan of pork tamales, a bowl of rice and beans, and fresh guacamole and pico de gallo. He was becoming known for his Mexican dishes, though he was also proficient in French and Italian cuisine. His grandfather on his mother's side had been born in Guadalajara, and Jeremy always made sure to mention this when he catered a Mexican meal. Of course, he made up other relatives who were either French or Italian as necessary, but the grandfather was actually a real person who still lived in Texas with his aunt Pat.

He arrived early at the condo in Henderson and could tell the woman didn't know who he was when she opened the door. She had hired him over the phone based on a recommendation from a friend, and it was likely she hadn't expected a man who looked like he belonged in a punk band instead of in the kitchen.

"I'm Jeremy," he said quickly, holding out his hand. "The caterer."

She smiled, and Jeremy smiled too, then he was inside assessing the space and asking when she wanted the dishes to come out. The woman, Virginia, was older, maybe late forties, but she had an excellent figure and Jeremy couldn't help but admire the curve of her ass beneath her jeans. He had her test the guacamole before the guests arrived, and she made a noise of appreciation that had the quality of a sexual moan. It was easy for him to imagine her in bed, and this imagining lightened the feeling of pressure he'd had in his chest ever since Gretchen had left him alone and gone to work.

The other women began arriving for the book club, and Jeremy got busy setting up the table in the dining room and heating the oven. He blended margaritas and salted the edges of the blue glasses Virginia had set out for drinks. There were six women and they gathered in a circle around the coffee table, three on the couch and three in chairs. Jeremy watched them through the opening over the counter as he made drinks.

One woman was younger than the rest and she looked like she'd been crying. Her hair was cut short and shone blue-black in the light from the window. Her heart-shaped face was familiar, though Jeremy didn't think he actually knew her; he'd just seen her somewhere around town before. She was not pretty exactly, but memorable, with a vibrating presence that sent sparks out into the room. It was her eyes, he decided, their small, darting vitality and black sheen, the arched brows above them as perfectly drawn as an old-timey movie star's.

Virginia put a protective arm around the woman and drew her back to the kitchen, where Jeremy pretended to be busy with the drinks while they murmured together in the corner. When they grew quiet, he turned and handed each woman a margarita, which brought the smiles he'd hoped for.

While the tamales were heating up, he washed his hands in the sink and looked out the window onto the sloping lawn and broad elm trees. Despite the nearby presence of other condos, the world was still, and Jeremy could almost imagine he was out in the country. His own apartment was near downtown, and the noise from the street below and the kids above him was at times unbearable. Gretchen's apartment wasn't much better, but he stayed there many nights now anyway, desiring the presence of her thin form splayed out in bed beside him. They had been dating for three months, and before that he'd had a surprisingly long dry spell, which had worried him to the point that he could now imagine asking Gretchen to move in with him just so he wouldn't have to go through so many nights by himself ever again. He had been married, once, for two years. The first year and a half had been like a dream, but the last six months had been the worst of his life.

The younger, red-eyed woman—he'd heard them call her Kristina—came into the kitchen and asked for another margarita. He made one on the rocks at her request, and she leaned against the counter waiting. A heated discussion rose up from the other room, but it made no sense to Jeremy. He supposed this was because he hadn't read the book they were arguing about, but it was also because these women seemed to exist on a different plane than he did, in a separate, more organized world that didn't include noisy streets, or sex on scratchy green couches, or old girlfriends you'd talked into selling pot for you in high school.

"Here you go," he said, handing over the fresh drink. He wished he could have one too, but knew that would be bad form on a job. In the old days he would have snuck half a dozen drinks in a two-hour period, then burned his hand on the oven or fallen over a kink in the carpet while holding a tray of fajitas. Both of those things had happened at the first restaurant he'd worked in after high school, but he was wiser now, an entrepreneur making a name for himself around town.

"Do you have a kid at Grant?" the woman asked him. "You look familiar."

He shook his head. "No kids."

"Did you go to Chaparral?"

He shook his head again. "Vegas High."

"Hmmm," she mused, studying him.

It was then that he remembered her. She'd been a waitress at that first restaurant, years ago, a witness to his bad behavior. "I have a familiar face," he said, wanting now to hurry her out of the kitchen. "Lots of people think they know me from somewhere." He smiled but was nervous, thinking her memory might somehow cost him this job. *Oh, you're the guy who fucked everyone over, the guy who stole all the cooks' tips your last night, right?* He imagined her revealing these bad deeds to Virginia, and word spreading everywhere about what a jerk he'd once been. No one would care that he was no longer such a bad guy. It was only his past that would matter to them.

She shrugged and thanked him for the drink, then returned to her seat on the couch. Relief moved through him as he removed the tamales from the oven and arranged them on a serving tray.

He brought out the tamales and cleared the almost empty bowl of tortilla chips, but left the pico de gallo and guacamole. Virginia hurried over from the couch and asked him to make another round of drinks, then looked at the food and said, "It looks wonderful. I can't wait."

These words lit a small light in the base of Jeremy's neck, creating a warmth that carried him back to the kitchen and eased his worry about the waitress from his past life. He'd worked in that dump—what was it called again? The Crescent?—over sixteen years ago now, and even if Kristina did finally recall who he was, it could no longer hurt him. Lots of people did bad things when they were young, then reformed. It was an old story.

Making this second batch of drinks, he risked a glance at Kristina. She'd had long hair back then and the same magnetic presence. Her boyfriend picked her up in the bar most nights after work, looking like he'd just walked off Wall Street in a neat suit, his dark hair slicked back. People gossiped that she would marry him and be rich, then never have to waitress again. They had also gossiped about the weird outfits he made her wear in the bedroom— one was an elf costume; he remembered that—but Jeremy imagined that little if any of that talk had been true.

Ivy had been long gone by then, off to Wisconsin with Frank to go to college. He could remember calling her once, drunk, from the bar of The Crescent, and the way she had listened to him patiently even though it was obvious he was in bad shape and not making much sense. He had asked her to come back—he could remember that moment clearly—and the pause over the line, then the catch in her voice when she told him that wasn't possible. At that point, she hadn't yet married Frank, and Jeremy realized much later that he should have flown out there to see her in person, while she still had that catch in her throat. But he had been busy making a mess of his life and then he had met his wife, Stacy, at a party out in the desert, and he had forgotten all about Ivy for a long while.

Virginia came into the kitchen and helped him carry out the drinks, then followed him back and said, "Can you stay for a while? A few of my friends want to book you for things and they have some questions."

"Oh, sure," he said, wiping his hands on the apron around his waist. There was a promise hidden in her words, but he wasn't sure if it was just about the extra work, or if there would be something else expected after everyone left. He couldn't really fuck this woman, could he? He was with Gretchen now, and he had just found Ivy again, and he didn't even know this person.

She touched his shoulder. "Okay. And feel free to make yourself a drink."

He did make himself a margarita, and he sipped at it as he waited for the women to finish eating, then he cleared away the plates and serving pans and washed them all by hand in the sink, looking out at that green lawn. He was not expected to wash this woman's dishes, only what he had brought himself, but the warm water over his hands was soothing, and the view of that lawn in the slanting orange light was something he could watch all day. He could hear laughter from the other room now. Everyone was loosened up from the alcohol, and their bellies were full of his good food. This was the part of the job he liked best: feeding people something that brought them happiness. He had not made many people happy over the years, but now he was able to do that. His food could do that.

Later, driving home through the dark streets, he tried to remember that feeling he'd had at the sink, of doing good, instead of Virginia's soft mouth against his neck in the hallway, his hands up under her shirt and down the back of her jeans before his head cleared and he politely refused her. She had given up easily, but he did worry she would bad-mouth him now. He would deserve it, he guessed, for having let things go as far as they did, for leading her on.

The worst part of the night, however, had come before that. After talking to several of the women about parties they were having or planning to have, he had gone to gather his things in the kitchen, then turned to find Kristina watching him with a creased brow and narrowed eyes. "I remember you now," she said in a soft voice, no longer friendly. "I do remember you."

IVY

"I think you should give him a call," Frank said, sipping his gin and tonic. "What the hell? It will make the party more interesting, that's for sure."

Jane nodded. "Yes, definitely more interesting."

"Plus you need some help," Frank said. "It's a sign that you ran into him. Call him. Book it."

The three of them were sitting around the pool drinking in the moonlight. Jane's kids and Lucky were asleep. The night was balmy, perfect. Jane was stretched out on a deck chair. Frank sat on the pool's edge nearby, swinging his legs through the water. Ivy was sprawled out in a chair beside Jane, drink cradled in her lap.

This was not the way Ivy had imagined the conversation going when she brought out Jeremy's card, brandishing it in the air before her friend and husband. There had been wine with dinner. Two drinks since then. She had almost fallen into the pool after swinging the card around over her head, and when she sank down into the deck chair the sky spun very slightly above her.

As she looked up at the sky now it seemed to widen, then narrowed to the white, pocked half-moon, then widened again to include the only two stars she could find. "But I thought you hated him," she said to Frank.

"No," he shook his head. "Water under the bridge."

"You used to call him a loser."

Her husband shrugged. "He was kind of a loser."

"I always sort of liked him," said Jane.

"But he was a loser, admit it," Frank said.

"Maybe," Jane agreed.

"He was also kind and talented and smart," Ivy said, frowning at Jane. What was she doing taking Frank's side?

"Okay, take it easy," Frank said, smiling. "That's enough praise."

Jane laughed. "Remember that time he talked us into skipping school and going to the hot springs? We couldn't get the cooler down that sort of cliff thing, so Ramona rigged up a rope and Jeremy waited at the bottom with Kevin—is that who I brought?—and the cooler came loose and crashed, and all the Cokes inside it exploded?"

"But the rum bottle didn't break," Ivy said.

"I know, it was some kind of miracle," Jane said.

"A fucking act of God," Frank smirked. "Meanwhile, I was busy learning calculus so I could get into a good school and then get a good job so I could win you in the end."

Ivy laughed. "Is that what you were doing?" She watched her husband smile over at her. Unlike Jeremy, his appearance had changed a great deal since she began dating him eighteen years ago during their senior year of high school. His hair, once lush and wavy, curling over his forehead and down to the collar of his shirt, had thinned and was now cut short, befitting his position of authority as a principal. His jaw had softened a bit as had his stomach, and he'd long ago traded his faded-out T-shirts with ironic sayings for striped polos and khakis.

Despite these changes, it was obvious women still liked him. The secretary at school greeted him with a certain smile. Waitresses always straightened up in his presence, tried to hold his gaze even when Ivy was sitting right across from him.

"So you think Ramona is going to show?" Jane asked. "I hope so. I haven't seen her since Fern was born."

"I don't know. She reminded me that she hasn't set foot in this town since high school. I guess I didn't realize that."

"Well, her mother made it pretty clear she didn't want her around," Jane said.

"But she's been dead for five years now, hasn't she?"

"Six," Jane corrected.

"She did say she had a great present for Lucky," Ivy said.

"I bet she sticks it in the mail and writes a funny note," Jane said.

"No, she'll show," offered Frank. "She'll want to see Lucky."

"You should have seen her with him in LA," Ivy said. "He was only two months old then, and she wouldn't set him down except to go to the bathroom or when I had to nurse him. She even held him on her shoulder during meals."

"She should have a kid," Frank said.

"Another one, you mean," Jane reminded him.

"How old would her son be now?"

"Nineteen," Ivy said. "His birthday's this week sometime. I remember it was almost the same as Lucky's. That would have been weird, if it had been the same day."

"Wow," Frank shook his head. "Can you imagine having a nineteen-year-old son?"

"We will one day," Ivy said.

"True."

The three of them were silent for a moment. Ivy tried to imagine Lucky eighteen years from now. Would he look like Frank had in high school? She thought he would look more like her because he resembled her now. She hoped her too-big eyes and wild hair would work better for him than it had for her. She had grown into the hair and eyes eventually, but it had taken a long time.

"Sometimes," Jane said, "I imagine leaving the kids and returning when they're twenty or even twenty-five. When they're grown. That seems like it will be the rewarding part, having grown-up kids who are out of all the bad and awkward phases and just beginning to appreciate their mom. We can meet for a cocktail, go out to dinner, talk about current events, books, movies. It will be great, I think. That part."

"I love this part," Ivy said.

Jane shrugged, and Ivy noticed again that her friend didn't look quite right. She was too thin and angular, thinking of something else even when they were talking.

Later, lying in bed next to Frank, Ivy whispered, so as not to wake Lucky several feet away in his crib, "I'm sort of worried about Jane."

"She seems good," Frank said.

She turned onto her side and saw her husband's profile etched against the dark. "Earlier, when Rocky was sitting on her lap after dinner, Jane looked like she wasn't listening to him at all. She was in a different world. And she usually doesn't drink as much as she did tonight. Also, she's too skinny, and what's with that pink stripe in her hair—is she in junior high?"

"I like the stripe."

"You would," she said and lightly pinched his leg.

"And maybe she's just tired from her trip. And we all drank a lot tonight."

"True," she agreed. "Why do you have to be so reasonable? Why can't you just let me worry?"

He turned on his side and faced her, though it was too dark in the room to make out his eyes. "Okay, go ahead and worry." He put a heavy hand on her hip and pulled her toward him. She turned onto her side, facing away, and they fitted their bodies into their customary position: spooned together, his hand cupping the soft skin of her stomach, knee matching knee. Later, they would separate and sleep on their backs, and later still Lucky would cry and she'd carry him to bed and set him between them, where he would nurse then flop onto his back, deeply asleep, and stretch out his arms as wide as he could, taking up more room than it seemed possible for a baby to occupy.

Ivy tried to recall the position she'd slept in with Jeremy, in her single bed in that depressing bedroom all those years ago. After her father had gone out for the night, Ivy would sneak Jeremy in and they would have sex on her small bed, then curl into each other and sleep until the sound of her father coming in late and bumping into things woke them.

They had faced each other in sleep, his head tucked just beneath hers, his warm breath on her chest and throat. His arms would be curled up, fists beneath his chin, and her free arm flung over his shoulder. Her knees had been bent into his smooth, white chest. Even though she had been the one home alone, her mother already gone, it had seemed as if she were protecting Jeremy, cradling him against her for comfort.

She had loved him then almost as if he were a child, wanting to keep him close and safe from whatever dangers he faced outside her door. Usually she loved him with just plain infatuation, with teenage passion and intensity, but during those nights her love had been different, tender and mature. She'd stroke his back, his spiky hair, murmur to him as he slid toward sleep. It was not clear to her how this dynamic had developed, or if she'd even noticed it at the time, but she had liked it. She remembered that. It had felt like a relief after the back-and-forth passion. It had felt like she was learning to be a grown-up.

Frank was close to sleep; she could tell by the way his breathing slowed and steadied, and she was almost there too when a long whimpering cry sounded nearby. Ivy was up on an elbow and swinging her legs over the side when Frank pulled her back down. "That wasn't our kid."

"Are you sure?" She padded over to the crib and peered down at Lucky, who was soundly asleep.

In the next second, they heard Jane's voice. "Shhh," her friend said. "It's okay, sweetie. Just a dream. Be quiet or you'll wake up Rocky."

Ivy resettled herself against Frank and listened closely but the voices were quieter now, a murmur coming through the bedroom door, which was slightly ajar. She wondered if she should get up and help Jane, then decided against it.

"Told you," Frank said and pulled her closer. She wondered how she could have possibly mistaken Fern's cry for Lucky's. This error struck her as a flaw, tiny now, just a tear in the fabric of her role as mother, but as she lay there listening to Frank breathe, she imagined the tiny tear growing wider. Maybe that was how it had begun for her own mother: first she didn't recognize her child's cry, then she didn't care whether she did or not, then she no longer even listened for it.

TUESDAY

JANE

When she woke at seven, the house was still quiet and her first thought was of Adam—or, rather, Adam's absence. It had been a long time since she'd woken up in a home that didn't also contain him. They hadn't slept in the same bed for the past two weeks, but his presence could still be felt from the moment she awoke until he left the house for the bar at three. She couldn't decide when he had begun to grate against her insides so that she could barely breathe. The simple act of brushing her teeth and going downstairs to make coffee in the morning had become an agonizing routine.

Downstairs, Adam would either be asleep, his body emanating a sort of primal heat through the French doors of the living room, or awake in his chair by the window listening to his headphones and eating a piece of toast.

She knew that part of his oppressiveness was brought on by her own guilt over what she'd done, but another part of it was just about him, about who he'd become during their eleven years of marriage.

Here at Ivy's house, despite the inkling of a hangover, Jane already felt lighter, and she got out of bed and stepped over Fern's sleeping form on the air mattress, then wandered out to the kitchen.

At the table, she found Rocky seated beside Ramona, both of them eating cornflakes. "You're here!" Jane said, and moved around the table to embrace Ramona, who rose and opened her arms. "I didn't even hear you come in."

"This kid let me in." She pointed an elbow to Rocky. "I could see him watching cartoons through the window, so I just knocked lightly and he heard me."

"You're not supposed to open the door without an adult nearby," Jane scolded.

He shrugged. "I could see who it was. I know her."

"You don't think he should have let me in?" Ramona asked.

"No, of course not, sorry."

Ramona smiled and sat back down to her bowl of cornflakes. Her skin was tan and her long black hair hung in her usual two braids halfway down her back. Her sky blue tank top had LONG BEACH MUSIC FESTIVAL printed on it in white cursive letters.

Jane started a pot of coffee. "We weren't sure you'd make it," she told her friend.

"I know," she said. "Me either."

"But she has a boyfriend named Nash, who told her she should go," Rocky said.

"He thought it would be a good thing for me. A healing thing." She smirked, then shrugged and ate another spoonful of cereal. "Rocky thinks Nash is smart."

Rocky nodded. "He is."

"But he has this goofy walk—more of a *strut* really—and I don't think it's going to work out," she told both of them.

Jane laughed. "A strut. That's not too bad."

"You haven't seen it."

"Musician?" Jane asked.

Ramona shook her head. "He has his own company, something to do with heating and cooling."

"Age?"

"Not sure."

"Sounds serious," Jane said, pouring herself a mug of coffee before the pot was finished brewing. The sizzling sound of hot liquid hitting the base of the coffeemaker jarred her, and she quickly slid the pot back into its space, then sat down between Ramona and Rocky.

Ramona shrugged. "He's very sweet. And he has these laugh lines around his eyes that sort of remind me of the rays of the sun."

"So he's old?" Jane asked.

"No." Ramona shook her head. "Weathered. He used to surf, I think. He's cute, trust me. Except for the strut."

Rocky laughed, then cleared his bowl and disappeared back into the family room.

"I like your hair," Ramona told her now.

"Thanks." She pulled on the stripe, then lifted the pink section of hair toward her eye for a better view. "It's fading now, so it looks better. It was hot pink at first, really fucking bright. You should have seen the face Ivy made when she saw it. She pretended to like it but I saw the look. You know which one I mean."

Ramona nodded. "Sure. I'm thinking I should chop mine," she said, pulling a braid around to the front and yanking at it. "I'm a little too old for braids."

Jane waved a hand dismissively. "You look great."

"You don't look so good."

"I drank too much last night, after Ivy and Frank went to bed I kept going. Big mistake."

She had gone inside the house with the two of them, put on her short red nightgown, and brushed her teeth. She had even gotten into bed beside the air mattress that held her two kids. Then Fern had cried out for her pillow and Jane had been required to lie down beside daughter until she fell asleep. Rocky slept beside his sister, already unfolded into a splayed-out and delicious-seeming slumber. She had felt resentful then for Fern's need to have her nearby. It was midnight and Jane considered herself off the clock. But of course a mother was never off the clock, especially with Fern, who was a light and troubled sleeper.

When Fern's breathing deepened and slowed, Jane had slunk carefully off the air mattress, as cautious as if she were leaving a crime scene, then wandered out to the kitchen and poured herself more gin with a little tonic. She downed that one quickly, then poured another and stepped back out onto the pool deck. Around three in the morning she woke up on the deck chair, still half blasted, under a sheet of moonlight so brilliant it hurt her eyes.

"I drank coffee all night playing at this club," Ramona said, "then couldn't sleep, of course, so decided to leave around three in the morning."

"Why were you drinking coffee?"

"To avoid drinking booze."

"Why?"

Ramona looked toward the window, then back at Jane. "Just trying to be healthier, you know? Also, I think I sing better with coffee, something about the warm liquid soothing my throat. I suppose decaf would do the same. Or tea. It didn't occur to me at the time."

"How's the new album coming together?" Jane asked, then immediately worried the question would be unwelcome.

"Okay. Good, I think. Slow. Eric and Sally had another baby so that set us back a bit."

Jane nodded. "Babies will do that."

Ramona rose and cleared her bowl to the sink just as Fern wandered in, looking sleepy and disoriented. She crawled onto Jane's lap, almost upsetting her coffee cup in the process, then Rocky appeared around the corner and draped his arms around her neck from behind, leaning his warm head onto her shoulder. "I want pancakes," he said.

"Me too," Fern added.

"Well look at this little beauty," Ramona sang, leaning in to kiss the top of Fern's head. "Remember me?"

Fern shook her head, and Rocky hit his sister's arm. "It's Ramona, dummy," he said.

"Go give her a hug," Jane suggested, but Fern shook her head and burrowed more deeply into Jane's lap.

"Later," Ramona suggested, then asked, "Can I go crash on your bed for a while? I'm burnt."

"Of course," Jane said, wishing she could return to her bed, but the day had begun and someone had to make breakfast for her children.

She sighed, then slid Fern off her lap, and extricated herself from Rocky's arms to search the cupboards for pancake mix. "Why don't you both go play while I do this," Jane suggested.

"No," Rocky said. "I want to help."

"Me too," Fern said.

She could feel her body contract. "No," she told them. "I can make them faster by myself."

"I want to help," Fern said. "Please please please, let me."

She didn't answer, just kept searching the cupboards. It occurred to her they didn't have pancake mix. Or even if they did, she could lie and say there wasn't any, that cereal would have to do, but then Rocky called out over her shoulder, "There it is, Mom. Right there, see it?"

She did see it. It was not the mix she typically used but something healthier with whole-wheat flour that required the addition of eggs, olive oil, and milk. She suspected her kids wouldn't like the pancakes created from this earthy mix, but she opened the box and got out a bowl, measuring cup, and frying pan.

Rocky did an excellent job of cracking in two eggs, and Fern was allowed to pour the mix, measured out by Jane, into the silver bowl. It was not as difficult as she had foreseen; still, their help felt like a burden. She wanted to do this by herself, to just get it done and serve it up, put this chore behind her. Something is wrong with me, Jane thought, watching Rocky stir the mix while Fern peered into the bowl. This is not oppressive, it is loving and sweet. This is my family.

Ivy wandered into the kitchen then with Lucky on her hip. "Look at you three little chefs," she said. "I hope there's enough in there for me."

"Yep," Rocky said. "We made a lot, right Mom?"

Jane nodded. "Enough for the whole household. Ramona's here," she said, and tilted her head toward the hallway. "Asleep in my room."

"Oh, good," Ivy said, a smile lighting her face. "I knew she'd make it."

"I want to pour the mix in the pan," Fern said.

"No," Jane told her. "Go play now. I'll tell you when they're ready."

"I'm doing that part, right Mom?" Rocky said.

"I am," said Jane. "The stove will be too hot. It's dangerous."

"It should be okay," Ivy said, "if you stand by and watch him."

"No, I'll do it," Jane insisted.

"But Mom . . ." Rocky whined.

"It's not fair," Fern whined now too.

"I said no." Jane made her voice sterner.

"Please," Fern said. There were tears in her eyes now. "Please please please please please."

"That's not fair," Rocky flared. His cheeks were red, and Jane knew he may begin to cry at any moment. He went easily from claims of injustice to tears.

"Why are you acting like brats?" Jane asked, feeling the anger building. It was a great river of anger, burbling low in her throat and threatening to crest the banks and overflow everything in sight. She couldn't explain where the force of this anger had come from; she knew only that she was tired of constantly having to argue for everything she requested. The resistance of her children tripped her up all through the day, exhausted her so deeply she didn't understand how other mothers did it. How did other people navigate these ordinary hurdles? "I said no," Jane told them again.

Fern started her "pleases" again, saying the word over and over until it droned through the kitchen like a chainsaw, constant and grating. "Please please please please please."

Rocky caught the feeling and chimed in with his own set of "pleases," lower and faster in tempo. Ivy smiled, obviously amused by this show of pleading.

Without meaning to, without any conscious decision, Jane yelled, "Shut up! Both of you, just shut the fuck up!"

Instantly, there was the silence she'd wanted. All eyes turned to her. She could feel the disapproval of her friend like a sharp pain in her side, could feel the shock emanating from Rocky and Fern, even Lucky.

Then her own disgust with herself swelled up and overpowered any other feeling in the room. It seemed the only way to amend this situation, to fix the fact that she had just yelled at her children to *shut the fuck up* in front of her best friend, was to leave the room, leave the house even, so this is what she did, hurrying through the kitchen and slipping on a pair of flip-flops sitting by the front door before stepping outside.

She was still wearing her nightgown but decided it could pass for a simple sundress with its spaghetti straps and cotton material. It hit her just at midthigh where there was a centimeter's hem of red lace, the only real clue, she hoped, of the garment's intended use. As she walked down the sidewalk she wished most of all for her sunglasses, because her head was pounding. Her second wish would be for a cold glass of water.

It was already hot out here, and sun burned the space between her shoulder blades as she trudged blindly up the walk. She expected to hear someone running after her, a voice calling her name, but there was nothing. Only the deep silence of these identical houses and the ragged hum of the cicadas.

The trees were young here, small and spindly, furthering the neighborhood's sense of desolation, of sterility, artificiality, unkindness. It seemed to Jane that she should cry now, that at last here was her chance to weep and prove herself human, but nothing came, only more waves of anger, their red power diminishing a little bit with every step. Her eyes were dry as sand, her heart pounding. She couldn't imagine ever going back into that house and facing Ivy.

She could just go to her parents' house, but they would want a reason for the change of plans, wouldn't they? And she was sure Rocky would be all too happy to explain the reason. "Mom told us to shut the fuck up," he'd happily relate. "And Aunt Ivy kicked us out!"

Her thirst became more prominent the further she walked beneath the hot, white sun. She had only drunk coffee this morning, a mistake with a hangover, and she was paying for it now, but she could not turn back. Wasn't there a park around here with a water fountain, she wondered, scanning the long empty street, the rows of homes with no break for green space. In Madison, she would have passed three parks at least by now; she would have been offered water by strangers on the street.

Jane turned a corner, then another, then took a pathway through a row of homes to another street. The trees were slightly more mature here, the yards more tightly packed with shrubs and cactus. Some had patches of yellowish-green grass. Further down the street, she even heard the sound of children playing, a dog barking, water hitting pavement. Turning another corner, she saw the kids running up and down a long driveway. A man was spraying both them and a large black dog with a hose. Water fanned out in the air, catching the sunlight, sparking and leaping as two little bare-chested girls in denim shorts ran in and out of the spray, laughing and calling to each other.

Jane approached the scene, then slowed and stopped to watch from the sidewalk.

"Hello," the man with the hose called to her. He was bare-chested too, pale as a cloud with white-blond, cloudlike hair floating down to his shoulders. Despite his sturdy, well-muscled chest and arms, the hair and his pale color made him seem frail. She thought he might even be an albino, but then he wouldn't be out in this bright sun, would he? He smoked a cigarette with the hand that didn't hold the hose.

"Hi," Jane said, waving. She wondered if he could tell she was wearing a nightgown, then decided it didn't really matter since she had on more clothing than anyone else in the yard.

"New neighbor?" he called.

"No, just visiting. Taking in the sights," she said, spreading her arms wide.

"Pretty exciting shit, no?" He grinned and took a drag from his cigarette.

"Extremely exciting. I can't get enough of it." She looked around, realizing for the first time that she had no idea how to get back to Ivy's house. "Actually, I think I got so entranced that now I'm lost."

The man walked over to her, keeping the hose in his hand as he crossed the lawn and turning it as he walked so that it continued to spray the girls. Up close, she saw that he had dark brown eyes. So, not an albino.

"What street are you looking for?" he asked.

"Um," she thought for a moment, crossing her arms over her chest. "Pigeon Way? No, Cardinal Alley? I don't know, something with a bird in it. My friend lives in that house with the crazy red door?"

"Oh, I know that door." He looked immensely pleased. "That's on Mourning Dove Way, right around the corner."

"Mourning Dove Way. That's it." She smiled. "I don't suppose I could have a sip of water from that hose. I'm parched."

"Be my guest." He lifted the hose her way and she leaned to take a sip, a lock of hair falling into the water as she drank deeply from the spray. It had been years since she'd drunk from a hose, and the pleasure of it was unexpected, the cool mist in her face, the cold, cold water sliding down her throat. "Thank you," she said, straightening up.

"My pleasure."

He explained the way to get back to Ivy's street and she realized she'd looped in some sort of huge circle, because it was not far at all.

"How old are your girls?" she asked him. They both had the same cloud hair he did, striped in wet, white strands down their backs.

"Six and eight," he said. "The perfect ages, in my opinion."

"Why's that?"

"They're on autopilot. They know what to do and they do it by themselves, but they're still little enough to play with."

"Do you stay home with them?" Jane asked.

"Not usually. I just got laid off."

"Me too," she said.

"Isn't it awesome? You get paid by the government to laze around with your kids."

Jane wasn't sure whether he was being serious or sarcastic, but could detect no bitterness in his tone. "I liked my job," Jane told him.

"I did too, but this is better." He spread out the hand holding the cigarette to include his driveway and daughters, the dog, his house, which was only half the size of Ivy's and not very well kept from the looks of it. The lawn was scruffy and covered with two pink Huffy bikes, a half-empty baby pool, and, inexplicably, a tall pile of palm fronds stacked beside an aluminum chair.

"Here." He handed her the hose. "Let me get you a real drink," he said, then crossed the lawn to the front door before she could respond.

She stood there, still on the sidewalk, spraying the two blonde girls with water. They didn't seem to notice that operation of the hose had been transferred to a strange woman in a nightgown.

Several long minutes passed, and Jane considered leaving—setting the hose down and walking away—but it seemed unfriendly, even callous, so she stayed put, wondering if Ivy and the kids were worried about her yet, wondering too whether or not they would forgive her. Out here beside this house with its messy lawn, it seemed to Jane that Ivy would be able to overlook her cursing. Of course she would. She had not, essentially, done anything terrible. Surely she had been forgiven for worse.

The man emerged through the front door carrying two tall green glasses. He had discarded his cigarette and put on a red T-shirt that said REHAB IS FOR QUITTERS in black letters. She tried to decide if this was a pro-rehab shirt or a slam against it.

He handed her a glass, then took the hose out of her hand. The liquid inside the glass was pale yellow. Ice cubes chimed against the side as she took a tentative sip, unsure what to expect. To her relief, it was simply lemonade. "Thanks," she told him. "This is perfect."

"No sweat," he said. "So where are you visiting from?"

"Wisconsin. But I'm from here originally."

They exchanged the usual information about neighborhoods and high schools. It turned out he had gone to Las Vegas High School too, but three years later than she had.

"So when I was a puny freshman, you were a senior," he said, then gave her a smile that was roguish, familiar. It suggested a shared intimacy. "Remember me?"

Jane shook her head and took another long swallow of lemonade, then moved slightly away from the man despite an impulse to step closer. Her skin tingled from his proximity, and the hairs on her arms stood up in goosebumps. "Do you remember me?" she asked.

He gave her a long, probing look, as if he were running through every face he'd ever seen, then shook his head. "Nope. But I was kind of a goody-goody. I ran with the Mormon crowd."

"Are you Mormon?"

"Used to be."

"I used to go to those Mormon dances sometimes with one of my friends. I come from a long line of atheists though."

A cell phone in the man's pocket buzzed. He set down his lemonade, still holding the hose, and extricated the phone to check the number. "Oh, shit," he cursed, but didn't answer the phone. "I forgot something. I just need to run one block over real quick. Would you possibly mind watching the girls for a sec?"

"Um," she hesitated.

"C'mon," he smiled. "We went to high school together, after all."

He held out the hose to her, and Jane's automatic impulse was to accept it. "Okay," she agreed. "Sure."

"It will only be five minutes, tops. I promise." He shoved the phone back into his pocket and hurried off down the sidewalk, in the direction Jane had come from.

She stood for a minute on the sidewalk, holding the hose and sipping the lemonade. The girls didn't seem to register the fact that their father was gone, and Jane wondered at this. Did he often leave complete strangers to watch them? Would her children notice if she slunk away while they were absorbed in play?

Adjusting the hose as she walked, Jane crossed the lawn and pulled the aluminum chair over by the driveway, then sat down. What was she doing here? She'd left Ivy's house to escape her own children and now here she was, responsible for watching two girls she didn't even know and would likely never see again. She supposed she could leave, but of course she would not. The responsibility bore down on her, made her aware of the girls' every movement. "Slow down," she called, when the smaller one raced down the driveway and almost slipped in the pooling water.

"Okay," the girl yelled back, then stopped and turned to see who had spoken. She ran over to Jane's chair; the bigger girl followed her, then they both stopped in front of Jane's knees, looking down and dripping water onto her thighs. Neither of them had their father's brown eyes; instead, they were light blue and widely spaced. "Who are you?" the big girl asked.

"A friend of your dad's," she said. "Sort of. He'll be right back."

"Why are you wearing a nightgown?" the little one asked.

"It's a dress," Jane said.

"No it's not," the bigger girl said, frowning.

Jane shrugged. "I don't know."

"It's cute," said the little girl. "I like the lace."

"Thanks," Jane said.

"Do you know how to play Mother May I?" the little one asked.

"Sure," Jane said, hoping beyond all reason she would not be asked to play. She hated that game—its ridiculous premise and snail's pace. As if a child would ever ask permission to take a step.

"You're the mother," the big girl instructed. "Let me turn off the hose first."

She ran over to the house and cranked an unseen spigot behind a sagebrush, then ran back and got in line with her little sister, several yards away from Jane.

"Take three giant steps," Jane called out, looking at the taller girl.

"Mother may I?" she asked.

"Sure."

"No, you have to say, 'Yes, you may.'"

Jane rolled her eyes and let out a sigh, then said what she was supposed to say. The game continued in a haze of heat as Jane waited for the man to return. To pass the time, she imagined these were her kids and that man her husband. What a different life it would be. She would be at work now, she guessed, as his wife must be now. After that, Jane would come home to this place where there was a definite sense that anything you did would be considered okay. Adam would not be sulking in the corner in his headphones—all the years between them somehow getting in the way of being honest. She had wanted to tell him why she'd been fired, but could never bring herself to do it, wasn't even sure it was the right thing to do. This new man, on the other hand, might be amused by her story of the long, groping kiss with her coworker in the cloakroom.

After fifteen minutes or so had passed, Jane began to worry. What if he didn't come back? What if he'd been planning to leave for days, months even and had just been waiting for his opportunity? His wife would come home at five to find a strange woman playing Mother May I with her two daughters, unable to explain the whereabouts of her husband. *He got a call and just ran around the corner*, she'd say, pointing. *He was wearing his rehab shirt.* The wife would be pale with cloud hair too, Jane imagined. Lined up in a row, they would look like a family of ghosts or fairies.

Pink sunburn was beginning to spread across the shoulders of both girls, and Jane stopped the game and asked if they had any sunscreen. "In the house maybe," the older one said and ran inside.

"What's your name anyway?" Jane asked the little one, who had moved close to her knees again and was eyeing the lace on her nightgown.

"Calliope. My sister is Polyhymnia."

Jane nodded and smiled. "Those sound like fairy names."

"Actually, they're muses," the girl said.

"Oh, right," Jane said, remembering now that they were, indeed, the names of two of the Greek muses. "They're beautiful names."

"Thank you," she said.

The older sister returned and handed Jane a bottle of Coppertone number four, which did not seem sufficient for their white skin, but she rubbed it into both of their shoulders anyway, then dabbed it on their faces too.

She was rubbing some into her own shoulders when the man tapped her lightly on the arm. "Hey, thanks, I owe you one," he said.

Jane rose and handed him her empty glass. She had been planning to say something cutting to him when he returned or at least shoot him a rude look, but the sight of him only engendered a sense of relief. She almost threw her arms around him she was so grateful for his return.

"How long are you in town?" he asked.

"All week."

"We should get a beer. Talk about old times."

She wondered what old times they would discuss since they had no real shared history, but didn't point this out. "Okay," she agreed, then wondered why she had. Surely having a beer with this man was not a good idea. "Maybe," she added.

"Stop by whenever you like." He grinned at her and she had an impulse to touch his white skin. She thought it should feel cool and solid like marble, though of course it wouldn't.

"I'm Jane, by the way," she said.

"Rex." He offered his hand for a shake.

His skin was cool and smooth but soft, and Jane found herself disappointed by his ordinary name. She thought he might have an exotic name like his children: Mercury, perhaps, or Dionysus.

She waved to all three of them, then set off in the direction of Ivy's house, feeling slightly revived, lighter than when she'd arrived.

When she finally reached Ivy's house, she found Ivy and Ramona sitting side by side on the front step. They both stood up when they saw her, a frown crimping Ivy's brow as she said, "We were worried."

"Yeah, she was so worried she woke me up," Ramona said with a smile.

"She was gone a long time," Ivy said.

"Sorry," Jane said. "I shouldn't have cursed in front of the kids."

"That's what you're apologizing for?" Ivy crossed her arms over her chest. "Saying fuck in front of the kids?"

Jane nodded, uncertain. Was there a grander offense she hadn't registered?

"How about sorry for disappearing for an hour and a half in your nightgown? How about sorry for not telling me what the hell is wrong with you?" Ivy was speaking quietly but with a steady anger Jane hadn't heard from her friend in many years.

"Nothing is wrong with me," Jane said, feeling an odd calm settle over her. "I'm just hungover, and the kids were driving me crazy, and I snapped. That's it. It happens sometimes."

"It's more than that," Ivy said. "I can tell."

"Well, I did lose my job."

"More than that," Ivy insisted.

"That's not enough?" Here was her chance to tell them both about Adam, about the months of discomfort and sadness, about her stupid kiss with that coworker and her realization that she no longer wanted to be married, but she found the words were stuck deep inside her, and she had no idea how to lodge them free.

REX

He did remember her now. After she'd left, walking away in the red nightgown he'd wanted to ask her about but hadn't, an image from high school floated into his brain out of nowhere. He had been at the Mormon dance on a Friday night one of the first weeks of school, and he'd noticed a girl who obviously did not belong. She was dressed in what had looked like a costume to Rex at the time: a hot pink dress, sort of Madonna style he understood now, with a tight bodice and frilly short skirt covered in black polka dots. Beneath this, he'd been shocked to see her black fishnet tights, ripped across both knees and cut off midcalf, paired with scuffed biker boots completely inappropriate for the dance. He was awed that she'd been allowed past the chaperones. Her hair, almost as white-blonde as his own, had two thick pink stripes in the front, which is how the memory came loose now all these years later. They were bolder versions of the thin stripe of pink he'd noticed in her hair today.

He wanted to call her or go find her and tell her about this memory. It seemed important, though he couldn't say why. But the idea of walking over to that house with the red door and knocking felt wrong. He had a sense that he would be deeply unwelcome.

He called the girls in from the driveway and asked them to go take a shower. Calliope argued against this for a few minutes but was eventually dragged away by Polly to the bathroom. When he heard the water running, Rex went back out front and lit a cigarette, then sat down in the folding chair where Jane had been less than an hour ago. He thought about what he'd looked like at that same dance all those years ago. His short, skinny frame encased in dark slacks, a short-sleeved white button down and striped tie. His hair was short, almost a buzz cut then, and his face had been pudgy and dotted with zits. That girl in the crazy outfit, *Jane*, had been standing only across the room but seemed to have landed from another planet. He recalled a strong desire to go over and speak to her—no one else was near her at all—but just as he was working up his nerve and walking toward her, a giant, beefy boy swooped in and took her off to dance.

"Dad?" He turned around in his chair and saw Polly on the front step. Her hair was slicked back from the shower, and she had changed into a pink leopard-print sundress her mother had picked out that Rex always thought was too grown-up for his daughter, bordering on slutty. Leopard print had crossed the line into mainstream, he knew, but his old Mormon self still thought of it as the fabric of dancers and hookers.

"What's up, kitten?" he smashed his cigarette out on the driveway, then rose and walked toward her, tossing the butt behind the sagebrush.

"What am I supposed to pack to go to Death Valley?"

The question stopped him cold. He'd forgotten Kristina was taking the kids there tomorrow. "I guess you pack very cool clothing and sunscreen. And a hat. And maybe a snakebite kit since there are a ton of rattlesnakes there."

"I don't have a snakebite kit."

She looked upset now, a crease in her young, perfect skin, and Rex regretted his words. "You're only going for the day, right? You should be fine. Besides, your mom will take care of the first aid stuff."

Calliope appeared beside her older sister on the step, and it was obvious from her troubled expression that she'd heard his warnings about snakes through the screen door. "I want to stay here with you, Dad."

"I want you to stay here too," he told her but then amended. "But it's important to spend time with your mom. She's going through a tough time."

"Are you going through a tough time too?" Polly asked.

"Sure I am," he said. "But that's okay. That's what life's all about, getting through these times together." He almost added "as a family" but caught himself.

Inside the house, the front room still possessed the museum-like quality Kristina had cultivated, but every day the order was being chipped away, despite Rex's struggle to keep the space intact. The long white couch, which the kids were now forbidden to sit on, had a stripe of black across a back cushion, and a pile of comic books had been left on the kidney-shaped coffee table. The framed photos above the buffet were coated with a thin skin of dust—he could see that now with the sun burning through the front windows—and the wood floor was cluttered in one corner with toys. He considered telling the girls to get their crap out of the front room, as he did almost every day, then decided against it. He was tired of this command; he would clean it himself before Kristina came to get the kids.

It was essential that she saw he could take care of this place, since one of her numerous complaints had been his inability to help out with anything, including cleaning up the house. Sometimes he wondered if that would have been enough. If he had simply cleaned once or twice a week, would she have stayed? It seemed too simple, not a true solution to their multilayered marital problems, but the idea still nagged at him that a few minor actions would have kept her close, if only for a few more years.

Kristina arrived at exactly two o' clock to pick up the girls. Rex ushered her inside then called out for Polly and Callie. The front room was now spotless. He'd spent an hour going over it and hoped

Kristina wouldn't walk beyond this space into the rest of the house, which had not been given the same care.

It had been a week since he'd seen her, and she seemed smaller than he remembered, with darker hair. She'd had it cut, that was certain, and he told her it looked nice.

"Thanks," she said, reaching up to tug at her new bangs. "I needed a change."

Rex chuckled at this—he couldn't help himself—and immediately understood this was the wrong thing to do, but how could she talk about change with such a straight face? They'd been officially divorced for four months—separated for three before that—and every single thing in his life felt different.

She frowned, then walked past him to the hallway and called out, "Light a fire, guys. We've got things to do."

"Their stuff's all ready, right here," he said, pointing to the twin backpacks beside the front door.

She seemed not to hear him, but walked deeper into the house, down the hallway toward the kitchen. He followed, wishing he'd finished this morning's dishes or wiped the crumbs off the counter, but she didn't give any of it a second look, just moved to the screen door and slid it open. At the sight of their mother, the girls jumped up from their space on the grass and ran to throw their arms around her. Rex watched the three of them as if from a distance, wondering how he had become an outsider when the four of them had once been a single, breathing unit. The sight made his chest feel tight, and he placed a hand over his heart as if to still it, then leaned over the sink and pretended to inspect something in the depths of the garbage disposal.

When he could breathe normally again, he righted himself and left the kitchen, then sat on the white couch in the front room and waited for them to leave. Kristina emerged from the hallway first; she perched on the arm of the couch beside him and crossed her legs. "Polly's trying to find her magnifying glass. She wants to bring it to Death Valley."

"Seems like a long drive for one day," he said.

"We're going to spend the night. At some place called the Furnace Creek Inn."

"Oh," he said. "I didn't know that."

She nodded, and they were both quiet, listening to the distant sound of their daughters' voices.

"Who are you going with?" he finally asked.

Her skin flushed at the question, but she shook her head. "Just a friend."

"Anyone I know?"

She shook her head again.

The knowledge that she was bringing someone on this trip—a new boyfriend, he guessed—filled him up with a slow buzzing, so that he couldn't hear his own thoughts. The information was both new and something he seemed to have known all along. "I'm going to take them camping next week," he told her, just now deciding. "Up to Pine Creek."

"That will be nice."

Polly and Callie seemed to explode into the room, all bright laughter and yelling, and Rex was anxious to have them gone now and just sit here in utter silence. He hugged and kissed them each good-bye, then stood on the front step and waved as Kristina drove them away.

Instead of heading back inside to the silent house, as he'd imagined, Rex started walking up the street, shoving his hands into the pockets of his shorts and staring at each foot as it hit the pavement. He tried not to think about Kristina, but his thoughts kept circling back to her, each one with an image attached: a day at the beach in San Diego, her smiling face shielded by a giant floppy hat as she turned to him; her sleeping form the morning after she'd given birth to Polly and the desire he'd had to crawl into the skinny hospital bed beside her; her red-eyed look of pleading over a plate of pad thai at the restaurant they liked on

Eastern; her stiff, angry form when he'd recently arrived at her work unannounced.

When he reached the end of the long street, Rex stopped and looked up toward the Black Mountains, then turned and headed back in the direction of his house. It was only one night, he told himself. His daughters would only be gone for one night, then they would be back home, and their presence would distract him from his thoughts. He didn't want to picture the man they might meet tonight at the Furnace Creek Inn or how this new man might be introduced. Rex would try with every cell of his being not to ask his daughters about that part of the trip, though he could already feel the hairline cracks forming in his resolve, and the questions that would stream through those cracks and damage everyone a little bit more.

RAMONA

Ramona watched Jane's kids play in the shallow end of the pool as she held Lucky on her lap under the blue umbrella. He was starting to fuss, so she bounced her knee a bit, then lifted him and made a face. She finally solved the fussing by handing him one of her long braids.

"I can take him," Ivy said.

Ramona shook her head. "He's happy now."

Ramona and Jane were wearing their bathing suits and drinking iced tea, but Ivy was wearing a silky blue cover-up over her suit and had forgone the iced tea for a margarita in preparation for Jeremy's visit. He was bringing over a tray of food, samples of what he would make for Lucky's party on Friday, if Ivy decided to hire him.

"I still can't believe he's a caterer," Ramona said again.

"He always liked to cook," Ivy said and shrugged.

"I was hoping not to have to see anyone else from high school while I'm here," Ramona told them. "Other than you guys and Frank I mean."

"Sorry," Ivy said.

In fact, Ramona had already had one run-in with a person from high school. On the drive in, she'd stopped at a gas station to find Jim Wall from art class peering into her window, asking her questions, telling her all about his pregnant teenage daughter as if Ramona were some sort of expert on the subject. She hadn't been able to place him at first since his long hair had been buzzed off and he'd added at least thirty pounds to his frame, but then she saw his broad, square hands and recalled the time she'd let him rest his palm on the growing mound of her belly, the way he'd covered most of her stomach with his giant hand, then lifted it quickly away and shook it out as if he'd just burned his fingers.

"I especially don't feel like seeing that jerk," she said now about Jeremy, recognizing that she was still thinking mostly of Jim Wall, mentally blending the two men into one person for her to despise. She hadn't told either Ivy or Jane about the early morning run-in with Jim and considered doing so now, but decided against it. Lucky gave her braid a sudden tug, as if defending his mother's ex-boyfriend, and Ramona looked down at him and gave his back a light pat. "No offense," she told him, then looked over at Ivy. "But I never liked the way he treated you."

"I know," Ivy said. "We can just try his free samples, then send him on his way and never see him again. I haven't officially hired him yet or anything. I don't even know why I called him, to be honest."

"Frank and I talked her into it," Jane said. "It seemed like a good idea at the time. I don't remember him being such a jerk."

"Well, he was," Ramona said.

"Not all the time," Ivy said. "He could be very kind and loving too."

"Whatever you say," Ramona said, then smiled to soften the comment.

The doorbell rang, and Ivy ran inside, then reemerged with Jeremy, who looked exactly as Ramona remembered: skinny and tall with badly cut black hair, tight black clothes, black shoes. He carried a large silver tray covered in wax paper and ran his eyes all over Ivy as they crossed the pool deck together, talking.

He said hello and set his tray down on the table, then lifted off the wax paper to reveal a colorful array. "Okay," he said, clapping his hands, then rubbing his palms together. "Black and white minicupcakes, sweet potato purses, goat cheese and honey canapés, salmon and dill on rounds of pumpernickel. Oh, and these are

peanut butter and jelly sandwiches, right here, for the picky kids."
He pointed to a cluster of tiny sandwiches in cut-out shapes of
hearts, stars, and moons, then looked up at Ivy and smiled expec-
tantly. "Dig in," he said, and Ivy reached for a sweet potato purse,
which looked sort of like a soft fortune cookie.

Jane reached for a salmon and dill round, and Ramona picked
up a minicupcake and popped it in her mouth. The flavor was rich,
true vanilla with dark chocolate. It was a lush, perfect cupcake, and
Ramona had to admit she was impressed.

"Wow, this is amazing," Ivy said. "What's in this thing?"

"Well," Jeremy said, "It's sort of like a wonton wrapper on the
outside, then the inside has sweet potato, of course, and a little
bit of shallot, but it's the sharp cheddar that makes it sing. Oh, I
almost forgot, I have one more thing in the car." He rushed back
inside and they could hear the front door open and close.

"I think you should hire him," Jane said, popping one of the
canapés into her mouth. "This shit is good."

"Maybe he bought it all at a gourmet food shop," Ramona said,
"then put it on his own tray."

"Why would he do that?" Ivy asked, frowning.

Ramona shrugged. "To get back into your good graces. To rob
your house, sell Ecstasy to your kid, raid your liquor cabinet." She
smiled to show she was half-joking, then popped one of the sweet
potato purses into her mouth, bouncing Lucky on her hip as she
stood and chewed. "Wow, this is good."

"You're crazy," Ivy said, and the three of them all started to
laugh.

When Jeremy appeared through the sliding glass doors with
a Tupperware container a moment later, the three of them were
laughing even harder.

"What'd I miss?" Jeremy asked.

"Nothing." Ivy waved a hand through the air. "Inside joke."

"I was reminding Ivy of what an asshole you are," Ramona said.

He smiled uncertainly, and Ivy shook her head. "She's kidding."

Jeremy nodded and lifted the lid of the Tupperware to reveal three neat rows of peanut butter cookies with candy kisses pressed into their centers. Ramona looked at Ivy, who had begun to tear up, so she called Jane's kids out of the pool to come and eat the cookies, to distract her sentimental friend.

"You remembered," Ivy said to Jeremy, picking up a cookie.

"Of course," he told her.

For a moment, it looked as if Ivy and Jeremy were together in a private room, and Ramona watched them with a deep sense of foreboding. She remembered the night Ivy had found him with another girl at the park by their apartment building. He and the girl had been lying together inside the tunnel slide, the girl's pants pushed down around her ankles. Ivy had run to Ramona's apartment sobbing, calling out for her at the top of her lungs until Ramona answered the door and Ivy fell against her.

Somehow they had gotten back together after that night, but Jeremy had failed her again and again: cheating on her, showing up on her doorstep half out of his mind on drugs, leaving town for a week without letting her know. Ramona had a list of the grievances in her mind but she wasn't sure Ivy had the same list. She wasn't sure Ivy really remembered how awful he had been.

"So what's your story, Jeremy?" Ramona asked. "Did you ever get married? Have kids? Go to college? Not necessarily in that order."

"Ramona," Ivy scolded. "He's not here for an interview."

"Actually, he sort of is," Jane said.

"No, it's all right," Jeremy said, then sank down in an empty chair under the umbrella and stretched out his legs. "Married once, a million years ago. No kids. No college. I cooked in restaurants after high school and started doing this on my own about two years ago. It's actually going really well. I quit my day job about six months ago."

"So that wasn't your wife I saw you with yesterday?" Ivy asked.

"Her?" He waved a hand through the air dismissively. "We hang out off and on. More off than on I'd say. She's not really my type."

"So your career as a punk rocker never took off?" Ramona asked him. She could hear how mean she was being, how invasive, but couldn't seem to stop herself. It felt instinctual to drive him away.

"No," he laughed. "We were terrible, I admit it. I hear you made it all right though. I actually bought your first album. Not my thing really, but I could appreciate the artistry of it."

Ramona sat down, still holding onto Lucky, and began to bounce him on her knee. "Thanks," she said.

"Are you going to do another one?" he asked.

"Working on it now."

"It's been a while, hasn't it?"

She shrugged and could feel everyone watching her. "A few years." She didn't add that the indie label, which had released her first album, had gone bust, her drummer had a baby and quit the band, and the bass player had recently gone back to school to study patent law. Now it was just her and Eric, but they were the core really, and both of them still enjoyed sitting on his porch in Long Beach writing songs, though playing in local clubs was starting to get old. Luckily, she raked in a decent income teaching private guitar and piano lessons.

Lucky suddenly began to cry, a long piercing wail she'd never heard from him before, and Ramona quickly handed him to Ivy, who excused herself to put him down for his nap.

Ramona expected Jeremy to leave since Ivy was gone, but he reached for a cupcake and popped it into his mouth. "What's it take to get a drink around here?" he asked, looking first at Ramona, then Jane.

"I'll grab you one," Jane said, standing up. "Beer?"

He nodded and she disappeared through the sliding glass doors. Fern and Rocky were back in the pool now, and Ramona watched them closely.

"Was it something I said?" Jeremy asked Ramona, smirking just enough to reveal his dimple.

She realized she'd been frowning over at the pool and turned to him now, willing herself to relax, to forget who he had once been. "No," she said, shaking her head. "Sorry for grilling you. It's just being back here, I guess. I'm not very fond of this city."

"Oh, c'mon. It's not so bad. There's some really cool clubs now and more of an art and music scene. There's even a museum at the Bellagio. It's much better than when we grew up."

She shrugged. "Okay, I'll take your word for it."

"You know, I think I saw your mom a couple of months ago. Does she still work at the Golden Nugget?"

Ramona shook her head. "She died six years ago."

"Oh, shit. I'm sorry. I had no idea."

"It's all right." She had booked a room at the Golden Nugget for the night, wanting a place of her own for this trip, for the search she was about to begin. Jane and Ivy still didn't know that she wouldn't be staying here with them.

Jeremy shook his head slowly. "Remember all those times me, you, and Ivy hung out at your place?"

"Drinking my mom's wine."

"Exactly. Remember that time she came home and caught us? She was so cool about it, didn't even scream and yell like my mom would have. She just took the empty bottles off the table and put them on the kitchen counter, then asked me and Ivy to leave."

"Then she yelled. At me," Ramona said, though the truth was she couldn't remember her mother ever really yelling. Instead, she exuded an air of disappointment, of utter silence and contempt, which managed to be worse than any shouting.

Ramona would have done anything to make it up to her, to have her forgiveness.

Jane emerged from the dim house holding three beers and passed them around. Ramona shook her head and handed hers back, wondering how long it would take for someone to ask why she wasn't drinking.

Jane set the third beer between her and Jeremy. "We can share this one," she said.

He nodded. "Perfect. Wow, this tastes good." He tilted his head back and took a long swallow. Ramona watched him, noticing that he had aged slightly. She could see it in the lines around his mouth, the worn look of his hands around the glass bottle of beer. Still, he was mostly intact, a perfect relic of her past.

By the time Ivy came back outside, Jane and Jeremy had finished off the three beers and the kids were settled onto their towels, laid out neatly by Jeremy alongside the edge of the pool. Fern lay facedown on her belly, and Ramona guessed she was asleep, thinking it was fortunate she had Jane's olive skin so she wouldn't burn to a crisp out here. Rocky, however, was another story. He had his father's pale skin, and his shoulders were turning lightly pink. Jane seemed to notice this at the same time because she called him over and held him on her lap in the shade of the umbrella.

"You need some more sunscreen," Jane told him. "Or maybe a break."

"Why don't I set the kids up inside with a movie?" Ivy suggested. "Then we can hang out and finish off these samples. Lucky will be out for a couple hours," she added.

"Actually," Jeremy said, standing. "I have to take off. I've got a gig at the Rotary Club tonight. Just desserts, but still, a lot of them."

Ramona could see disappointment spread across Ivy's face like a shadow, but her friend smiled and said, "Okay, I'll walk you out."

When they were gone, Ramona turned to Jane and said, "This is a bad idea, you know. Her spending time with him."

"No," Jane shook her head. "It's fine. Since when did you become such a worrier? He's changed anyway. Maybe they can become friends so Ivy doesn't feel so alone here. Who knows? Stranger things have happened."

"Don't you think that would bother Frank?"

Jane shook her head. "Nope, not at all. Frank is secure. That's always been one of his best qualities. Besides, Ivy loves him like crazy."

"Who do I love like crazy?" Ivy asked, walking back onto the patio.

"Frank," Jane told her.

"Oh, I do. That's true." She smiled, then ate one of the cupcakes.

Later, after dinner and books and bedtime rituals, Ramona drove the three of them downtown for a drink. It was a little after eight o'clock and the sun was gone, but its light still tinted the sky a pale tangerine. Shredded rose-colored clouds were scattered along the horizon like petals. Ramona's duffel bag still sat in the trunk of her Mustang, and she planned to call a cab later for Jane and Ivy, then check into her hotel room at the Golden Nugget. They would try and talk her out of it again, she knew, but she looked forward to the single, empty room with its absence of smells or personality, its utter lifeless quiet.

They parked in the Golden Nugget's lot, then walked outside and up the road to Fremont Street. Ramona had heard about the Fremont Street Experience, basically a giant arched screen that now covered the entire length of the street, but seeing it was more depressing than she'd thought it would be. The covering shut out the darkening sky. It dampened the effect of the giant neon cowboy atop the Pioneer hotel, swinging his thumb back and forth, beckoning. The covering had also helped to dispel some of the street's seediness, and Ramona missed that too. There were too many families wandering back and forth along the street now, children running in circles and stopping to gaze at the dome above, which had begun to show images of race cars speeding around to loud music. Couples strolled together holding plastic cups of beer. Where were the derelicts of her youth? The men drinking from paper bags? The homeless woman with the red lipstick and pink crocheted beret who always stood outside the Four Queens?

"This is ugly," she said to Ivy and Jane.

"Let's go drink it away," Jane suggested, pulling them toward the entrance to the Golden Nugget.

Inside, they quickly found a place called Rush Lounge and settled in at a curved glass table where they had a good view of the casino. Ivy ordered a margarita, Jane a gin and tonic. Ramona asked for a club soda with lime.

"What's the matter?" Ivy asked. "You're not driving."

Ramona shrugged and leaned back, avoiding the eyes of her friends. "My stomach's upset. It's probably from something Jeremy made."

"I bet there was some kind of narcotic in those cupcakes," Jane said. "They were almost too good."

"Stop," Ivy said, but laughed.

Ramona laughed too, then sat up straight and smoothed out her jeans beneath the table. She'd taken out her braids, and the sweep of hair against her arms and the bare top of her back felt alien, almost as if another person were touching her. The casino was crowded and loud, and she put a protective hand over her stomach. This night of noise and secondhand smoke could be harming her child right now. She would take a test in the morning to confirm her missed period, then she would know for sure.

She wondered what Nash was doing right now back in Long Beach. It was likely he was sitting in a bar with his friends too, the one he liked to go to on Seventh Street that was dark and gloomy with fishing nets strung around the ceiling. The nets held shimmery stones and fake fish, and if you drank too much the effect was both disconcerting and somewhat magical, those stones glinting in the dim light like treasure overhead, those fake fish with their pale, sickly bellies reminding you of death.

This place had nothing to remind you of death with its updated gleaming façade and packed game tables, and that seemed to be the point. There were no clocks, no dingy corners, no pockets of stillness. It was too artificial—even more so now that the place had been refurbished and glamorized. The white marble and chandeliers of the lobby, the deep red walls of this bar with its black leather chairs were a bit too perfect, and Ramona began to doubt her commitment to staying here instead of with her friends.

"So tell us about your new boyfriend," Ivy said, as if reading her thoughts.

"He's not actually that new," Ramona said. "We've been together almost a year."

"Practically an old married couple, then," Ivy said.

Something in her friend's tone irritated Ramona. "I hope we're not like that."

"It's not such a bad thing to be," Ivy said, shrugging as she took a sip of her drink.

"Yes, it is," Jane said.

"Jane," Ivy said. "You're supposed to be on my side here."

"I wasn't aware there were sides," Ramona said.

"Just a joke," Ivy said. "Of course there aren't sides."

"Nash is sort of a cross between Mark and Adam," Ramona said, trying to smooth out the discomfort she could feel knotting among the three of them. "He has Mark's solidity or reliability I guess you'd call it. Or what I remember as Mark's reliability—we were only seventeen after all—and he has Adam's nature thing going for him." She nodded to Jane when she said this. "He's always taking me out of the city on these crazy hikes, showing me places I'd never even heard of before. We went to the Santa Monica Mountains last weekend and hiked for about an hour to this gigantic waterfall. It was amazing."

"Have you been in touch with Mark?" Ivy asked.

"I was just making a comparison," Ramona said, her irritation flaring again. "I haven't spoken to him since graduation."

"I heard he's a policeman in North Las Vegas," Jane said. "That's kind of sexy, don't you think?"

She was smiling, and Ramona could see that there were, indeed, sides. It was her and Jane against Ivy. Ramona returned her smile. "I should go find him and ask him out. Start the whole thing all over again. Then I could move back here just like you, Ivy, and we could go on double dates and relive our high school days together."

"Cut it out," Ivy said. She frowned and slumped a little in the booth, then reached for what was left of her drink and cradled it close to her chest. "I was just asking. You don't need to get so defensive."

Silence shrouded the table again, and Ramona wondered why this was so difficult tonight.

"Maybe we should go dancing somewhere," Jane suggested with a look of despondence. She was hiding something too, Ramona decided.

"I don't feel like it," Ivy said.

"Me neither," Ramona agreed.

The waitress hadn't yet reappeared, so Jane went up to the bar to get another round of drinks for her and Ivy. Ramona was still sipping at her club soda, wishing she could add a couple shots of vodka, thinking that maybe alcohol would help to loosen the hard knot of anxiety that had formed in her stomach during the last hour. She looked toward the bar and saw that Jane had wedged a spot for herself between an older woman with a gray twist in her hair and a young guy who was leaning close to hear something Jane was telling him.

Jane had a way of drawing people toward her. Ramona remembered this about her now, the way a certain type of boy had flocked to her in high school, hoping to coax a hello out of her. This guy beside her was a grown-up version of those boys: dark clothing and chunky black glasses. His floppy, artist's hair covered half of his left lens. Jane had long ago shed her costumes—tonight she was in jeans and a white tank top—but she still managed to evoke an aura of knowing things nobody else did, of having entrance to a hidden world. It was the sealed-off quality of her presence, Ramona decided. She was the opposite of welcoming, revealing nothing with her expression or gestures.

Ramona had been drawn to her too, when they'd shared an art class freshman year. Jane sat in the back of the room wearing a wide-brimmed black hat. Her lips were painted bright red. A peacock feather the size of a thumb was painted on the skin of her cheek. When Ramona sat beside her, Jane didn't say hello, didn't smile or even glance her way, but she wasn't unfriendly or cruel either. Somehow Ramona was certain of this. Later they'd worked on a project together, making stained glass, and something between them had opened wide.

She and Ivy, on the other hand, had been friends for much longer—since the third grade, when her family moved into the same crappy apartment building where Ramona lived with her mother—but right now they seemed to be having trouble finding things to say to each other. Ramona tried to make an effort. "How's your dad?"

Ivy shrugged. "Okay, I guess. He finally remarried. Did I tell you that?"

"I think so. Some lady from his church, right?"

"He met her at the library, and now he goes to her church. She's actually very nice but the complete opposite of my mom. I guess that's a good thing though. He doesn't need someone else skipping out on him."

"Your mom had good qualities too."

"Sure. I know."

They were quiet again, the noise of the bar churning around them, and Ramona thought she'd probably misstepped once more by mentioning Ivy's mother.

"I think I saw her the other day," Ivy said quietly, not looking up from her hands on the table. "A woman getting into a car at the park reminded me of her. It was just a feeling, but it was a strong one."

"Wow. Really? Did you tell your dad?"

"There's nothing to tell really. I just had a feeling that someone across the park looked like my mother, but how would I even know what she looks like since I haven't seen her in twenty years? She could even be dead by now. Who knows?"

"I don't think she's dead," Ramona said, then instantly regretted it. She didn't have any idea whether or not Ivy's mother was still alive.

"Well, it doesn't matter anyway, I guess."

"Of course it matters," Ramona said. "Dead is different than absent. A lot different."

"Not really," Ivy said. "Not in this case."

"How can you say that?" Ramona thought of her own mother, the way she'd avoided coming to see her until it was too late. Ivy must not understand the breadth of her regret, a regret as wide and empty as the desert. But how could she? Ivy's mother was the one who had left, not the other way around. "I'd give anything for the chance to talk to my mom one more time."

Ivy looked up from her hands and furrowed her brow with concern. "But she didn't want to talk to you."

Ramona considered this. It was true, of course, but also not true. Something about the line her mother etched between them had never felt absolutely solid or uncrossable. Ramona had just chosen to view it that way. She could feel herself slipping into a dark, ruminating mood now—her knot of anxiety turning harder and brighter, glowing from the depths of her chest like a radioactive stone—when Jane reappeared at the table with two fresh drinks.

Ivy began to tease Jane about the man in black glasses at the bar, and the rhythm among the three of them grew looser and varied as they joked, so that after a while it was almost possible for Ramona to ignore the stone that had taken up residence in her chest.

JEREMY

He was just finishing up with his gig at the Rotary Club when he remembered it was Gretchen's birthday. It was past nine o'clock already, and by the time he got all these trays and leftovers loaded up in his car and on the road it would be close to ten, but he guessed a store somewhere would still be open. This was Las Vegas, after all.

A man from the club walked back to the kitchen and handed him a check. Jeremy shoved it into his back pocket and thanked him. The man wore a dark suit and had a kind face, but Jeremy could not, for the life of him, remember his name. Doug, possibly. Or Dirk. He wasn't the man who'd hired him, but he was the one who had requested chocolate mousse. Jeremy did remember that.

"Did you like the mousse?" he asked the man. Like every event, this one could lead to other contacts, and forgetting the guy's name wasn't going to help.

He nodded and smiled. "So what's the secret ingredient? There was a bit of an extra zing—am I right?"

"A little lemon zest," Jeremy told him.

"That was nice. Different, but nice."

"Thanks."

"I'd tone it down just a bit next time though. It was a little too lemony."

Jeremy nodded. "I'll make a note of that." So he was essentially here to criticize. The mousse had been perfect, and they both knew it. This man should stick to what he knew—being in the Rotary Club, whatever the fuck that was—and let Jeremy handle the food.

Outside in the parking lot, a circle of men stood smoking under a streetlight. A hearty laugh carried across the lot to Jeremy, and it felt specifically aimed at him, though he knew that was unlikely. Something about these people made him feel inadequate. That man in the kitchen, Doug or Dirk, reminded him of his younger brother, Ben, who was now an accountant for a firm in Los Angeles. He'd been the smart, focused one, and Jeremy, according to his mother, had been the late bloomer. He wondered if she would now consider him to be in bloom, but both of his parents had died years ago in a car accident on the Baker Grade, so there was no way of finding out, ever.

His old Subaru was parked just beyond this group of men, so Jeremy had to trudge past them, carrying his stack of silver trays and backpack of Tupperware containers.

"Let's hear it for the chef," one of them called out as he passed, and a brief bout of hearty clapping and whooping ensued. Jeremy pretended to tip his invisible hat, then waved good-bye, deciding he'd been wrong to judge these people so quickly. The applause had felt genuine and added a lift to his step that had been missing since the book club the evening before.

On his way home, he stopped by Target and roamed the aisles for half an hour, trying to figure out what he could possibly buy this woman he was dating whom he barely knew. He was only aware it was her birthday because she'd been reminding him of the fact for the past five days. That's what people did in their twenties, Jeremy recalled, advertised their birthdays for the whole world to hear. She was twenty-nine today and out with a group of her girlfriends right now, but Jeremy was supposed to show up at her place around eleven, and he'd better arrive with a gift or it was likely he wouldn't be let in. He could just not show up at all, he thought, eyeing a long row of colorful scarves, but then he'd be sleeping alone again, and he'd been alive long enough to know that he hated that.

Without noticing where his meandering path was leading, Jeremy ended up in the baby section staring down at a shelf of blankets and bright, miniature socks. He picked up a pair of sky blue booties embroidered with tiny green grasshoppers and fingered the stitching. A memory rose out of the socks in his hand: sitting in the clinic waiting room with Ivy, sweating with fear. During their junior year, she had been three weeks late getting her period and they had finally gone to a clinic for a test. The stress of those weeks and then that final twenty minutes in the waiting room had been heavy, a steady pulsing of fear in his skull. He had almost cried with relief when he found out he was not going to be a father.

His own parents had still been alive then, and would have punished him severely. They also would have made him keep the baby and propose marriage. He had high hopes back then of his band's punk rock stardom. He'd be too busy touring the country to take care of a wife and kid.

But if Ivy had been pregnant, if they had married and had the baby, at least he would have something to show for his life right now. He would have a twenty-year-old son or daughter to keep tabs on, to worry about, to help out when they were broke or stranded. He would have saved some money and be helping them with college right now. He would cook them meals and teach them to play the bass. Instead, he had only a Subaru full of silver trays and a girlfriend he didn't love and likely never would.

He finally decided on a lavender nightgown for Gretchen, very short with a lacy bodice, but somehow classy, better than the things she usually wore to tempt him to bed: leopard print teddies and skimpy black garter belt contraptions that seemed better suited for bad porn movies. In the checkout aisle, he realized he still clutched the baby socks in his left hand, that he'd been holding them the entire time he was looking for a present for Gretchen, so he paid for those too. He would wrap them up for Ivy's kid, Lucky.

At eleven o'clock, he arrived at Gretchen's apartment, but she wasn't there. He'd already gone home, showered and changed, neatly stacked his catering trays in the kitchen cupboard, and stored the leftover mousse in the fridge. He'd wrapped Gretchen's present in yesterday's *Las Vegas Sun*, then wrapped the baby socks, too, in the comics section of the paper and set them on the coffee table, pleased with himself. Buying a present for Ivy's child felt like a step in the right direction. It was the action of a reliable, thoughtful adult.

He sat on the stairs beside Gretchen's apartment for five minutes, then decided to get up and walk. He had gone three blocks when he realized how close he was to Ivy and Ramona's old building. He took a right, then another right onto Bonneville, and halfway down the block there it was, the U-shaped building with the fountain in its center where he'd spent so many afternoons during high school he couldn't count them if he tried. How had he not noticed the proximity of Gretchen's place to this one?

Lights were on behind three windows, but the rest of the units were dark. The white, tiered fountain was dry and gave off an eerie green glow as if it were emitting a poison of some sort. Jeremy had been standing exactly where he was right now—across the street—when he witnessed Ivy's mother leaving in May of their junior year.

He'd snuck out of Ivy's bedroom after ten at night, left her sleeping soundly, and crept through her window, hanging from the second-floor ledge by his fingertips, then using the lip of the window below him as a foothold down to the green Dumpster, before he took one last leap onto the graveled lot behind the building. It was a maneuver he'd perfected over the past year.

On the sidewalk, across the street, something had made him turn for a last look. He couldn't say what it was—a dog had barked so that might have been it, or he may have heard the door clicking closed—but he'd felt the hair on the back of his neck rise, and turned around.

He was hidden in shadows in front of a dark house, so he'd been able to watch the figure emerge from Ivy's apartment and walk down the stairs. At the bottom of the stairwell, she stepped into the light of the hallway, and Jeremy saw it was Ivy's mother. Her blonde hair, usually swept up in a bun, had been loose around her face, giving her a more youthful appearance, though she looked young either way. She was only thirty-five at the time of her departure, a year younger than he was now. She was wearing an outfit he'd never seen before, a straight beige skirt and matching jacket over a white shirt, as if she were off to a business meeting. Her heels clicked as she walked to the sidewalk, then around the side of the building. Jeremy stepped further back, his feet touching dry lawn, hoping she wouldn't notice him watching her, wouldn't find out that he'd just snuck out of her daughter's bedroom. Of course, if he'd known that Ivy's mother was leaving for good, he wouldn't have worried about being caught. Could a mother who left her family be bothered to care if her teenage daughter was having sex?

In the days following, he tried to remember if she'd been carrying a suitcase or a large bag, but he didn't think so, and he told Ivy over and over, "She'll be back soon. I'm sure she will. She can't be gone for long."

"How do you know?" Ivy would ask, tears streaking her fair, smooth skin.

"I just have a feeling." He worried that telling would somehow make him an accomplice, so he kept quiet.

A light came on now in the apartment that used to be Ivy's, and he stood for a while watching a shadow move behind the blinds, then turned and walked back to Gretchen's.

IVY

When Ivy and Jane got home around eleven thirty, climbing out of the cab with an awkwardness brought on by several cocktails, Lucky was still awake, sitting on Frank's lap outside by the pool playing with a straw, presumably one that had been inside Frank's empty drink. The glass still sat on the table beside him, its melting cubes of ice catching the moonlight and creating a strange effect, as if he'd been drinking a poisonous potion that still bubbled and sparked beside him.

"I couldn't do it," he told Ivy, lifting Lucky off his lap. "He wants you."

Ivy slipped off her sandals and crossed the deck, then scooped Lucky up and held him against her chest. "Hi, baby," she whispered and kissed the warm top of his head, then sat down in one of the chairs across the table from Frank.

"My kids are asleep?" Jane asked, sitting down between them.

"Soundly," Frank said. "I just checked."

"You deserve a medal," Jane told him.

"Yeah, thanks sweetheart," Ivy said, attaching Lucky to her breast and letting him drink himself to sleep in her arms. Across the table, her husband looked tired. Ivy couldn't help but recall Jeremy sitting in the exact same chair earlier today, looking a lot more vibrant than Frank did right now.

It was difficult, she realized, to watch Frank age, since they had known each other as teenagers. She thought that would make it easier because his face and body would always hold the memory of those days when they'd been young together, but instead she was more aware of what she was missing. His boyish, handsome features sank further away every year into his softening jaw and body, and there was nothing she could do to retrieve them.

"Fun night?" Frank asked, tilting a chip of ice into his mouth and crunching down.

Ivy nodded. "I wish Ramona were staying here though."

"You have Jane," Frank said, then turned to her friend. "You need to move back here. We miss you."

"This part is pretty nice," Jane said, gesturing to the backyard—its lit-up pool and palm trees, the pot of lantana spilling a long trail of orange and yellow flowers at her feet. "But the neighborhood is a little scary. Sort of like a maze. Or a hall of mirrors—made with stucco. I've been meaning to ask you if you painted your door so you wouldn't get lost." Jane asked Ivy with a smile.

"I painted my door because I drank too much one night last week and it seemed like a good idea at the time."

"It's really a great door," Jane said. "There's no way I could have managed something that creative right after having a baby. Fern seemed to suck out my soul for a few months. I think I have it back now, but I'm not sure."

Ivy shrugged. "Lucky inspires me."

"Did he inspire the painting of the skull or the vodka bottle with wings?" Frank asked, his eyebrows raised.

"I meant he just inspired the general creative impulse."

"The impulse to deface our door?" Frank asked. He was smiling, but Ivy sensed his irritation. He wanted the old beige door back.

"Don't be such a drag," Jane told him with a smile. "You should feel lucky to have such an artistic wife."

"I do," he nodded. "Don't worry, I do."

"He wants me to go back to work," Ivy told Jane.

"Not until Lucky turns one," Frank said, raising his palms as if in surrender.

"He'll still need me when he's one."

"And you'll still be here for him. You'll just be gone during the day."

Ivy sighed and looked down at her baby, who had pulled away and was nuzzled against her bare skin now, almost asleep. She'd once made twice the amount of money Frank did now. They were still living off some of the riches she'd stored away working at Elysian, but that money wouldn't last much longer.

"Let's talk about it another time," she told Frank.

"You brought it up."

"True," Ivy said.

"How's Adam, by the way?" Frank asked Jane.

Jane shrugged. "Same as always. Party-boy naturalist."

Frank laughed. "The perfect combination."

"It was in college, at least," Jane agreed.

"Move here and we'll whip him into shape. Do you want me to get rid of the party boy part or the naturalist?" Frank grinned.

Jane laughed. "Neither." She looked around the dark yard, then added, "I don't think I could live here again. It's not really home to me anymore. I've been gone too long. You know, I've now lived in Wisconsin longer than I ever lived in Las Vegas."

"It's just like riding a bike," Frank said. "Give it two more days and it will feel like home again."

"No, it won't," Ivy said.

"Don't listen to her," Frank said, rising from his seat and moving to kiss Ivy, then Lucky, on the top of the head. "I'm heading to bed," he told them. He turned away, then back, and leaned to kiss Jane's head as well. "I'm really happy you're here," he told her.

After Frank went inside, Ivy rose slowly, holding Lucky. He appeared to be deeply asleep, but the minute she was fully upright his eyes popped open and he smiled at her, struggling in an effort to switch positions. She put him over her shoulder and patted his back, swaying. He murmured against her, making all the new sounds he'd recently learned. "I can't believe he's still awake," she told Jane.

"Let's go sit on the edge of the pool. You can dangle his feet in the water and cool him off. That might help. It's still really warm tonight."

The water did feel good on her feet and calves, and she held Lucky on her knees so that his feet were submerged in the pool too. He kicked and laughed in delight and Jane laughed too, watching him.

"I think that's Orion's belt," Jane said, pointing to the sky.

"No," Ivy told her. "I don't think so. It's not straight enough. Or bright enough, but it's hard to pick out the constellations here— too much afterglow from the casinos, so maybe you're right."

"I'm probably telling my kids all the wrong constellations," Jane said. "Then they'll grow up to tell their kids the wrong things and it will be a never-ending vicious cycle of misinformation."

"You hear that, Lucky?" Ivy said, kissing the top of his head. "Don't let Auntie Jane explain the stars to you."

"I was thinking the other day, we could tell our kids the wrong information about lots of things—history or nutrition, anything— and they would probably believe us. Then think how long it would take them to unlearn it," Jane said.

"Why would you want to do that?"

"I don't *want* to. I'm just saying it's possible."

"I guess I never thought about it," Ivy said.

"I know. You wouldn't."

"What's that supposed to mean?"

"It means only a fucked-up person like me would think of something like that."

Ivy didn't like the defeated sound of Jane's voice. She watched as her friend looked down into the pool. A shock of blonde hair was tucked behind her ear and the sharp lines of her profile were cleanly pressed against dark sky, but her eyes were shadowy, unreadable. "So are you going to tell me what's going on with you and Adam?"

Jane sighed. "No, I don't think so. I can't."

"You mean it's a secret, or you can't put it into words?"

"Both, I guess."

Ivy frowned and patted Lucky's back, considering what to say. She had never been one to force a confession; on the other hand, she had never had to force anything out of Jane.

Lucky was almost asleep in her arms now, content with his cool, damp feet. The water lapping against her feet felt lukewarm and silky.

Ivy recalled the gigantic and freezing cold pool at a junior high school where she'd gone with her mother in the summer. She waited for Ivy, waist deep in her red one-piece, hair up in a bun, tortoiseshell sunglasses, the plump curve of her cheeks. Had her mother wanted to leave, even then?

"Do you think my mom's still alive?" she asked Jane.

Jane appeared unsurprised by the question and merely shrugged. "Probably. She's not very old. Fifty-five? Fifty-six?"

"That doesn't matter," Ivy said. "Ramona's mom was younger than mine when she died."

"Don't you think you would have heard something?"

"Why? How?"

"I don't know. It just seems like something that momentous couldn't happen without you hearing about it."

Ivy tried to recall the moment in the park last week, when she thought she'd seen her mother. What had been familiar about the woman ducking into the car? Lots of older women had blonde hair—that didn't mean anything. There was something else, a certain way she had moved or bent her head. Ivy couldn't pinpoint exactly what it was that had affected her. She was considering confiding this information to Jane, as she had earlier to Ramona, when something small and light sailed over the adobe wall of the backyard and landed in the water, on the steps of the shallow end where it remained, bobbing in the water.

Jane got on her knees and leaned out over the pool, then plucked it up with two fingers and brought it to Ivy. It was an origami bird woven from a palm frond, green, delicate, and perfectly crafted. When she held it up, moonlight backlit the wings. "Weird," Ivy said. "Let's go see who threw it."

Ivy led Jane through the dark house and out the front door, Lucky heavy against her chest, and they stood together on the driveway scanning the street. It was completely empty, dead silent as if no one lived here at all and this was just a movie set or a ghost town. Lights were on in one house down the block, but otherwise the homes around them were shuttered and dark.

"Does origami get thrown over your wall often?" Jane asked with a smile.

Ivy laughed and held up the bird again. "It's pretty, don't you think?"

"It is pretty. Maybe your neighborhood's not so bad after all."

Ivy shrugged and looked up and down the street. "It's the door," she suggested. "Attracting weirdos."

"Artsy weirdos."

"Right." She turned and looked at her red door, slightly ajar from their recent exit. The night she'd painted it Ivy had felt almost frantic in her desire to escape, to leave this place behind. Frank's father had been over for dinner earlier in the evening, and his sadness had seeped into her, infecting the entire house, so that just sitting on her couch later alone, reading and drinking a glass of wine, was almost unbearable. She had been unable to sit still. Her mother used to paint in moments like those, and Ivy thought she'd do the same.

"The bird on the cliff is my favorite," Jane said, walking to the door and outlining the painting with her finger. "You're really good."

Ivy shrugged. "A lot of good it does me. It's not exactly a practical talent, covering doors with strange images."

"So what? Why does everything need to be practical?" Jane said, then turned and gestured for Ivy to follow her back inside. "C'mon, let's go to bed. The kids will be up in five hours."

Ivy scanned the street again, looking for the person who'd sent this strange gift sailing over her wall, but there was not a soul in sight.

WEDNESDAY

RAMONA

In the morning, the hotel room looked better than it had the night before. Sunlight improved the beige damask wallpaper and pale green carpet. It gave life to the rich brown satin bedspread, lit the mirror above the dresser with reflected light. Last night it had seemed like an old person's room, a room of luxury for someone who had given up, and she'd almost turned around right away and driven back to Ivy's place except for the fact that she'd been so exhausted.

It was only eight o'clock right now, but she guessed that Ivy and Jane had already been up for hours, tending to breakfasts and clothes and all the other needs kids had to get the day started. Suddenly she felt completely isolated from the world here in this strange room. Why had she chosen to separate herself during the one week she was among friends?

She dressed quickly and braided her hair, avoiding her eyes in the mirror. There was no nausea this morning, nothing to indicate she might be pregnant other than the ten-day delay of her period, and she decided to wait another day to take a test. It would be too much information to take in this morning, pregnant or not. It was enough to absorb just being here, back in her hometown.

Downstairs she bought a cinnamon raisin bagel and a cup of coffee to go, then drove to the family division of the district courthouse on Pecos Road. The building was inauspicious—a pale, sandstone rectangle—and Ramona got out of her car and strode across the lot and through the glass double doors before she could change her mind. Inside, the air-conditioning was on overdrive so

Ramona shivered a bit as she asked where and how to find the information she was seeking.

It was easier than she had ever anticipated. During the past ten years every Termination of Parental Rights document had been scanned onto microfilm, and all Ramona needed to do was tell the older woman behind the desk her name and the year of her child's birth. Her voice was shaky as she spoke, and as she stood waiting for the woman to return, Ramona considered leaving. She didn't feel well standing here, and she had a sudden need to lie down in a dark room and close her eyes. Her surroundings were innocuous enough—sage-colored carpet, long rows of fluorescent lights, an assortment of strangers waiting in various lines or hunched over their own microfilm images on the bank of machines by the window—but the place had a feeling of desolation, of utter despair.

Ramona was considering her escape when the woman appeared, cleared her throat, and said, "Here you go." She handed Ramona a small flat container and pointed in the direction of the microfilm machines.

The black square of film was cool in her hands, and she took it to a machine by a window and sat down beside a skinny man with acne in an expensive-looking suit. It took her a few minutes to figure out how to insert the cartridge and get the view she wanted, and then there it was, in black and white on the screen: her signature—Ramona White—signing away the rights to her newly born child.

She touched her name on the screen, noting how her writing had been loopier then, neater. It was girlish handwriting, she supposed, and that is what she had been back then: a girl. The screen was cool beneath her fingers, and she wished she had the actual paper before her, something more alive than this cold machine.

The document was only five pages long, mostly with legal explanations of what she was giving up, and on page four she found what she was looking for. Near the bottom were the signatures and printed names of the adoptive parents and beneath this, their county and state of residence. Jim and Celeste Dillman, Clark County, Nevada.

Something about the sound of the names relieved her, especially Celeste. It was a soft, welcoming name that evoked a woman with wispy hair, a demure, high-collared shirt, a tray of lemon cookies and tea. She had met the parents once, very briefly right after the birth, but she couldn't recall a single aspect of their appearance, and she had never been allowed to know their names.

It was also a relief that these two people lived in Nevada, or at least they had at the time of adopting her baby. Ramona wrote down their names on a sheet of paper, though she couldn't imagine ever forgetting them, then returned the microfilm to the desk and asked for a phone book.

There were only twelve Dillmans listed, and Ramona was able to rule out many of them based on their first names or initials. What remained was a list of three. There were two J. Dillmans, and one James Dillman. She added these addresses and phone numbers to her sheet of paper, then surveyed the information, calculating where each of these homes might be on a map of Las Vegas, before folding the paper four times and sliding it into her bag.

The first J. Dillman lived fairly close to Ivy's neighborhood, so Ramona decided to swing by the address and park outside, then decide what, if anything, she might do. It was almost eleven o'clock now, and the day had warmed just enough to make swimming a possibility. She could check out this address then be at Ivy's in time for a dip in the pool before lunch. The cold brick in her chest was beginning to melt, and Ramona felt the first inklings of anticipation or hope. The piece of paper folded in her purse seemed to emit a subtle hum of promise.

The neighborhood she found was wealthy, with grand stucco homes traveling up the bottom rise of the Black Mountains.

Ramona found the address on her list, then parked across the street. Her old Mustang was conspicuous here—it was a place of shiny, expensive cars—and she worried someone might call the police.

The home she watched was surrounded by a high wall, but she could see the doorway and a large portion of the front yard through a wrought iron gate. It was a Spanish-style house with a red-tiled roof and dense, textured walls; the yard, however, had a distinctly Midwestern feel. Beds of tulips flanked the path to the door, and grass rolled out on either side, lush and perfect, as if this place existed in an ecosystem of its own and not in the desert.

Ramona scanned the street and watched a silver BMW pull into a garage up ahead. A girl stepped outside of another house half a block down and began jumping on a pogo stick. The noise echoed over the quiet street and began to give Ramona an immediate headache. She tried to ignore it and focused her gaze on the house across the street, which, as far as she could tell, was empty.

Fifteen minutes passed, and Ramona considered walking up the path and knocking on the door, but just then it opened, and a woman emerged, walking with a jaunty step down the walkway to the gate. She was tall and thin with dark hair cropped close to her delicate skull, and she was walking a German shepherd. She glanced at Ramona's car, directly across from her gate, and Ramona fought the urge to duck down out of sight. The woman's gaze was cool and apparently unfazed by the aging Mustang that contained a woman with long, black braids. Ramona tried to guess her age—forty-five? Fifty-five? She turned right with her dog and headed up the hill.

It occurred to Ramona to follow her, but that seemed pointless. What would she say? Are you Celeste Dillman and did you adopt a boy nineteen years ago? It sounded so raw and invasive, even inside her own head, so she stayed put and continued to watch the house. She was soon rewarded by the sight of a tall, gangly boy who ran down the path and out the gate. "Mom!" he called after the woman. "Mom!" But she was too far away to hear him and didn't look back.

The boy stood there for a moment, as if deciding. He had dark red hair that curled down over his ears, and a nice face covered in freckles and possibly a little acne. He looked nothing like Ramona, or Mark for that matter, but he also looked nothing like the woman with the dog. Had there been redheads in Ramona's family? She mentally searched what little she knew of her relatives: two uncles with black hair turning to gray; a grandmother, long dead, who had also been dark-haired. There was a bald grandfather—a possibility—but she doubted the hair that used to be on his head was red since he had dark eyes and olive skin.

She knew very little about Mark's family. He was dark-haired, as was his mother. Ramona had never met his father or any other relatives despite the fact that she'd dated him for over a year. She wondered whether or not this was normal in a high school relationship. Were other people introduced to families? Were they invited to gatherings of aunts and uncles, grandparents, and cousins?

Ramona remembered with sudden vividness the day in the school lunchroom when Mark had begged her in front of everyone to marry him and keep the baby. Ramona had been very far along then, her belly swelling her white XL Hanes T-shirt to the limit. Under that she had on black leggings and Converse high tops, refusing to wear maternity clothes even at the end. Instead, she'd shopped in the men's section of thrift stores or Kmart. Would she do that a second time around, or would she buy the happy, sleek-fitting maternity outfits she always walked past in Target and JCPenney?

She remembered, too, the constant dark circles under her eyes throughout the pregnancy, the blemishes that had formed on her back—red spots under her hair like a secret garden—then disappeared again once the baby had been born, the insistent craving she'd had for cigarettes. No, she had definitely not been one of those lovely pregnant women. There had been no glow to her skin, no placid smile of contentment on her face.

When Ramona told Mark "no," that day in the lunchroom, he'd turned and punched the kid closest to him right in the face, then run from the room. After that, most of the attention had turned to the kid who'd gotten punched. Ramona couldn't remember his name but he'd been well liked, more so than she or Mark, and blood streamed down his face. Ivy had hurried Ramona out of the lunchroom to a semiprivate niche between two buildings. Jane had been there too. The three of them huddled together in the small cove of concrete against the wind, not talking. What was there to say? They had both urged her to get an abortion many months ago, though neither friend said a word about it now that it was too late. After the death of her brother, Ramona couldn't bear the thought of killing anything, no matter how small and unknown.

The kid standing across the street right now looked too young to be nineteen, but age was such a difficult thing to gauge. He also seemed too tall to be hers, too fluid and lanky. She possessed a compact, athletic frame, and Mark had been husky in high school, heading toward a middle age of fat just like his mother.

The boy loped after the woman with the dog, breaking into an awkward run to catch her. Ramona watched until he reached his mother, then closed her eyes, not wanting to see them together. She doubted very much that this was her child; still, there was a pain in watching him with this other parent that she couldn't explain.

When she opened her eyes, the woman and boy were far ahead on the sidewalk, and the girl on the pogo stick had gone inside. The street was empty, so Ramona stepped out of her car and walked across the road, through the gate and up the tulip-lined pathway to the front door. She held the paper with the address in her hand, and carefully checked the numbers with the ones beside the door. This was the right place.

She knocked and rang the bell, and when there was no answer she tried the doorknob and found it unlocked, as she somehow knew it would be. Without giving herself time to consider what she was doing, Ramona opened the door and stepped inside the house. A high ceiling soared over her. A wrought-iron, spiral staircase led from the expansive foyer to a shadowy upstairs. "Hello?" Ramona called out, first with a hoarse, unused voice, then louder. "Hello?"

She stepped across the red-tiled foyer then slipped off her flip-flops before padding onto the creamy carpet of the living room, soft beneath her feet. The room was more lived in than she'd expected. Coffee mugs sat on an end table beside an open newspaper; a pair of hockey skates—strange to find those here in the desert—were set in the corner by the television; a discarded pink robe was slung over an armchair. But even these items seemed artfully arranged, as if set in place for a photo shoot.

One more room, she told herself, crossing the carpet to the tile of the kitchen. One more room, then she would leave before the woman and boy and dog came back and arrested her for trespassing. There was nothing in the kitchen of interest, so she headed upstairs, where three open doors revealed bedrooms in various states of disarray.

One door was closed, so Ramona turned the handle of that door, feeling as if this were the important room, the one that would reveal all the home's secrets, and peered inside.

What she saw made her heart stop: an old man snoring lightly on a twin bed. Ramona closed the door as quietly as possible, her heart beginning to pound with a fury now, and took the stairs two at a time, holding her breath. She stopped at the bottom of the steps and listened but heard nothing. Even the man's snores were eclipsed by the heavy bedroom door.

Her hand was on the knob to leave, when a stack of mail on a nearby table stopped her. Of course. She would just check the names on their mail. Why hadn't she thought of that before? There were five letters: James Dillman, Jim Dillman, J. Dillman, James Dillman, and finally, one addressed in slanted handwriting to

Barbara Dillman. Barbara. That must have been the woman she'd just seen walking the German shepherd.

A dog barked outside, breaking the silence, and Ramona set the mail down and looked out a window, already planning how she might escape through a back door if Barbara and the kid were coming up the front walk, but there was no one, so she opened the door and pressed it closed behind her, then ran down the walk and made sure the street was empty before crossing to her car and sealing herself back inside.

It was only when she was five blocks away that Ramona realized she'd left her flip-flops in their foyer. She was driving barefoot and hadn't even noticed. That's what adrenaline could do, she guessed, rev your nerves up to the point that you didn't notice you were shoeless. So they would know someone had been inside, but Ramona couldn't imagine they would do anything about it, once they realized nothing was missing.

At least the information she'd found had been valuable. Of course it was possible the woman with the dog was Jim Dillman's second wife, Barbara, and the red-haired boy was still Ramona's son, but she felt certain this wasn't the case. That boy could not be hers.

When she parked outside Ivy's home, Ramona found a pen in the glove compartment and crossed that particular J. Dillman off her list, then slid it back into her bag and got out of the car.

JANE

Jane pushed the stroller up the incline, noticing how much nicer it was than the one she had at home—lighter and sleek as a bird. Also, the awning completely covered Fern so that Jane didn't have to hear complaints about the bright sun in her eyes.

Rocky ran up ahead, and Ivy pushed Lucky in another, slightly larger stroller. It was warm outside but not too warm yet, and the air was dry and perfect. Mountains rose up in the distance, their cool, dark gray forms pasted onto the blue sky.

"Let's just walk by, and if we see him, we see him," Jane suggested again. "I want him to know I don't wear a nightgown around every day."

Ivy laughed. "Why would you possibly care what he thinks?"

Jane looked down at her current choice of clothing: sandals, blue shorts, a white tank top that complimented her already darkening skin. She couldn't explain her need to see this man, to have him see her looking decent. It was an indecent urge, she was sure. "I don't care," she said. "Never mind."

"It's no big deal," Ivy said. "His house is on the way."

The origami bird was shoved into Jane's pocket, and it poked her hip as she strode forward. They turned the corner and were nearing his house, but she couldn't hear the shouts of his daughters as she had yesterday morning. Even though it was the man's daughters who had the names of muses, and she knew the man's name was Rex, Jane had begun to think of him as "The Muse" in her mind, imagining he had some creative pull on her, though if asked, she would have been unable to explain what, exactly, this meant. She had dreamed about him last night. He floated on his back in the pool, white hair streaming out behind him, the origami bird perched on his chest. She had gotten into the water and walked toward him, and the bird had lifted and flown away, its wide green wings still made of palm fronds. She woke with the certain knowledge that The Muse had made the bird for her. Of course he had.

They slowed in front of his house now, and Jane looked at the empty yard and driveway. The chair was gone, as was the stack of palm fronds. Or maybe Jane had imagined them? She had not yet confessed to Ivy who she believed was behind the bird.

Through the large front window Jane saw movement: a woman with short black hair walked into view. She was wearing a cap-sleeved red dress that nipped in at the waist, then floated out in the style of a 1950s party girl; she picked up a stack of mail from the table and leafed through it. The Muse was nowhere in sight. "His wife, I think," Ivy said, continuing to walk.

Jane realized she had completely stopped and gave the stroller a push to catch up. "I didn't imagine her looking like that," Jane said. "I thought she'd have that white fairy hair too."

"I guess you'll have to show him your nonnightgown look another time."

Jane laughed, embarrassed, and changed the subject. "You don't really hate it here, do you?" she asked, looking around at the clean, empty street, breathing in the dry air.

Her friend shrugged. "It's just a little lonely. That's the main problem. I can't find any people I like here."

"Do you think Ramona will be upset we left without her?"

"We left a note. She's taking forever."

Jane nodded and looked ahead to Rocky who was running in a serpentine pattern half a block ahead.

"Faster, please," Fern's disembodied voice called up to her through the awning.

Ivy picked up her pace immediately, and Jane hurried to catch up. She had brought along a travel mug of coffee, and they were now going too fast for her to reasonably take a swallow without spilling. For some reason this began to fill her with irritation—with her daughter for ordering them to speed up, with Ivy for instantly obeying. She lengthened her stride and looked around the neighborhood, willing her good mood back into place.

The homes they passed were now smaller versions of Ivy's, the front yards and gardens all that served to differentiate the owners' personalities: gravel and decorative boulders; an ornate cactus garden, complete with pathways and statues; lush grass, broken only by a young mulberry tree.

They reached the end of the street and turned right. To Jane's surprise they were done with the neighborhood. The street ended, and over a low concrete barrier the base of the Black Mountains rose up before them. Garbage collected along the edge of the wall—an empty bag of Doritos, two beer cans, a purple brush—but beyond this the slow rise was clean and inviting, crowned with green bundles of sagebrush, rocks, and low, spiny cactus. Rocky had already jumped the barrier and begun to run up the hill. Ivy and Jane parked the strollers and Jane unlatched Fern, who leapt to follow her brother over the barrier. Ivy fitted Lucky into his sling, then gently stepped over the wall, cradling her baby with one hand.

Jane was the only one left on the other side of the wall, and she hesitated, watching Rocky pick up a rock. Fern squatted beside him and peered underneath. "Be careful," Ivy called to them. "Sometimes there are scorpions under rocks."

Jane turned to look at the street behind her, the asphalt beginning to lightly steam with the increasing heat of the day. There was something so inviting about the emptiness, about the clean, straight lines of the new road. She imagined The Muse and his wife in the kitchen, drinking coffee and reading the newspaper before she left for work. Jane wondered what the wife did for a living and guessed it was something professional from her smart dress. Jane felt an ache of longing for her old cubicle, the view from her second-story window of the side lawn and parking lot where she liked to watch people arrive and step out of their cars as she pulled together the strings of her interviews until a story rose up, fully formed.

Her flirtation with the crime editor had begun in that very cubicle. It was not a place she should remember so fondly. Jane shook away the image of him, leaning over her shoulder to read her lead. He had always smelled of Earl Grey tea and mints to hide the cigarettes he smoked during breaks. She had never been able to figure out why someone not particularly attractive or even all that interesting had lit such a fierce craving in her bones.

They hiked up the hill, over a rise and down, then back up another easy slope. Lucky fell asleep against Ivy's chest and the kids were tireless, running ahead, then looping back to show Jane and Ivy what they'd found: a smooth red rock, a handful of cicada shells, a stick shaped like a Y. The street and houses were out of sight now, and the sky had turned the washed-out blue of noon. The sun bore down, and Jane began to feel sweaty and out of breath. "I think I've lost my heat legs," she told Ivy. "I'm dying."

"I bet it's not even eighty-five degrees," Ivy said. "The Midwest has made you wimpy."

They sat down on a large boulder, and Ivy pulled a bag of snacks from a large pocket on the sling. Grapes and crackers were handed out, and Jane retrieved the two water bottles she'd put in her small backpack and passed them around. Ivy pulled an elastic band out of her back pocket and looped her long hair into a makeshift bun at the nape of her neck just as Lucky woke up, whimpering slightly. Ivy pulled him out of the sling and passed him to Jane while she extricated herself from the contraption.

He started to cry in earnest the moment he was in Jane's arms, so she stood and put him over her shoulder, patting his back and bouncing lightly. He wailed louder, and Jane felt as if she might begin to cry herself; she was so awkward with this baby even though she had two of her own. How was it that she had even managed to make it this far? Adam had done much of this part, Jane recalled now. He had perfected a swaying rhythm that calmed Rocky, and a bouncy energetic walk that Fern liked.

"Here," Ivy said, taking Lucky and settling down on the rock where she lifted her shirt and attached the crying baby to her breast. The silence that followed was sweet and absolute. Jane sighed and plopped down on the rock across from her.

Her friend looked like the Virgin Mary herself, sitting there nursing her baby, the sun creating a glow in her hair and over her soft skin, dewy with a sheen of sweat. Over the years, Ivy had become the undisputed beauty among them. In high school, she had been too scrawny, with eyes too big for her head and unwieldy hair that never quite looked right. Now, however, she had been made curvaceous, almost plump, by motherhood, and had grown into her too-large eyes; their luminous brown drew you toward her. Her hair floated in long, brown waves over her shoulders, and she had a look of innocence, of saintly purity that drew you in. You wanted, Jane thought now, not only to look like her, but to think her thoughts, to feel the grace she must inhabit.

"I could really go for one of those sweet potato purses right about now," Ivy said, looking up from Lucky.

"Or a minicupcake." Jane glanced over at the kids. Rocky was drawing a circle on the ground with a stick several yards away, and Fern was trying to sit inside it. "You hired him for the party, right?"

Ivy nodded. "We're meeting to plan the menu tomorrow."

"So what's it like spending time with Jeremy again?"

Ivy shrugged, looking up to the pale sky as if for guidance. "It's nice. I'm surprised, but it feels good to be around him. I know you guys—well, Ramona at least—think he's a jerk, but I think she's wrong. He's always been good at the core. I don't care anymore about the other girls or everything else that happened. He's just an old friend now."

"You two looked like more than friends yesterday when he brought out those cookies. I think they cast a spell on you." Jane smiled. "He used to make you cookies after your mom left—that's it, right?"

"He didn't cast a spell," Ivy said dismissively, but she looked down at Lucky and stroked his hair, appearing to avoid Jane's gaze. Her tone had hardened when she spoke again. "And yes, he did used to make those for me after my mom left. That was something really kind that he did for me, and it affected me a lot. Not many people were doing kind things for me then, you know?"

"Okay, I know, I understand. No need to get defensive. I like the guy." Jane tried to recall whether or not she'd shown particular kindness to Ivy when her mother left. She had been her friend the same way she always had been, but nothing more. It now seemed she had been remiss, had failed Ivy when she could have buoyed her somehow.

Lucky pulled away and Ivy deftly pulled down her bra and shirt then sat him up on her lap and patted his back. The baby's expression was dreamy now, and Jane reached for him. Ivy passed him over.

"Sorry," Ivy said, then stood up and stretched her arms over her head. "I used to have to defend Jeremy all through high school to everyone—my father, Ramona, even you sometimes—and now look at me, doing it again, and we're not even a couple. I don't know if I'd even call us friends."

"You're loyal."

"Or stupid."

"No," Jane shook her head. "Definitely not stupid." The baby leaned his back against her chest and kicked out his pudgy legs. His happiness seeped into her so that she felt a momentary infusion of pleasure. The air smelled so familiar out here, of sand and some type of plant she couldn't name—maybe creosote, she thought, or sage? She rose and walked over to see what the kids were looking at in the sand. At first she thought it was a stocking or a gauzy scarf they were prodding with sticks, then Jane registered the pattern and realized it was the cast-off skin of a rattlesnake. She looked around on the ground quickly, as if expecting the skin's owner to be nearby, but there was no movement on the sand.

"Who found this?" Ivy asked.

Rocky raised his hand, tentatively, as if he might be in trouble.

"They say that if you put a rattlesnake skin in your pocket, you'll have good luck. Or if you tie it around your neck, it will ward off illness," Ivy said.

"Really?" Rocky asked.

"It's true." She handed the skin to Rocky and he glanced up at Jane, who nodded at him.

He rolled the skin into a ball then gently slid it into the large side pocket of his cargo shorts.

"Let's head back," Ivy said, taking Lucky from Jane and settling him back into the sling.

The hike down the mountain seemed longer, now that the sun was higher in the sky. Also, Jane was getting hungry, and she was sure the kids were too.

When they finally reached the concrete barrier by the street, Ivy stepped over the wall, then swung her stroller around and frowned. Placed in the seat of green cloth was a present the size of a shoebox wrapped in baby blue paper and topped with a silver bow. She picked up the package and looked at Jane. "That's strange."

"Any card?"

Ivy inspected it, then shook her head.

"I want to open it," Rocky called out, leaping over the barrier and holding out his hands to Ivy.

She passed it to him and he ripped into the paper with glee to reveal a Nike shoe box. Inside, there was a piggy bank, white porcelain with black letters and a red heart on the side: I Love NY. There was no note inside the box either.

"A gift for Lucky?" Jane suggested. "From a secret admirer?"

"Who gives a baby a piggy bank?" Ivy asked, taking it from Rocky and turning it over in her hands.

"Do you know anyone from New York?"

Ivy shook her head.

"Maybe it's a bomb," Rocky said.

Jane turned to him and frowned.

"I don't hear any ticking," Ivy told him, holding it to her ear. She set the piggy bank back in the box on the ground, then got Lucky into the stroller and handed the gift to him. He inspected it closely, then cradled it to his chest as if it were a real creature, a pet pig.

They discussed possibilities on the way home. Ivy seemed to think it was from Jeremy, or maybe a woman she knew named Mia who lived around the corner. Jane agreed that Jeremy was a good possibility but didn't see why he wouldn't want credit for the present. There was no need for him to be secretive with a baby gift, was there?

"No, but he just likes being secretive. That's how he is," Ivy said.

"Maybe there's a plane ticket inside the pig for you to meet him in Acapulco. Or a hotel room key. Or maybe just the key to his apartment. I guess he wouldn't need to get a hotel room to be with you since he lives alone."

Ivy laughed, then stopped the stroller, gently removed the pig from Lucky's hands, and shook it. "Empty."

"What if there was a key inside, just hypothetically? Would you use it?" Jane asked.

Ivy shook her head. "No way. I'd never cheat on Frank, especially now."

"Why especially now?"

"Well, because of Lucky. Now anything I do to Frank will hurt Lucky too, don't you think?"

Jane considered this. "I don't know. I guess you're right. For some reason I like to still think of myself as a separate being."

"Well, you're not anymore, so get used to it."

REX

He was in the dining room, crouching to retrieve the arm of a Barbie from behind a chair when he saw Jane again through the slatted blinds, pausing in front of his home with a stroller, and her friend, the one who lived behind the crazy red door. He'd noticed the friend on several occasions—she was too pretty not to notice—but it was the sight of Jane, pausing and peering toward his house, shading her eyes with her hand, that sent a tremor of feeling through him. The feeling was two parts lust, but one part a simple desire to talk to her again, to remind her of her strange outfit at the Mormon dance all those years ago.

He would have gone outside and said hello, but Kristina was here, rifling through her mail in the front room and collecting a few more of her things, a slow, drawn-out process that he imagined might last several years. This time, she was seeking an alleged vase she'd bought in La Jolla one summer. He couldn't remember any vase from La Jolla, but she was intent on finding it and she probably would because that's the way she was: efficient and thorough with a flawless memory.

With the Barbie's arm clenched in his fist, he returned to the kitchen, got out the superglue, and reaffixed the arm to the doll waiting on the kitchen table. The girls were in the backyard, filling up the baby pool, and he watched them from the window, relieved to have them back here with no visible wounds from their trip to the desert. He was waiting for Kristina to leave so he could ask them more about the trip.

"Found it," she said, coming into the kitchen with a vase so pale blue it was almost white. He reached for it and she handed it over. It was cool to the touch, the size and shape of a small gourd. Turning it over, he tried to remember buying this with his wife. It seemed essential that he recall that moment on their long-ago trip to La Jolla.

"It's from that shell shop," she told him. "We had calamari at that place, the little one with the weird drip candles, then we walked down to that shell shop and bought this."

Calamari. Drip candles. He couldn't picture any of it. It sounded like a scene from a bad novel. He handed back the vase and shook his head. "Wow, I'm getting old," he told her. "My mind's a blank."

She shrugged. Their shared memories were no longer of importance to her. Color striped her cheeks and nose from the recent trip, and she wore the red dress that had always been one of his favorites. He considered touching her then, just on the shoulder or lower back, but a voice inside told him this was a bad idea. "You're going to be late for work, aren't you?" he asked.

"Yep," she said. "I've gotta take off." She stepped outside and kissed each girl good-bye, then was through the house again and gone. Gone.

Rex went into the backyard and checked his small garden. He watered the basil and pulled out three weeds surrounding the serrano peppers, then coiled the hose and set it on the patio. Polly and Callie were in the baby pool now, laughing about something, and he walked over and asked, "So how was the trip, really?"

"Fun," Callie said, looking up at him. "Mom's friend Peter showed us how to find scorpions."

So his name was Peter. It had been almost too easy to unearth the first detail. "I could have shown you that. Pick up a rock, and there might be one underneath."

"Well, there's a certain kind of rock to look for," she explained. "And you should use a stick to lift it. We didn't see any scorpions though."

"I ate cactus," Polly offered. "At the restaurant. It was gross."

"Why would you order cactus?" he asked, his stomach roiling at the thought.

"I just tried Peter's. I had a quesadilla for my own dinner."

The image this evoked—a strange man offering his older daughter a forkful of cactus across a table—filled him with a sudden rage. "Oh, all right," was all he could bring himself to say. He turned away from them, so they couldn't detect his anger, the tight fire of it burning his insides, so that he could almost feel the skin over his chest blackening from within.

"Will you practice ball with me, before it gets too hot out?" Polly asked.

She was starting softball next week, and they had been working on throwing and catching at least once a day.

"Sure," he said, his voice sounding choked off to his own ears, not like himself at all. "In a minute."

Inside, he went to the front room and lay down on the white couch, setting his dirty tennis shoes on the armrest, then lifting his legs to see the gray splotch they'd made. What difference did it make anymore if this room remained clean? He closed his eyes and tried to calm himself with deep breathing, but he kept seeing images of his wife beside a different man. He wanted to know what this particular man, Peter, looked like, just so he could know and be done with it. He imagined a shorter man with dark hair, dark eyes, someone completely different from him. A clean-cut executive maybe, or a military officer.

A hand on his ankle. "Dad?"

He opened his eyes to Polly. "I'm ready," he told her. "Go get your glove."

In the street, he felt cleaner, his anger-blackened chest fading back to its normal pale pinkish white. The ball was sure in his hands as he hurled it toward his daughter's mitt. She was a natural, like he had been, still *was* he guessed, though he no longer played ball anymore. Callie watched from the sidelines, sitting on the curb.

Even though she didn't possess her older sister's talent, he should throw a couple of balls to her too, after he was done helping Polly.

The old lady next door came out on her front step, hands on hips in her yellow housedress, and watched them for a long minute. Her gaze was an irritation, and Rex felt his calm begin to ruffle once again. She had complained to him, on more than one occasion, about the loud fights he'd had with Kristina those final months together, and he still held this against the old bag. Couldn't she hear that his marriage was imploding? Did she need to make it worse by complaining?

She made her slow way across her lawn to where Callie sat on the curb, and Rex saw her leaning down and speaking to his daughter, but he couldn't hear what she was saying. The ball thwacked softly into Polly's waiting mitt, and she threw it back with more force this time, which made him smile. She was improving. Despite the divorce and this new boyfriend of her mother's and every other sad distraction in her life, she was getting better at catching and throwing, and it was all because of him, because of his work with her. He held this thought out before him like a crystal, gleaming and warm from the sun, sending its refracted rainbow against his skin.

Rex sent the ball back to her, not using all of his force but giving it a little more kick each time. She was only eight years old, after all. The sound of it hitting her glove was a soft thud of air, his own catch a slightly louder version. Thud, toss, thud, toss, thud, toss. He could do this all day long.

The old woman—Rosemary was her name, that was it—sat down on the curb beside Callie and was watching them too now, and actually smiling. Her perfect dentures gleamed across the asphalt, a wind lifting the edges of her gray, bobbed hair. Callie was leaning against her, whispering something. Having this audience of two enhanced his feeling of well-being, reminded him more fully of high school when everyone had watched him play, waiting for something amazing to happen. It was why he had left the church—well, one of the many reasons. He didn't want to break his career trajectory with a two-year mission to some faraway country. After graduation, he pitched for the High Desert Mavericks for two years in a California town even more desolate than Las Vegas, but his game had fizzled there, and he'd quit after being passed over for promotion to the big leagues for the second year in a row.

Thud, toss, thud, toss. They hadn't dropped one yet. The air was growing warmer as the sun climbed, but he liked the feel of the heat through his black T-shirt. Maybe Jane would walk this way again with her friend and see him playing catch out here with his daughter. That had to be appealing to a fellow parent, didn't it?

Polly's face was stern with concentration beneath her lavender ball cap. She got the same vertical crease between her eyebrows that her mother did when she was thinking hard on something. She had Kristina's arched brows and finely shaped mouth, too, and sometimes when she pursed that mouth into a pout of disapproval, it was like looking at a miniature, white-haired version of his ex-wife.

Watching Polly and listening to the rhythm of their game, he suddenly remembered buying the vase. They found it in a shop on the water with a long, winding stairway in the back that led down beneath the store to a cave that opened out onto the sea. You paid extra to climb down to that cave, and he could still smell its dark scent of wet earth and saltwater. Waves poured in, but he and Kristina were safe, up on a wooden observation platform. That was all he could see: that platform and the two of them standing on it, watching the waves unfurl in that dark, mysterious space. He couldn't picture the actual store, or the restaurant she'd mentioned, but he felt better, remembering that cave.

"I threw the ball with Peter a little bit," Polly called over to him, "in Death Valley."

Her voice broke into the memory, and he heard her as if from a great distance. Then the meaning of the words became clear, replacing the image of the cave with a new one: a dark-haired man throwing a ball to his daughter, to Polly. The pain of this image was like a wave breaking inside of him, curling up in the base of his chest and unleashing its powerful fury through his long, outstretched arm as he threw the ball back. She caught it, stumbling from its force, and immediately started to cry.

Rosemary reached her before he did—he'd never seen the old lady move so quickly—and then Polly was removing her glove with a whimper and holding up her crooked finger for all to see. It was obviously broken.

"Oh, honey." He cradled her in his arms, lifting her and holding her small frame close to his chest. "I'm so sorry."

"You threw it too hard," she said, her voice angry even through the tears. "You know you can't throw it that hard to me."

"I know," he whispered. "It was an accident. I'm so sorry."

Her tears increased then, and through a broken sob she said, "I want Mom. I just want Mom."

"Me too," he whispered into her hair, then met the old woman's eyes and felt a flush of embarrassment run through him. Why was this person once again witnessing his weak moment?

"You take her to the hospital," Rosemary told him, "and I'll watch Callie." Her voice was kinder than he expected.

"Okay," he agreed. "Thank you."

He folded Polly carefully into the backseat, and left for the emergency room, looking once in the rearview mirror to find the old lady and Callie holding hands in the middle of the street, waving good-bye.

IVY

Ivy grabbed a beer for herself from the icy bucket that Frank liked to bring out by the pool whenever people were over and sat down beside Jane. Ramona was drifting nearby on a pink raft, and Frank swam laps, back and forth past their knees. "Don't tell Frank about the piggy bank," she whispered to Jane. "I don't want him to make a big deal out of it."

"Fine," Jane agreed, then looked toward the shallow end, where Rocky was splashing Fern in the face.

Lucky was asleep in his crib, and Ivy leaned back and raised her face to the sun, feeling the beer move through her faster than she'd expected. She was secretly pleased by Jeremy's gift. He had mostly been a selfish boy back in high school—even the cookies he'd baked for her typically came with an unspoken expectation of sex—but this gift seemed simple and pure, particularly since it had been anonymous.

Ramona paddled over to them, avoiding Frank's lap across the pool, then lifted herself out and sat on the edge beside Ivy.

"Where were you all morning, anyway?" Ivy asked her.

She shrugged. "Nowhere. I slept in. I think I might go by the old apartment building later though, or tomorrow. You want to come?"

"Why?" Ivy asked. "That place is awful."

"I don't think anyone we know lives there anymore," Ramona said.

"Of course they don't," Ivy said, shaking her head. "I won't go near that place ever again."

"It wasn't that bad," Jane said.

"You never had to live there," Ivy told her.

"True," Jane said, sipping her beer. "I was always jealous that you two got to live in the same place though. That part seemed fun, and the fountain was cool."

"It was fun," Ramona said, nudging Ivy with her elbow. "All the sleepovers, playing hide and seek in the hallways, the guy in number four who always lent us his moped."

Ivy nodded and said, "You're right," but she was recalling only the bad times: The day in fourth grade when Ramona's brother had died. The morning after her own mother had left and she'd stood waiting for her on the balcony. The long nights of listening for her return and hearing only snoring in the next room or shouting down the hall, or the distant sound of weeping. Ivy had always associated the weeping with Ramona's mother, but she lived all the way across the courtyard and emerged every morning dry-eyed in her cocktail uniform, looking small and fragile with all that black hair piled up on her head. She surely cried at night, but not within Ivy's hearing.

Jane brought her another beer, which Ivy finished quickly, then set the bottle on the edge and slipped into the pool just as Frank lifted himself out of the deep end and disappeared inside. She swam the length of the pool twice before coming up for air in the shallow end.

The sliding glass door opened, and Jeremy appeared, carrying a plate of sandwiches. Frank walked out behind him, holding a large bowl of grapes and a fistful of napkins. The two men turned to face the pool, and standing like that, side by side, Ivy had the feeling of seeing her old life beside her current one. Frank was taller, broader, and more self-assured. He held the bowl of grapes casually, under one arm like a basketball; whereas Jeremy held the plate of sandwiches formally out in front of him, as if serving a table of diners.

"What are you doing here?" Ivy asked from the pool, then added, "Hi."

"We're supposed to meet, remember?" Jeremy said. "Go over the menu for Friday?"

"I thought you said tomorrow."

He shook his head. "I can come back if you like; it's no big deal."

"No," Frank shook his head and patted Jeremy on the back. "She can go. We'll watch the kids," he told her.

"We can just talk in the living room really quick," Ivy suggested.

"I was hoping to show you the commercial kitchen where I rent space too," Jeremy said. "That is, if you're interested."

"Of course she's interested," Frank said, and Ivy couldn't tell if he was just being polite or mildly sarcastic.

Ivy hesitated, not wanting to step out of the water in front of Jeremy, feeling embarrassed by the slight pooch of her belly still leftover from having Lucky, by the small starburst of spider veins on her left thigh which she hadn't yet had time to cover with a summer tan. Ramona, who was sitting under the yellow umbrella, seemed to read her mind and brought a towel to the pool's edge where she held it out for Ivy as if for a child. It was enough to propel her out of the water, then into the bedroom where she changed into a skirt and T-shirt and ran a brush through her wet hair.

In the bathroom mirror, her eyes were tired, but her skin was slightly flushed, giving her a healthy glow, and the leftover plumpness in her face from having the baby made her look younger, she decided, but slightly naive. She swiped on pale lip gloss, checked her teeth, then left the bathroom.

Jeremy's car did not have air-conditioning, and the breeze through the open windows quickly dried Ivy's hair as they drove out of her neighborhood. The two beers hummed in her, relaxed her, and she leaned back against the seat and watched Jeremy shift gears, then ease onto Eastern Avenue. Should she thank him for the present now, she wondered? Or would it be better not to say anything?

They'd been driving for several minutes before it dawned on Ivy how far they were going. Her new neighborhood was left behind along with the landscaped sidewalks and ornamental medians. The palm trees were further apart now, and shaggier, the homes along the road more like white boxes than Spanish bungalows. They passed a Chevron, a Circle K, an endless block of beige strip mall, a white stucco house with a picket fence, then more strip mall. "How far are you taking me?" Ivy asked.

"The kitchen is over by Vegas High, in an old building near downtown. It's a really cool space."

"Not to be rude, but why do you want me to see it?"

He shrugged. "I don't know. Since my parents died, I don't have anyone to brag to, or show stuff to anymore. I guess I just want someone who knows me to see the things in my life that are important."

This made sense to her, so she tried to relax back into the ride and just take in the scenery. She hadn't ventured to this part of town since she moved back and was surprised when they passed Jaycee Park where she'd sometimes skipped school with Ramona and Jane. She hadn't realized how little time it took to get back here, to travel to the places where she'd grown up. The slide, once covered in graffiti, looked new, and the grass was green and neatly trimmed. Her brief vision of the park's familiar hills and picnic tables, the baseball diamond off to the right, calmed her. Maybe she was making a mistake by so completely avoiding her old haunts.

When he turned left onto Charleston and started driving toward their former neighborhood, agitation stirred inside her. "You're not taking me by my old apartment building, are you?"

"Nope."

"Because I have no desire to see that place."

"I understand. There's just one quick stop I want to make before we see the kitchen."

"Where?"

"It's a surprise."

"I shouldn't be gone too long," she told him. "When Lucky wakes up, he'll want some milk, *my* milk. He won't take a bottle."

Jeremy frowned and looked over at her. "So you think if you disappeared forever Lucky wouldn't survive, that he'd never accept formula or cow's milk?"

"I didn't say that."

"That's what you're implying." He grinned at her and tapped his thumbs on the wheel in a snappy beat.

"I'm just saying I shouldn't be gone too long, okay?" She said this sternly, the hum of the beer beginning to wear off and irritation settling more firmly into place. Why had she agreed to leave the house with him? Why had she hired him in the first place?

"All right, take it easy. I'll get you back as soon as I can." He moved as if to pat her bare knee, but she shifted her leg away, out of his reach.

"Wow, you've gotten so uptight. What did you do with the old Ivy? I'd like to see her again."

She rolled her eyes and leaned back against her seat with a huff. She noticed for the first time that there was a sparkly plastic flip-flop wedged into the space between her seat and the gear shift. "Whose is this?" she asked, plucking it out and waving it around. It was purple, size nine.

He glanced at the shoe and shrugged. "Probably Gretchen's. I don't know."

"You don't recognize your own girlfriend's flip-flop?"

"I told you," he said, giving her a slow smile, "she's not my girlfriend."

He made another right turn, then a left, and parked the car. Ivy hadn't been paying attention—the flip-flop angered her, though she couldn't say why—and looked out to find they were sitting beside Las Vegas High School, now a school for the arts called the Las Vegas Academy.

Despite the school's new purpose, and a new coat of coral paint, the building was the same. It had been designated a historic landmark after they graduated, and she admired the art deco façade, the latticed windows and clean lines. This was a structure from her past that she actually liked, the only building in her small radius that wasn't ugly.

"C'mon," he said. "Follow me."

He retrieved a minicooler from the trunk and slung a duffel bag over his shoulder then crossed the empty street and led her to a metal gate through which she could see a portion of the school's central courtyard, the lunchroom hulking behind it. "Here," he said, handing her the duffel bag, then he dug into the pocket of his jeans and retrieved a key.

Ivy followed him to the open-air courtyard where she used to meet him between classes. She'd talk to him while he smoked a cigarette, then they'd share one deep, lingering kiss, an embarrassing memory to her now, before heading off to their separate classes. Frank had always refused to kiss openly at school, which Ivy had come to admire, though she'd originally felt slighted by it.

Jeremy looked around, seeming to consider the open space, then doubled back to a shadier corner beneath a stairwell among a quad of classrooms and set down the cooler and duffel bag. He produced a red-and-white checked blanket from this bag, which he shook out and laid on the ground, then motioned for her to sit. Because it was spring break, there was not a student or teacher in sight, and the place was eerily empty, her voice echoing lightly when she spoke. "How did you get that key?"

"A buddy of mine is a janitor here."

"And let me guess, you sell him drugs."

He looked up from the open cooler and shook his head. "No way, I don't do that anymore. I can't believe you think I still do that." He opened a Tupperware container and set it in front of her. It contained a sandwich on crusty French bread, with what looked

like thinly sliced carrots sticking out of its sides. She picked it up
and took a bite, surprised by its spicy complexity, the crispness
of the carrots against some type of meat, ham, she guessed, and
there was cilantro too, and maybe sliced radish? "This is great," she
said. He passed her a cold thermos, and she unscrewed the lid and
sniffed, expecting the pungent ammonia of alcohol, but instead the
aroma was slightly sweet, lemony. She took a sip and recognized it
as iced tea, though it wasn't a typical black blend.

"The sandwich is called a *bahn mi*," he told her. "It's sort of a
Vietnamese-French fusion. I know it won't work for your party,
but I wanted you to try it." He bit into a sandwich of his own, then
grabbed the thermos. "Iced green tea with mint and lemon," he said,
before taking a long swallow.

"This sandwich could work for the grown-ups," she said.

He shook his head. "Not everyone will like it. Too risky for a
mixed crowd. I knew you would like it though. So I'm thinking of
a corn and red pepper salad that I do and some empanadas for the
adults, both sweet and savory. Also a green olive tapenade, some
tomatillo salsa, cheeses, things like that."

She nodded, unsure what empanadas were, but decided to
trust him on the food. "Sounds perfect."

He finished his sandwich quickly, then leaned back and crossed
his legs at the ankles. "Listen, I'm sorry I took you all the way out
here. I just thought it would be fun."

"It is fun," she admitted. She'd finished her sandwich too and
was drinking tea. A sparrow swooped under the stairwell and
buzzed their heads, causing them both to duck and then laugh. Ivy
looked up and noticed a nest tucked under one of the stairs, and
she pointed it out to Jeremy. "We're in her territory."

"This is *our* territory," he said. "We were here long before she
built that nest."

"True," she agreed, leaning back against the cool concrete wall.
It was oddly comfortable under here, tucked away from the sun

and the noises of the neighborhood. Jeremy stretched out his legs, and his foot, in its black tennis shoe, touched her sandal.

"Sort of like old times, isn't it?" He smiled and she felt something familiar zigzag through her insides, a buzzing expectation.

"Not exactly," she said.

"I keep expecting Mr. Tripoli to peer under here and say, 'Get your sorry asses to class.'"

"Mr. Tripoli never talked like that."

"He did to me."

"Well, you probably deserved it."

He nodded slowly. "Yes, I probably did." He leaned to rummage in the cooler again and brought out another, smaller Tupperware container. This one contained a row of four tiny cakes, perfect rectangles covered in glazed icing and each topped by a delicate decoration: a violet set against white, an espresso bean pressed into a dark chocolate glaze, two raspberries pressed side by side on top of a pink cake, and a white curlicue scrolled across a deep lavender background.

"Petit fours," he told her. "I want to make a whole tray of these for the party. They take a while but they're worth it."

"They're beautiful," Ivy said, picking up the one with the raspberries and taking a bite. There was chocolate inside layered with vanilla and raspberry. She'd never tasted anything so good.

She was biting into her second petit four, the one with the violet on top, when they heard the gate clang open and then shut with a heavy click. Ivy stopped chewing and looked over at Jeremy, who shrugged and held a finger to his lips. From their position beneath the stairwell, they saw a woman's feet, wrapped in gold gladiator sandals. The woman passed nearby, then stepped out into the courtyard, where they could see her entire form from the back: short brown hair bounced over a purple top as she crossed the concrete, swinging a green canvas bag.

"A teacher?" Ivy whispered.

Jeremy nodded. The woman stopped suddenly, and just as she turned toward them, Jeremy looped an arm around Ivy's waist and pulled her close, out of the woman's line of sight and into the deeper shadows of the stairwell. The woman peered in their direction, then turned and continued across the yard.

"That was a close one," Jeremy said.

Ivy turned to Jeremy, his face inches from her own, and breathed in his familiar scent of cinnamon and tobacco. Strange, she thought, how a person could still smell the same after all these years. His hand rested lightly on her waist, and he tightened it and pulled her a millimeter closer. She'd always liked the contrasting colors of his face—the shiny deep black of his hair against the pale skin, the unexpected green of his eyes. Without thinking, she swept her fingers over his forehead and smoothed back his hair. He leaned toward her then, expectant, but she scooted away before he could reach her, understanding that she had just barely avoided doing something she would regret. What was the matter with her?

"This is going to sound strange," Jeremy said, now sitting at a safe distance, "but I think I should tell you something."

Here it comes, Ivy thought. He still loves me. She could see it in his face, had felt it in his hand on her waist, could taste it in his food. "Okay," she said, preparing a response in her mind that would damage him the least.

"I'm pretty sure I saw your mother the other day."

His words knocked her back. Cool shivers of sweat emerged beneath her clothes, and Ivy closed her eyes, not so much thinking as absorbing what he'd said. Then she opened them and gave him a hard stare. "You're lying."

"Ivy," he said softly. "I would never lie to you about something like that."

She shook her head. He was right. "Where?" she asked.

"Your neighborhood. She was in a silver car, maybe a Monte Carlo?" He shook his head. "I'm not good with cars. And it might not have been her—it's been a really long time since I've seen her—but I don't know. She looked familiar—blonde hair, those big tortoiseshell sunglasses she always wore. Maybe I shouldn't have said anything. It seems so unlikely."

"No," she shook her head. "I thought I might have seen her the other day too. A different day last week. So . . ." she trailed off and shrugged. "She might be back in town."

"Maybe she heard about Lucky," he suggested.

"Possibly. Doesn't matter. I don't want to see her again, ever." Anger burbled up, and she pulled her knees up to her chest and took a deep breath. What was the point in being angry, after all this time?

"Here, have another petit four." He offered her the Tupperware and she selected the dark chocolate one, but the first bite wedged like a wood chip in her throat.

"We need to go," she told him.

"All right," he said, popping the lid back on the container. He patted her knee kindly, and she let him touch her this time. Just as they were packing up, they heard the clack of shoes again and the woman reappeared in the courtyard, this time coming toward them. Jeremy nudged Ivy in the side, then whistled, the long, cat-calling whistle of a construction worker. The woman stopped, squinting with accusation in the direction of the stairwell. Even though Ivy thought they were sufficiently tucked into the shadows, she froze, heart pounding as she held her breath. The woman took several steps in their direction, then stopped at the edge of the courtyard and peered once again into the shadowy area where they crouched beside the remains of their picnic. Ivy didn't think the woman could see them, but she had a sudden urge to step out of the gloom, to make herself known.

"You're not supposed to be in here, you know," the woman called out. "The school is closed."

Ivy glanced over at Jeremy and noticed that he was shaking with laughter. This was the kind of thing he'd always loved, almost getting caught at something. She recalled all the nights he'd stayed over longer than he should have, then climbed out her window at the exact moment her father was walking through the front door. For a while, when he'd been banned from her apartment, Jeremy would peer into her living room windows at dusk, waving to her over the sullen form of her father in front of the television as she did homework at the kitchen table. If her father had adjusted his vision even slightly to the left, he would have seen Jeremy, but he never did.

The woman squinted toward them once more, then turned abruptly and strode off in the opposite direction. When she'd disappeared from view, Jeremy allowed himself to laugh fully, tears of mirth appearing in the corners of his eyes.

"Why was that so funny?" Ivy wanted to know. "We could have gotten in trouble."

"Oh, I know her," Jeremy said, waving a hand through the air dismissively. "She's a pain in the ass. I was just trying to cheer you up." He took a deep breath and wiped his eyes with his knuckles, then grinned over at her. "And what kind of trouble could we have gotten into? Is she going to call the cops because we're having a picnic? C'mon, it was funny, admit it."

Ivy frowned. "How do you know her?"

"I don't know, from a party or something. She used to run around with a friend of mine."

"What friend?"

"Nobody you know."

Ivy wondered why she was grilling him, and forced herself to relax and finish packing up. It all felt too familiar: the strange woman that Jeremy knew, the friends of his she didn't know, the keys to places he shouldn't be allowed to enter. "Let's go," she said, brushing off her lap and standing up.

"We didn't really talk about the party yet," Jeremy said.

The school's courtyard was empty now, and Ivy felt slightly ill emerging from their shady space beneath the stairs. Out here, the many ghosts of high school swirled around her, choking off her air, and Ivy hurried to the gate and waited for Jeremy to let them out.

"We should discuss the menu," he said, unlocking the gate. "But I guess we can do that at the kitchen."

"You know, I'd rather just go home if that's okay. I don't feel so good. Just make all the things you brought over the other day, and what you mentioned earlier for the grown-ups. I trust you."

"You do?" He turned toward her, looking hopeful and some-how younger than he had just a moment before.

"Well, about the food at least," she said.

RAMONA

When Lucky woke up, about half an hour after Ivy left, he quickly became inconsolable, searching for his mother with those big, weepy brown eyes; he looked like a cartoon child those eyes were so oversized, so sad and dreamy. Ramona took him from Frank and held him close to her damp swimsuit, circling the pool and patting his back in an effort to soothe him but to no avail.

Jane tried a bottle of formula, then Frank tried it. Ramona had the last go at it, but by this time Lucky was so upset with that fake plastic nipple, he batted it out of her hand. The bottle flew and hit the pool deck, then rolled into the water with a soft bloop of sound. "Maybe something else to eat?" Ramona suggested to Frank.

In the kitchen, Frank mixed up some rice cereal and got a jar of pureed bananas out of the fridge. Lucky turned his face away to both offerings and continued to cry and whimper against Ramona.

Frank tasted the food himself, then frowned before laughing. "This stuff is not very good. Why can't a baby's first food be ice cream or chocolate pudding?"

"Or mashed potatoes and gravy."

Frank sank into the chair across from her and set the spoon down in the bowl of rice cereal with a sigh. "Where the hell is Ivy?" he said, but not with any real anger.

Lucky, who was still whimpering, settled down completely as Ramona rocked him gently on her knee. He seemed to have given up on finding his mother and turned in toward Ramona to nuzzle her chest and pull on one of her braids. She thought about the baby that was probably growing inside of her right now and decided that if she could guarantee her baby would be a replica of this one on her lap, she would definitely have it.

Frank got up and poured two glasses of water, then set one down in front of her. He didn't return to the table but instead leaned against the sink and drank his entire glass in three long gulps, then placed it on the counter. He was composing something important to say—Ramona could see that by the look of concentration on his face—and she sat patting Lucky and waiting with a slight ripple of unease. Had he somehow found out about her search?

"Do you remember that day when you were in the hospital and I came to see you?" he asked. "You'd just had your baby the night before, and they had you on a whole bunch of sedatives, so you might not remember, but I came in to visit. Ivy had a test and Jane was in a ballet recital or something, so they sent me to keep you company."

"Sure, I remember," she said, wary.

"Do you remember what you asked me to do that day?"

Ramona did—of course she did—but she shook her head no, not wanting to say the words, but not wanting Frank to repeat what she'd asked of him either. "You know, let's not talk about that," she suggested with a weak smile. "It's such a nice day. Let's not talk about the hospital."

"But I've always felt guilty about that, that I couldn't do what you asked of me, that I couldn't help you."

She shook her head again and leaned down toward Lucky in an attempt to hide her face from Frank. She didn't want him to see the tightening around her mouth, the squinting up of her eyes in her effort to prevent tears. "You have nothing to feel guilty about," she said into the soft top of Lucky's head. "It wasn't fair of me to ask you that."

"Well, for the record, I'm sorry."

She took a deep breath and raised her face, calmer now. The moment of threatened tears had passed. "Well, then, for the record, I accept your apology, even though none is necessary."

He smiled down at her, and she took in, for the first time since she'd arrived, the new lines around his mouth and eyes, the single twine of white in his deep brown hair. His wrinkles were of the happy variety, brought on by smiling and sleepless nights with a new baby, and he looked like a softened, slightly worn version of his high school self. He was no longer as handsome as he had once been, but he looked content and friendly, like a person you could trust, which he was.

Just then, Lucky let go of her braid and reached for the bottle of formula, which sat on the table beside the bowl of rice cereal. Ramona picked it up, and he accepted the drink hungrily, holding the bottle in both hands as he lay in her lap and drank.

"Well, look at that," Frank said with a smile. "He decided not to starve himself just because his mother's gone. I knew he was a smart kid." He leaned down and kissed the top of Ramona's head, as if she were a little sister, then said, "Be right back."

Ramona tried to smile, but she was remembering the hospital now with a vividness that sometimes came to her: the cool periwinkle color of the walls in her room, the sound of nurses walking back and forth outside her door, the pain of having to bind her chest to stop the flow of milk, and the sickly sweet smell of its insistent production.

That day, she had asked Frank to help her get the baby back, told him that she had changed her mind about the adoption. By then, however, it was really too late, and there was nothing Frank could do. He'd told her to talk to her mother about it, or the nurses, but she hadn't done that. She had asked only him, then never spoken of it again.

Lucky yanked on the bottle as if to remind her of his presence. He was gripping the thing with both hands now, looking gloriously happy as he continued to fill up his belly. Ramona hadn't planned to ask Frank for help that day in the hospital. She hadn't planned anything really. She just remembered seeing his face—he had a broad, gap-toothed smile that inspired confidence—and thinking that if anyone could help her, it would be Frank. He possessed a sense of calm authority even then, and Ramona guessed he made an excellent principal.

Later, when she'd had the opportunity to ask a nurse about it, she'd changed her mind. She was too young. Her mother was too sad, even though she offered to raise him. No, this baby needed a different family, one that hadn't been marked by her brother's death.

Lucky was almost finished with the entire bottle of milk and was making a sort of contented humming sound as he sucked the last bit down. Ramona stroked his cheek with her thumb. She allowed herself to imagine that she was seventeen again and this baby was hers. It was not particularly difficult to do. Those days in the hospital had always felt close to the surface, as if they were easy to access and change. They also felt distant, unreal. Had she really given away her child? Had such a thing actually occurred?

She made a bargain with herself long ago that she must accomplish something important. It was only fair. If she chose not to raise her own child, then it had to be worth it somehow. For a while, it seemed she was on her way to doing this. Her first album had been very well received in small, artistic circles. Other musicians thought it was excellent, and the reviews were luminous, even if not that many people actually purchased the CD. But since then she had faltered. She was still writing good songs, still singing one or two nights a month for decently sized crowds, but there had been no second album, nothing to follow up her original spark of promise, and she couldn't explain why. What, exactly, had been lost?

After Ivy returned, looking shaken and slightly guilty, Ramona made an excuse about running an errand to the store, then left to find the second J. Dillman on her list. This address was easy to locate because it was in the older section of town, Huntridge, and close to where she had lived as a kid.

The house was on Sweeney Avenue, a street that had seen better days. She found the number and pulled into a space under the
shade of an old elm tree, then cut the engine and sat, staring at the
small, yellow ranch house across from her and waiting for something to happen. It was 4:10 p.m. on a Wednesday, and the street
was quiet except for two boys on a yellow lawn several houses
down floating a green Frisbee back and forth between them. They
were surprisingly good, sending each other into the street for high
leaping catches, turning and grabbing the Frisbee from behind
their backs, and Ramona's gaze kept straying from the door of the
house to the boys and their game. She decided they were definitely
brothers, and one was likely nine or ten, the other eleven, possibly
twelve. It was hard to watch them without thinking about her own
brother, his angular face, the chipped front tooth, his dark, lovely
eyes looking oddly large once his hair was completely gone.

She tried to clear this image and focus all her efforts on the yellow house. That's why she was sitting here, after all. The grass was
green, which indicated sprinklers, but overly long and neglected. A
pomegranate tree. Oleanders blooming pink and white flowers. A
gray, block wall fence shielding the backyard from view, etched with
ivy. The roof appeared to be older, perhaps leaky, and the yellow
paint peeled in a few, almost unnoticeable spots. It was a decent
home, one of the nicest on this block as far as she could tell, and
Ramona decided it wasn't a bad place for a boy to grow up, better
than her old building.

She considered taking a peek in the mailbox, which was right
beside the front door, but she dreaded getting out of the car and
being observed by those two boys as she crossed the street and
lifted the black lid of the box.

After another fifteen minutes of watching the house and the
boys playing Frisbee, Ramona gave up, deciding to try the place at
a different time of day. She had told Ivy she wouldn't be gone long,
that she'd be home in time for dinner and bring wine with her, and

dessert, but she was too close to her apartment building not to go and see it.

In under five minutes, she was in her old neighborhood, which alternated between wealth and decay as it had when she lived here. Old stately homes surrounded by tall elms were followed by small box houses with dried-out lawns and an abundance of chain-link and plastic toys. She passed an empty desert lot with rolling tumbleweed; a comely, stucco law office; the back of an apartment building marred by graffiti. Palm trees, telephone wires, a cracked, wide street that led to her apartment building, still standing right where she'd left it almost twenty years ago.

The two-story, thirty-unit building was pale pink stucco in the shape of a U. In the scoop of this U were dry grass, two benches, and a white, tiered fountain. She parked at the curb, then got out of her car and went to sit beside the fountain, which was dry. At a house half a block away, two men worked together on a car; other than that, the street was empty.

When she was growing up here, the fountain gurgled and sang. It reminded Ramona of a wedding cake, and she often sat on the bench beside it, just watching the water cascade from the top tier to the bottom. Sometimes she sat here with Ivy, usually at dusk, each of them tossing pennies into the water and making impossible wishes. Ramona used to wish her dead brother back to life and for her mother to be restored.

The bench was warm beneath her legs, and the sun had lowered just enough to bore into her shoulders with a force she'd almost forgotten. California's sun, at least near her apartment, was never so obvious or harsh. Ramona shaded her eyes and scanned the row of apartments on the second floor, holding her breath. There was her old door, number sixteen. A white slip was flung over the rail of the balcony, a red ten-speed parked beside it. Both were evidence that her mother was no longer alive. She would never have hung a slip out for everyone to see, and she had never ridden a bike, at least in Ramona's presence.

There was a light tap on her shoulder, and she turned to find a teenage boy leaning down from what seemed like a great height, his braces glinting in the sun as he asked, "Are you Cecilia?"

"No," Ramona said and shook her head. The boy had bad skin and lank, greasy hair, but he smelled good, like limes or oranges.

"Oh, sorry." He straightened up and smoothed down his hair, making it look even worse.

"Do you live here?" Ramona asked, looking around for the apartment from which the boy had just emerged, but every door she could see was sealed shut.

"Just during the week," he said.

"Why aren't you at school?"

"School's over. It's five thirty."

"And who's Cecilia?"

The boy held up both hands, as if fending off a blow. "Jeez, what's with the questions? I'm not doing anything wrong."

Ramona watched him for a moment with a solemn stare, wanting to intimidate this kid for no good reason. Sitting here beside this dead fountain made her unbalanced, skittish, and wary. She shrugged her answer then turned away, hoping the boy understood he was officially dismissed, but instead of leaving he moved past her and sat on the other bench.

He crossed his legs and swung one back and forth. "I know Cecilia online but I've never met her in person. She's supposed to be sixteen and have short red hair, but it would be easy to lie. She could be anyone. Even you."

"Even me," Ramona said and nodded her head.

"I doubt she'll show," the boy said, turning his head to look up and down the street.

"Why not?" Ramona asked, suddenly wanting to make it up to him, to erase her rude behavior. "You seem like a nice kid."

"The problem is she doesn't have a car. She said her friend would drive her over here, but she's already ten minutes late, so I'm thinking that didn't work out."

"You never know," Ramona said. "Maybe they just hit some traffic."

They were both quiet for a moment. The buzz of a power tool broke the air into pieces, so that only now, Ramona recognized how quiet the street had been. It was the two men down the block, working on the car. After a few seconds, they shut off the tool, and there was silence again, then whoops of congratulation.

"I guess they fixed it," Ramona said.

"Doubtful," the boy said, but didn't explain.

She noticed that he was wearing a very thin black tie with his black shirt. She wondered at the point of a tie you could hardly see, but decided she liked the gesture of it, dressing up to meet a girl from the Internet.

Ramona watched the balcony with the slip as if expecting her long dead mother to emerge. She could almost see her standing there, calling down that dinner was ready. Every Monday, she made spaghetti sauce with ground beef and peppers, and this meal would last them through the entire week. The sauce had always been a little too thick and spicy for Ramona, who ate most of it anyway.

Her mother would be wearing her cocktail waitress uniform at the table, a tight scarlet sheath with a high collar and cutout oval in the back that emphasized her small, boyish frame. Her long black hair would already be coiled neatly in a braid on the top of her head, gold earrings dangling beside her cheeks. The smell in the apartment was ground beef and tomatoes mixed with intense lilac perfume, a smell so potent it made Ramona's head ache. Neither of them spoke during dinner at the round table in the kitchen. After the meal and her mother's departure for the casino, Ramona would wash the dishes. Her mother had only been twenty-eight or twenty-nine at the time, almost ten years younger than she herself was now.

"Did you know a woman named Charlotte who used to live here?" Ramona asked the boy. "Or Mrs. White? Sometimes people called her Charlie too."

"No, but my dad might have," the boy said. "You want me to go ask him? He's just watching TV." He pointed toward a door across the courtyard.

"No, that's all right."

As if on cue, the door the boy had pointed to opened, and a heavyset man stepped out and crossed the dead grass to stand beside the boy. "Time for homework," he said, giving the kid's head an affectionate pat. "And you didn't finish your pasta or clear your plate. That means you owe me, let's see, one load of laundry and two nights of dishes now."

The boy rolled his eyes and huffed, then said, "Dad, this lady wants to know if you knew someone named Charlotte who used to live here."

The man turned to Ramona and smiled, revealing an acne-pocked face, similar to his son's. "Charlotte White?"

Ramona nodded.

"Yes, in fact, I did. She was a really sweet lady."

Ramona's throat had gone dry.

"Were you a friend of hers?" the man asked.

"She was my mother," Ramona said, her voice emerging hoarse and tentative.

The man smiled at this news. "I didn't know Charlie had any kids," he said. "Well, I heard about the son who died—I'm so sorry about that—but I didn't know she had a daughter."

So her dead brother was known, but not her. This did not surprise Ramona. She stood and held out her hand to shake. The man took her palm, and his handshake was weak and floppy, what her boyfriend Nash would call a "flounder."

"I'm so sorry for your loss," the man said when he released her hand.

Ramona nodded, unsure how to accept this kindness. Her loss had happened long ago, much longer ago than her mother's death; still, it was nice for this man to be sorry for it. "Thank you," she said, then rose and looked at the boy who was still searching the street.

"She's not coming," Ramona told him, then shrugged. "Sorry."

"Who's not coming?" the father asked.

"Nobody," the boy said. "It's nothing."

Ramona waved good-bye then walked over to her car and got inside where she sat for a while looking up at door number sixteen. What did it mean, she wondered, to be disowned by your mother? It wasn't a question she had allowed herself to ask in a very long time. Up on the balcony, the bike propped by the door shone in the sun, and the white slip hung beside it like a ghost or a discarded skin.

JEREMY

After dropping Ivy back at her house, Jeremy circled the neighborhood for a while in his car, not yet wanting to leave her proximity. As he drove, he searched again for her mother, slowing to look inside parked cars, trolling alongside the low wall at the end of the neighborhood beside the mountain, but the silver Monte Carlo he'd noticed over a week ago now was nowhere in sight. If only he'd pulled over on that day, rapped on the woman's window, and said hello, then he would know for sure whether she was Ivy's mother or not, and would have something valuable to offer, rather than a glimpse of a possible stranger.

When he finally left Ivy's radius, streaming with evening traffic away from the newness of her part of town and toward the center of decay, as he was now coming to think of his part of town, he felt the usual pressure begin building in his chest, a gray mass circling beneath his rib cage the way he imagined a tornado formed, with swirling, excruciating suppleness.

Gretchen wouldn't be home from work yet; in fact, she didn't get off until ten thirty tonight, and he didn't have any catering jobs until tomorrow afternoon. The specter of his empty apartment rose in his mind. He hadn't slept there in over a week and the place was neat, unlived in, as lonely as a stone.

When he glimpsed the neon blue sign for the T-bird Lounge ahead on his left, he pulled into the lot and went inside. It was early, just now five o'clock, and only a handful of people hunched in the red booths or ringed the small bar in the restaurant's center. Two girls who looked underage—long glossy hair streaming down their backs—played pool in the far corner.

Jeremy got a beer at the bar, then slid into a booth and sipped at it. He had imagined just having this one beer and then heading back on the road toward home, newly fortified, but now that he was inside he had an itch to see someone, to hang out and talk, so he flipped open his phone and called Mark to come and meet him. They hadn't seen each other in at least six months, but he had news for him, now that he'd seen Ramona, so Mark would be the perfect companion. Talking about Ramona could lead into talking about Ivy, and then it would feel like old times, sitting here in this bar where they'd spent many hours together during and after high school, talking about the exact same thing. Maybe the pool table would clear out soon and they could play a couple of games.

Mark picked up on the second ring. He'd just gotten off duty and agreed to swing by for one drink on the way home. Jeremy got another beer, then went to the jukebox and looked through all the song choices. They had the same music they had always had, with the addition of a few new bands, and Jeremy picked out a string of five songs that appealed to him: Prince, Bowie, Springsteen, and two Green Day songs for good measure. He had once bemoaned the music choices here, could even remember standing at this very jukebox with Ramona, bitching about the lame selection. Why no Black Flag, no Misfits or Social Distortion? But since then his musical tastes had expanded to include just about everything, and it was a rare occurrence when he felt the need for the harsh sounds of his old favorites.

Back inside his red booth, he listened to the music with anticipation, savoring the taste of his beer and the feeling of peace that was finally seeping into him. His nerves had been jangled all day with the expectation of seeing Ivy and then with actually seeing her, and now that their meeting was behind him he could feel his insides finally begin to unwind.

Across the room, he watched the two girls playing pool. They were older than he'd first thought, maybe even thirty, and he considered going over to talk to them, but he wanted Mark's full attention when he arrived, so he stayed put. The door opened and he watched for his friend's hulking form to appear, but a couple slunk in and crossed the room and sat in a booth closer to the pool table.

He watched the couple holding hands across the table and leaning their heads close, and realized the woman was Kristina, from the book club and the old restaurant. Jeremy didn't recognize the man. What were the odds of running into her twice in one week? It struck him as a sign, an omen, and he decided it meant that he should make amends. This woman represented his past of drunken thievery, of every bad decision he'd ever made, and if he apologized to her, maybe he'd feel free.

Even as he rose and made his way toward her table, he knew his goal was absurd, that she would not want to lay eyes on him let alone listen to some belated apology for an entire era of bad behavior, but he felt a pressing need to speak to her again. "Thunder Road" was playing now, and he hummed along as he walked toward their table, trying to devise what he wanted to say.

They both looked up when he reached them. Kristina wore a red dress, bright as a blinking siren, and her lips were painted the same color. The man reminded him of a newscaster, with his neat, dark hair and false smile. Jeremy felt unsteady gazing down at them, though not drunk or even buzzed, far from it. Kristina scowled at him, as if he'd interrupted something serious, and he tried to smooth out her expression with a smile. "Hey, Kristina. We meet again."

"Hi," her lips pressed tightly together, then she seemed to decide something and sighed. "This is Peter. Peter, this is . . ."

"Jeremy," he quickly filled in and offered his hand to the man, who gave him an overly hearty handshake.

"We used to work together," Kristina said, "at this place called the Crescent that caught fire about ten years ago and thankfully burned to the ground."

"Someone probably set that fire on purpose to get rid of the smell," Jeremy said.

"Fried food," Kristina explained to Peter. "And smoke and mustard, all swirled together."

The man smiled agreeably, but didn't say anything. It was obvious he didn't care about the Crescent or Jeremy or even any detail from Kristina's past. He was wearing a suit with no tie, the collar of his white shirt open, and he reminded Jeremy a little of the man who used to pick Kristina up after work, the wealthy one who liked the elf costume. He wondered if this man was wealthy too, but he didn't think so, just comfortable, just organized and middle class. It was amazing how much wealth you could accrue at a young age—and this man looked to be several years younger than him and Kristina—if you traveled a straight line from high school to college to a professional job. Jeremy had learned this from his younger brother, though too late to do himself any good.

A silence hovered around them now, and Jeremy knew he should say his good-byes and return to his booth, but he didn't feel finished. "I wanted to tell you, the other night at that book club, that I'm sorry I was such a jerk back then, at the Crescent."

"Book club?" Peter asked, frowning.

Kristina shook her head as if to say "don't ask." "Okay, thanks," she said, and smiled at him, though it was a fake smile, a smile to hurry him away.

"I mean, I guess we were all young and doing stupid things, but I seemed to do more stupid things than most people," he was rambling now but unable to stop. "It's just that my heart was broken when my girlfriend left me and moved away, and then my band broke up, and all I'd ever wanted to do was be some sort of underground punk star but instead found myself as a prep chef—the lowest person on the totem pole—at that shitty restaurant, and I was just so angry, so disappointed with everything in my life. But really it turned out to be a good thing because I found out that I actually like cooking, *love* cooking, and now I have a career doing just that, and I'm finally almost happy."

They were both staring up at him with slightly stunned expressions, and he was embarrassed but also relieved, unburdened. Two large hands pressed down on his shoulders, and for a minute he thought it was the bouncer and he was being kicked out, but when he turned he saw Mark's broad face. "Hey, buddy," Jeremy said, and he hugged him, something he'd never done before. The sheer bulk of Mark felt good, but Jeremy released him quickly, sensing Mark's discomfort, and pounded him on the back. "Let's go over here. I have a booth."

He didn't introduce Mark to Kristina or Peter, or even tell them good-bye, have a nice night, just turned away with his friend and crossed the room to his booth where his empty beer glass sat waiting.

"What was that all about?" Mark asked, nodding toward Kristina's booth. "Those people didn't look very happy to see you."

"I used to work with her," Jeremy said.

Mark nodded, apparently satisfied with this answer. He was still wearing his police uniform, and Jeremy couldn't help but admire the sight of him, all that bulk neatly packaged in his dark blue shirt. He had been almost chubby in high school and not particularly athletic, but now he was mostly muscle and gave off the impression of a bear at rest.

"How are the kids?" Jeremy asked, though he couldn't remember how many there were or even their genders.

"Great. Delilah is almost finished with junior high, which was rough, brother, let me tell you. And Rory and Cole start third grade next year. Kat wants to put them in this private school because they're having some discipline problems at Williams, but I don't see how that's going to happen unless a rich uncle dies, and I don't have any rich uncles." He laughed, then signaled to a waitress and ordered two more beers.

So three kids. Jeremy remembered their faces now from his one visit to Mark's house a couple of years ago. They had their mother's curly hair and Mark's sleepy, dark eyes. The daughter already looked like trouble, and the boys were rowdy, wrestling and tumbling around the living room for his entire visit.

"So I saw Ramona this week. She's at Ivy's place."

"Ramona," Mark rolled the name out slowly, seeming to savor the syllables. "Wow, I haven't thought about her in a long time."

"Really?"

"I'm busy, brother. Busy. I don't have time to think about old girlfriends." The beers arrived, and Mark swallowed half of his pint in two gulps, then swiped a hand across his mouth. "How's she doing?"

"Okay, I guess. She looks good—same long braids, nice tan. She still thinks I'm a piece of shit, but I guess that's to be expected."

Mark laughed. "Good for her. I could always count on Ramona to call you out."

"She's staying at the Golden Nugget for some reason. I guess she likes her solitude." Even the word—solitude—gave him a shiver. His empty apartment. The neatly made bed, his TV set atop a vegetable crate. The single, overstuffed chair in the living room. He would buy a couch, a TV stand, and a coffee table next week. Surely that would help.

"I always liked that about her, the way she could just be quiet and listen to music or play her guitar. We didn't have to talk all the time. That's my main issue with Kat. I get home, and she wants a long story about my day in real time, and I'm just burnt. I just want to sit and not speak for an hour. Ramona got that about me, or maybe she was just that way too, who knows?"

"Did you know her mother died?" Jeremy asked.

Mark nodded. "I saw the obit. A buddy of mine sent it to me. I sent her a condolence card but never heard anything back. I guess you're not supposed to respond to those cards though anyway.

That's not the point. I sent a picture of the kids with it and wondered later if maybe that was in poor taste. Kat told me it was, but Ramona's never seen them or anything, so I thought, what the hell?"

A condolence card. This information shocked Jeremy. The notion of sending a condolence card struck him as the domain of grown-ups, particularly women, and the image of Mark sitting down at a desk to send one was absurd. "I didn't think you two kept in touch or that you even knew where she lived."

"We don't. Just that card. It seemed like the right thing to do. And I know everything that's going on here or with people who used to live here, brother. I have my finger on the fucking pulse."

Jeremy smiled at this. Mark had always known everything about everyone, that was true.

"I hear you're doing well," Mark said. "Cooking up a storm."

Jeremy nodded. "It's paying the rent, finally. Though the rent isn't much right now."

"That's good. Keep it that way. Keep it simple."

"That's my motto," Jeremy said and raised his glass in a toast.

Mark clinked his pint against Jeremy's, and the impact of the two glasses was sweet to his ears. The Prince song was on now, "Purple Rain," and despite the slow, shadowy splendor of the music, the mood in the bar had turned festive. While they'd been talking, every single booth had filled up, and the bar was packed. Jeremy glanced across the room and saw that Kristina and Peter still sat in their booth, sharing a plate of chicken fingers. The girls at the pool table had been replaced by a trio of middle-aged men in bright polos. "Look at this place," Jeremy said. "I've never seen it so crowded."

"It's always like this now," Mark said. "Good thing you got here early."

"Yeah, good thing." He was oddly proud of himself, for creating this evening with his old friend, for making amends with his ex-coworker, and he brimmed with an unnamed excitement. "We should take a trip," he told Mark. "A road trip. We could go to the Grand Canyon or Valley of Fire, spend a couple of days roaming around."

"I used up all my time off over Christmas."

"Well, then . . . just a drive out to the lake, right now. What do you think?"

Mark smiled, sipping his second beer. "I can't, brother. Wife. Kids. You know the drill. They're expecting me. I have to help Delilah with her math homework. Kat refuses."

"Oh, of course," Jeremy said, feeling the excitement spill out of him in a rush. He allowed himself to slump, ever so slightly, and took the final swallow of his beer. "Another time, maybe."

"Sure. Sure. That sounds good. We can make it a family thing—you can bring a girlfriend. You still seeing Louisa?" He shook his head. He could barely remember Louisa. Dark hair, a limp, those beautiful, poufed-out lips. The image flicked through him, then was gone. Maybe it had been longer than he thought since he'd seen Mark. "A woman named Gretchen, but it's not serious."

"Well, bring her along. What's her story?"

"I don't know," Jeremy said, looking around. He suddenly wanted to be free of this place, but Mark still had half a beer to go. "Um, she works at the Stardust, at the front desk. She's getting a hospitality management degree at the community college part-time, and I don't know how she ever expects to finish because she only takes one class a semester. She works full-time," he added, not wanting to imply she was lazy.

"Lots of people do it that way. It will just take her a little longer, that's all."

Jeremy nodded. Actually, she would probably finish. He could tell she was determined, but he didn't care. He barely cared about her at all.

"I should head out," Mark said and rose, the last quarter of his beer unfinished.

"Me too," Jeremy agreed.

Outside, the sky was dark, and a wind had picked up, sending debris across the parking lot. He waved to Mark and watched as his black pickup truck pulled out into traffic. Jeremy felt a sudden longing to be inside the cab of that truck with his friend, heading home to a family, homework, dinner, the bustle of middle-class living. It wasn't a life he'd ever thought he wanted, but right now it struck him as ideal. He imagined Mark's home as a glowing hub of activity that would leave him worn out at the end of a day, ready to rest, whereas Jeremy was growing restless. There was too much energy inside him right now, and it threatened to unleash itself in the usual unhealthy ways: drinking, roaming around through the night, waiting up to fuck Gretchen when he knew he needed sleep, when he didn't even like her. He got inside his Subaru, then turned on the music and just sat there for a while, waiting to see what he would do next.

JANE

Jane watched her children running on the sidewalk up ahead as she strolled slowly in the direction of Rex's house. She'd made everyone spaghetti and meatballs for dinner tonight and it had been a big success, with second helpings for all, including Fern and Rocky.

She'd left Ivy and Ramona behind with the dinner dishes, and it felt good to be outside and relatively alone. Earlier on the phone, she'd fought with Adam, and the conversation still clung to her, sucked at her heels as she stepped lightly up the sidewalk beneath a sky beginning to turn the exact color of a ripe peach. She tried to immerse herself in the beauty of it, in the warmth of the air. She'd begun to associate Adam with winter, she realized, and thinking of him also made her think of the graying roadside snow, the bone-racking cold.

"Watch out," she called to Rocky as he reached a curb up ahead. "Wait for me."

Her son stopped, and Fern bumped into him, then turned to watch Jane approach. The origami bird was shoved into the pocket of her shorts, and she could feel its wing poking her leg with each stride. She had dreamed about The Muse again last night. This time he'd been sitting up in the apple tree in Jane's backyard at home, watching her through the bare branches as she crossed the grass.

On the phone, Adam told her that she needed to come home, that he didn't want to be separated, that he missed her and missed the kids. Jane wished that she wanted to go home to Adam, but the truth was she didn't.

At the corner, each kid took one of her hands before they crossed the street and turned left. At the next block she led them right, and up ahead was a familiar scene: two blonde girls in the driveway, this time playing with skateboards rather than the hose. Closer, Jane expected to see The Muse sitting in a chair or standing by the porch smoking, but when they reached the house, no parent was in sight.

"Hi," the two girls called out to Jane. Their voices sounded happy enough, but the older girl had a splint on her ring finger, and the younger one looked as if she might have recently finished crying.

"Hello," Jane said, stopping at the bottom of the drive. "These are my kids," she told them, unable to think of anything else to say. She wanted to ask where their father was, if their mother was home, but both questions felt weighed down by the wrong kind of desire.

Rocky helped her out by asking to try the older girl's skate-board, and Jane felt slightly relieved as he followed them up the drive. Now there appeared to be a purpose for her presence here.

Just as Rocky put a tentative foot on the board, The Muse appeared in the doorway, and Jane was surprised by his appearance. He looked nothing like he had in the dreams. His hair seemed less white and silky; his face and body were more ordinary than she'd imagined. The name she'd devised for him suddenly seemed silly, and she reminded herself that his real name was Rex, and he was just a regular human being like everybody else.

"Oh, hi," he said, smiling. "It's you again." He wore a plain black T-shirt and worn jeans. Very-white, bare toes poked out beneath the fraying denim as he crossed the driveway to Jane. His hair was coiled in a small bun at the nape of his neck. "How goes the vacation?"

Jane shrugged, suddenly embarrassed to be standing here on his driveway again, despite the fact that she'd hoped to see him. "This is my daughter, Fern," she said, pushing her forward as if she were a sacrifice. "And that's my son, Rocky."

"Rocky," he said. "What a great name. Are you going to be a boxer?"

Rocky shook his head, and Jane said, "He's named after the mountain range, not the fighter."

"Oh, even better," the man said. "We were just about to look through the telescope, out back. You can see Saturn's rings tonight. Care to join us?"

"Okay," Jane agreed, and she and the kids followed him through the house, which, to Jane's surprise, was spare and dimly lit, like a museum.

"My wife's influence," he said, gesturing to the almost empty living room. "If I had my way, this place would probably look like a junkyard. I like stuff."

"What does your wife do?" Jane asked, stopping to run her hand along the length of a black walnut buffet, topped by a white vase containing four purple irises. On closer inspection, she saw that the flowers were made of silk.

"She's a concierge at the Flamingo."

"Oh, the Flamingo! That's where we spent our wedding night," Jane said, without thinking.

"How long have you been married?"

"Eleven years." She thought about explaining her separation or the fact that she didn't want to be married anymore at all, but she kept quiet.

"I have you beat. We just had our fourteenth anniversary."

"Congratulations," Jane said, sounding oddly formal to herself. She followed him into the kitchen and watched as all four kids disappeared through the sliding glass door, then dispersed into the backyard.

"We need drinks for this, I think," he said opening the fridge and peering inside. "You probably don't drink beer, do you?"

"Of course I drink beer," Jane said.

He passed her a Miller Lite, smiling, then righted himself and touched his bun, as if to make sure his hair was still there. Now that she'd been with him for a few minutes, she'd rediscovered his allure. It was the dark contrast of his eyes against the white skin, she decided, and the broad, bony sweep of his shoulders beneath the T-shirt.

Behind him, on the refrigerator, there was a photograph of the entire family on a beach somewhere. The wife wore an old-fashioned swimsuit, the kind with a modest cut on the thigh and a built-in bustier. It was red, reminiscent of a '50s-era bombshell, and she looked great in it with her short black hair and movie-star sunglasses. The rest of the family seemed ragtag beside her, with their wild white hair blowing in the wind.

The backyard, unlike the house, was cluttered with stuff: a baby pool, two bikes, a multicolored climber. Rocky swung back and forth on an old metal swing set, and the three girls were crammed into a sandbox. Beside the sandbox, Jane saw the stack of palm fronds that had been out front on her last visit. So she hadn't imagined them.

The sun was long gone now, but the sky was still light, and a white half-moon was visible, embedded into the deep pink and bronze sky like a chip of bone in the desert. A telescope was set up on a square of concrete by the back fence, and Rex led her over to it and leaned down to set his eye against the lens. "It's still too light right now," he said, straightening up and pointing. "But right over there we should be able to see Saturn in a bit."

"How do you know about this stuff?" Jane asked him.

"My father," he told her. "We used to go out to Spring Mountain Ranch and watch meteor showers, lying on the grass. When I was older we got this telescope so we could see more stuff."

"We used to go there too," Jane said, remembering. "But during the day, for picnics. I love that place." She took a sip of her beer and looked around the yard. Behind the baby pool, there was a pomegranate tree covered in deep orange-red blooms. She had a sense that she was gathering details in her mind for a reason. She noted the hummingbird feeder, a plastic flower filled with red syrup, hanging from the branch of a mulberry tree in the yard's corner, the pink scooter propped against the side of the house, the bowl of cat food beside it.

"Come see the garden," Rex said, leading her to the other side of the yard. In the corner was a neat square of dirt planted with rosemary, mint, chives, and thyme. "What's that one?" Jane asked, pointing.

"Thai basil," he said. "It's really nice in a green curry. And those will eventually be serrano peppers, but it's too early for them yet," he explained, pointing to a small plant. "If you're still here this summer, I'll have you over for this jicama and black bean salsa I make that's so fucking good you'll die happy."

"I'm leaving this weekend," she said.

"Oh, really? That's too bad." His dark eyes stayed on hers as he said this, and Jane felt her face heat up.

"Did you make this?" she asked, pulling the origami bird from her pocket.

Rex frowned and took the bird. "No," he said. "But I wish I had. That's really cool."

He handed it back to her and she inspected it again. Who else could have possibly thrown this into Ivy's pool? She walked over to the telescope and set the bird on a small table, then took a long swallow of beer, trying to cover her embarrassment. "I was sure you made that," she mumbled. Why would she assume this man she'd met only once before had tossed her a present over the wall? She must have imagined the attraction between them. This was all one-sided, and she should leave before his wife came home and there was a misunderstanding.

"I guess I'd better get going," Jane said, setting her empty bottle on the table.

"But we haven't seen Saturn yet. You have to stay for that."

He smiled at her, then picked up her empty bottle and went inside.

Jane looked over at Fern, still in the sandbox. She was listening closely to something Calliope was saying. Her daughter appeared to be spellbound, as if the older girl had hypnotized her, and Jane wondered if she were under some sort of spell as well; what else would explain why she was in a stranger's yard, waiting for Saturn to appear?

Rex reemerged with another beer and passed it to her. She cracked it open and took a sip, thinking about how Adam would scorn this beer. He was a snob about his coveted microbrews, and would have judged Rex for the Miller Lite, but it tasted good to her right now: airy and clean and cold. Adam would scorn this man for other things as well—the bun, the cluttered yard—but he would admire the telescope, Jane decided. He would like the fact that Rex knew his constellations.

"So what did you do before you lost your job?" she asked him.

"Construction. I think I might try and get into nursing school though."

Jane nodded. This struck her as a good idea. She liked the notion of a sensible, helpful profession, one with obvious goals and rewards.

"How about you?" he asked.

"I was a reporter at a newspaper."

"They've had a lot of layoffs, I bet," he said.

"Well, they have." Jane paused, then added, "But I was actually fired."

"Oh?" he said, watching her.

Here was her chance to unburden herself. This man seemed like a good choice. She sensed no judgment in his gaze as he waited to hear what had happened.

"I was caught with a coworker." She took a deep breath then said quickly. "We were caught making out in the office. It was assumed we had done more, but really it was just the kissing, just that once. But we were caught, and our boss didn't want to hear any explanations. It was probably an easy way to lay off two more people." She paused and took a deep breath, then added, "It was really humiliating."

Rex laughed at the news, tilting back his head and letting loose a loud hoot. Then he noticed her serious face and said, "Sorry. You just seem so proper and good. I never imagined you'd do something like that in a million years."

"Proper and good?"

"Don't look so offended. It's a compliment." He smiled at her. "You seem classy. That's what I meant."

"Well, thanks, I guess," she said. "But apparently I'm not." She was aware then of how she was sitting, perched carefully on the edge of the chair, her posture erect, one leg crossed over the other. In an effort to relax, she uncrossed her legs and slid to the back of her chair, then took another swig of beer and felt the muscles in her face begin to loosen.

"We all make mistakes," he said. "It sounds like you just made one in the wrong place at the wrong time."

"It was more than a mistake," Jane said.

"What was it then?" He tilted his head, waiting, one white eyebrow lifted over his dark eye.

Jane thought for a moment. "It was a revelation. I realized that I no longer wanted to be married."

"Hmmm." He nodded and leaned back in his chair.

"We're sort of officially separated. At least that's what I would call it. Adam would say something else—'taking a breather' is how he'd probably put it. He likes to mitigate situations, which is one of the many things he does that makes me mad." Jane paused to wonder if Rex knew what the word *mitigate* meant, then felt guilty for wondering and plundered forward. "I mean we had a gigantic fight last week, over this trip actually, and he referred to it later as a 'minor disagreement.' It was a fight. Definitely a fight. But he's in his own world where everything is just fine between us." She shrugged and crossed her legs again. Rex sat watching her, sipping his beer, as if waiting for her to continue.

"But I don't have any good reasons not to be married," she told him. "My husband is a bit of a slacker, and he's been working on his dissertation for at least six years, which is annoying, but he's kind and smart and he loves me and the kids. It's just . . ." She paused and looked up at the sky, clear but devoid of stars. "It's just that sometimes, so much of what's fun about life feels like it's behind me now." Hearing herself say these last words out loud, she felt them to be true, and a blue shade of depression pulled down through her.

"We all feel that way sometimes," he said. "It's the human predicament."

"Maybe," she shrugged, embarrassed again for having said so much to a stranger. "Can I use your bathroom?" she asked, setting down her beer and rising, wanting to put some space between the words she'd just uttered and her physical self.

The mirror above the sink in Rex's bathroom revealed pink across her nose and shoulders from today's sun. She ran the water and splashed her face, then dried it on a slightly dingy, white towel. Sitting on the closed toilet lid, she felt decidedly lighter for having told him her story. So what if Rex judged her—though she didn't think he would. Now at least one other person knew what she had done wrong, and it was a relief.

Jane thought about the editor who'd also been fired from the paper and wondered what it was he'd seen in her. They hadn't spoken at all since their mutual dismissal, though he'd emailed her twice. Both times she'd deleted the messages without responding. At the office, his interest in her, his desire, had seemed like such a gift. But the emails—both asking her to meet him for coffee or a drink, to talk over what had happened between them—made that gift feel small and suddenly worthless, though she couldn't explain why. It was his physical presence that had affected her, the heat of his desire rising from his skin like a visible force. That desire had made her walk around the office with a lighter step. It had glowed secretly within her while she performed her daily chores, helping her to be more patient and loving with her children.

It had even, in some strange way, brought her closer to Adam. The editor compared poorly to her husband in many respects. He was not as funny. He couldn't throw a Frisbee or set up a perfect campsite in twenty minutes. He didn't like to have a drink on the back porch at dusk just when the fireflies appeared for their brief, radiant light show.

But the editor had made her feel happy, or, at least, expectant. He had lightened the feeling of overwhelming despair she had many mornings upon waking. Her whole day sometimes seemed like a series of chores—dress and feed the kids through a maze of arguing and cajoling; go to work for eight hours; pick up the kids at day care and feel guilty about having left them with strangers all day; fix a dinner that Rocky and Fern wouldn't like; do dishes and laundry and give baths and read books and solve ridiculous disputes; then finally, at last, sleep. Adam would slip in beside her late at night after working at the bar, smelling of liquor and laying a heavy arm across her middle as if pinning her, unwittingly, to the bed.

The two final emails from the editor had felt like one more chore to attend to, one more heavy presence to weigh her down, which she guessed is why she had deleted them.

Jane looked around Rex's bathroom and took in the details, willing her mind out of the past and into this moment. There was a black comb and single green toothbrush stuck into a cup. The shower curtain was clear and slightly moldy. A naked Barbie doll sat on the back of the toilet. If I lived here, Jane thought, I would get a new shower curtain and brighter towels, hang a picture on the wall and ditch the Barbie. I would tan my skin as dark as I could to see the sharp contrast of my limbs against Rex's white ones in bed at night.

Back outside, everyone was in the same position in which she'd left them. Rex standing by the telescope, kids in the sandbox.

"Okay, it's time," Rex said, when he saw her. He set his beer down on the concrete and clapped his hands together. "It's dark enough now, I think. Hey, Rocky," he called across the yard, "why don't you do the honors?"

Her son jumped off the swing and ran to the telescope as if he'd been given a military command, then leaned to look through the lens, adjusting the eyepiece as Rex instructed, and moving the position of the scope just slightly to the right. Jane realized she was holding her breath. For some reason, she did not think they would actually see Saturn tonight.

The girls were gathered on the concrete square now too and formed a line behind Rex and Rocky, waiting for their turn to view the planet. Jane was surprised that Fern even knew what Saturn was; she couldn't recall teaching her daughter about the planets. It would have been Adam, she realized. He liked to tell the kids about things like the stars and planets, mountains, canyons, oceans, all the natural wonders.

"There it is!" Rocky suddenly cried out.

Jane felt a rush of energy move through her as she let out her held breath and laughed with delight. He had found it! Her son moved away from the scope with a huge grin on his face and looked at Rex, who nodded in approval. "Good work," he told Rocky, lifting his beer in a toast. "I knew you could do it."

Calliope went next, then the other two girls each took turns gazing through the scope. Each viewing brought a sigh and smile, a laugh of delight. Fern clapped her hands as if she'd just seen a show, then ran to hug Jane's legs.

When it was her turn, Jane handed her beer to Rex, then leaned down and placed her eye against the cool lens. It took a moment for her vision to adjust to the scope, and she squinted, then relaxed until the sky came into clear view. And then, there it was floating before her: Saturn. It was smaller than she'd expected, and paler, almost black and white with just the faint glow of orange; there were the rings too, darker reddish-orange loops that looked absolutely still, though she knew they were in orbit. The sight made her heartbeat quicken. She had never seen Saturn before, nor thought she cared to, but there it was, glowing before her right eye with unexpected beauty and promise.

"Wow," she said straightening up. "That's amazing."

Rex grinned and passed back her beer, then leaned to take his turn at the scope. "It's my favorite planet," he said, his eye pressed to the lens. "I guess it's sort of an obvious choice because of the rings—I should pick something obscure and unloved like Mercury—but I just think it's radiant."

"It really is," Jane agreed. She was light-headed for a moment and sat back down in her chair. The two beers were working on her now, but it was more than that. She was excited, filled up with simple, awe-inspired joy. The two younger girls and Rocky had taken up residence on the swing set now, but Polyhymnia remained, hovering nearby. "What's your favorite planet?" Jane asked her.

"I like Pluto," she said. "Even though it's not considered a planet anymore. It's still my favorite."

"I know, what a rip-off," Jane said. "It will always be a planet to me."

"They thought about naming it Zeus before it became Pluto," the girl added. "Right, Dad?"

Rex turned and put a hand on his daughter's shoulder. "That's right; I guess they considered hundreds of names. But Zeus was one of them."

The two of them standing before her, Rex's hand lightly on the tall girl's shoulder, reminded Jane of Adam standing in exactly that position with Rocky on their back porch. Instead of stars, however,

Adam liked to point out birds—cardinals, starlings, crows, the occasional hawk. It struck Jane that this man and his daughter were simply stand-ins, actors replicating scenes from her life at home, an absurd idea that flitted through her, then was gone.

Jane realized how dark it had become and stood, knowing that Ivy and Ramona would be worried. "We should head back," Jane told them. She called her kids over, finished the last swallow of her beer, then shook Rex's hand. "Thanks so much," she told him. "That was really great."

"Come by whenever," he said. "The telescope is always open."

Passing back through the house with Fern and Rocky—Rex had stayed outside with the girls—Jane noticed another photo, framed and hanging on the wall near the front door. It was a picture of Rex, she decided, though he looked to be only fourteen or fifteen, with close-cropped hair and a nervous smile. He wore a thin black tie over a blue shirt and was standing in front of a white building, possibly a church. He looked vaguely familiar, and Jane thought that perhaps she did remember him from high school. An image flashed through her of a boy sitting beneath the palm tree in the quad, all alone, eating a sandwich. She'd seen that boy sitting there by himself on many occasions, maybe even wearing the exact outfit Rex had on in this photo.

"Mom," Fern said, pulling on the leg of her shorts. "Let's go."

Outside on the front lawn, Jane realized she'd left the origami bird behind. She instructed the kids to wait exactly where they were, then let herself back inside and made her way through the living room and down the hallway where she saw Rex coming toward her. He met her halfway and set the bird into her outstretched palm.

In this close, dark space, Jane felt a desire to touch his skin, which glowed in the dim light reaching them from the kitchen. But before she could react to this strange urge, he stepped toward her, then leaned down and kissed her, wrapping his hands around her waist and pulling her into him so that she could feel the boniness of his chest through his T-shirt. The bird was in her left hand and she held it out and away from her body and put her free hand briefly around his neck before pushing his shoulder away and taking a step back. "My kids are waiting," she said, feeling guilty, but also humming with the kiss, with the sensation of his hands on her waist.

He let her go and nodded. "Sorry," he said. "But once you said you were separated from your husband, that's all I could think about doing."

"But you're not separated."

"Actually, I'm officially divorced. For about five months now. I should have told you before, but I don't like to talk about it."

"Oh," Jane nodded, thinking about the morning she'd seen the wife through the front window. Was he lying to her?

"I have to go," she said, then turned and walked through the dark house to the front door. Her children were waiting for her outside, right where she'd asked them to stay, and she took each one's hand and began walking in the direction of Ivy's house.

REX

He should have lied and said he'd made the bird; perhaps that would have kept her there longer, against him in the hallway. She'd felt sturdier than he'd imagined, not bony at all, and he'd enjoyed the firm curve of her waist in his hands, the lemon smell of her hair. But now she was gone, and he was alone again with his daughters, thinking about Kristina, who was likely lying in a bed somewhere beside a man who now had a particular presence in his mind and a name: Peter.

The girls were still out in the sandbox. He couldn't imagine sinking back into that lawn chair and drinking another beer, thinking and thinking about things he didn't care to think about, so he said, "Let's go girls, we're taking a drive."

Inside the car, leaving his neighborhood behind, Rex continued to feel an anxious buzzing in the pit of his stomach. He needed a sanctuary, somewhere without memory, because every street he passed called up some time from his life before the divorce—there was the square park with the tunnel slide where he and Kristina used to take the girls, there was the coffee shop where he picked up her espressos on the way home from work; they passed Rhonda's house, where he'd spent many evenings at raucous poolside barbecues. Now Kristina would likely take Peter to those gatherings.

The girls were quiet in the backseat, as if they knew better than to speak and interrupt his growing discontent. He turned off of Eastern and drove into another neighborhood. The yellow squares of lit windows lined the street. At nine o'clock, it was too late for kids to be playing outside, he realized, and knew that his own daughters should be in bed too. In the rearview mirror, Callie looked tired, like a mournful wood nymph with her wild blonde hair and pixie features. He couldn't even bring himself to look at Polly. Since the broken finger, she'd been cheerful enough, but Rex could detect a distinct undertone of despair in her every movement.

He was not fully aware of where he was going until he was there. The church loomed up on his right, a dark presence that pulled him to the curb where he cut the engine, and sat for a moment in silence.

He'd been parking outside of this Mormon church for a couple of months now, swinging by after he dropped the girls at school and sitting beside the building in his car. It did not look like the church he'd once attended with his family, but it did remind him of that time, that feeling he'd had of belonging to something.

Finding the church had been an accident. On his very last construction job, he'd driven by it, noticing the place without stopping. Later that month, after he'd been laid off, he considered going back, possibly joining the congregation, but he had never ventured inside, never looked it up online or called to inquire about the hour of services. It was a medium-sized building—nothing special to look at—but Rex found a certain comfort in just sitting beside it, knowing he could get out and open those wide front doors if he ever decided to do so. The pale beige stucco of the building's walls looked bumpy in the moonlight. The high-peaked roof cut an angle out of the dark sky.

"Why are we here?" Calliope asked him from the backseat.

"No reason," he told her. "I just felt like sitting for a minute."

"I'm tired," Polly said. "Can we go home?"

"In a few."

Rex could tell they were aware something was the matter but were uncertain how to proceed. He should get out of here and take them for a cone at Baskin-Robbins, but the thought of leaving this dark curb and venturing further overwhelmed him. He needed to be here, just for a few minutes, then he'd be able to face whatever needed doing next.

He'd left the Mormons for baseball but stayed away for Kristina, who was Catholic. He wouldn't have gone back anyway, Kristina or not, because during his time apart from the church, he'd begun to understand its intolerance and rigidity. He didn't think the Catholics were much better, but it really didn't matter because he and Kristina had never gone to church, not once during their entire marriage. His daughters had never seen the inside of a church, despite efforts from both grandparents, and Rex decided that he would take them at least once, maybe this summer, just so they could see what it was like.

He stepped out of the car and stretched, then looked up and down the block lined with homes. Across the street, a curve of green park reached around the corner. Not a single human being was in sight. This was his first visit to the church at night, and he felt emboldened to take a closer look, so he stepped over the sidewalk and stood on the lawn, leaning back to take in the roof, then moving his gaze down the building until his attention was caught by something sitting on the concrete step by the front doors. It was a dark bundle, the size of a backpack.

Halfway up the walkway, his breath caught. The pinkish arm of a baby was stretched out of the bundle. He rushed over to the step, all his nerves firing at once. He'd heard about this sort of thing occurring—of course he had, everyone had—but the sight of an actual child on an actual church doorstep seemed unreal, out of a movie.

When he reached the bundle and crouched down, he saw that it wasn't a real child inside the scrunched-up blanket but a doll. Rex sat back on his heels and looked at the naked, plastic infant. His heart was still pounding from the shock of seeing the baby's arm; an instinctive panic had propelled him here, and now it felt as if he'd been knocked over. He realized that he'd wanted the child to be a living being, that he'd already imagined the comfort he would provide, picking it up and patting it on the back as he bounced lightly, circling this yard.

Polly appeared behind him, then crouched down and lifted the doll out of the blanket, turning it over for careful inspection. "Can I keep it?" she asked.

Could she keep it? He didn't think so. "No, honey. It's not ours."

"Let me hold it," Callie said, crouching to join their half-circle on the step. Polly passed the baby to her younger sister.

Rex rubbed his eyes, then stood and looked across the lawn. When he turned back, he noticed a white slip of paper inside the whorled depths of the blanket and he leaned to retrieve it, then unfolded it slowly. *You pretend to give, but all you do is take and take.* The writing was slanted and neat, done in blue pen. The words sent an unexpected shiver through him. Had someone lost a child? Given one up for adoption? Abortion? What could the meaning of this message possibly be? He slipped the note into his pocket, not wanting his daughters to see it, and watched Callie, sitting on the dark grass talking to the doll. Polly sat beside her. Rex settled down on the grass nearby, then lay back and looked up at the sky.

The idea surfaced, quietly at first, then with more persistence as he watched the crescent of yellow moon overhead, that he had taken a lot from Kristina over the years—her love and kindness, her time, her patience—and then left her empty these final years. He had imagined she had endless reserves, but it turned out she didn't. Maybe nobody did. He felt empty now too, as if she'd scooped out his insides and taken them away. His heart pounded in a cavernous, echoey chest. His gut was sucked in with starvation. His eye sockets felt dry and fragile. This evening, holding Jane in the hallway had momentarily filled him up once again, but now the emptiness was more prominent, having met its opposite.

Rex sighed and closed his eyes, then felt Callie set the baby on his chest.

"He won't sleep," she told him. "Do something."

"This is dumb," Polly said. She rose and returned to the car, then shut herself inside.

Rex covered the doll with his hands and hummed, pretending to comfort it, stroking its smooth, plastic back. The weight of this toy was so unlike the feel of an actual baby. He could remember lying in bed with Polly on his chest, humming to her exactly like this. She had softened against him, matched her breathing to his, and fallen asleep. He'd loved resting like that during Polly's very first year, closing his eyes and feeling the rapid heartbeat of his daughter, her steady breathing, the small stripe of drool she left on his T-shirt. When Polly's fists unclenched, Kristina knew she was truly asleep and transferred her to the crib.

The horn honked, and he startled, sitting up quickly and sending the doll to the grass. It was Polly, leaning over from the backseat and pushing on the horn. "Stop it," he hissed loudly, not wanting to shout on this quiet street. He leapt up and ran to the car, then opened the door and pulled his daughter's hands off the horn. "Do you want to wake the whole neighborhood?"

Her angry face stopped him cold. She had not been cowed at all by his stern tone. "I want to go home," she said in an even voice. "Now."

"All right, fine. Okay." He returned to the step where he folded the blanket, then took the doll from Callie and set it on top. They were halfway home before he remembered the note, still shoved into his pocket. But it had been meant for him, in some sense, hadn't it? It could have been an exact line from a fight with Kristina. He could even picture her red mouth forming the words—*You pretend to give, but all you do is take and take.* And he could hear his anguished response as well: *I didn't mean to,* he would shout back at her. *I didn't know what I was doing.*

THURSDAY

IVY

In the morning, they drove out to Red Rock Canyon, then parked at Sandstone Quarry, hiked in, and found a flat, salmon-colored stone large enough to hold all five of them. Ivy dumped her pack of food at her feet, then stretched her arms overhead and looked toward the V in the distance where two mountains of rock met. Their deep rust color, cut through with paler shades of carnation and beige, revealed the sky to be bluer than she thought possible. That is where she would like to hike, she decided, to that V and then up as far as she could go. At the top was a shallow pond, if there had been enough rain this spring, and beyond that pond a view of the city. She wanted to see the water, then sit on a shelf of red rock and look out at the city.

Frank had stayed home with Lucky today, and Ivy experienced her third heart-racing moment of worry that she'd forgotten the baby. She had grown so accustomed to having him attached to her chest or resting on her hip that she was unbalanced without him. Instead of feeling free, she was oddly panicky. The view from the top would calm her. She knew this from experience.

Jane appeared beside her and dropped another backpack onto their home base, then sank to one knee to tend to Rocky's untied laces.

Ramona stepped onto the rock next, helping Fern climb up before turning to spread the green blanket over the wide, pale stone. She sat down and smiled. "Perfect," she said. "A perfect day."

"I know, the weather's just right," Ivy said. "Not too hot—not too windy. I think we can make it all the way up today if we help the kids."

"That might be a little out of Fern's league," Jane said, releasing Rocky's foot and turning to watch him leap off the rock. "Besides, she'll want to jump in that pond if there's water."

"I'll stay with her," Ramona offered. "I don't like heights anyway." She kissed the top of Fern's head, then looked up at Jane. "There's a pond here?"

"Just this scooped-out rock area that sometimes fills with water. I guess pond is the wrong word. You've never seen it?"

"I've never been here before," Ramona said.

"Really?" Jane said. "That can't be possible."

"I only came here because Jeremy brought me," Ivy said.

"I guess I only came here with my family," Jane said. "I was sure we'd brought you along once or twice."

Ramona shook her head. "Nope."

"Wow, that's so sad," Jane said.

"No, it's not," Ramona frowned. "Don't act like I was deprived because no one ever took me to Red Rock. Big deal."

"But you were deprived!" Jane said, sitting down beside Ramona. "There aren't that many things of beauty here, and this is one of them, and you never even drove the thirty miles to see it."

Ivy was the only person still standing, and she looked down at both of her friends. Ramona caught her eye and an old, familiar understanding passed between them. It was one they had never vocalized, but it was still there, solid as a wall: Jane lived on a separate plane from the two of them. Growing up, they had both envied her well-kept, middle-class neighborhood, her attentive and kind parents. Did this difference still matter, Ivy wondered. Had it ever?

"Sit down," Ramona told her, and Ivy obeyed. "Let's have a snack, then you two go up that giant rock, and Fern and I will explore down here. Rocky's already halfway there."

"I'm not hungry yet," Ivy said, turning back to Ramona. She pulled a bottle of water from her pack and took a long drink.

Both she and Jane tried to convince Ramona to hike up with them, but to no avail. Ivy offered to stay with Fern, and so did Jane. They explained that it was a fairly easy hike, that she didn't have to go to the edge and wouldn't notice the height if she hung back a bit, but Ramona was not going. So Ivy and Jane set off with their backpack of water bottles and a camera.

They caught up with Rocky quickly, then followed his pace through the maze of boulders, smaller sandstone outcroppings and flat dusty ground toward their destination. Small manzanita bushes grew up between the rocks, their red branches covered with the pale green leaves of spring, and in some of the shaded crevices, lichen grew with neon vividness.

"Why is she so stubborn?" Jane asked when they stopped at the foot of the mountain for a drink.

"I don't think she liked being called deprived."

"Well, she was deprived. Besides, she picked that word, not me."

Ivy smiled and shook her head. "Was I deprived too?"

Jane shrugged, then tilted the bottle of water and drank deeply before passing it back. "I don't know what I'm talking about."

"That's right. You don't." Ivy agreed pleasantly enough, though she felt irritation flash through her.

"She had no one to show her things," Jane continued. "Imagine if Lucky didn't have you or Frank to take him places and teach him about the world."

"He'd figure it out."

"How can you say that?" Jane frowned and shook her head.

Ivy tucked the water bottle back into her pack without answering, then pulled the arm straps snug and started climbing up the first ledge of the mountain, motioning for Jane and Rocky to follow her lead. Jane was right, of course. Compared to Lucky, Ivy had been deprived, but she felt unwilling to admit this out loud, at least to Jane.

The climbing grew more difficult the higher she went, so that in a few spots she needed to grip the rock with her hands and pull herself up to the next plateau. Below, she watched as Jane assisted Rocky, letting him climb first, then boosting him up when necessary. Jane had come home after dark from her walk last night, smelling of beer and seeming happier and more relaxed than she'd been the entire trip. Her story of looking through the neighbor's telescope with the kids sounded innocent enough, but Ivy knew something more had happened.

They were halfway to the pond now—if there was a pond today—and the climbing was easier now. Ivy stopped on a solid rock and turned to look down, then out toward Ramona and Fern, who were small, faraway figures sitting on a patch of green blanket. Ivy waved and shouted out "Ramona!" and her voice echoed nicely but didn't appear to reach them because no one waved back.

Watching their distant forms, Ivy recalled a picnic with her parents when she was no older than five or six. She didn't think they had come here, but somewhere similar, a place with red mountains and Joshua trees, wildflowers creating small flags of color in the dusky, pebbled ground. She remembered her mother that day as plump and happy, her blonde ponytail shiny against the fair skin of her back in a halter top, her brown sunglasses goofily large on her face. She had made ham salad with pickles—Ivy's favorite—and brought three giant oranges that Ivy's father peeled then passed around. Between each offered slice of orange, Ivy held her mother's hand, or pressed her palm to her mother's leg, or played with her ponytail. It was as if even then Ivy understood her mother's presence was temporary, insubstantial.

"Tired?" Jane asked, climbing up beside Ivy. Rocky kept going.

"No. Just taking in the view. My parents took me on a picnic somewhere near here, I think. When I was little. Where do you think it could be?"

"Maybe Spring Mountain Ranch?"

"No, there weren't any picnic tables, or grass or anything. Just rocks and wildflowers."

"I don't know. Why don't you ask your dad?"

"He won't remember," Ivy said. It was actually very likely he would remember, but he would not want to be asked about anything having to do with her mother. It was an unspoken rule between them not to mention her name.

"Lucky really looks like your mom," Jane said. "Around the mouth, and his eyes too, don't you think?"

"He has Frank's eyes," Ivy said, hearing how defensive she sounded.

"Oh, I can see that, I guess."

The only sound for the last part of the climb was her own breathing. Ivy shook away thoughts of her mother and concentrated on getting the correct hand and footholds to lift her onto the plateau. When she pulled herself up the last section of rock, she could see that there was indeed a small pond. Rocky already crouched beside it, peering into the water's shallow depths.

"Fish," he said, pointing.

Ivy walked over to him and took a look at the water. "Actually, those are tadpoles."

Jane appeared at the top of the ledge and joined them by the pond. "If there are tadpoles in here now, how come we never see frogs on our hikes?" Jane asked.

Ivy shrugged. "Good question. It's too hot for them here. They must die."

"Then why would they be born here in the first place?" Jane asked. "That doesn't make evolutionary sense."

"Where's Adam when you need him?" Ivy asked. "He'd be able to explain it."

Jane nodded, looking uncomfortable. "That's true. He would."

Ivy watched her for a moment, then turned back to the pond. The scooped-out crater of water looked as if it could be on the moon, or Mars, with its red shelf of rock rising up on the far side. Only the small boy, kneeling beside the water, made the lunar landscape human.

Ivy circled the pond and climbed up past the crater to the flat space beyond, then stood surveying the valley below. The city winked in the distance as sunlight struck the tall, glassy hotels. The easiest one to pick out was the Luxor, its black pyramid further proof of this place's strangeness.

Up here, thoughts of her parents vanished, and Jeremy replaced them. He had taken her to this place on several occasions. They had sat together on this very piece of rock and watched the city's dim, daytime glow as they shared a beer or a joint. Later, they had sex standing up against a flat, hidden rock near the pond. It was the only spot not immediately visible when you first climbed up. Ivy recalled the surprisingly cool feel of that rock against her back and how nervous she'd been that someone would discover them. She had never much enjoyed the outdoor sex, but she had loved this spot, this view, her feeling of being someplace very far away from home.

"I don't think I ever climbed up this far," Jane said, appearing at her elbow. "Wow, look what I've been missing."

"Now who's been deprived?" Ivy asked, and they both laughed, the tension between them finally drawing tight and snapping so that Ivy felt the relief as something physical, a loosening inside her chest. They sat down together and absorbed the view without speaking. Rocky appeared behind them, then sat down on Jane's lap.

"So when do you think Ramona's going to tell us she's pregnant?" Ivy asked.

"What?" Jane's eyes widened. "What do you mean?"

"She's not drinking. She's moody. Her skin's glowing like a beacon. What other clues do we need?" Ivy asked.

Jane nodded, as if going over the information in her mind. "Maybe you're right."

"Of course I'm right. I just want to know why she won't say anything."

"Too early?" Jane suggested.

"Maybe. Or maybe she's not going to keep it so she doesn't want to tell anyone."

"She'd still tell us, I think," Jane said.

"Maybe." Ivy could feel the pull of tension again. She considered badgering Jane to tell her about Adam but didn't have the energy. To fill the silence, Ivy began pointing out landmarks to Rocky—the Strip, Las Vegas Boulevard, Sunrise Mountain across the valley—then the three of them rose and started the trek back down the rocks.

It was on an easy part of the hike back, climbing over the last cluster of boulders before the straight sandy run to the picnic rock, that Ivy slipped and fell, cutting her bare leg open on an oddly shaped, sharp rock. Jane was kneeling beside her in seconds, along with Rocky, and Ivy tried to offer a smile of reassurance that she was fine, but the sight of blood seeping out of a long gash on her left inner thigh stopped her, and tears beaded in her eyes.

"Go get Ramona," Jane told Rocky, and he ran off.

Jane pulled a long-sleeved shirt out of her backpack and pressed it to Ivy's wound, then wrapped it around her leg and tied it before helping her up. "I think this will need stitches," Jane said, helping her over the last of the rocks and down to flat ground.

There wasn't much pain, but Ivy did feel dizzy. She had always hated the sight of blood. "No, it's not that bad."

"Yes, it is," Jane said.

It turned out Jane was right. In the emergency room of Spring Valley Hospital, Ivy got twenty stitches in her leg. Jane took the kids home, but Ramona stayed and was sitting beside Ivy's bed now, gazing up at the television screen only partially visible due to the curtain separating Ivy's bed from the other two patients in the room. "Go ahead and pull my curtain back a little," she told Ramona. "I don't care."

"No, I'm not really watching," she said, turning her gaze back to Ivy.

Ramona's face floated before her, soft around the edges as if growing out of focus. They had given Ivy a drug of some sort, to dull the pain that she hadn't felt at Red Rock but had come surging through her in the van on the way here, and Ramona's voice felt far away and inconsequential. The stitches were done, and now they were waiting to be seen by one other doctor before her release.

On the other side of the curtain there was a girl and her father. The girl had hurt her ankle skateboarding and was waiting for an X-ray. Jane and Ivy had heard the whole story while they waited for the first doctor to arrive.

"Where's Mom?" she heard the girl ask now.

"On her way," the father said.

Through the haze of the drug, Ivy imagined her own mother rushing to be here. What did she even look like now? Ivy's mother had tried to leave them twice before the last and final time: Once when Ivy was in the third grade, her mother had disappeared for two weeks without a word, then returned with no real explanation; the summer before Ivy started junior high, her mother had walked out again, this time for three months. The third time she left, during Ivy's junior year in high school, Ivy was certain she'd be back. It was just something her mother needed to do: spend periods of time away from her family. But then a year passed without a word, then another, and Ivy had graduated from high school and moved to Wisconsin with Jane.

"Do you ever miss your mom?" Ivy asked Ramona.

"Sure," Ramona said. "Of course."

"Me too," she admitted. She closed her eyes again, falling into the drug's sleepy pull, and thought again of the picnic with her parents.

Later, her mother had set up her easel and painted several wild-flowers. Ivy had still been young enough to think that her mother was exceptionally talented, though the truth was her paintings were amateurish and choppy. Ivy still owned one of them, an oil of the fountain in the courtyard of their old apartment building. The lines of the painting were coarse and unskilled, but the colors were right. She had gotten that pinky orange sky exactly, and the blue shadows beneath the tiers of the fountain were true. It was in the back of Ivy's closet, wrapped in brown paper. She hadn't looked at it in years.

"Hey, look who's here," Ramona said, nodding toward the door.

Frank appeared at the edge of the curtain, looking pale but smiling. He moved toward her and found her foot beneath the thin sheet, then held onto it.

"You didn't need to come," Ivy told him. "I'm fine."

"I know I didn't need to," he said. "I wanted to. And fifty stitches is not fine, by the way."

"It's only twenty."

"Okay, then, twenty. I'll go home." He turned and began to walk away.

Ivy laughed and called out for him to come back, which he did, grinning. She could tell, however, that the grin was forced, and she understood then how worried he was. He pulled up a chair next to Ramona's and leaned forward to take Ivy's hand. "I called your dad to let him know."

"Why would you do that?" Ivy asked.

"Believe it or not, parents like to know when their kids get hurt."

"But he can't do anything for me. He'll just worry now." Ivy sighed and leaned her head back against the pillow. That was all she needed: her father driving over to fuss. Ever since he'd stopped drinking, he'd become a worrier. It was not unusual to get an article in the mail that he'd clipped out, detailing the dangers of rubber bands, or describing the death of a family swept off a cliff in Maine by a giant wave.

A nurse appeared at the edge of the curtain and asked Ivy how she was doing.

Ivy was about to say she was okay when Frank said, "It's sort of depressing in here. How about some music? Or better lighting?"

The nurse looked at him and smiled. She was young and pretty, curvy beneath her white and lavender scrubs. "I forgot my candles and boom box," she said with a smile and shrug, obviously flirting.

"So when can we get her out of here?" he asked, tilting his head toward Ivy. "What's the holdup?"

"I'll check and see what's taking so long," the nurse said, then smiled and left the room.

"Thanks for coming," Ivy told Frank, squeezing his hand. Her leg was beginning to ache through the haze of drugs, and the tightness of the stitches was unpleasant, alien. She had never had stitches before, and just thinking about the skin laced together over her wound made her stomach churn. She pressed the button to increase the drug coursing through her, then sank deeper into her pillow and closed her eyes. Her mother's face swam over her, and Ivy reached up to touch her features, or she thought she was reaching up—she wasn't sure. The blonde hair was thinner now and shorter, going white at the crown. As she watched her mother's face shift in and out of her half-dream, she could hear Ramona and Frank talking. Their low murmurs were a comfort and reminded her of being young and in bed, listening to her parents talking in the living room. She had been loved then and happy, but she hadn't even realized it. If she'd known how tenuous that feeling was going to be for the next ten or twenty years, she would have cherished it, held the emotion close and memorized its every slope and valley.

JEREMY

The grocery store was practically empty. Jeremy pushed his cart down the aisle, scooping up champagne grapes and fresh figs, cucumbers, mangoes, and raspberries. Six perfect pears, a ripe mango. This was the Vons where he'd run into Ivy only three days earlier. It felt as if a lifetime had passed since then.

He didn't expect to see her today, thinking that would be much too lucky, but he had driven across town to shop here simply because he liked the idea of having Ivy nearby. Also, the drive helped him to think about what he could make for the sweet sixteen party he was catering tonight. The girl's mother had been vague about what she wanted, saying only that he should make snacks and dessert for twenty-five people and "nothing spicy please." He'd devised several possible menus, all of which were shoved into his back pocket, but he was buying on impulse now, imagining the birthday girl's homely, freckled face as he threw in blue cheese, goat cheese, Brie, Edam, fontina. Eggs, pickles, onions, bacon. He would need honey, he decided, and also some type of flatbread that he would bake himself.

Back out in the parking lot, he began to sweat as he loaded the bags into the backseat of his car. The sun was high and sharp today, burning the parking lot to a faded husk. Inside his car, he rolled down the windows, realizing the drive had been foolish because the fruit would overheat, and the cheese might begin to soften, which would work all right for the Brie, he guessed, but not the others.

He was almost out of the lot when he saw her—the older blonde woman who was or wasn't Ivy's mother. She was loading a bag into the front seat of a white car, and he couldn't get a good look at her face. This might not even be the same person he'd spotted last week, but something told him to wait, so he did, idling close to the exit.

When she drove by him, he recognized her large tortoiseshell sunglasses, and on impulse he followed her out of the lot and to the right, toward Eastern. She drove slowly, as if uncertain of her destination, pausing at a stop sign for an inordinately long time. His honk made her jump, and he felt guilty for startling her. The white car was a rental, and he'd been right about the make; it was a Monte Carlo.

She screeched away from the stop sign, as if propelled by his honk, then he was forced to wait for a slow-moving pickup truck, and when he crossed the small intersection, the white car was no longer in sight. He was in Ivy's neighborhood now, and he looped through the quiet streets, seeking out the Monte Carlo. He saw a couple of white cars parked in driveways, but not the same rental. A blonde woman trimmed her pomegranate tree on one front lawn, and Jeremy slowed, but when she looked up he saw it was a different person. The fruit in the backseat was beginning to smell overripe, its sweetness signaling its doom. Soon he would need to turn around and drive to the kitchen as quickly as he could.

Just when he'd given up, he passed a small pocket park, and there was the car, parked and empty at the curb. He pulled in behind it, looking for the woman through his window, but the park was shaded with several large mulberry trees blocking his view, and he couldn't see beyond the bathroom in the park's center, so he cut the engine and rolled down his windows, then stepped outside.

He found her sitting on top of a picnic table just past the bathroom. The paper bag from Vons sat beside her, and she was making a sandwich from its contents. First, she lifted out a loaf of bread, then a package of lunch meat, a block of white cheese.

Approaching her slowly, he tried to decide if this was Ivy's mother. She was definitely familiar, though smaller than he recalled, and thicker around the middle. She was wearing white tennis shoes, dark jeans, and a red T-shirt that said THE BIG APPLE. New York's smoky skyline was etched beneath the white letters.

He tried to remember her first name. It was something strange and foreign-sounding, like Ostrich. Astrid. That was it. It was a name he'd never heard before or since. He said it softly to himself, then stepped closer and said the name again, "Astrid?"

She looked up from making her sandwich, then pushed her sunglasses back onto the top of her head and stared at him. Her eyes were the same giant gray-blue as Ivy's.

"Do I know you?" she asked.

"I think maybe you do," he said. "It's Jeremy, Ivy's old boyfriend, from high school?"

The information made her smile, a wide, apple-cheeked smile he hadn't expected. It made her face instantly younger. "Jeremy, of course," she said, getting down from the table and walking over to stand directly in front of him. "I always liked you."

"You did?" She didn't hold out her hand for a shake, and Jeremy wondered if she was expecting a friendly embrace, but decided against any contact.

"Of course I did. Remember that show we used to watch together, while Ivy was getting ready? It was a game show of some sort—I haven't watched TV in years—but I do remember that one."

"*Wheel of Fortune*," he said, recalling now how they used to sit together on the couch, figuring out the words while Ivy curled her hair, applied her mascara, spritzed on perfume. "You always knew the answers."

She shrugged. "It was a useless talent. But fun."

"Does Ivy know you're here?" he asked, knowing of course that she didn't.

Astrid shook her head. "And please don't tell her."

"How long have you been in town?"

"A couple of weeks."

She returned to her seat atop the picnic table and patted the space beside her. "Join me?"

"I can't," he said, remembering the food in his car, but it was more than that. Sitting beside Ivy's mother and eating a sandwich would be a betrayal. He cleared his throat, suddenly nervous, and asked, "Where have you been? All this time?"

She shrugged again. "Oh, here and there. Most recently Phoenix."

Phoenix. Such an ordinary place to escape from your family. He had always imagined her in Paris or Rome, sitting at a sidewalk café sipping wine, an image instantly erased by the word *Phoenix*.

"When are you going to go and see Ivy?"

"When I'm ready." Astrid had finished making her sandwich and she took a large bite, then closed her eyes as she chewed and swallowed. "This could really use a pickle," she said and opened her eyes. "Or red onion."

He had both of those items in the grocery bags in his car, but he said nothing. Why was she acting as if meeting him in a park after twenty years was an ordinary experience? Her nonchalance unnerved him. "I saw you," he said, hoping to jar her into the moment, to coax out a stronger reaction. "You know, the night you left. I was standing across the street. I should have told Ivy about it, but I never did."

She raised her thin, blonde eyebrows, as if waiting for him to say more, then bit into her sandwich again. When she finished chewing, she said, "You did the right thing. It wasn't your place to say anything and it's not your place now. So keep out of it."

There was a threat in her sentence, despite her continued calm, her sugary tone. Jeremy took a step back, glad to have elicited a greater show of emotion, though now he didn't know what to do with it. He had to ask her something important, gain crucial information for Ivy's sake, so he tried the simplest route: "Why did you leave?"

"Why did I leave?" she echoed, then nodded, and looked down at her knees. A fine peach fuzz of hair was lit by the sun along the curve of her cheek, and her face had tightened into concentration or pain. "You wouldn't understand," she told him finally.

Though this was likely true, it struck him as unfair. He hoped she would not give Ivy the same answer. "Where are you staying?" he asked, trying for the next best thing, a solid piece of information to offer Ivy.

"A friend's, over in Henderson."

"What's the address?"

She gave him a long appraising look, then said, "None of your business."

"Okay." It was true, he guessed. It was none of his business. "Maybe I'll see you around," he said, and waved, feeling foolish. The exchange was too mundane, and he found it difficult to believe that this was it. They had talked about nothing, and now he was waving good-bye. But there was nothing left to be done, so he turned, walked across the grass, and got into his car.

The smell of ripe fruit was sickening now, and he drove quickly through the streets, hoping the groceries could be salvaged. Guilt overwhelmed him as he hit Eastern and headed toward his apartment, which was closer than the rented kitchen. He should have said more to Astrid. He should have yelled at her, cussed her out, pushed her onto the grass, done something to express the rage he'd felt toward her, that both he and Ivy had felt toward her all those years ago. Instead, he'd chatted pleasantly about *Wheel of Fortune*.

His apartment building appeared sooner than he'd expected—traffic was light today—and Jeremy parked in his spot, then climbed to the second floor of the beige stucco building carrying all four bags of groceries and setting them down on the concrete hallway to unlock his door. He carried his groceries inside and quickly put half the items in the refrigerator, which was empty except for a jar of capers and a bottle of Tapatío sauce. The fruit and cheeses appeared to have survived the journey.

He flopped onto his overstuffed chair and stared at the ceiling, thinking. He should call Ivy to tell her about Astrid. This duty sat in his gut like a stone. It would be best to tell her in person, but he couldn't afford the time to do that until tomorrow. Still, a phone call would be awkward. Her voice would be wary; he would be unable to read her face; she might even cry. It was possible she would be angry about the delay if he waited until tomorrow to go over there and tell her, but he had a lot to do before the party he was catering in seven hours. He closed his eyes, and a menu began to take shape in his mind, clearing away his other worries: fig and goat cheese crostini, deviled eggs with horseradish and red onion, a cavatappi pasta with bacon and blue cheese that everyone always liked, as his safety. A fruit plate that would include the champagne grapes and mango. His assortment of cheeses and olives. Dessert would be a gingered pear pandowdy he'd been wanting to try and a simple chocolate mousse for the less adventurous. He'd make extra mousse in case the pandowdy didn't work out. The ingredients for all of these things drifted in his mind, pictures floating through his vision with a vividness lacking in the rest of his life. He got up, poured himself a glass of water, then got to work.

RAMONA

She was looking forward to dinner at Jane's house. Ramona had always liked her friend's parents, and it felt good to leave that new, sterile neighborhood behind and travel back into the overgrown trees and uneven sidewalks of the older section of town, the one that felt more like home. Ivy had stayed behind to rest, still drugged up and sleepy, and Frank was so good at caring for her that Ramona and Jane were practically in the way around his competence.

"I hope your mom makes those spinach crepes with goat cheese," Ramona said. "I always loved those."

"Don't get your hopes up," Jane advised. "I don't think they eat cheese anymore. Lactose intolerant."

"Both of them?"

Jane shrugged. "Not sure, but they're a united front. If one is lactose intolerant, then they both are."

"That's sweet," Ramona said.

"And a little bit annoying."

"I feel sort of bad leaving Ivy," Ramona said.

"She probably wants to be alone to sleep. That was an outrageous cut. I thought she was going to bleed to death for a minute. The shirt I tied to her leg was soaked through."

"I know," Ramona said, shaking her head. Recalling the sight of Ivy hobbling toward her across the red rocks, Ramona felt again the dread of that moment. If anything happened to Ivy or Jane, who would she have left to love? She supposed there was Nash, and the possible baby, but would they be enough?

They turned left and headed into Jane's old neighborhood. This had once been a fairly well-kept area, with tall leafy elms and neat lawns, and Ramona was surprised to see how much it had changed. Cars were parked on grass. Chain-link fences were erected here and there to keep in large, angry looking dogs. Dusty front yards held plastic play sets.

At the end of the block, Ramona saw that Jane's old home was still a haven of cool green trees. The house was painted a bright, sky blue now—it was gray when she'd last been here—and the cheery color only served to emphasize the decay of the homes around it. "No offense," Ramona said, "but this house should be airlifted out of here."

"I know. Sad, isn't it?" Jane said, parking at the curb and cutting the engine.

"What's sad?" Rocky asked.

Ramona turned, surprised to hear his voice. She'd completely forgotten the kids were in the backseat. This forgetfulness struck her as a bad omen, a mark against her potential as a future mother.

"It's sad that the neighborhood where I grew up looks so crappy now," Jane said, stepping out of the car.

"I like it," Rocky said, getting out and stepping onto the lawn. "I like the trees."

"The trees are nice," Ramona agreed, looking up into the broad arms of the elms.

Fern had fallen asleep, and Jane was trying to carefully lift her out, so Ramona took Rocky's hand and led him to the front door.

Jane's mother, Sheila, answered, wearing an apron with the name of a vineyard on it. The green cloth was spotless, as if she hadn't actually worn it while cooking. "Ramona!" she cried and pulled her into an embrace. "Look at you," Sheila said, holding her at arm's length. "You haven't changed a bit."

The attention made her blush, and she smiled, then said, "You haven't either," though of course she had. Her light brown hair was striped with gray now instead of blonde, and her skin had a nice crêpey softness that it hadn't back in high school.

"Nonsense," Sheila said. "I'm an old lady now." She smiled to reveal even, white teeth.

"Ancient," Jane said, coming up behind Ramona and leaning to kiss her mother on the cheek before moving past her into the house. Rocky and Fern each grabbed Sheila around one knee and she leaned down to coo at them.

Inside, the house was just as Ramona remembered: green walls, parquet floors, and the clean lines of pale Swedish furniture. A Matisse print called *Blue Nude* hung over the fireplace, and Ramona recalled that she'd planned to buy that print one day and hang it in her own home, something she hadn't yet accomplished. She made another mental note to do so, but couldn't quite picture where it would fit in her tiny apartment. There must be a smaller version of the print, but that wouldn't be the same, would it?

In the living room, Jane's father, Gary, sat on the couch holding a glass of white wine and talking to Jane's brother, Russ. Ramona stopped when she saw Russ and felt a brief flush of nervous wings beat through her. She hadn't known he was going to be here tonight.

Both men rose to greet her, first bestowing a kiss on Jane, then hugging Ramona and telling her how good she looked after all these years. She wasn't sure she actually looked very good at all—her hair definitely needed cutting (Ivy was right) and she could feel a painful blemish forming on her chin—but she guessed this was the standard offering to a friend, or a friend of your daughter's, whom you hadn't seen in twenty years.

"You guys aren't looking too shabby yourselves," she said, gratefully accepting a glass of wine from Jane's mother and sitting in the coral-colored armchair beside the couch.

On her third sip of wine, she remembered she wasn't supposed to be drinking, so she set her glass on an end table, then tried to get a good look at Russ as he listened to Jane. Jane's brother had aged well so far. His slight scrawniness had turned into an appealing wiry build, and his hair was still blond and shaggy. The new, square, black glasses were a nice addition to his face, which had pale lashes and brows, and his laugh was the honky guffaw she recalled from the many nights and afternoons she'd spent in this house. She'd always liked that laugh, its utter lack of decorum or self-consciousness.

For dinner, they gathered around the long, polished oak table and spooned piles of Thai food—green curry with beef—into sky blue bowls. A dog brushed by her legs, and Ramona leaned down expecting to see the beagle Jane had in high school, but found a white Pomeranian instead, looking up at her with giant brown eyes.

"Don't feed him," Gary advised.

"I wasn't planning to," Ramona said.

"You always used to feed Daisy under the table," Sheila reminded her. "Don't think I don't remember! That dog had the worst habits. We're trying to be stricter with Casper."

"Just like you were stricter with me than you were with Russ," Jane said, chewing.

"I never fed Daisy under the table," Ramona protested. "Must have been Ivy."

"We were not stricter with you," Sheila said to Jane. "Why would you say such a thing?"

Jane shrugged and took a long swallow of wine.

"Your mother wasn't strict with anyone," Gary said. "If you'd asked her to fill your pillow up with whipped cream, she probably would have done it."

"Whipped cream," Sheila repeated, shaking her head. "That's ridiculous. We never even keep that in the house."

"It was a metaphor, Mom," Russ said.

"I get it," Sheila said, frowning at Russ, then breaking into a broad smile. "Remember that time you girls had the ice cream social here, and that boy went around in a bowtie offering whipped cream to everyone out of our silver bowl."

"That was Jeremy," Jane said. "He's a caterer now."

"That wasn't Jeremy," Ramona argued. "It was that kid Felix, the foreign exchange student."

"Are you sure?" Jane asked, knitting her brow. "I think you're wrong."

"All I remember," her father cut in, "is the doofus who broke my stereo."

"*That* was Jeremy," Ramona said.

"Actually, it was your boyfriend, Ramona," Russ said. "Mark."

"Oh, right," Ramona said, shaking her head. How had she forgotten that? "I felt awful about that."

"You shouldn't have, dear," Sheila said. "Why do we always feel like our boyfriend or husband is our responsibility, like they're some extension of ourselves?"

"Because they are," Gary said.

"No, our children are, to a certain extent. But you're not. I don't have anything to do with your personality."

"Yes, you do," Jane said. "You two have melded into one person. You're lucky."

"That doesn't sound very lucky," Russ said.

"What do you mean by that? That's a ridiculous statement," Sheila said and looked slightly annoyed even though she smiled her graceful, hostess smile.

"You two agree on everything, that's all," Jane said.

"Not true," Gary said.

"Okay, give me one example then," Jane said.

"Your mother hates my friend Craig."

"Don't be ridiculous." Sheila shot her husband a disapproving look, then turned back to Jane. Ramona felt a bubble of discomfort work its way up her gullet. She'd forgotten the way Jane liked to subtly poke and prod at her parents.

"Just admit it, Sheila. It's no big deal. You've always disliked him."

"I will admit no such thing."

"See, Jane," Russ said. "That's how you do it: Deny, deny, deny. Never admit to anything."

Jane laughed and shared a look with her brother that made Ramona envious. If her own brother were still alive, would they share jokes around the dinner table? She couldn't picture it. Even before he'd gotten sick, her brother had been a picky eater, so the idea of him at a dinner table for any length of time struck her as wrong.

"So, what's the matter with Craig?" Jane asked.

Sheila sighed and looked around the table, then took a swallow of wine and said, "He's just a little bit crass for my taste, that's all. I *do* like him."

"What does crass mean?" Rocky asked.

"Sort of gross and rude," Russ told him.

Sheila shared a look with her husband, as if to say *See what you started?* She stood and began clearing the table.

After dessert of lime sorbet and small, strong cups of coffee, they reconvened in the living room. "Play us a tune, Ramona," Gary said, settling back into his place on the couch.

"Oh, I didn't bring my guitar," she said, sitting down in the coral armchair.

"Mine's still here," Russ offered.

Before she could protest, he rose and disappeared then returned with his old guitar. Once, they had played a duet together in a talent show, back in junior high school. Russ set the guitar on her lap with a smile, and Ramona saw that she would have to play something. She was used to playing in front of people, but this was different. These were the people she had once wished were her real family. This was the boy she had once wished to marry.

She tuned the guitar while Fern and Rocky fought over who got to sit beside Russ. Jane and Sheila were on the opposite love seat, talking quietly with their heads bent toward each other. Ramona knew she should play one of her new songs, but suddenly they all

struck her as rubbish. Running through the lyrics in her mind, the
songs sounded hollow and stunted, the product of someone who
didn't understand much about life.

Instead, she settled on a song from her first album called *One
Night in the Desert* about a girl who can't find her way home from
a party. It was one of the more melancholy songs she'd written, and
halfway through, it felt like a huge mistake. Why hadn't she chosen
something more upbeat? Her voice was out of practice from this
week of lazing around, and it sounded slightly hoarse to her ear,
the acoustics in the living room not very good.

When she was finished, everyone clapped and she smiled and
even blushed when Russ caught her eye and winked his approval.
She felt, for a moment, as if she were still in high school, still hanging out in Jane's living room pining over Jane's older brother. As
if her life hadn't happened yet. As if she were still on the verge of
everything. No terrible decisions made. Her skin was hot, and she
held the guitar close against her chest and tried to smile without
looking as if she were about to cry.

"Oh, honey," Sheila said. "That was just beautiful. We are so
proud of you."

"Thanks," Ramona said. The compliment settled a pillow of
warm air around her, and the feeling that she was about to cry
passed.

"Really great," Gary added. "We brag to all our friends about
you, by the way."

"It's true," Russ said. "I've heard them."

Ramona set Russ's guitar carefully on the floor, said "Thanks"
again, then left the room to get a glass of water.

She didn't turn on the kitchen light but found the glasses in
the same cupboard where they always were. Running the tap, she
looked out the window by the sink at the dark shapes of the backyard: the hulking forms of the oleander bushes against the fence,
the arms of the mulberry tree that held a hummingbird feeder,

gleaming in a spoke of light from the neighbor's back porch. From the living room she heard murmurs, then a bright crack of Jane's laughter. It occurred to her that she had pined for Jane's parents more than she had ever pined for Russ. He had simply been the crush she could admit to.

Ramona had an overwhelming urge to sneak out. The backyard had a gate that led to the street. It would be easy to leave without anyone hearing her. How long would it take them to notice she was gone?

The glass of water was cool on her throat, and after she finished it, she set it on the counter, where she noticed Jane's car keys. On impulse she pocketed them, then stepped outside. The night was chillier than usual, and the smells of a barbecue reached her as she wound behind the house toward the gate. The sight of the lit windows of the living room stopped her. Just one more look, she promised herself, then she would go.

Rocky was curled onto Jane's lap now, his head on her shoulder as she talked to her mother with animated pleasure. Russ and Gary were talking on the other couch, and Fern sat between them, combing the hair of an old, ratty doll that rested on her lap. The guitar still lay on the floor where Ramona had left it. She pulled Jane's car keys from her jeans pocket and held them in her hand, considering.

Fern looked up toward the window, and Ramona stepped back, then realized the girl couldn't see her. It was too dark outside, too bright inside. This was where she belonged, on the outside of Jane's family, staring into their lit-up living room. The gate squeaked a little as she opened it, but not at all when she closed it. She crossed the lawn and didn't look back.

Driving toward the hotel, she realized she was close to Sweeney Street, where the second J. Dillman on her list was supposed to live. She found the street easily and turned right, then parked in the same place she had yesterday afternoon, beneath the elm tree.

The lights were on inside the yellow house, and a white pickup truck was parked in the driveway. Ramona waited, watching the windows and the door, and wondered why she was doing this. Even if she did, indeed, find her son, would he want to speak to her?

She sat for fifteen minutes, then considered leaving. She was tired from hiking and from the emotion of Ivy's fall and seeing Jane's family. The muscles of her arms ached from carrying Fern around this morning at Red Rock, and she needed to use the bathroom.

Then the porch light came on across the street and the front door opened and she held her breath and waited, feeling her heart beat as if to break apart her chest. The person who stepped outside was male, on the short side, and slightly husky, with dark, shaggy hair. He looked out at the street, then sat on the edge of the porch and lit a cigarette. It was difficult to discern his age. He could be nineteen or thirty-five from this distance in this dim light. The porch light revealed the shape of him—the tufts of hair curling out on either side of his neck, the wide shoulders and solid bulk of his chest—but his face was cast in shadows, and Ramona began to send him a silent message to turn his head to the side. A profile would help her somehow; the shape of the nose and chin might mean a lot, might reveal his true identity. She touched her own nose as she sat watching, then traced the curve of her chin.

Ramona definitely felt more connected to this kid than she had to the red-haired boy in the fancy house. This boy shared her loneliness, her need to be separate from the people inside. It pained her that he smoked, but she understood that too, since she'd done it herself for several years after high school. His build resembled Mark's, and the kid had her black hair. This might be him, she told herself. This could be your son.

The boy stood, then walked across the grass to the street and began strolling in the opposite direction of Ramona's car. When he was three houses down, Ramona got out and locked her car, then decided to walk around the block in the opposite direction in the slim hope of running into him on his loop back home. Of course, he could be going somewhere, she told herself as she rounded the corner and began walking up the opposite street. It was just as likely he was going to a friend's house or down to the 7-Eleven as it was that he was taking a walk around the block.

This was not the best section of town, but the street was quiet and peaceful. She passed a woman dragging her garbage bin to the curb. They exchanged hellos.

Ramona was about halfway down her side of the block now, and she searched the circles of light beneath the street lamps up ahead, hoping to catch sight of the kid. She felt guilty suddenly for having run out on Jane and her family. What if they were searching the streets for her right this second? But, of course, they'd see that her car was gone, so seeking her out nearby wouldn't make sense. She would apologize later, either call Sheila or write her a note. A note would be best, she decided, easier but more thoughtful. Jane's mother always appreciated gestures of that sort.

A form appeared at the end of the block, and Ramona recognized the boy instantly, even from a distance. He had his hands shoved into his pockets now, and he trudged along, as if hunching himself against a cold night despite the air's silky warmth. Her heart started to pound again, and Ramona tried to make a plan for the moment when they crossed paths on the sidewalk.

And then the moment was there. As they each stepped beneath the brief glare of a streetlight, their gazes locked, and Ramona took note of his blue eyes surrounded by dark, curly lashes. This boy's eyes were far superior in their beauty to either hers or Mark's, though Mark's were the same color blue. Other than the eyes, his face was ordinary: his cheeks sweetly packed with baby fat, a nose a little too big for his face. He bit his lower lip nervously and nodded at Ramona. She nodded back, then the moment was over and she was past him, the empty sidewalk unrolling ahead of her into the night.

She turned and looked back at his retreating form, wanting to call out to him, but what could she say? "Excuse me," she cried, lifting her voice to be heard. He turned and stopped, several lengths of sidewalk away from her already. Ramona jogged over to him, then asked, "Do you have the time?"

"Um, sure," he said, and pulled a cell phone out of his pocket to glance at its bright face. "8:56." His voice was deeper than she expected, and up close, with more time to observe his face, she saw that he was definitely older than nineteen, possibly nearing thirty. The recognition she'd experienced in the car seeped out of her. This man was not her grown-up son.

"Thanks," she told him, wanting to be back in her car now, driving to her hotel room, but she had to navigate the remainder of the block first. "I appreciate it."

"No problem," he told her, then turned and continued on his way.

Ramona stood where she was, watching him until he turned the corner back in the direction of his home.

JANE

Just as Jane pulled into a parking space at the Golden Nugget, Adam called. She was on the top level of the ramp and got out of her mother's car to stand in the windy night and look down on the streets and people below as she said "Hello" into the phone and waited for her husband's voice to answer back.

"How's it going?" he asked, sounding tired and slightly hoarse, as if she were the one who'd called and woken him up.

"Fine," she said, then added, "Is everything all right?"

"No, everything is not all right. I miss you guys."

Jane nodded, as if he were there and could see her. "The kids miss you too," she said, though she wasn't sure this was true since they hadn't asked about him for a day or two. "Ivy got hurt at Red Rock today and had to get a bunch of stitches. It upset Rocky a lot because he saw her fall. And Ramona was just over at my parents' house for dinner, and she ditched us without saying good-bye, just escaped out the back door. I'm trying to find her right now."

"Wow," he said. "Sounds like there's a lot more going on there than there is here. Can I talk to the kids?"

"I left them with Mom and Dad. Tomorrow I'll have them call you," she promised. She waited for more follow-up questions about Ivy or Ramona, but none came. She felt almost grateful for his lack of empathy about her closest friends. It was good to tally up another of his flaws rather than more of hers.

After they said good-bye, Jane stood looking at the street below and tried to imagine what it might be like to live here again. Being this far from Adam wasn't fair and might not even be legal—she wasn't sure what types of divorce statutes there were about leaving the state—but she couldn't shake away the appeal of an entirely new life. A new life in her old town.

She found Ramona in her room and was let in without a word. Jane had been planning to demand an explanation for her friend's sneaky departure, but now that she was actually standing beside Ramona in this hotel room, the urge to gather answers dissipated. Instead, Jane asked, "Is it all right if I stay here with you tonight?"

"Of course," Ramona said, then stepped away from the door and plunked onto one of the beds.

Jane set her purse on the other queen bed by the window, then pulled the curtains aside and looked at the view: the lit shell of the Fremont Street Experience, a sliver of moon, people walking up the side streets toward their cars. She couldn't help but wonder which direction Saturn was in. "Let's take a walk," she suggested.

Outside, the lights in the ceiling of the Fremont Street Experience danced blue, green, and purple across the high, curved archway, and the music was Donna Summer. It seemed to Jane that she was on a strange new planet—a loud one with a colored, blinking sky—and the feeling was unsettling but also liberating. This was not the street she'd visited growing up; it had been so thoroughly altered it now felt new.

"Where should we go?" Jane asked, taking Ramona's arm. She had a notion to play one hand of blackjack and have one drink in every casino along the street, then run back to the room together, half-drunk in the cooling air and either richer or poorer from their night's efforts.

"How about the drugstore?" Ramona said flatly. "I need to take a pregnancy test."

They found a Walgreens much further down, out from under the canopy of the Fremont Street Experience. Here, at the end of the street, it was quieter, darker. The forlorn sign of a Motel 6 blinked at them from a block away, and Jane noticed a pack of teenagers on

bikes huddled in the motel's parking lot, talking loudly. The sound
of a bottle breaking from within their huddle sent a wave of anxiety through Jane but only stirred up raucous laughter among the
group. The air smelled drier out here and somehow wild, as if this
were not a place people should inhabit.

Inside, the store was bright and empty save for the clerk, a
young girl filing her nails as she leaned against the cash register.
Ramona picked out the generic brand pregnancy test and held it
up for Jane's approval.

"Why don't you just take it here?" Jane said. "In the bathroom."
She pointed to the door marked LADIES ROOM right beside their
aisle. She had the notion that if Ramona were not pregnant they
could continue on with the night as planned, filling themselves up
with mindless fun all the way back to the Golden Nugget.

"I can't do that," Ramona said, shaking her head.

She paid at the counter then they were back out into the night,
which had grown very windy. Great, warm gusts sent dead leaves
and debris flying against their knees as they trudged back up the
street toward their hotel room.

Jane laced her arm through Ramona's and pulled her friend
closer, wanting to shield her from the wind, to protect her from
the elements and also from the possibility of pregnancy. A baby for
Ramona did not strike Jane as happy news.

Once they were back under the canopy, the wind slowed, and
Ramona tugged gently away from Jane's grasp.

"Why did you leave tonight?" Jane asked her. "Why would you
just sneak out without saying good-bye or anything? I thought you
liked my family."

"I do like them," Ramona said, then added only, "I'm sorry."

"Was it because they made you play a song? Is that it? They
sort of put you on the spot there, I know."

Ramona shook her head. "No, that was fine. I didn't mind."

"Then what?"

"I'm not sure."

They walked in silence for a while, and Jane saw the great crown of the Four Queens pulsing with lights, then the arched sign of the Golden Nugget.

"I've been looking for my son," Ramona said, keeping her eyes forward as they trudged together up the sidewalk.

"Really?" Jane stopped and turned to face her. "Any luck?"

She shrugged. "I have one more name to check on. The other two didn't pan out."

"Wait a minute. You've been doing this while you're here?"

Ramona nodded.

"Why didn't you tell us? Why didn't you let us help?"

Ramona shrugged again and gave her a half-smile. "You can come with me tomorrow if you want."

"Of course I want to," Jane said. "I just don't understand why you've been so secretive. This is big news." She smiled to soften this and understood that she was being secretive as well. No one but Rex knew the real reason she'd been fired or that she and Adam were separated.

They resumed walking but Ramona stopped near the hotel entrance and said, "I think I'd rather take the test in the morning. You're supposed to do it first thing when you wake up, right?"

"I think you can do it any time of day."

Ramona clutched the paper drugstore sack and frowned. With a braid slung over each shoulder and her face free of makeup, she looked suddenly very young and scared, and Jane remembered the day in high school when Ramona had pulled her aside and told her she was pregnant. Ramona had been crying then, with stripes of black mascara crisscrossing her pale cheeks. Jane had pulled her friend against her body and held on tightly. She had no idea what to say to a pregnant friend then and realized she still didn't know the proper words to offer. "Do you want to be pregnant?" she asked Ramona.

"I'm not sure," she said, then laughed a weak, nervous laugh and added, "I guess I'm not sure about much of anything today."

"Well, let's go find out, then you can be sure about one thing." Jane took her arm again and led her inside.

Waiting on the bed while Ramona was in the bathroom, Jane tried to keep her thoughts neutral. It seemed important not to impose her wishes on the pregnancy test, even though she knew her thoughts could hold no sway over whatever was happening inside Ramona's womb. If she is pregnant, Jane decided, I'll suggest we celebrate. They could order up room service—french fries or chocolate ice cream, something Ramona loved—then sit cross-legged on the bed and talk about the future.

If she were not pregnant, Jane decided she would talk Ramona into the night of drinking and gambling Jane had previously envisioned. Her friend would protest, she knew, but Jane could persuade her.

She rose from her position on the bed and went to stand at the window, imagining Adam wandering through the rooms of their house in Wisconsin. Even though it was after midnight there, he would still be awake, either watching TV or reading a magazine in the big red chair by the window. He had often been the one to tend to Rocky or Fern in the middle of the night since he was usually up anyway and Jane needed her sleep for work in the morning.

The day she had found out she was pregnant with Rocky, Adam had brought her a giant chocolate milkshake to celebrate. They sat together on the back porch sharing the shake, Jane on Adam's lap, and he had made jokes about how she would soon be too heavy to sit this way. Jane thought of that day, sometimes, as the highest point of their marriage. Every detail had been exactly right, and for once, the weight of her worry had been so much lighter than the solidity of her joy.

Jane crossed the room to the bathroom and knocked lightly. "Almost done?" she asked.

"Almost," Ramona said. Her voice sounded faint and shaky.

"Everything okay?"

"Yes," she said.

"I'm going downstairs for a sec," she told Ramona through the door. "Give you some privacy."

Down in the lobby, Jane was uncertain of her purpose. She had come with the idea of a drink, but it seemed depressing to sit alone at a bar, so she wandered to the gift shop instead, thinking to buy something for Ramona and maybe for Ivy too. The small shop had several gaudy baubles with the Golden Nugget logo—shot glasses, ashtrays, blinking key chains, and glittery snow globes. All of these items were obviously wrong as gifts, but Jane picked each thing up anyway, turning it over in her hands as if seriously considering a purchase. There were a couple of racks showcasing T-shirts and extremely short dresses, then half a wall of stuffed animals. What did you buy a person who may or may not be pregnant?

A shelf of piggy banks caught her eye and she wandered over and hefted the weight of one in her hand: I LOVE LAS VEGAS was written in red on the side, and the pig's tail was a curly dollar sign. This was the one for Ivy, a match for the gift they'd found in her stroller yesterday.

A pig was not a good choice for Ramona's gift. If she were not pregnant, the childish gift would seem like a slap, and if she were pregnant it was too small an offering.

There was a rotating cylinder of birthstones on the checkout counter, and Jane considered the garnet earrings, but Ramona was not one for adornment and would likely never wear them. A series of embroidered coin purses were pretty, but not Ramona's style. Finally, Jane settled on a single red rose in a small tube of water, the kind a guy might buy for his prom date. She wound her way back through the crowded casino, holding the rose out in front of her, then caught the elevator back upstairs.

Inside the room, Ramona had pulled the curtains closed over the sparkling night and turned on a lamp. She sat in the armchair by the table writing, and Jane stopped and waited for her to look up. When she did, her eyes were red and slightly swollen but her smile was luminous. "I'm pregnant," she told Jane. "I'm going to have another baby."

REX

The date was not going well. Jessica was a friend of a friend he'd agreed to go out with weeks ago, but from the moment he'd picked her up the whole thing felt wrong. For one, she had a large tattoo of a hibiscus flower displayed on her bare left shoulder. It was a deep pink with green leaves and very nicely done, but Rex had never liked tattoos, especially now that they were ubiquitous. It seemed wrong that this young woman—a third-grade teacher, for God's sake—would choose to permanently ink an image onto her skin. Then there was the perfume, something spicy and rich that drifted over to him across the front seat of his car and made him sneeze. He couldn't picture kissing a woman who smelled this way, or even sitting close beside her in a restaurant, but he had managed the restaurant—a Thai place she'd suggested—and now they were wandering Fremont Street, seeking out a lounge she'd heard about at the Golden Nugget.

This was only his second date since the divorce, and it still felt strange walking beside someone other than his wife. Jessica was tall, close to six feet he guessed, and sturdily built with long red hair, freckled skin, and a loose, pretty smile. He wondered if he should take her hand as they strolled, but decided he didn't want to.

"Almost there," she said, and pointed to the Golden Nugget on the corner. "My friend Becky—well, you know Becky—told me they have this great piano player. Sort of cheesy but good."

He nodded and smiled, allowing her to grab his hand and pull him more quickly through the crowd. He had no idea who Becky was.

It felt good to step inside the dim casino after the neon, crowded street. The Rush Lounge was only half full, pulsing quietly with ambient music. A baseball game played on the plasma TVs scattered throughout the dark, amber-colored space of the bar. They slid into a booth, and Jessica looked around and pouted her lips. "Damn it." She pointed to a small sign by the bar. "The piano guy's only here on the weekend."

Rex smiled, beginning to relax. He hated piano music. "Maybe we can catch him next time."

She nodded, smiling back at him, and he realized he'd practically promised her another date, a promise he wasn't sure he would be able to fulfill.

They ordered drinks from a waitress in a short, slinky black dress—a pomegranate martini for her, a beer for him—then talked for a while about her job, his kids, what he thought of the school. "It's done us right so far," he said, and shrugged. "Some girls were bullying Polly last year, but the principal took care of it, and she's been happy this year."

"Oh, the principal is amazing. He was new last year and the school has just transformed under his care. Frank Jacobsen. Have you met him?"

He nodded. "At open house." He couldn't quite remember the man's face, but he did recall a charm emanating from his ordinary presence. He remembered the man's wife better, her slightly plump, luscious body, those beautiful gray-blue eyes. She had the name of a plant. Fern. But no, that was Jane's daughter's name. Something else.

"When I started there, I had such a difficult time of it. No support at all for discipline issues, but all that's changed. I'm so happy there now," Jessica said.

He nodded. "Great. Liking your job is a good thing."

"Oh, I know. I was so miserable there for a while that I was no fun to be around. That's why Matt and I broke up, I think, because I was so pissy all the time after work. But now, I'm just in heaven."

There was something else woven into her words. A crush, Rex decided. She had a crush on the new principal. It struck him as sweet but also slightly sad. Jessica was no competition for that wife. Ivy, her name was Ivy. Then another detail: she was Jane's friend, the one who lived in the house with the red door. For some reason, this connection pleased him immensely.

Their drinks arrived and he took a swallow of beer. It was warmer than he liked it, but it didn't matter. He would only have this one, because he was driving but also because he didn't want to get involved more deeply with this woman because of alcohol. That's what had happened on his first date, and he still regretted it. Sandra, the manager of the coffee shop he'd been going to for years, had always flirted with him, but their date was awkward, too long. The sadness he'd felt after fucking her, when his buzz had worn off and he lay beside this woman who was at once familiar and a complete stranger, had been overwhelming. Maybe that's what you had to do though: get through a certain number of new women before you could cleanse the old one, the true one, out of your system.

"Oh, look," Jessica said, pointing out into the casino. "See that guy with the ball cap? The tall guy? We used to be engaged."

"Matt?" he asked, proud to have remembered the name of her last boyfriend.

She shook her head. "No. Someone from a long time ago."

He doubted she was a day over thirty, so it couldn't have been that long ago, but he didn't press it.

"Oh no, he's coming over here. Don't look at him." She picked up her martini and took a long swallow, avoiding the gaze of the man walking toward them through the casino and into the bar.

"Jess," the man said when he reached their table. "Long time, no see."

She smiled up at him and said hello, then introduced Rex as her "friend." Rex stood and shook the man's hand, taking in his lean, brown face beneath the ball cap, the narrow shoulders inside a white T-shirt. His name was Jamie, and he looked like a tall ten-year-old, though Rex guessed he was somewhere in his twenties.

"Why don't you have a drink with us?" Jessica suggested.

Rex assumed the man would protest—wasn't it obvious they were on a date and Jessica was just being polite?—but he immediately slid into the booth beside her and took a sip of her martini. Jessica looked over at Rex and shrugged, with a small frown on her face.

The waitress returned, and another round of drinks was ordered. Rex got another beer, against his better judgment, then finished off the first one quickly, listening as this man who used to be engaged to his date explained his new job setting up networks for local companies. Jessica looked interested, but Rex was bored, and also slightly relieved to no longer bear the burden of conversation. He excused himself to the bathroom and left the bar, deciding to wander a bit before returning. He found a restroom off to the side of the craps tables, and when he was finished, he walked a bit further away from the bar, thinking he might not return at all.

As he was passing the gift shop, a blonde head bent over the glass display case caught his eye, and he slowed and watched as Jane straightened up then plucked a rose from the carousel by the cash register and paid for it. She didn't see him standing there in the hallway, and he wanted to go over and say hello but couldn't bring himself to do it. It was as if he were at that Mormon dance again, watching her from a distance, wanting to talk to her. Their kiss in the hallway two days ago had circled through him again and again. Just watching her now ignited his body with desire. She was not even all that pretty, really, but there was something about her that he wanted to crack open and reveal, a hidden self he'd seen briefly, beside the telescope and then again in the hallway.

He watched as she left the gift shop through the opposite entrance, then he looped around the outer edge of the shop and followed her through the casino. It was crowded here, but he found it easy to keep her in his sights: her blonde hair lifting above her slim neck, the bright white of her shirt. She moved through the crowd with ease, then stopped in the space between the banks of elevators and waited. Before he reached her, she stepped out of view and was shuttled upstairs.

He decided she must be staying here, or maybe visiting a friend. The thought that she was meeting a man bothered him, and he allowed a picture of her in a hotel bed with someone else to flicker through his mind, before the image faded and went dark.

Back in the lounge, he found Jessica sitting alone, staring into her martini as if it might speak to her, her broad shoulders slumping a little, causing the tattoo to curve and catch the light.

A flash of guilt shot through him for having left her alone. "I'm sorry," he said, sitting back down. "I ran into a friend."

She smiled, as if genuinely happy to see him, and pushed another beer and a shot of tequila toward him. "Here, I ordered you this."

"Thanks," he said. "But I won't be able to drive if I have tequila. You take it."

"I was thinking," she said, twirling her glass at the base and avoiding his eyes. "Maybe we should just get a room. My friend works here and she could comp us, then we wouldn't have to worry about driving home either."

He nodded slowly and leaned back in his seat, then took a sip from his new beer, deciding. Half an hour ago, he would have said no, without question. An excuse would have arrived without effort. But seeing Jane had stirred him up, made him dread his empty house, his large, unmade bed.

Kristina had the girls tonight, and he imagined them all sitting on the couch together, watching TV with Peter. He hadn't seen Kristina's new place, but she had taken their orange velvet couch to her apartment, so he could picture this part clearly, his daughters' pale limbs against the brilliant, plush fabric, huddled together. Callie would be leaning against her mother, who in turn would be leaning against her new boyfriend.

"Okay," he said, and shot the tequila down his throat then sucked on the lime beside it. "Sounds like a plan."

The room was dark and sleek and smelled of nothing. The ruby curtains were pulled open, but a sheer, white fabric was closed over the night, so that the lights of the city were muted and distant. Jessica turned on the lamp by the bed, then pulled her yellow blouse over her head and stepped out of her flats and jeans. Her underwear was white cotton, as was her bra, and the sight of these simple garments filled Rex with relief. Racy lingerie would have been too much for him to bear in this situation. He felt uneasy enough as it was, having never slept with a woman, other than Kristina, in a hotel room. The setting struck him as tawdry and secretive, and Rex wished he'd had more beer and tequila or that he'd been raised differently so this situation wouldn't seem so unnatural, but he'd left the rest of his drink on the table, and it was too late not to be a Mormon.

She sat on the edge of the bed and fluffed out her long, red hair, tossing it over her shoulders so that the tattoo was completely covered. His first girlfriend back in high school had also been a redhead. Laura, a girl from his church who'd given him his first hand job in a car overlooking Lake Mead, an act for which he remained eternally grateful. After graduation, they'd had sex a couple of times the summer before she left for college, but it was that moment in the car he remembered most vividly, the moon skimming over the lake as he felt her cool hands wrap around him. The silence of the night. The dark shapes of the bluffs in the distance.

"I just got divorced," he told Jessica now. "Bradley probably told you."

She nodded. "And I just got dumped, so maybe we can just have a good time and not think about those creeps."

"Kristina isn't a creep."

"Sorry," she shook her head. "Of course. I meant Matt, that's all."

He nodded and walked over to the bed, then removed his clothes with quiet efficiency, pulling his black T-shirt over his head last and adding it to the pile on the floor. He sat down beside her, completely naked, finally feeling the liquor take hold and erase his hesitation.

She removed her white underwear, and he appreciated the pale haze of freckles above her small breasts, the smooth, taut muscles of her stomach. The fact that she was the physical opposite of Kristina helped him, and when she leaned to turn off the light, then crawled beneath the sheets, he felt relief that they would be covered up and in the dark.

Their coupling was quick and intense, Jessica moving beneath him with quiet concentration, the only sound her faint, steady breathing. He wondered if she was thinking about Matt, or the man from the bar, or really just thinking about him, the actual person moving inside of her. He closed his eyes and thought of Jane, and then Kristina, and then nothing at all but the feeling of rising.

Afterwards, lying flat on his back, he experienced an acute sadness once again, so he closed his eyes, trying to erase the feeling with sleep, but he was wide awake. Jessica was sound asleep beside him, and he listened to her steady breathing, hoping it would work on his restlessness, but it was no good.

He needed to get up, so he rose and pulled on a complimentary robe from the closet, then fished a bottle of whiskey from the minibar and sat sipping it directly from the bottle, looking not at the lights outside but into the depths of the dark, foreign room.

FRIDAY

IVY

In the morning, her leg throbbed lightly upon waking, but her head was clearer than it had been the day before, and she hoped she'd feel well enough to finish shopping for tomorrow's birthday party. Lucky was in his typical splayed-out position in the middle of the bed, and Frank was on his side, both of them still deeply asleep. Ivy swallowed four ibuprofen from the bedside table, then slipped out of bed as quietly as she could.

The house was silent, and Ivy wondered how her friends were faring downtown. She had a brief flash of jealousy at having been left here, but in the next second she was grateful for her night of sound sleep and the peace of the morning. Her leg had to heal so she could host this party.

After starting a pot of coffee, she stepped outside, still in her robe, to retrieve the paper. It wasn't yet seven o'clock, and the street was still. The sky was a clear, pure blue. Ivy scooped up the paper, then padded barefoot back up the walk where something on the front door stopped her. There was a new painting. A white and gray pigeon perched on a brown branch had been added, just below the gecko. Ivy stepped closer and touched the image with her fingertip. The paint was already dry so it must have been done last night. She stepped back and inspected it.

The placement of the image was perfect. It hadn't ruined the door's balance, and the bird was nicely done with sure, efficient strokes. As she stood looking at the painting, apprehension began to coil up inside her limbs. She thought she recognized something in the colors, in the shape of the bird.

Ivy hurried inside, then hunted in the back of her closet until she found what she was looking for. Both Frank and Lucky were awake now—she'd made so much noise going through the closet—so she set the square package down on her side of the bed and untied the twine. Then she carried the painting of the fountain outside and set it next to the door. The lines of the pigeon were cleaner and more finely drawn, but despite the considerable improvement in technique, the style and colors were still very much the same. This painting on the door had to be done by her mother.

She looked up and down the street quickly, almost expecting to see her walking up the sidewalk toward the house or crouched behind the oleander bush, but there was no one in sight. Back inside, she returned to bed, dropped the old canvas on the floor, and scooped up Lucky, holding him close to her chest, then lying back down and opening her robe to latch him to her breast.

Frank was at the dresser now, stepping into orange boxers, and he watched her with concern, an expression she had seen on his face many times since yesterday at the hospital. "What's going on?" he asked her.

"Apparently, my mother is in town. She painted a pigeon on the front door."

He laughed at this, then realized she was not joining him. "Oh, you're serious?"

"Go see for yourself."

He pulled on a pair of shorts and a T-shirt and left the room. Ivy looked down at Lucky and touched the soft, silvery top of his head. Her mother's nearby presence settled into her chest—a spiny, cold ball of worry that hurt when she breathed in. It struck her for the first time why she hated it here: she didn't want to become her mother. Something about being in Wisconsin had diffused this worry. There was nothing in the green Midwestern landscape that reminded her of home. But here, there were constant reminders of who she was, of all the fault lines that crisscrossed her insides.

She was her mother's daughter, and if her mother could just up and leave her own child for no discernible reason, then surely that impulse lived inside of Ivy as well.

Lucky pulled off of her with the small sound of a suction cup's release and lifted his brown eyes to hers. This weekend he would turn one, and the distance between them would grow every subsequent day after that. He smiled and gurgled his contentment, then clutched a piece of her hair and pulled it toward his mouth.

Frank appeared in the doorway and said, "Probably some kids in the neighborhood painted it. I can't see how you came to the conclusion that your mother did that. You haven't heard from her in over twenty years. And if she wanted to talk to you, wouldn't a phone call be simpler?"

Ivy considered this. She had never told Frank about the possible sighting of her mother at the park, and now it felt too late. "She must know about Lucky. She wants to see him."

"Possibly," Frank said. "But I wouldn't get your hopes up."

"Get my hopes up? I don't know if I'd even let her see Lucky if she was in town. I don't know if *I'd* even agree to see her."

"Well, I don't think she's here."

"What type of kid does such a nice job vandalizing a door?"

"A nerdy hoodlum?" He wanted her to smile at this—she could tell by his lifted eyebrows—but Ivy couldn't bring herself to do it.

"Well, why don't you decide whether or not you'll agree to see her *if* she actually appears," he said. "Until then, get up. We have stuff to do."

"My leg hurts," she told him, though it was actually beginning to feel better from the ibuprofen. "I think I'll just stay here for a while longer."

Frank came to the bed and sat on the edge beside her. He ran his palm from her shoulder down to her wrist, then leaned and kissed her cheek. "I can take Lucky," he said, reaching over her. "You go back to sleep."

"No," she stopped his hand. "I'll keep him here with me."

"Okay," he agreed, seeming to hesitate. "Okay, you two stay here, and I'll go shop for party supplies."

Ivy was almost asleep when the doorbell rang. Lucky was sitting up beside her playing with a loose string on the blanket, and she picked him up and went to the door, then peered cautiously through the peephole, not wanting the person on the other side to detect her presence, in case she didn't feel like letting them in.

To her great relief and disappointment, the person outside was not her mother. It was Jeremy, looking off to the side and toying with his necklace. Ivy wasn't sure about letting him in either, but then Lucky let out a squawk of delight for no apparent reason, and Jeremy's head turned, and it looked as if he could see right through the peephole and into her eyes. She took a step back and opened the door, but not all the way. She was still wearing her robe and she wanted to get rid of him quickly and return with Lucky to bed.

"I was sleeping," she told him, without saying hello.

"Oh, sorry." He turned to look over his shoulder at the street, as if expecting someone else to join him on the porch, then he turned back to Ivy. "I wanted to drop off the menus for tomorrow. I had them printed up." He held up a thin rectangle of pale blue paper, and Ivy leaned closer to read it. Frilled letters at the top said, *In celebration of Lucas Jacobsen turning one year old*. Below, there was a list of the food to be served: empanadas, petit fours, and about six other items.

"I didn't ask for a menu," Ivy said. "I can't pay extra." This was actually the first time money had been discussed at all, and she felt how it instantly shifted the tone of their interaction.

Jeremy stepped back and pulled the stack of menus to his chest. "I just thought it would be a nice touch. Free of charge, of course."

"Oh, thanks then," she said. To make up for her rude behavior she stepped back and gestured him inside.

He crossed the entry hall and placed the blue stack on the dining room table, then turned to face her, hands behind his back. He looked very young to her just then—almost exactly the same as he'd looked back in high school—and it was not so difficult for her to imagine that he was her husband and this was their baby in her arms right now. There had been a scare once—didn't everyone have a scare during high school? A two-week delay in her period had sent Ivy and Jeremy to a clinic for a test. The twenty-minute wait afterward had been nerve-wracking but also packed with tender feeling. They would have the baby, she decided, then move to California and camp on the beach. Ivy had imagined the sandy floor of the tent, while she waited in that dingy Planned Parenthood behind the library. She had pictured fresh fish in a pan over the fire and the stripe of sunburn that would cross Jeremy's cheeks and nose, making him look healthier than he actually was. Ivy had constructed an entirely new life in that twenty-minute wait, then disassembled it and left with the news that she wasn't pregnant after all.

She limped over to him now, feeling the pain in her leg more acutely than she had this morning, and picked up a menu for inspection. The paper was card stock, good quality, and not a single menu item was misspelled. It surprised her that Jeremy remembered Lucky's real name, and she set the paper back down then smiled up at him. "Thank you."

"What happened to your leg?" he asked.

She told him about the fall and the stitches, and he frowned with concern, then put an arm around her shoulders and led her back down the hallway to her bedroom. "You should be resting it," he said, releasing her from his hold at the doorway and watching as she limped to the bed and set Lucky down in the middle.

"It's okay," she told him, sitting on the edge of the bed. "It will heal."

He seemed nervous today. She watched him hesitate on the threshold, then nod, apparently deciding. He walked over to sit beside her on the edge of the bed. Ivy felt the need to lean into him, to feel his hand move over her hair and down her back in comfort. Jeremy had known her mother. He had actually spent time with her while he waited for Ivy in their small, yellow kitchen, or sat beside her mother on the couch watching TV. He would remember those first months of her absence, and the way Ivy had been unable to sleep at night. Often, he had woken up in her bed to find Ivy on the floor, sitting cross-legged playing solitaire in the light of the street lamp coming through her curtain.

"My mom's back in town," she said softly. The words sounded strange on the open air, like a misremembered lyric.

"I know," he said. "I spoke to her yesterday." He explained seeing her at the grocery store and following her to the park.

Ivy absorbed this information slowly, not quite believing him, even though she knew what he was saying was true. There were a million questions crowding her mind, but none of them seemed adequate to get the answers she wanted, so she sat in silence for what felt like a long time, Lucky cooing and flopping on the bed beside them. She turned and rubbed her baby's stomach through his green onesie, then sighed. "So she talked about *Wheel of Fortune* but she didn't ask about her grandchild."

"Maybe she doesn't know about Lucky."

"She knows," Ivy said, certain this was true. "I just feel it." She turned away from Lucky and leaned against Jeremy, giving in to the urge for comfort. Ivy closed her eyes as he ran his hand over her hair and down her back, just as she'd imagined him doing a moment ago. The touch wasn't sexual, but it made her feel guilty, so she moved away and stood up.

"I won't let her hurt you," he told her, looking down at his hands. "If you don't want to see her, I can find her again and let her know."

"No," she said. "I'm not sure yet what I want to do."

"Okay," he lifted his gaze to hers. "Just let me know."

She sat down next to him again, but farther away this time. "Would you like some iced tea or something?" Ivy asked.

"No, please, just rest. How about if I get you something?"

Before she could protest, he disappeared and she could hear him in the kitchen, opening and closing drawers, then the fridge, turning the tap on and off. Ramona would have said he was stealing the silverware or drugging her drink to have his way with her, but Ivy felt at ease listening to him rummage around her kitchen. She wasn't even particularly nervous about Frank coming home and finding Jeremy here. It just felt natural, she guessed, to be cared for by him. She lay back down on her pillow and put a hand on Lucky's belly to keep track of his movements, then closed her eyes and waited.

He returned to her room carrying a yellow tray she'd forgotten they owned. It held a poached egg in a small white bowl, a plate of sliced cantaloupe, and a glass of tomato juice. Ivy sat up and scooted against the bed's headboard, then accepted the tray on her lap and took a bite of the egg. "This is wonderful," she told him.

Jeremy sat beside her knees, not touching her but looking as if he wanted to. His hair wasn't spiked up today and a black strand fell across his forehead. Ivy noticed for the first time that a thin stripe of gray traveled through the black. She also noticed that the pendant on his necklace was a turtle, not a marijuana leaf. This struck her as a good sign. Lucky crawled over to her tray, and she fed him a piece of cantaloupe, then handed a piece to Jeremy but he shook his head.

"At least she's alive," he said. "That's something."

Ivy nodded. "You're right."

The specter of Jeremy's own dead parents rose up between them, though neither mentioned their presence. They had died in a car crash while Ivy was in college in Wisconsin. She had sent him a note, but that was all. It now struck her as a meager offering. She had loved Jeremy once, and he had become an orphan in one night. Didn't that warrant a phone call at least?

"Where is everybody, anyway?" he asked, looking around.

"I'm not sure." She knew Frank was shopping somewhere and would be home soon, and she'd expected Ramona and Jane to show up this morning, but it was already edging toward noon. Even though she'd told everyone to go, that she was fine, Ivy now felt left alone. Once again, the only person around was Jeremy.

This wasn't fair, of course. Frank had been with her through many difficult times—her father's cancer scare two years ago, the ultrasound predicting birth defects that led to a very stressful amnio, the birth itself. All those essential moments, however, faded away now, and the morning of her mother's disappearance was all that remained. She worried that Jeremy's presence at that crucial moment in her life would link them forever, in a way she didn't want to be linked to him.

The doorbell rang and they both jumped.

"I'll get it," he said, rising.

"No," she set the tray aside and quickly stood, feeling the blood rush out of her as tiny stars appeared in the blackness before her eyes. Then her vision returned and resettled and she sat back on the edge of the bed. "Light-headed," she explained.

Jeremy left the room and she heard him speaking softly, then he appeared in her doorway and said, "Some guy named Rex looking for Jane."

Ivy frowned at this news, then tightened her robe and tried rising, more slowly this time. The room held and she felt okay, so she picked up Lucky and brushed past Jeremy on her way to the door. Rex stood leaning on the doorframe, almost needing to duck beneath it due to his extreme height. His white hair was wet and combed into neat grooves against his skull, and he wore a black polo shirt and khaki shorts. His clothes were too preppy, too nicely pressed, and Ivy had a hard time believing they actually belonged to him. She imagined him raiding one of the houses of her neighbor's on the way over, maybe the tax accountant on the corner who golfed every weekend.

"I'm sorry, but Jane's not here," she said. "Can I help you?" She propped Lucky against her hip and bounced him lightly, waiting for a response.

"Will she be around later?" he asked. His voice was warm and lazy, and she actually liked the sound of it.

Ivy shrugged. "Not sure. But you can leave a message with me if you like."

"Well, I just wanted to see if she'd like to swing by later and check out some constellations. The sky is supposed to be really clear tonight from all the wind yesterday. You and your husband are welcome to come too, of course," he said, then nodded over her shoulder. She turned to find Jeremy a couple of steps away.

"Oh, he's just a friend," she told Rex, uncertain why she was bothering to explain. "And I just got out of the hospital, so I can't make it. But thank you."

"Well, just Jane then," he said.

"She's married, you know, but I'm sure she mentioned that."

"She mentioned that she's recently separated."

Ivy blinked, then took a deep breath, feeling as if she'd been pushed back by the force of his words. So that was what Jane was hiding. "I'm sure they'll work things out," she said. "They've been together a long time, and he's a really nice guy."

Rex shrugged and pressed his lips together, and Ivy felt the urge to slap him hard across the face. Would that scar Lucky somehow? Watching his mother slap a stranger at the door?

"I'm sure he is," Rex said. He met her gaze, then looked over her shoulder, presumably at Jeremy.

She understood now that he thought he'd caught her in the middle of something illicit. This wasn't her husband. She was in her robe. But the baby on her hip disproved him, didn't it? How could she carry on an affair with a baby on her hip? "I'll tell her you stopped by," Ivy said, "if I see her today." Then she turned around and said, "And I'll see you later, Jeremy. I really need to rest my leg." She ushered both men out at the same time, then shut the door and leaned against it, pulling Lucky into her arms and kissing the warm top of his head. Outside, she heard the murmuring of conversation and she strained to hear what these two people could possibly be saying to each other, but was unable to make out any words other than "Jane" and "baseball."

Back in her bedroom, the yellow tray sat on her skewed, blue sheets like a raft adrift at sea. She sat beside it and fed the last piece of cantaloupe to Lucky, then drank the tomato juice and gazed out the window behind the bed. It seemed fitting that the white-haired neighbor had broken up her morning with Jeremy, that one conniving man had reminded her to be careful of another, or to be careful at least of her instincts and feelings, no matter how seemingly natural.

Of course, she didn't know if Rex was actually conniving. Jane had told him she was separated after all, but wasn't he married? More importantly, why hadn't Jane told Ivy that she had left Adam? Wasn't that the sort of information you imparted to your best friend?

Ivy lay back on the cool sheets and pulled Lucky close to her. What if her mother was watching the house right now? What would she think about the parade of strange men arriving at her daughter's door? She would not bother explaining anything to her, Ivy decided. Let her think that I've turned out badly, Ivy thought. Let her think the worst.

JEREMY

It was standing outside Ivy's house, having just been kicked out, that Jeremy knew he needed to break it off with Gretchen. The decision came to him with perfect clarity, and he realized he'd known for weeks that it was the right thing to do.

The tall, white-haired guy was still standing beside him. Neither of them had moved since Ivy shut the door, and they heard the lock click into place, as if the two of them were a pair of criminals.

"So," Jeremy said, turning to the man. Rex, that was his name. "Jane, huh? You dig her?"

"She's interesting," Rex said. "I like her."

They turned away from the door at the same time and began walking toward the sidewalk, in step.

"And you're in love with Ivy," Rex said, as if stating a fact.

"Me? No, man. She's married. We're just old friends."

"Right," Rex said, making it obvious with his sarcastic tone that he didn't believe this.

"Well, I guess I do still love her, a little bit, but it doesn't matter." He couldn't say why he was telling this to a stranger, but he kept going. "She was my first real girlfriend, and we were close, you know? Things happened then that connected us and probably always will, but she doesn't want anything to do with me, and Frank's a good guy."

Rex nodded. They stopped together in front of Jeremy's car. This odd-looking person was familiar, Jeremy realized. "Hey, did you used to play baseball for Vegas?"

"Yep," he nodded. "A long time ago."

"I used to go to the games after I graduated with a friend whose brother played. Manny DeVetas?"

"Sure." He nodded, smiling. "Good old Manny. He got kicked off, you know, senior year."

"I know," Jeremy said, remembering it had something to do with drugs. "A shame."

"Well," Rex shrugged. "You have to follow the rules. But he did have a great arm."

The rules. So he was that type of person, Jeremy thought.

While they were still standing on the sidewalk, a car pulled into the driveway, and Frank stepped out. Jeremy couldn't help but admire his athletic movements, even just emerging from a vehicle, the way he sort of leapt onto his feet, then strode over with purpose. "What's up, gentlemen?"

Frank was taller than Jeremy by several inches, but still half a foot shorter than Rex, which made Jeremy feel better in Frank's presence than he usually did. "I just dropped off some menus for the party," Jeremy said, nodding his head toward the house.

"I'm Rex," the other man said, offering his hand, which Frank shook. "We've actually met before, at open house. My kids go to Grant."

"Sure, of course," Frank said. "I thought you looked familiar. Calliope and Polyhymnia, right?"

Rex smiled, as if it were an automatic reflex in response to the names of his children. "Wow. Pretty impressive memory," he said to Frank.

Jeremy fought the urge to roll his eyes. How difficult was it to remember two of the freakiest names you'd ever heard?

"I try," Frank said, actually sounding modest.

Jeremy was used to the slightly mocking tone Frank typically used around him. It had to do with Ivy, he understood now. Frank singled him out this way to make a point—it wasn't the way he spoke to every man. Why hadn't he recognized this before?

"Well, I gotta run," Jeremy said, then added. "See you tomorrow, Frank."

He got into his car and started it up, while the two men continued to stand on the sidewalk talking. Frank laughed and shook his head, and Jeremy guessed that Rex was praising him again, as if Frank needed any more praise, any more affirmation that he had the better life.

But Jeremy wouldn't want to be a principal, would he? He couldn't even picture himself wearing a polo shirt like the one Frank had on right now, let alone standing on a blacktop greeting parents. In his mind's eye the image he dredged up was ludicrous, and also apocalyptic: the never-ending blacktop, heat rising from its rough surface, the parents all white-haired giants like Rex, coming toward him like some futuristic race of humans. He shuddered and pulled away from the curb.

The day felt ruined now, but also filled with purpose. Gretchen would be home getting ready for work or studying, and he may as well get it over with. He had spent last night at her place, arriving late after the sweet sixteen party. They had lazed together on the couch watching a cooking show, then gone to bed and made love carefully before falling asleep. Everything had been fine last night, maybe even better than usual, but after seeing Ivy today he just knew. It wasn't right.

Gretchen answered the door in her robe, though it was a little past noon, and Jeremy had a strange sense of déja vu, since Ivy had answered the door in exactly the same getup. The robes were even the same color, a pale, grayish blue that illuminated Ivy's eyes but only served to make Gretchen's skin look unhealthy.

"Hey." She smiled and ushered him in, then leaned to kiss him. She tasted as if she'd just brushed her teeth, but her hair smelled slightly stale. "I've just been studying since I got up. I have an exam at four."

"I thought you worked today."

"After the exam. I'm going in late."

"Oh." He grabbed a glass and filled it with lemonade from the fridge, then sat down at the kitchen table, across from her. "What class?" he asked, nodding toward her open notebook.

"Finance."

The word's solidity, its sense of purpose, caught him off-guard. He'd imagined hospitality management as a series of classes on taking orders, filling up glasses, and booking rooms, even though he knew this wasn't the case. Gretchen was poring over a page of numbers and equations. "I should leave you alone," he said.

"I need a break anyway." She closed her book and refilled her cup of coffee, then sat on his lap. She weighed next to nothing, and he didn't like the feeling of her light, birdlike form. He craved a more hefty weight, a plush curve of ass against his bent thighs.

Now, he told himself. Break it off now, then go.

She kissed his temple, played with the hair at the base of his neck. "I'm sort of nervous about this test," she said. "It's going to suck eggs."

This made him smile and shake his head. She sounded like a teenager. "Rodney says just to do some breathing exercises right before, and not to smoke too much the day before."

He almost asked who Rodney was, then remembered it was a guy who worked the front desk with Gretchen. "Why no smoking?"

She shrugged. "Limits oxygen to the brain or some shit like that."

"Look, Gretchen," he said, ready to do it now. "Um . . . I need to tell you something." He had broken off relationships so many times, he ought to have a ready script, but suddenly his mind was a complete blank. A soft voice was essential. Vague reasons were better than specific ones. Still, nothing.

She was watching him intently, her green eyes only inches from his own. He liked her pale lips and paler skin, unbroken by a single mole or freckle, the clarity of her eyes when she was sober and alert, as she was right now. "Why do you look so sad?" she asked.

"I do?"

She nodded and smoothed his hair off his forehead. "Did something happen?"

He considered this. It felt as if many things had happened this week and were still in a state of unfolding. Also, he'd found himself thinking about his parents more than usual, the red and white checkered scarf his mother had worn on her head for years, like a kerchief from the old days. The clarinet she brought out once a month and played alone in her room. The boom of his father's voice calling him to supper, his broad hands flecked with color after a day of painting other people's houses. His rogue's smile with the discolored front tooth. All of this felt too large and unwieldy to say out loud to anyone, especially Gretchen, so instead he offered, "Something sort of weird happened at the party last night."

"Tell me."

He turned away from her gaze, uncertain why he'd called the incident, if you could even call it an incident, "weird." But it had been strange and unsettling. "There was this band playing at the party, this really awful sort of rockabilly band, and I didn't see what set him off, but this kid sort of flipped out after one of the numbers. He was the guitarist and he screamed a bunch of curse words and threw the guitar on the ground, then stormed off, all crazed. The room was dead silent for about thirty seconds, then the party sort of resumed, but it was muted, you know, not quite a party anymore. Anyway, the weird part is that I saw him outside maybe an hour later, when I was loading up my trays. He was hiding in the bushes by the driveway and he scared the crap out of me. He stepped out of his spot and whispered, 'Hey, food guy. Do you think they'll take me back?' He meant the people at the party, and I didn't know what to say, so I asked him what happened."

Gretchen was still listening intently, rubbing his neck. The movement of her hand was helping him to tell the story. The kid's face came back to him now, those dark eyes lined dramatically in black, his soft, childish voice. "He wouldn't tell me what happened. *Some girl*, was all he said, and I guess that was explanation enough, right?"

"So did you tell him to get the hell out of there?" Gretchen asked.

"No," Jeremy shook his head. "I said he should go back and apologize, that they'd forgive him. So he did. He followed my advice. I watched him go up to the door. It was opened, and he said something, then was let back in." Jeremy had been inside his Subaru, watching from the driveway through the front windshield. He'd been nervous, incredibly nervous, though he didn't know why. This kid didn't matter to him, not really. But that open door with the light coming through, the mother's bulk in the door frame, her head nodding as she listened, then her hand on his shoulder, ushering the boy back inside, had made every part of his body ache.

After the door closed, he was relieved, so relieved that he'd been right: the kid had been forgiven, or at least allowed back into the party. Jeremy imagined him walking through the crowd and onto the makeshift stage, where his guitar, which hadn't broken, would be lifted up and handed to him.

Of course he identified with the kid because he was in a band, because he was a troublemaker, but it felt like more than that. It had felt, last night in that driveway, as if his fate were linked to the boy's.

"Wow, you're like an oracle or something, dispensing wisdom and shit." Gretchen smiled and hopped off his lap.

He wasn't sure what she meant by oracle, but it sounded nice, so he smiled. "I'd better head out," he said. "Good luck on the test."

"See you tonight?" she asked. "After work?"

"Sure," he said. "I'll be here at eleven."

JANE

The neighborhood she and Ramona drove to that morning was three blocks away from the university, and the address led them to a small apartment building made of beige stucco. Ramona parked across the street and cut the engine, then rechecked the address from the piece of paper in her lap. "Yep, that's it," she said.

They got out and crossed the street, found apartment number seven on the ground floor near the stairwell, then walked over to the small courtyard, shaded by palm trees and palo verde, and sat down on a bench to wait.

In the last hour, clouds had been pulled across the sky like a dark curtain, and Jane wondered if it would actually rain. "How are you feeling?" she asked Ramona, both about sitting here waiting for her possible son to emerge from this depressing building and about sitting here potentially queasy with morning sickness.

"Fine," Ramona said with a decisive nod. "A little bit anxious."

"So you arrived in Las Vegas with no kids, and you might be leaving with two. An instant family."

Ramona nodded again. "I guess I should tell Nash. About the baby, I mean."

"How do you think he'll react?"

She shrugged. "He'll probably feel trapped at first, so I'll tell him he doesn't have to be a part of it and can just leave. Then he'll storm out but come back two days later full of regret and apologies and we'll have sex on the living room carpet, then make a bunch of promises that may or may not pan out."

Jane laughed. "A fairy tale ending."

Ten minutes later, the door of apartment seven opened, and Jane held her breath and reached for Ramona's hand, which was clammy. A thin girl appeared, wheeling a ten-speed and wearing a purple helmet over long, silvery blonde hair. Her face beneath the helmet was sullen, concentrating on getting the bike through the door. "I wonder who that is," Jane whispered, though they were far enough away that whispering was unnecessary.

"Maybe a daughter? My son's half-sister?"

Ramona and Jane looked at the paper again. This was the last name on the list: James Dillman. That was the father's name, but couldn't it also be the son's? Many kids were named after their fathers, adopted or not. The apartment number was right, so they settled back on the bench, watching as the girl, who looked to be seventeen or eighteen, slung a long leg over her bike and pedaled away, out of view.

"Your son's girlfriend?" Jane suggested.

"I can't even think about that," Ramona said. "A girlfriend. But I guess most nineteen-year-old boys have girlfriends, don't they? I'd better get used to the idea."

"She was pretty," Jane offered. "And I liked her bike."

Ramona frowned at Jane just as another person emerged through the door, a young man with caramel-colored hair and black glasses. He followed the path to the sidewalk then turned right and broke into a light jog. His legs were thick, almost stout, and he ran clumsily, as if it were a rare occurrence.

"That's him," Ramona said, standing up.

They tailed him around the corner to Maryland Parkway, walking quickly, then watched as he disappeared down a stairwell to the lower shops of a two-story strip mall. They followed him downstairs, but could no longer see him when they reached the bottom level. They were in an open-air hallway lined by various shops: Kinkos, Patty's Pizzeria, Subway, The Word. The boy wasn't anywhere to be seen.

They checked out Kinkos first, but saw only two Asian girls standing languidly behind a loud, humming copier. The man at the cash register was middle-aged and red-haired.

At Subway, they found a line of people waiting to have sandwiches made, but none of them were the boy they'd seen at the apartment building.

The Word was a coffee shop, and they entered to raucous punk music and the whirring of an espresso machine. A girl with fringy black hair sat in front of a laptop wearing white earbuds. Two men in suits leaned together over a square table, having an intense conversation. The woman working the coffee machine was pale as a ghost and wearing a bowler hat. The place was distinctly grimy, with purple pendant lights and posters of old horror movies framed and hung above scarred wooden tables. As she and Ramona stood surveying the scene, the punk music was suddenly turned down, then changed to something more grungy and mellow, and Jane guessed the manager had arrived and switched it up.

Ramona approached the counter, and Jane followed her, hoping they had time for a cappuccino, then she noticed the boy coming out of a back room behind the counter, tying on an apron. He stopped to consult with the girl in the bowler hat, pushing his black glasses up onto his nose as he spoke. Ramona turned to Jane and gave her a look that asked, *What do I do?*

Jane said, "Let's get a drink and discuss things, over there," she pointed to a table by the window.

At the counter, the woman took their orders, and Jane paid, then led Ramona to the table to wait. The boy was making their espresso, and Ramona was staring at him so intently that Jane took her hand across the table and pulled on it to get her attention. "Take it easy," she said. "Don't bore holes into him."

"What?" she said, looking confused, then asked, "Do you think it's him?"

Jane turned sideways in her chair for a better look, but tried to be subtle about it, pretending to read the menu, written on a chalkboard above his head, but really stealing a solid look at the kid. He was an average height and build with a square, appealing face. His cheeks and chin were dusted with a five o'clock shadow, despite the fact that it was only 10:00 a.m., and Jane noticed that his hair was actually dyed that pretty caramel color. It must be darker, she thought, noting the color of his stubble and the slight hint of dark roots when he bent his head to inspect the coffee machine.

The question was: could she see Ramona or Mark in him? There was nothing obvious to suggest this boy belonged to her friend, but he did have a similar shape to his eyes, behind the thick glasses, and his mouth was thin and prettily shaped, like Mark's.

She turned back to Ramona. "I don't know. Maybe?"

"Hey, James," they heard the girl in the bowler hat call out. "Check the cookies."

"James," Ramona repeated, looking over at him again. "I never would have chosen the name James. Isn't that strange? He must be a James Jr. I always had a name picked out and so now, knowing his real name, it feels like I can't have given birth to him."

"What was the name you picked out?"

"Keith, after Keith Richards. That was my Stones phase. I know," she said, holding up her hand. "It's a terrible name. James is actually much better."

"Keith," Jane said, and nodded.

"It's Scottish and means 'man from the forest.'"

"What does James mean?"

Ramona shrugged. "Who knows?"

James called out Ramona's name to come and pick up their coffee order.

"You go," she told Jane, looking pale. "I can't."

Jane rose and walked over to the counter. The boy stood waiting, not smiling, but somehow exuding calm welcome. He had wide, strong hands, browned by the sun, and Jane found herself watching them closely as he handed her the cappuccino and soy latte. "Thanks," she said, looking up into his face and feeling a nervous current run up her spine. What if this was, indeed, the baby Ramona had given away? His eyes were wide-spaced and dark green, just like Ramona's, but there was more—an intense quality to his gaze that seemed familiar. "Do you go to UNLV?" she asked him, then tilted her head toward the campus.

"Not yet," he said, but didn't explain further. His voice was soft and confident, but he turned his eyes to the window when he answered, as if uncomfortable with her scrutiny.

"I grew up here," she said, "but I didn't go to college here. Just high school. Vegas."

"I was at Valley."

She nodded. This was going nowhere. What question could she possibly ask that would confirm this boy's identity? *Were you given away by a girl with long dark braids?* She could ask whether or not he had been adopted, but what if he was and didn't know it, or what if he was but had been born somewhere else, far away from here? Or, of course, there was the very real chance that he hadn't been adopted at all. She thought to ask if he was born at Sunrise Hospital, but that wouldn't narrow her search much. The futility of Ramona's quest struck her then, and she realized she did not want to return to a table and sit with her friend while they tried to figure out whether or not this was her son. Perhaps this was the reason Ramona had kept her search a secret. She did not want to be pitied or cajoled into believing this might work out in the end.

"Do you need something else?" the boy asked.

She realized she'd been just standing there, staring into her mugs of coffee, and she looked up and gave the kid a quick smile. "Um, can you recommend any snacks?"

He shrugged. "We have biscotti, but it's kind of hard."

"Biscotti's supposed to be hard," Jane said, without thinking, then added, "Give me two, please. The lemon rosemary ones."

He turned and retrieved two cookies, then put them on one plate and handed them over to Jane. She passed him a five-dollar bill, though they only cost $1.10 each, and said, "Keep the change." It was the least she could do for making the poor kid feel uncomfortable. She must seem overly interested in a boy almost twenty years her junior and noticed for the first time that the woman in the bowler hat was listening to the exchange. She thanked him again, then carried the cups of coffee back to the table and sat down.

"Well?" Ramona said, a hopeful lift to her eyebrows as she accepted her mug of coffee.

What was she expected to say? Jane wanted both to offer her hope and to not get her hopes up too high. "He has your eyes," she said, then heard that this was too definite, so she amended. "Well, the color is similar, and the shape reminds me of yours."

"I wonder if Mark wears glasses now," Ramona said, glancing again at the boy. "Doesn't one of the parents have to wear glasses for the kid to need them?"

"I don't think so," Jane said. "It's not that clear-cut."

"My mom wore reading glasses," Ramona said.

"Everyone wears reading glasses eventually, don't they?"

Ramona shrugged, then asked, "So, what do I do next?"

Jane took a bite of biscotti, which was harder than it should be—the kid had been right, and she'd been snotty about it—and thought for a minute. "Talk to him?" Jane suggested.

Ramona cringed at this idea. "I can't even think of how to begin."

"Are you sure you even want to know?" Jane glanced over at the counter and saw that the boy was talking to the girl in the bowler now, making her laugh. She tried to imagine not knowing who her children were. Would she be able to recognize Rocky in a crowd if she hadn't seen him for the past nineteen years? There must be some link, Jane thought, some pull between you that would reveal the connection of parent and child. Or maybe there was nothing. Maybe this person you'd given birth to was just another stranger in the end.

"I think so," Ramona said.

The boy was laughing now, leaning back against the counter and listening to the girl beside him. This might be the girlfriend, Jane decided, rather than the girl on the bike. He looked happy, at least in this moment, and she imagined how he might feel if he discovered his mother was sitting here watching him. It wouldn't necessarily be a good feeling, Jane thought. It would be jarring and upsetting, something he'd have to mull over for many nights before deciding how, exactly, he felt about the matter.

"I should have let her raise him," Ramona said softly, watching the boy.

"No. No way," Jane shook her head with vehemence. "Your mom would have sucked the life out of him. She couldn't have handled it."

"Or maybe it would have helped her. Maybe it would have been her second chance. Then she wouldn't have cut me off and died alone and I wouldn't have to feel so guilty all the fucking time." Ramona closed her eyes and shook her head, then blew out a poof of air and opened her eyes again. "Sorry, never mind."

Jane didn't know what to say, except to repeat, "Your mom couldn't have handled raising another kid. You did the right thing."

"Okay, whatever you say." Ramona gave her a half-smile, then stood. "C'mon, let's get out of here. I can't figure out what I'm supposed to do yet. I need to think."

Outside, they walked slowly this time, back around the block toward their car. A sign for an open house caught Jane's eye, and she suggested they go check it out. "Just for fun," she said, "to take your mind off things."

It turned out to be an open house for a condominium that looked almost identical to several other stucco buildings on the street, but once they were inside, Jane appreciated the spare cleanliness of the place, its blonde wood and white walls, the view of a community pool through the balcony doors. The idea had been to take Ramona's mind off her son, but now that they were inside, Jane understood she was here for her own purposes. She plucked a statistics sheet off the kitchen counter and considered the price and size, then asked the realtor about condo fees and what a typical electric bill might look like.

"Is there something you're not telling me?" Ramona asked when they were back outside. "Does Adam need some desert soil samples to finish his degree?"

Jane shook her head, looking down at her feet as they moved along the pavement. "I'm leaving him. Well, we're separated. Nothing's official or anything yet."

Ramona didn't respond for several strides. Slowly, drawing out the word, she said, "Okay," then, more softly and to herself, "Wow."

Jane waited for her to say more, but they walked in silence for the last half of the block, then turned the corner. Up ahead, across the busy street, Jane could see the simple white buildings of UNLV settled in stretches of green grass. Students milled about on the lawn as if classes had just let out. If she somehow managed to buy that condo—she did have some savings and decent credit—Jane imagined she could find a job on campus and walk to work, picking up a coffee from Ramona's son every morning on the way.

When they were heading back to Ivy's, Jane finally asked, "Aren't you going to offer your two cents about what I should do?"

"Nope," Ramona shook her head. "Unless you want me to?" She glanced over at Jane, then back to the road.

"I guess not," Jane said.

"I will say that I don't think you should move back here."

"It would be good for the kids, to be near my mom," Jane explained.

"True," Ramona agreed. "But better for them to be near Adam, don't you think?"

Jane nodded. "Yes, of course. But he's not tied to Wisconsin. He could bartend out here, I'm sure." Even as she said this, the absurdity of the idea struck her. She would divorce Adam but make him move across the country and live where he knew no one but her. "Okay, that's a dumb idea, but it just sounds nice to have a fresh start somewhere, you know?"

"Las Vegas would not be a fresh start."

Jane considered this. Ramona was right—of course she was, about everything—but the image of that spare condo stayed with Jane as they wound their way through a city that was both new and old, both familiar as her own hand and completely unknown.

RAMONA

Frank greeted them at the door with a pale, worried face. "She's in there with Lucky," he said, nodding toward their bedroom. "And says she's fine, but she won't get out of bed."

"Well, it's her leg, right?" Jane said.

"Her leg looks pretty good, actually," Frank said. "It's healing well."

Ramona brushed past him into the house, and Jane followed. Half the room was hung with blue and yellow streamers, and a cluster of balloons sat on the floor by the couch. The streamers were haphazardly hung, crisscrossing the space above the dining room table and dangling unfinished in the corners.

"I'm not done with that yet," Frank explained, walking over and catching the end of a yellow streamer in his hand. "When I add the balloons, it will look better."

"No, it looks nice," Jane assured him.

"Isn't the party tomorrow?" Ramona said.

"I wanted to get a head start," Frank said. "Since I have no idea what I'm doing."

"We'll help you," Ramona said, though to her recollection, she'd never hung a streamer in her entire life.

"Go see Ivy first," Frank suggested.

The bedroom door was shut tight, so Ramona knocked lightly, and when she got no reply turned to Jane and shrugged, then entered Ivy's bedroom.

She was sitting up, propped against the pillows in her robe, watching Lucky crawl back and forth across a small hillock of bunched-up sheets. Ivy's hair was unwashed and tangled, and her skin looked dim, its usual glow of health gone. She looked up at them and offered a wan smile, but said nothing.

"What's up?" Ramona said, trying to sound cheery as she settled on the bed beside her friend. Jane circled around and sat on the other side so that they both faced her.

"I'm resting," Ivy told them.

"I can see that," Ramona said. "How's the leg?"

For an answer, Ivy turned down the sheets then pulled back her robe to reveal the long, sewed-up cut on her inner thigh. It was red and puckered around the dark seam of the stitches, but there was nothing particularly gross about it, Ramona noted. She had never had stitches before and was surprised by their neatness. She had expected oozing blood and pus, a haphazard crisscrossing up her friend's leg that would turn her stomach.

"Does it hurt?" Ramona asked.

Ivy shrugged. "A little bit. Not much. Just if they rub against something too hard, like a pair of jeans." She threw the robe back over her leg, then yanked the sheets up and across her lap with a single motion.

"Ramona has some news," Jane said.

Ramona glanced at Jane, uncertain how to begin. The events of the morning seemed more real than the baby growing inside of her. She was still thinking about the boy with the black glasses, tilting his head back with laughter as she and Jane exited the coffee shop. That laugh had pierced her skin, wounded her in some unseen way that pained her even now, sitting here on Ivy's bed.

Before Ramona responded, Ivy turned to Jane and said, "I want to hear *your* news first."

"My news?" Jane scooped up Lucky and set him on her lap, almost, Ramona thought, as if she were using the baby as a shield against Ivy's anger, because she could feel it now, emanating from her friend like the uncomfortable heat of a campfire.

"You know what I'm talking about."

"Did Adam call you?" Jane asked, as she stroked Lucky's smooth cap of golden brown hair. She would not meet either of their eyes.

"Rex came by," Ivy said.

"Rex?" Ramona asked, feeling suddenly lost.

"The albino," Ivy told her.

"He's not an albino," Jane said, finally lifting her eyes to Ivy's. "And I only told him because I didn't think he would judge me, the way you're doing right now."

Ramona thought this was likely why Jane had confided in her as well, but instead of feeling included she felt extraneous, like a faceless sounding board rather than a true friend. She should have offered Jane something more this morning, a bit of wisdom scrounged up from her past.

"I'm not judging you," Ivy told Jane. "I'm worried about you."

"Well, there's no need to worry because I'm fine." She smiled at both of them, but Ramona could see it was a forced smile, a smile to hide pain.

"But why?" Ivy asked. "How could you leave Adam?"

"How could I?" Jane adjusted the baby on her lap and began to bounce her knee. Lucky giggled with delight, and the emotion was so out of place it raised the level of anxiety in the room. "It was easy, actually. Much easier than I ever imagined."

Ramona nodded. Of course it was easy to leave. This was something she had learned long ago.

"But you're going to try and work it out, right?" Ivy asked. "For the kids?"

Jane looked at Ramona, but she couldn't interpret her glance. "Maybe she hasn't figured it out yet, Ivy," Ramona offered. "Why don't we hear her out before we assume she's going to do what you say?"

"I know that's what I should do," Jane said, turning again to Ivy. "But I just don't feel happy lately. Being with him."

"So what?" Ivy said, crossing her arms over her chest. "It's not about feeling happy. You have to make the decisions that are right for Rocky and Fern, that's all. Period. Unless Adam is beating you or abusing you in some way, then you have to stick it out."

"That seems a little harsh," Ramona said.

"Oh, really?" Ivy turned her anger toward Ramona now. "That's great. Get advice from the person who's left everybody."

"What's that supposed to mean?" Ramona asked, feeling her own anger rise like a thin stream of red up the center of her chest.

"Nothing," Ivy said, shaking her head. "Sorry." Tears pooled in her large eyes, and then she was sobbing, turning her face into the pillow behind her.

"What is it?" Ramona said, scooting closer and putting a hand on Ivy's back. "What's wrong?"

"I don't want to abandon Lucky," Ivy said.

Her words were muffled by the crying and the pillow so that Ramona wasn't sure she'd heard her correctly. She turned and looked at Jane, who shook her head as if to say *Don't look at me—I don't know what she's talking about.*

"Lucky," Ivy said, turning to face them now.

Jane handed the baby over, and he clung to the lapels of Ivy's robe and nuzzled his face into the bare skin between the cotton.

"I'm worried that I'm going to leave Lucky one day just like my mom left me."

"I don't think it's genetic," Ramona said with a smile, trying to lighten the mood.

"I keep thinking I'm being ridiculous. Of course I'd never do that. But I'm sure my mom never thought about leaving me when I was a baby. People don't plan on doing terrible things to their children."

"She didn't do it to you," Jane said. "I'm sure it had nothing to do with you at all."

"It had everything to do with me," Ivy told her. "How can you even say that?"

Jane shrugged, then stood up and walked over to the window beside the crib. "Parents have lives of their own. That's all I meant. You shouldn't take it too personally."

She stood looking out at the oleander bushes for a moment, then turned back to Ramona and Ivy. "So why did Rex come by anyway?"

"I knew you were going to ask that," Ivy said with a frown. "Who cares? He came by to ask you to stargaze, all right? But you're not going."

Jane frowned back at Ivy but didn't say anything, and Ramona admired her restraint. She wasn't sure why Ivy was acting like Jane's mother, but it wasn't very pleasant to be in the room with the two of them.

Ramona rose and patted Ivy's knee through the sheets. "I promised Frank I'd help with the streamers," she said.

"But wait," Ivy said. "What was your news? We never got to that."

"Oh," Ramona looked at Jane, but she didn't appear to be paying attention. Her back was to both of them as she looked out the window. "It's nothing. I'll tell you later."

JANE

She left while Ramona and Frank were busy with the decorations, explaining that she should go and pick up her kids, but now that she was outside and sitting in the driver's seat of Ramona's Mustang, Jane had no intention of going to her parents' house.

The route to Rex's place was familiar now, and she drove there in under a minute and parked out front, trying to decipher who was home. There were no cars in the driveway and no signs of life on the front lawn, which was free of its usual clutter. The curtains were pulled back from the front window where she'd seen his wife or ex-wife only two days ago, but no one passed by.

Jane couldn't explain, even to herself, what she was doing sitting in front of this man's house. Despite Ivy's annoying way of reprimanding her, Jane knew that, essentially, her friend was right. When she and Adam had decided to have children together, she'd understood in a solid, uncomplicated way that this was the end of her selfish viewpoint on the world. She was no longer first—it was that simple.

It hadn't felt like any sort of loss those first years with Rocky. When Fern was born it had gotten more difficult, exponentially so, but still, Jane had been happy, for the most part, with her life.

What had happened since then? At some point, her family had begun to drain the life out of her—it was almost a physical feeling, similar to hunger or fatigue—but you couldn't admit this to anyone, could you? You couldn't tell someone that your loving husband and kids were turning you into a lifeless husk.

The notion that she had chosen the wrong life for herself had begun to surface last night in Ramona's hotel room as she lay alone in bed looking through the gap in the curtains toward the mountains, waiting for dawn to make them visible. She had fallen asleep before that happened but in the morning had felt her usual pleasure upon seeing the mountains' pale peaks against the clear sky. Maybe she belonged here, in the desert surrounded by mountains.

She didn't miss the flat green of Wisconsin that was currently iced with spring snow. She didn't miss her husband or her house or her friends. When, she wondered, would a pinch of longing hit her? Would it ever? And the question was: If she'd chosen the wrong life, then what did the right one look like?

Jane unlatched her seat belt, then checked her teeth in the rearview mirror. She was here to tell Rex that she couldn't come by and stargaze later, but thanks for asking. That was it. It would be rude to ignore him completely. If he wasn't here, she could leave a note on the door.

Outside of the car, she felt exposed. The sun pounded down on her bare shoulders as she took the concrete walkway up the lawn to Rex's front door. A boy on a scooter watched her from half a block away. His gaze felt sharp with judgment, and she wondered if he was a friend of Polyhymnia and Calliope. Jane waved to him, but he didn't wave back, just turned and rode in the opposite direction.

Her knock on the door sounded loud and angry, and she wished she could erase the sound and start over, tap the door gently with her knuckles. There was a doorbell, she noticed, but thought pushing that button would be overkill now, after the aggressive knock. She was wearing a straight, cream-colored cotton skirt, and she saw there was a spot of coffee near the hem. Checking her dark pink tank top she saw there was coffee on that too. These two stains were enough to make her want to turn around and get back into Ramona's car, but just then the door opened, and Rex stood before her, smiling.

"It's a little early for constellations," he said.

"I know. I can't come by later. I just wanted to tell you that."

He nodded at this news, then stepped back from the door and held out his arm, gesturing toward the dim recesses of the living room. "Well, come in and we'll figure out something else to do."

"I can't," Jane said, but she made no move to go. "I have to pick up my kids."

"I do too. But not for an hour or so. They're over at a friend's, around the corner." He pointed a thumb over his shoulder, indicating the direction.

"Mine are being doted on by my parents and probably having the best time they've had since we got here."

"Well, then, you should let them stay a little longer." He reached out and looped his thumb and forefinger around her wrist, then tugged her gently over the threshold before she thought to protest. "It's hot out. Have some lemonade with me, then go."

In the kitchen, he poured lemonade into two ice-filled glasses. Jane tried to avoid looking at the photo on the fridge, but she was drawn to it, to the dark-haired woman that he either was or wasn't married to. She wanted to ask what had happened between them to cause the split or to ask why the photo remained on the fridge if he was, indeed, divorced, but these questions were too intimate, so she kept quiet and accepted the lemonade with a smile. Maybe his wife had chosen the wrong life for herself as well and just recently figured it out.

They sat at the round kitchen table by a window looking out on the backyard. The telescope was in the exact same place it had been on her last visit, and a row of empty beer bottles surrounded its base, as if to create a sculpture or a shrine. She had almost expected to fall into this man's arms the moment they were alone—they had kissed last time they'd been together, after all—but it was awkward between them now, and Jane could hardly meet his eyes across the table as she sipped her lemonade.

"My wife left me because she said I didn't contribute enough, that I was just living here as if I were a renter," he said.

Jane looked up quickly, still not quite meeting his gaze. "Oh, I'm sorry."

"It wasn't true, not completely, but I could have done more."

Jane nodded, uncertain how to respond. "You seem like a good dad."

"I'm trying. I'm getting better, that's for sure."

"How are your kids doing with it all?"

He tucked the loose strands of hair behind his ears and sighed. "They're okay, I think. Kids are resilient, right?"

"Right," Jane agreed, though she had never believed the truth of that statement. Kids were affected deeply; they harbored pain for years and years and remembered this pain again as adults when they had kids of their own.

"She has them two nights a week and every other weekend, but they live here with me the rest of the time."

"Oh, that's good. Nice for you, I mean."

"Definitely," he nodded. "Now I just have to find a job."

"What about nursing school?"

"That's one possibility," he said. "I'm weighing all my options."

Finally, she forced herself to look directly at this man across from her. The skin around his eyes was marked by soft crow's feet, and their color was such a deep black-brown she could hardly make out the pupils. Jane still couldn't figure out how he had such pale skin and hair and such dark eyes. It must just be some genetic blending of his parents, she decided, that didn't show up very often. It made him seem constructed of spare parts, a face created by someone's imagination rather than born from a woman in a hospital.

"I've been thinking about you a lot," he said.

Jane could feel her cheeks grow hot. "I'm sorry if Ivy was rude to you."

"Oh, she wasn't really. She just assured me that you and your husband would get back together and I should get the hell out of the way." He shrugged and sipped from his glass.

"She might be right."

He nodded slowly, not speaking.

"Or not. I'm not sure yet."

At her words, he rose abruptly, knocking the table with his knees, and the lemonade in Jane's glass sloshed out and onto her tank top.

"Oh, crap. I'm sorry," he said, then got a towel and wetted the corner at the sink before handing it to Jane.

She worked at the spot just below her left breast then realized she'd left a huge wet circle that looked worse than the actual lemonade.

"It will dry fast," he said, seeming to understand her discomfort. "I'm glad you came by."

So she was being dismissed. He began walking down the hallway toward the front door, and Jane followed him, suddenly desperate to stay here now that she was no longer welcome, to be close to him for a while longer. "How about a tour of the house?" she suggested when they reached the foyer.

"Um," he looked around the small room by the front window. "There's not much to see."

"I don't care."

He shrugged and went back down the hallway. Jane followed, understanding that she'd shifted the current between them. What had almost been finished was now about to begin.

He led her to the girls' room first. Jane peered in at the pink metal bunk beds, the disco ball hanging from the ceiling. Diaphanous, pastel clothes were strewn across the beige carpet as if there had recently been a party or a dance production of some sort.

The den had several bookshelves, which Jane took to be a good sign, as well as a flat-screen TV and a wraparound green suede couch. The house was clean but not particularly neat. Stacks of magazines and open mail sat on the coffee table. Two purple socks rested on one of the bookshelves, and there were several pairs of tennis shoes strewn along the hallway. She wanted to inspect some of the titles of his books, but Rex crossed the space quickly and led her down a hallway.

He had turned businesslike and brisk, and Jane wanted to draw him back out, to coax him into offering up his lazy, half-formed smile, but couldn't think how to do it. Her flirting skills were rusty and in fact had never been that effective. Besides, her last attempt at this sort of relationship had ended in such embarrassing disaster that she was hesitant to open herself again to that sort of danger.

"Last room," he said, stopping on the threshold of the master bedroom. A skylight above the unmade king-sized bed imprinted a rectangle of yellow sun on the navy sheets, and she felt shy even looking at this giant bed together, so she stepped into the room and pretended to admire its other furnishings: a green La-Z-Boy, a boom box atop a cheap-looking oak dresser, a rowing machine covered with stuffed animals.

This room seemed to confirm the truth of Rex's divorce. A few T-shirts hung in the open closet, but the rest of the space gaped with emptiness. There was nothing feminine in the room either. The only picture on the wall was the logo for a motorcycle shop in San Diego, complete with flames and vicious-looking skulls. The absence of his wife's belongings was an actual presence in the room, and Jane tried to ignore it. "Looks like this gets a lot of use," she joked, pointing to the rowing machine.

He smiled. "My girls like to pretend it's a guillotine or something. These are the animals being sent to the gallows."

Jane laughed, thinking these girls would get along perfectly with Rocky, then turned and stepped closer to Rex. He faced her, the bed directly behind him, and Jane thought she might walk around him and just sit there on the bed, in that rectangle of sun, but she couldn't work up the nerve.

"Your shirt's almost dry," he said.

She looked down at the fading water mark and nodded, and then he was next to her, placing a palm over the spot that covered her rib cage. It was an awkward place to touch her, but it sent a desire through her so absolute she knew she needed to follow it through or be left wondering, so she raised her face and leaned to kiss him on the neck.

This kiss transmitted her current of yearning into him, and they began to undress without speaking, then got onto the bed with silent purpose.

Rex's body was long and thin and finely muscled, like a piece of carved ivory. He was virtually hairless, and Jane searched his skin for a freckle or mole. When he turned to the night table for a condom, she saw the pink half-moon of a scar at his waist, and felt relief to find him marred in some way. She herself had four silvery stretch marks rising up from her pubic bone like smoke, and the tan lines from her bathing suit broke the smooth flow of skin in an unappealing way she'd never noticed before.

Their coupling was not particularly graceful. He was taller than Adam, and their bodies did not fit each other as well so that she found herself adjusting positions under him and moving her hips at the wrong times. A strand of his hair loosed from the tight knot at his neck and kept brushing Jane's cheek in an irritating way. But he touched her with a tenderness that felt particularly sweet, considering they were practically strangers, and his gaze was so guileless, so open, that she could feel herself unfolding toward him, wanting, even, to love him.

When he finished and separated his body from hers, Jane's knot of desire was not completely loosened; still, she felt deeply relaxed. They lay beside each other, the rectangle of sun warming their calves as the sound of a lawn mower raked the nearby air.

She tested her conscience for guilt, but found there was none. Even though she had been officially separated from Adam for several days—and had left him behind in her mind months ago—her body had not quite felt like her own until this moment. It was a sensation of lightness, as if she might lift off from this bed and float through the window toward the horizon.

But when she turned onto her side, she saw that Rex, staring up at the ceiling, had tears in his eyes. "What is it?" she asked, touching his arm and propping up on her elbow.

He shook his head, as if to deny he was crying, but said, "Kristina."

"Oh," Jane said, sounding stupid to herself. "I'm sorry. Should I leave?"

He shook his head again. "No, I'll be okay in a second. This always happens lately." He turned his face toward her and offered up a rueful smile.

Lately—Jane absorbed the word. Did this mean he'd taken several women to this bed since his divorce and cried every time? She could ask him but decided she didn't want to hear the answer, whatever it might be.

He turned onto his side, facing her, and swiped a hand across his eyes, clearing them before he reached out and touched her cheek, then smoothed back her short hair. The weakness she'd just witnessed made him less appealing, and Jane suddenly wished to be inside her car, driving across town.

"You should come back later with the kids. I'll set up the telescope."

"Maybe," she said.

They didn't speak as they pulled on their clothes and walked back through the house toward the front door. Jane recalled her tour of the place as something that had occurred long ago, instead of less than an hour before. At the front door, he leaned down and kissed her on the cheek, then squeezed her shoulder, and she stepped outside.

REX

He watched Jane get into her car and drive away, then was instantly coated in sticky regret. Why had he cried in front of her? It was the sadness again, that same grinding despair had descended immediately after they separated and lay back. It didn't make as much sense to him this time because he really liked this woman, but it had been waiting for him, and he had been unable to avoid it.

He brushed his teeth and combed his hair, then walked around the corner to pick up his daughters, feeling weighted down by the sun on his shoulders. The friend's mother, Andrea, opened the door with a tight smile, then made him wait on the stoop while she retreated into the dimness of her home and found Polly and Callie.

Andrea was a friend of Kristina's who had never liked Rex, even before the divorce, though he had no real idea why. She was younger than he was and had more conservative ideas about how kids should be raised, though he couldn't elaborate on what these ideas were except that they involved a lot of church and rules. It surprised him that she and Kristina were friends, but he guessed his ex-wife liked Andrea's generous supply of cocktails and frequent offers to have Polly and Callie over to play.

Andrea reappeared in the doorway, his daughters trailing behind her. The woman was so small he would have mistaken her for a teenage girl from far away, but up close her brown hair was graying at the temples, and her thin, unpainted lips were already beginning to form lines from pursing them so often. On the porch, she nudged the girls toward him grudgingly, as if she didn't think they should be in their father's presence. Each one latched onto a hip and he felt fortified by their physical attachment, as if they were propping him up.

"Hey, cutie pies," he said, putting his hands on their small shoulders.

"They ate some cornflakes," Andrea told him in a flat voice. "And some yogurt."

"Okay, thanks," he said, wondering why she was telling him this. "Did they have a good time?"

"Of course," she said, looking defensive now as she crossed her arms over her chest. "They always have fun here."

"Well, next time Beth and Angela can come to our house."

Andrea smiled, but Rex sensed her whole body tensing up at the offer. "Sure, sometime. We'll see. They're pretty busy right now."

When they were back on the sidewalk, heading toward home, Rex felt himself begin to relax. The remaining sadness from this afternoon lifted away as he listened to his daughters tell him about their day. There had been a bubble-blowing contest, a burial for a stuffed skunk in the backyard, and several long games of British Bulldogs, whatever that was.

"How did the skunk die?" he asked.

"Fell into the toy box from the top bunk," Callie told him.

"That doesn't sound too serious."

"Dad," Polly said. "It wasn't real."

"Oh, all right," he said. "That's good."

He began to think about Jane as he listened, wishing they could spend the evening together, that she could join him and his daughters for dinner and stargazing. He wanted to show her the constellations and explain their stories. He wanted to feed her fresh pesto made from the basil in his garden. He wanted to carry her back to the bedroom after the girls were asleep and toss her onto the bed, laughing.

They rounded the corner, and he picked up each girl's hand. "Should we set up the telescope tonight?" he asked.

"Sure," Polly said, sounding unenthusiastic.

"Is that lady going to come again? With her kids?" Callie wanted to know.

"No, I don't think so." he shook his head. "Maybe another night."

"Is she your girlfriend?" Polly asked.

He considered this, liking the sound of the question even though the answer was definitely *no*. "I don't have a girlfriend," he told her.

"Good," Callie chirped.

They rounded the corner, and Rex saw a large white SUV he didn't recognize parked in front of his house. Drawing closer, he felt a stirring of hope. Maybe Jane had taken her parents' car and driven back to see him. But then, from two houses down, he saw it was Kristina and a dark-haired man, sitting side by side on his front step, and Rex's stomach began to twist into a gnarled mass.

"Mom!" Callie shouted and ran toward her. Polly stayed close, and kept his hand in her own, a gesture that made him exceedingly grateful.

Kristina and the man both rose as he crossed the lawn, and she gave him a small, apologetic smile and a shrug. "I forgot my key and I need something."

"It's my night," he said.

"I know. I just need something."

"What?" he asked, wanting to say—*what the fuck could possibly be so important that you'd ruin our entire evening by showing up?*—but he restrained himself.

She shrugged again and mumbled, "Just a dress for this thing." Then she nodded toward her new boyfriend and said, "This is Peter. Peter, Rex."

The man held out his hand, and Rex considered not taking it, then decided there was nothing to be gained by acting childish and shook it quickly, noting with satisfaction that it was sweaty and petite. Everything about the man was small. He was Kristina's height, his hair was short, and his features were all undersized so that his face seemed to possess too much empty skin. Still, the man managed to be handsome. He was young and unblemished, with bright eyes and shiny teeth.

"We're going to a gala for my office," Peter explained. "And she needs a gown. I said we should just buy one, but she really insisted on coming by to get the one she already has."

"What can I say? I'm thrifty," Kristina said.

"That's not a word I would use to describe you," Rex said.

"I know, right?" Peter laughed.

Rex wouldn't even smile or meet the man's gaze. He was not going to compare notes about Kristina.

Rex unlocked the door, and everyone filed inside. The new smudges on the white couch were satisfying to Rex, as was the pile of Barbies under the buffet, but Kristina didn't notice anything, just walked quickly into the depths of the house toward his bedroom. Rex followed and waited in the doorway as she searched the almost empty closet. The sheets were on the ground from his afternoon with Jane, but other than that, he detected no signs that she had ever been here. He wished a silky undergarment of some sort were slung over a pillow for Kristina to see.

"It's not here," she said, turning to him. "I thought I left it hanging right here."

"Oh, I put it in the bottom drawer," he told her, remembering.

She retrieved a long, sage green gown from the dresser and shook it out. "This has to hang up. You can't just shove it in a drawer," she scolded.

He didn't bother to reply.

"I guess I will have to go and buy one. This needs dry cleaning now." She brushed past him, holding the balled-up dress to her chest.

They found Peter and the girls in the kitchen, where Callie was showing him a series of volcano drawings she'd been working on. They hung on the side of the fridge and Peter was only half looking at them. The man was obviously distracted, or maybe just bored. Rex didn't imagine that he had any children of his own. "Nice," Peter said, when Callie was done explaining the series.

This word filled Rex with a hatred he thought he'd banished days ago, when Polly broke her finger, but here it was again, steaming through his skin so forcefully he imagine he might catch fire. "Please leave," he told the man with more force than he'd intended. "I need to get dinner ready."

"Rex," Kristina chided. "No need to be rude. We're going."

"No," Peter raised his hands as if in surrender. "That's cool. I understand. It's your night. We're in the way."

Rex crossed the room to the volcano drawings, and aimed a finger at them. "*Nice*," he mocked. "These are fucking brilliant drawings for a six-year-old, but of course I wouldn't expect you to know that. Look at the detail here." He pointed to the varying shades of the lava, the way Callie had made it seem to bubble and spark, to come alive. "*Nice*. That's just fucking rude."

"Rex," Kristina hissed. "Stop it. You're acting crazy."

"Hey," Peter held up his hands in surrender. "I meant no offense. They're great drawings." He stepped back to the fridge and inspected them again. "Really amazing."

The man's tone bordered on sarcasm, and this made Rex angrier. The children were watching him, wide-eyed. He'd never cursed in front of them before. What he wanted to do was take this man's face and slam it against the volcano drawings, to make him feel the intense pain he was feeling right now, but he took a deep breath and closed his eyes, willing them to leave.

"Let's go," Kristina said softly.

Rex opened his eyes to see her hug each daughter good-bye. Peter stood motionless, looking at the ground, then turned at Kristina's touch and they walked out of the kitchen. When the front door clicked shut behind them, Rex sighed and sat down at the kitchen table, then lay his cheek on the cool, white surface.

A hand on his shoulder. Polly. "Dad. Are you okay?"

"Yes," he said, then closed his eyes. "Sorry about saying those bad words."

"It's okay," Callie told him. "We don't mind."

"It was actually sort of funny," Polly said, then giggled.

He sat up and looked at her, then pulled his older daughter onto his lap. Polly curled herself against his chest and he stroked her hair, pale and soft as corn silk. Callie leaned against his shoulder, and Rex looped an arm around her waist, drawing her into the circle. "He wasn't even paying attention, that's all," Rex said. "It just made me mad."

"I don't like him very much," Polly admitted.

The words infused his entire body with warmth, and he smiled. "He's not so bad. He looked closer at the pictures, once I told him to."

"True," she admitted.

"He bought us both Groovy Girls," Callie added.

"And those twisty suckers," Polly said.

"See, he can be nice. And your mom seems to like him, so I guess we'd better give it a try." Even as he said the words, he hoped the girls would both grow to hate that man. He hoped Kristina would break his heart, though Rex guessed she didn't yet have the power over him to do that. Soon she would. It wouldn't take her long.

He made spaghetti and baby carrots for dinner, and the three of them sat around the kitchen table and ate while the sun disappeared behind the fence and the light turned somber. He wondered what Jane was doing right now and guessed she was eating dinner with her kids and parents at this exact moment. Kristina would be at a department store with Peter, picking out a dress.

He looked out at the telescope, surrounded by beer bottles. After dinner he would clean that up and begin searching the sky, then tell his girls the same stories about the stars he'd already told them many times before.

SATURDAY

IVY

When she woke up much later, it was completely dark outside, and Lucky was no longer beside her. She sat up in a panic and checked the floor around the bed, the crib, the closet, before opening her door and walking down the hallway toward the living room.

Frank was asleep on the couch, and Lucky was strapped into his portable car seat and set on the ground nearby. Her baby was also sound asleep, and the sight of him, safe and peaceful, enveloped her in cool relief.

She noticed then that the living room was strung with blue and white streamers, so many looping from the edges of the room and meeting at the light fixture in the room's center that it created a canopy effect. Green balloons were hung in clusters at the edges like giant bunches of grapes, and a silver HAPPY BIRTHDAY sign hung over the entrance to the kitchen. All this had been done while she was asleep, and it disturbed her to think she could be that unconscious. What else might have occurred during the many hours of her slumber?

Ivy turned off the reading lamp beside the couch, then carefully removed the magazine from Frank's chest and set it on the coffee table. She considered taking Lucky out of his seat and transferring him to his crib, but he was content, so she decided it was better just to let him be.

In the kitchen, she poured herself a glass of pinot grigio from the fridge to settle her nerves, then tightened her robe and checked the clock on the microwave: 2:43. She hadn't taken any pain medication since early afternoon, and her leg was beginning to ache around the stitches, but she decided to try the wine first, hoping it would relax her enough to ease back into sleep without additional drugs.

Wandering through the house with her glass of wine, she found Ramona asleep in the back bedroom, her long black hair spread out around her on the yellow pillow. She was deeply asleep, but then Ivy noticed her frown and twitch and she guessed she was having a bad dream. Would it be better to wake her, Ivy wondered, or let her pass through it and remain asleep? She sat on the chair beside the bed and waited for several seconds, sipping her wine and watching her friend's face shift and change. When Ramona's expression settled back into calm, Ivy quietly left the room.

Jane's bed was empty, as was the air mattress beside it. Ivy sat on the twin bed that should have held her best friend and worried about their earlier exchange. Maybe she had been too harsh, too black and white in her views of marriage, but that had always been her way. The world was clear-cut, for the most part, and if you understood its rules and boundaries as vividly as Ivy did, it felt like a duty to explain those rules to your friends.

It must have been Ivy's own upbringing that had made her this way, she decided. Her parents had not been good parents. Her mother had abandoned her. Her father had drunk his way through her high school years and basically ignored Ivy other than to yell at her for bringing home Jeremy or to put the occasional meal on the table. Since then, he had reformed, but when she had most needed him, he had not been available. It may have been this lack of rules, of moral guidance, that had turned Ivy in the opposite direction.

She was not particularly bitter about her parents' flaws anymore. Well, at least about her father's. He had been deeply wounded by his wife's departure and uncertain what to do with a teenage daughter. He had done, as people say, the best he could.

A light came on in the house next door and illuminated Jane's room with a gray-blue haze, so that Ivy felt as if she were sitting underwater, looking at her friend's belongings at the bottom of the sea. An open suitcase beside the bed spilled out clothes. Two small swimsuits hung over a stool to dry. A glass of water sat on the nightstand beside a half-eaten banana and the wrapper from a granola bar. The detritus of small children.

Ivy imagined that Jane was at Rex's house this very second, curled against him in a big bed several blocks away. If this turned out to be true, Ivy didn't want to hear about it. She wouldn't listen to any details or offer any advice other than what she'd already said in the bedroom today, about returning to Adam. There would always be other people around to lure you into doing something wrong. Ivy knew this from experience, but she wasn't sure Jane did. In many ways, she decided, her friend was naive.

Ivy rose from the bed and finished off her wine, then set the glass on the bedside table beside the granola wrapper. Since she had not eaten in many hours, the wine seemed to have gone directly into her bloodstream, making her limbs feel light and heavy at once. She weaved slightly as she crossed the carpet and left the room.

In the living room, she reassured herself that Lucky was still sleeping, then slatted the blinds by the front window and peered out at the dark neighborhood. A white car was parked across the street that Ivy didn't recognize, and she thought she could see a person sitting in the driver's seat, but couldn't be sure.

As she sat there, watching the car, Ivy became filled with the absolute certainty that this was her mother, watching the house. It had to be her. Who else would sit in a car outside in the middle of the night? She closed the blinds and stood in the dark, uncertain about what to do next. The only sound in the room was Frank's deep breathing, and she considered waking him up and showing him the car, but then decided against it. She would go outside and see for herself.

She still had on the blue robe she'd worn all day but she didn't care. Her hair was a tangled mess, and she guessed her face could use washing, but she did not want to do a single thing to improve herself for this meeting. Her mother could see her at her worst. That was all she would offer.

The air outside was cooler than she expected, and she tightened her robe as she stood on the front step, trying to get a better look at the car. It was a white sedan, a generic looking car that Ivy couldn't identify and would never recognize if she saw it in a lineup. Now that she was out here, it became clear that there was, indeed, a person inside the car. The front seat was tilted back but she could see a profile, leaned against the headrest in slumber. It was impossible to say from this vantage point if the person was her mother. Ivy walked to the sidewalk, then crossed the street and stood in front of the driver's window.

Ivy's heart jumped and she stepped back, suddenly nervous. This person was not her mother, but a man, asleep. She was in the middle of the road now, several feet away from the car. Her heart was beating fast, and beneath this feeling of mild fear, she was soaked through with disappointment. She realized how much she had wanted this person to be her mother, how much she wanted to see her again.

As if sensing her presence, the man lifted his head, and Ivy was about to turn and run inside her house, when she realized that she knew the person in the car after all. It was Jane's husband, Adam.

JANE

A noise outside woke her, and she sat up in bed in the dark and listened. It had been a glass breaking on the street, she thought, or maybe the raw screech of tires. The sound had been ominous, foreboding, and she lay down and tried to find her way back into her dream about The Muse but couldn't.

The shapes of her old room loomed around her like ghosts in the dim light from the street. Here was her white dresser with the pink flower knobs, a relic from the third grade. Here was her lavender butterfly chair, her bookshelf, her rolltop desk. A mobile of gauzy dragonflies hung over her bed. She could still remember picking it out at the Boulder City Art Fair one summer in elementary school.

It struck her now that she had grown up in the room of a goody-goody. Where were the hidden stashes of cigarettes? The circular tray of birth control pills concealed in the underwear drawer? Sure, she'd worn strange clothes—ripped up fishnet tights and black boots, wide-brimmed hats and red lipstick—but the only colors in the room were pink, yellow, white, and seafoam green, and these colors told the truth about her life more than what she'd worn. Her wardrobe had been a feeble attempt at another persona, but these pastel colors were who she actually was.

There was nothing wrong, Jane knew, with being a good person, but this past year she could feel a rising craving inside of her to do something bad. It had begun with the editor at work and reached some sort of height today on that sunny bed with Rex. It may have something to do, she thought, with not getting enough wickedness out of her system in high school or college, but there was more to it than that. It was the mere act of being a mother that sometimes made her want to rebel against her better judgment.

One of the most difficult parts of having kids was that when you screwed up or failed there was an audience, an audience that was watching you in order to learn how to live, or how not to. Sometimes Jane just wanted to fuck up and be done with it. *Watch me, kids*, she might say, *this is what you're not supposed to do.*

She tried to recall when the shift had occurred, when she had slid from merely wanting to do something wrong into actually doing it. The editor had started it. One afternoon over lunch at the coffee shop down the block from the paper, he told her she had a sensual mouth. Jane had felt herself immediately drawn toward this comment, as if the simple words were a magnetic force. She was ashamed by how easily she had been wooed, but the truth was that she had never been a woman who men showered with compliments, and to receive one like that in the middle of the day after a difficult morning of making lunches and dragging the kids to day care against their will—Fern had cried and clung to her legs, infusing her with black guilt, then Rocky had pushed another boy off the climber, and she had been given a stern look by the kid's mother, all this making her late for work where Adam called asking her in a sleepy voice where she put the coffee (in the freezer, as she had for all eleven years of their marriage)—had lifted her up in a way nothing else had in a long time.

When she thought about the moment this way, it hardly even seemed like her fault. She had been on the verge of starvation, and this ordinary-looking, middle-aged man had offered her a plum.

Sleep was no longer possible, so she sat up, put on her robe, and wandered out to the kitchen for a drink of water. It was 3:01 a.m., and the yard out the window was as dark as she'd ever seen it. Hot tea seemed like a better idea than water so she filled the kettle, but when the teapot whistled several minutes later, Jane realized her mistake and waited for her mother to round the corner, which she did a minute later, tying her white robe at the waist and rubbing her eyes. Jane poured hot water into two mugs, then dropped in the bags of chamomile and set them both on the table.

"This is nice," she said, settling into the chair across from Jane's. "Insomnia?"

She smiled. "Just being with you. That's all. And the quiet. I've always liked this time of night."

The kitchen light was off, but enough moonlight came through the windows to make artificial light unnecessary. Still, Jane would have liked to see her mother's face more clearly. The shadows crossing her familiar features made Jane uneasy, and she tested her tea too quickly and burned her tongue. "Shit," she muttered. "Sorry. Too hot."

"You always burn your tongue," her mother said, shaking her head. "For as long as I can remember."

"One of my many flaws."

"Well, if that's a flaw, you're not doing too badly." Her mother blew across her tea, then took out her bag, expertly wrapping it around a spoon, and took a cautious sip.

"So who do you drink tea with in the middle of the night when I'm in Wisconsin?"

"You'd be surprised, but I actually sleep through the night sometimes now that you and Russ are out of the house."

"No one to wait up for?"

"Or worry about."

Jane nodded. There had been many nights when she'd arrived home on the exact dot of her midnight curfew to find her mother in a white nightgown at the window, or even sitting outside on the porch. "I wonder if I'll wait up just like you did when the kids are teenagers."

"Of course you will," her mother said with a smile. "It's the circle of life."

"But I don't seem to have the same natural maternal instincts that you have. It doesn't come so easily to me." Jane looked down into her tea as she said this and could feel her face burn from her mother's gaze. This was the closest she had come to admitting anything was wrong to anyone in her family.

"You don't have to be the exact same mother that I was. There was definitely room for improvement."

"I don't think I've improved upon your model in any way." She looked up now and saw that her mother wasn't watching her at all, but stirring her tea and staring into its swirling heat.

"Is anything going on at home, Jane? Rocky said something was wrong with Adam." Now her mother met her gaze, her green eyes serious and expectant.

"Adam's fine," Jane said, stalling. "What did Rocky say?"

"He said Adam wanted to come on this trip with you, but you wouldn't let him."

Jane shook her head. "That's not true."

"So why didn't he come?"

"He couldn't get the time off. And . . ." She shrugged and looked around the kitchen, as if hoping to find the answer written somewhere. "I needed some time by myself."

"Oh," her mother said. "Well, that sounds reasonable."

"Also, we're separated." Jane said this quickly, then took a long swallow of tea, hoping to drown her rising anxiety with the hot liquid. She watched her mother's face absorb the information. It began with a slight furrow between her brows, then moved through her eyes and cheeks and ended with a downturn of her mouth.

"Why?" was all she said.

"It's complicated," Jane began.

Her mother cut her off and set down her mug with a loud clunk. "No, it's not. You have two young children who need both their parents, and I don't want to hear anything else about it. Adam is a good person. You're a good person. That's all I need to know."

"You're not even going to let me explain?" Jane said, knowing as she said this that she couldn't really explain the situation clearly, even to herself.

"No, it's your business. I don't want to get in the middle of it." Her manner had become cold and efficient, a strange pairing with her robe and sleep-worn face.

"But Mom, what if I need some advice?"

"You've never wanted it before, even when I offered it."

"But now I *do* want it." As she said the words aloud she felt their inherent truth, though it was obvious her mother's advice was going to be the same as Ivy's: return to your husband. And that wasn't the advice Jane wanted, so what was the point in hearing it again? It was more of a need to be soothed, Jane understood, than to hear the truth. She wanted to crawl onto her mother's lap, wrap her arms around her neck, and weep into her shoulder, but she was taller than her mother now and heavier, and besides, she hadn't been able to shed a tear for many months. It was as if her sadness was something brittle and dry. It scraped against her insides when she swallowed or moved or even when she slept.

Her mother raised her thin shoulders. It was not quite a shrug, because the shoulders stayed up. It was more a gesture of cramped dismay, a motion used to absorb a blow. She didn't say anything else in response to Jane's plea for advice, merely shook her head.

This small movement hit Jane with such force that she rose from the table, set her tea cup on the counter, and returned to her bedroom. She shut herself in and quickly dressed, pulling on jeans and a tank top and slipping into her green flip-flops. She grabbed Ramona's car keys from the dresser along with her purse, then left the house without looking to see if her mother was still in the dark kitchen.

There was broken glass on the street beside her car, and she felt a moment of despair to think someone had broken Ramona's window, but the glass on the car was intact, and on closer inspection

Jane saw it was a broken bottle at her feet. Kicking it aside, she slid into the driver's seat and started the engine. The neighborhood closed in around her as she drove down her old street. It felt stiflingly narrow, and Jane wondered why she had always remembered her block as expansive, her street as a place of lovely trees and neat grass. It was a child's memory of a place, she decided, a memory that no longer held any truth.

The streets leading her back to Ivy's place were nearly deserted, and when she passed a bank she saw the time, 4:07, and the temperature, sixty-seven degrees, blinking at her across the dark sky. No one would be awake at Ivy's, and she imagined slipping back into her bed then getting up and eating breakfast with her friends as if nothing had happened yesterday. No one needed to know that she'd slept with Rex. She would skip that part of the day entirely and explain that she'd gone to her parents' house to be with her kids.

Just past Sahara, her gas light blinked on, so she pulled into a station and filled the tank, then bought a pack of powdered sugar donuts and a small jug of milk and stood eating and drinking as she leaned against the car and looked out across the strip malls and highway toward Sunrise Mountain, its dark shape collecting gray light at the edges, though it wasn't nearly time for dawn, was it?

Standing here reminded her of high school. It was something to do with the donuts and the time of night. On a few occasions she and Ivy and Ramona had stayed out until dawn at the lake—if Jane stayed the night with Ivy or Ramona, no one kept tabs on them at all—then driven back and stopped at a gas station for food, ravenous from a night of swimming and drinking wine coolers and telling each other ghost stories. It was likely those outings had been dangerous—Lake Mead was not necessarily a safe place at night— but it had never occurred to them to be truly scared. They had been lucky, she guessed, to have arrived home intact. Her mother hadn't known about those nights at the lake, and Jane wondered if she would ever tell her.

Back in the car, her stomach felt slightly sick from the sugary donuts, and she sat in her space at the gas station for several long minutes wondering if she should head back home or continue on to Ivy's house. Her certainty to return to her friends had begun to dissolve, and she worried she may not even be welcome, especially once Ivy found out that Jane had slept with Rex, for it suddenly struck Jane that the fact would be impossible to hide. It must show on her face, on her skin, in the way she would move across a room. The details of this afternoon played in Jane's mind like a movie, and she could feel her skin heat up at the memory. Her distaste for Rex's tears had vanished, and in its place remained a curiosity, a desire, even a need to see him again.

But first she must make things right with Ivy, so she started the engine and left the empty gas station. She would have to explain the separation from Adam to her friend in a way that made sense. This was a necessity. *My parents' marriage was so perfect and vibrant,* she might begin, *that the shock of my actual marriage, its meandering love, its many irritations and disappointments, knocked me over.* She had never explained the situation to herself in this way, but was struck now by the truth of it. Her expectations had been too high. She had been blindsided by the struggle of trying to continuously love another person for years on end. This was the advice she needed from her mother: how had she and Jane's father managed to be happy for over thirty years?

She was in Ivy's neighborhood now, and the rows of identical homes on either side of the street gleamed with newness compared to her parents' neighborhood. Seeing Ivy's now familiar red door gave Jane a leap of hope, as it had the first day she'd seen it, and she parked and got out of the car without hesitation. Coming here had been the right thing to do.

On the front step, however, she realized she had no key, and it wasn't yet 5:00 a.m., much too early to ring the doorbell. She tried to peer past the blinds into the front room but could see nothing, so she walked around the side of the house and noticed that the kitchen light was on. It would be Ivy, Jane knew, up with Lucky, and she walked down the narrow alley of pea gravel, then stood on her tiptoes and looked inside.

The scene before her made her insides contract. Adam was sitting at Ivy's table, drinking a glass of wine and nodding at something Ivy was saying to him across the table. She was drinking wine too and using her hands to describe something to Adam that Jane couldn't decipher—a waterfall? A boat ride? Everything about the vision was wrong. For one, it was almost dawn and they were drinking wine. Also, Lucky was nowhere in sight. Most of all, Jane couldn't fathom how Adam had materialized at Ivy's kitchen table in the middle of the night. Of course, he'd taken a plane and then a taxi or car from the airport, but it was too unlike him for the actions to be real. Adam did not take action; he waited for things to happen to him.

Jane flattened her feet and the scene disappeared from view, then she took a deep breath and lifted back up onto her toes to study her husband. He looked exactly the same as he always did. Her leaving him had left no visible trace. His light brown hair waved up from his forehead and down over his collar. His skin was slightly burned from reading in the hammock in their backyard. His profile revealed a nose that was a little too big, bumped at the top from breaking it during a tetherball game in junior high, lips that were thin and wide and a jaw that cleaved a neat, solid line, not yet softened by age. In five or six more years, she imagined it would begin to disappear like his father's, and his pale skin would weather around his eyes and mouth, but for now he still gave off the solid vibrations of youth. He was only thirty-four, two years younger than she was, and she understood as if for the first time how very young he had been, how young both of them had been, when they got married.

She felt a tenderness toward him then that she hadn't in a long time, and Jane placed her palm against the windowpane as if to touch him, expecting him to see her hand and turn toward her, wanting him to and not wanting him to at the same time. But neither Adam nor Ivy noticed her there outside in the dark, and the thought of knocking on the pane seemed impossible.

Her raised hand felt like a good-bye, and she lifted it off the glass, then walked back along the alleyway and out to the front of the house. Leaving the car at the curb, Jane began walking up the sidewalk. Her feet were leading her toward Rex's house, but she wasn't sure she wanted to see him. It would be a good destination, just to give purpose to her walk, then she could turn around and return to Ivy and Adam. In about an hour, Lucky would be up, then Jane could tap lightly on the front door and be let back in.

The dark air around her was clean and smelled of swimming pools, the familiar scent traveling from backyards and reaching her here as she moved in a straight line up the street. This smell alone was enough to call up an entire childhood, enough to press a painful fist against the back of her throat. Jane had been mostly happy here, growing up, and this seemed lucky. It was more than a lot of people had.

She had taken her happiness for granted, she saw now. She acted as if it was a birthright, but that wasn't true, and Ivy and Ramona already knew this. Being happy was a sort of perk, an extra that came to you in odd moments, then was gone. It was not continuous and steady. You could not rely on it to be there every morning.

Rex's house looked different in the dark, and she wasn't sure she was even standing in front of the right one. The row of oleander bushes along the edge of the yard seemed wrong, as did the circular stones leading to the front door. But that was his old blue car in the driveway, she decided, and the large front window where she'd glimpsed his ex-wife. When she noticed two skateboards leaned against the garage door, she finally felt certain this was the right place.

Jane sat down on the front lawn and pulled her knees to her chest. It wouldn't be light, she guessed, for another hour, so no one would see her sitting here. She wondered if Adam and Ivy were still at the kitchen table, but thought they had likely gone to sleep. Behind her, she pictured Rex asleep alone on that giant bed. He would have his arms flung out wide and welcoming, his white-blond hair a sharp contrast against the blue of his pillow. Jane felt an urge to climb through his window and slide in beside him. If she could manage that feat without waking him, she would do it, but she didn't see how that was possible.

She rose from her seat on the grass and began walking again, traveling the path she and Ivy had taken to the mountains the other day. It felt as if she were the only person awake in the entire city. Of course, a couple of miles away on Las Vegas Boulevard thousands of people would be up, playing cards and slot machines and eating cheap breakfasts, but out here the world was quiet and dark.

It took her hardly any time at all to reach the base of the Black Mountains, and she hopped over the low wall and began climbing, hoping she wouldn't step on a scorpion in her flip-flops. The sky was growing brighter now; the polished undersides of the clouds radiated a pale orange light that reminded her of winter skies in Wisconsin right before it snowed. Adam had first pointed those skies out to her, showing her the way the clouds were so full with ready snow that they cast a glow, even late at night.

Before they had Fern and Rocky, they used to stand on the back deck on nights like those, waiting for the first flakes to arrive. Usually, they couldn't wait long enough and they missed the beginning, going to bed after midnight and waking to a lawn of white in the morning, but once or twice they had witnessed the arrival of the snow, and it had felt, then, as if they had won a prize, together.

It struck Jane that this was the sort of memory that should lure her back to Adam, to their life together, but it felt more like a story about two people she no longer knew, rather than an actual vision of her past.

She sat down on a flat rock and looked out toward the city. She'd climbed higher than she had with Ivy and the kids and had a good view of the entire neighborhood and a glimpse of the streets and buildings beyond. Lights began to come on in houses; cars started in driveways. The sun was still behind the mountain, but the sky had transitioned to a pale, washed-out blue. The ground at her feet was visible now too, and she took in the low, green bundles of sage, the rocky, gray-black earth. Soon she would have to make her way back down the mountain, then walk to Ivy's house and see Adam, but for now she would just sit here, waiting for the city to awaken.

RAMONA

In the morning, Ramona felt a twinge of nausea and quickly ran to the bathroom, but once she shut herself inside and waited, the feeling passed, so she brushed her teeth and hair, then braided it and went to get dressed. It was as if learning she was actually pregnant had brought on the symptoms, which seemed absurd since the body knew what it knew and reacted accordingly. Still, in the kitchen she was hungrier than she'd been in weeks and was rummaging through the fridge for bacon and eggs when she felt a tap on her shoulder and turned to find Ivy, still wearing the robe she'd worn all day yesterday.

"We're out of coffee, if that's what you're looking for," Ivy told her.

"Bacon."

Ivy leaned in past her, reached behind a tub of cottage cheese, and produced a new package of bacon, which Ramona accepted gratefully and took to the stove to cook. Once the package was open, however, she hesitated, wondering if nitrates would harm the baby.

"Have you seen Jane?" Ivy asked. "Her car's here, or your car—the one she was driving—but I can't find her."

Ramona shook her head as she read the ingredients on the package, then resealed it and slid it back into the fridge. "Maybe she took a walk?"

"To that weirdo's house."

"I doubt that. It's pretty early."

"True," Ivy said, and sank into a kitchen chair. She sighed and rubbed her eyes, then ran both hands through her unwashed hair. "Adam showed up last night. He's asleep in Jane's room."

For some reason, this didn't surprise Ramona. "I guess I sort of expected him to show up sooner or later," she said, then poured herself a bowl of cornflakes and sat down across from Ivy. "The minute I heard they'd split, I had a feeling he'd come after her."

"Really?" Ivy raised her eyebrows in surprise. "I didn't see that coming at all."

"Jane always had boyfriends who couldn't live without her. Remember Arnold? And that other guy, Ricky? He used to stand outside her English class every day, waiting to say hi to her even after they broke up. He pretended he was there to get a drink at the fountain, but it was so obvious."

"I can't remember either of those people," Ivy said. "Are you sure you didn't make them up?"

"Nope. Arnold Richardson and Ricky Gonzalez. They weren't much to look at, but they were devoted."

Ivy laughed at this. "Okay, I kind of remember them now."

"You were too obsessed with Jeremy to notice our boyfriends."

"That's not true. I loved Mark. I thought you should have married him." The minute Ivy said this, she seemed to realize her error and covered it quickly with a smile. "Not really, about marrying him I mean. You were way too young."

"That's all right," Ramona said, taking a bite of cereal. It had gone soggy during their conversation, and she pushed the rest of the bowl away from her. "I know you think I did the wrong thing. I knew it then, too. Maybe you're right. I should have kept the baby and married Mark."

"No, that's not true." Ivy frowned and looked down at her hands in her lap. "Don't say that."

"I've been looking for him, you know. This past week."

Ivy looked up at this. "Mark?"

Ramona shook her head and watched Ivy's face absorb and then understand her comment. "But I haven't had much luck." The boy from the café flashed into her mind. Should she tell Ivy about this possibility or not?

Adam walked into the kitchen then, and Ramona was glad for the distraction. She didn't want to tell Ivy any more. In fact, she didn't want to talk about it at all, and she wished she hadn't told Jane about her search either.

He smiled when he saw Ramona, and she rose to accept his hug and kissed his warm cheek. "Welcome," she said.

A cry came from the back bedroom and Ivy stood and tightened her robe. "That's my cue," she said.

"I remember those days," Adam said, and sat down in Ivy's chair across from Ramona. "You're looking good," he said and smiled at her. "Sweet tan."

She laughed and looked at her brown arms. "You should see Jane," Ramona said. "Her hair is almost white from all this desert sun."

Adam frowned, then stood and began rummaging through the cupboards. "Where does she hide the mugs?"

"Bad news. No coffee," Ramona said.

He shrugged. "Tea will work. I prefer it anyway."

For some reason, this fact irritated Ramona, made her dislike him a little bit. She watched as he located a box of tea bags, then filled the kettle and set it on the stove to boil. He was wearing old jeans with a rip in one knee and a faded blue T-shirt. Ramona was almost certain he'd been wearing this exact outfit the last time she'd seen him, three years ago in Wisconsin.

"So, where is my wife, anyway?" he asked.

"At her parents'," Ramona said, almost too quickly. "She should be here soon."

"Do you think she'll be happy to see me?" He smiled as he asked this, but Ramona detected his nervousness.

"What do you think?" She said this as nicely as possible, keeping her voice low and gentle.

"I think I really fucked things up and I'm here to fix them."

"That's not the version I heard."

"Well," he shrugged. "It's the truth. I've been a crappy husband. Still working on my dissertation. Still tending bar like some sort of loser."

"I don't think bartending makes you a loser," Ramona said, rising and getting the orange juice out of the fridge. She poured two glasses and handed one to Adam. He accepted it without comment.

"Well, I've got news for you. It does."

Frank entered the kitchen looking tired and out of sorts. He said good morning and gave Adam a nod. "Too much wine last night," he told them, then opened the fridge and leaned down as if to crawl inside its cool interior.

"You mean this morning," Adam said. "We were up until five thirty at least."

"Sounds like I missed a party," Ramona said.

Adam shrugged. "Not really. Just catching up. We didn't want to wake you."

The teapot whistled, and they all turned to stare at the plume of steam rising from its silver spout. Adam filled his cup with boiling water. Ramona realized she hadn't actually eaten much at all, but her hunger was mostly curbed, so she grabbed an apple out of the silver bowl on the table and excused herself, explaining she was going to take a walk before it got too warm outside.

The sight of her car parked at the curb made her realize her exhaustion, so she fished the spare keys from her pocket and got inside, then drove away. The warm air moving through her hair helped Ramona begin to uncoil, and she understood that being around so many people was beginning to agitate her. She had lived alone for so many years now. The party was today, then she might stay most of tomorrow and head home in the evening, unless she found out that the boy at the coffee shop was her son, in which case she might have to extend her visit.

The ridiculousness of her quest struck her, not for the first time. What was she planning to do if she did, indeed, find her long-lost child? Would she uproot her life and move here to be close to him? Would she ask him to join her in LA? Or would he simply become a person she visited, talked to on the phone, emailed, met for coffee? A part of her just wanted to see him, once, then be done with it all. She wanted to hear the sound of his voice and smell his skin, touch his hair. The desire was more of an animal need than a rational human thought, and Ramona couldn't explain it to anyone, not even herself.

This notion of finding her child, then looking at him, touching his skin, smelling his hair, and saying good-bye was absurd, but she had not thought beyond this point in any concrete way. Any conversation or time spent together after the initial moment of discovery was murky and distant in her mind. That part did not seem likely or even, perhaps, desirable.

It was almost ten o'clock and she was beginning to sweat. It was only eighty-five degrees at the most, she knew, but Ramona had grown used to living close to the ocean and feeling the constant cool breeze that rose from the Pacific like a gift. She would never come here again during the summer, not for anyone. In her memory, the heat of summer meant miserable nights sweating in her apartment, the hum of the ineffectual swamp cooler taunting her from the next room. One night she had gone outside in her T-shirt and underwear and sat in the warm water of the fountain, looking up at the stars and wishing she lived somewhere far away.

Her drive had no specific purpose, but she was close to a Mexican restaurant named Ricardo's that her mother used to love. She was surprised to find the place still open, but there it was, sitting on the corner of Flamingo and Decatur where it had always been, and on impulse she pulled into the parking lot and cut the engine.

It had just opened for lunch, and Ramona got a seat in the Spanish-style courtyard beside a burbling fountain and ordered two beef tacos and an iced tea. Other than three waiters fussing with a long buffet table against the back wall, she was alone, and she ate the entire bowl of chips and salsa before her iced tea even arrived. "Sorry," she told the waitress when she set down Ramona's drink. "I'm pregnant."

"Oh, okay," the teenage girl said with a shrug. "You can have as much as you want. It's unlimited."

Unlimited. Ramona liked the sound of the word. It suggested freedom or abandon, an openness she rarely experienced in her hometown. It was peaceful out here, beside the fountain, and Ramona allowed herself to remember her mother sitting across from her in this very courtyard, eating a burrito in silence, but enjoying herself. Ramona had been a year away from getting pregnant, unaware that the fragile peace between them would soon be corrupted, made irreparable by Ramona's decision to let another woman, an unknown person, raise her son.

Her food arrived, and the tacos were drenched in too much cheese, but otherwise decent with a nice spicy kick. As she ate, she watched the waiters setting up the buffet and thought about Nash. He would be on his lunch break now, possibly at home if he were repairing a cooler in the neighborhood. He lived in a small, one-story house in an undesirable, slightly seedy part of town called Rose Park. Ramona was never afraid on his street, and the house was pretty with its low, curving archways and scuffed wood floors, but she didn't think she could be coaxed into moving any further inland.

She hoped Nash would want to move in with her, and eventually, maybe before the baby came, they could find a larger apartment with room for three. Ramona had never lived in a house, not growing up and not now. She wondered if having a baby meant she would eventually want a house as well. Maybe Nash could rent out his place in case the need arose for four isolated walls. This was all based on the assumption that he would want to live with her and have a child together. A phone call with the news seemed unfair, even risky, so she would wait and tell him in person. She had decided that it didn't matter whether he wanted to be with her or not. She would have the baby and keep it this time. That was certain.

It felt good to be sure about something, and she ran a hand across her shirt over her stomach and wondered if she would have a boy or a girl. Of course, it was early enough that something could go wrong—she guessed she was only six or eight weeks pregnant—but she wouldn't worry about that. There was nothing she could do but eat well and avoid her bad habits.

The tacos were gone quickly, and she accepted a refill on her glass of tea, then paid the bill and left. She felt fortified now, winding her way back to Ivy's, ready to smile and make small talk. Maybe she'd even offer to play a song at the party.

Turning off of Eastern back into Ivy's complex, an Eagles song came on the radio that her mother used to listen to as she washed the dishes, and the image of her mother was suddenly so clear and bright, wearing white shorts and a flowered apron over her T-shirt as she stood at the sink, a dark braid trailing down her back, that Ramona pulled to the side of the road, beneath the shade of a palm tree, and listened. She had forgotten that her mother wore a long braid on her days off, a solo version of the two braids she herself almost always wore, and she had forgotten about the song, too, until right now.

Ramona tapped her hands on the steering wheel, the name of the tune eluding her, and tried to remember past that moment at the sink: had her mother taken a walk after the dishes as she sometimes did, leaving Ramona alone for half an hour in the apartment? Or maybe she had scooped out strawberry ice cream for the two of them and then sat beside her on the couch and watched the news. Those had been the good nights, the ones with the TV and ice cream, despite the fact that there was no conversation, no physical contact.

Sometimes a man named Jonah came over and the three of them watched television together, then he led her mother to the bedroom and Ramona tried not to listen to the sound of their fucking, muted as it was, out of respect, she guessed, for her.

Ramona vowed to herself to be different with her own child. There would be books every night and cuddling and lying together on the sand watching the clouds move overhead. There would be singing and playing guitar and making cookies and visits to the library down the street. She could already picture the spot in that library where they would sit together by the window.

Of course, it was easy to imagine how wonderful you were going to be before you actually lived it. It was another matter entirely to be patient and kind on little sleep with little money or even with lots of sleep and lots of money. Sometimes it was simply difficult to behave as you should. Ramona knew this very well. And what would happen to her band once she had a baby? Would she leave just like her bass player?

Up ahead she could see Ivy's door, gleaming red halfway down the block, and Ramona realized her utter exhaustion again. It was the baby, she guessed—she could remember this exhaustion of the early months, like she'd just climbed a mountain. It was also the worry, the tenuous feeling of everything in her life right now.

JEREMY

Jeremy awoke in Gretchen's bed and was immediately seized by anxiety—he'd slept too late; he'd screwed up again—but then he saw it was only 7:00 a.m. and eased back onto his pillow with a sigh. Gretchen's side of the bed was empty, which is what had thrown him off in the first place because she was usually a late sleeper, but he could hear her now, very faintly, in the kitchen, walking on the tiles in slippered feet.

The sound reminded him of Ivy, quietly making cinnamon rolls while her father slept in on Saturdays, then bringing in a plateful to Jeremy, which they scarfed down before his escape. His own parents were told he was at a friend's house overnight. His brother knew the truth but upheld the brother code of keeping the information secret. These details shifted into a dream as he lay there, so that when Gretchen appeared in the bedroom doorway carrying a banana and a container of lemon yogurt, he was shocked to see her instead of someone from his past.

"Hey, lazy bones," she said, perching on the edge of the bed beside him and peeling her banana. She was already dressed for school in one of her long skirts and a skimpy tank top, hair coiled in a bun on top of her head. "Let's go for a walk before you go to the kitchen."

"Why would we do that?" he asked.

She shrugged. "Fun? Exercise? Health?"

"Oh, those things." He closed his eyes again. "All right."

Outside, it was cool and breezy, the light still soft. He hadn't been out this early in a long time, and it felt good to stroll the streets with

Gretchen, half listening as she told him about how well she'd done on her test yesterday. He slowed as they neared Ivy's old building, and decided to point it out. "That's where Ivy used to live. I practically lived there too in high school."

Gretchen glanced at the decaying structure and wrinkled her nose in distaste. "Poor baby," she said, taking his arm.

"My house wasn't much better."

"I know. You showed me before."

He nodded, trying to remember doing this. His family's house on Ballard was now dilapidated with a saggy carport and a lawn seared in spots as if fires had been lit then stamped out. It hadn't been such a bad place when his parents were alive, and he thought to tell Gretchen this now, but he liked the way she was holding his arm, stroking it a little, and being called "poor baby" filled him with surprising comfort.

They circled back toward her apartment, and Jeremy was glad that he hadn't broken it off with her yesterday. They'd had a nice evening together. He made butternut squash soup, and they ate at the kitchen table then played gin rummy until late, a game he'd somehow never heard of until last night, which was unexpectedly fun.

He spent the remainder of the morning making empanadas for Lucky's party. He rented the commercial kitchen on an hourly basis; the space, which was small but well equipped, was typically used by a bakery, and Jeremy was always finding chocolate chips underfoot, or dollops of icing on the handles of drawers. Today, there was a fine haze of powdered sugar on the cutting board, but he wouldn't complain. They rented it to him for cheap, and it was easy enough to spray his water and vinegar solution on the counters and run a rag over them before getting to work.

He'd settled on Peruvian-style empanadas, which he favored, since they were a good size for snacking and baked rather than fried. He made twenty with cheese; twenty with ham and cheese; and twenty traditional ones with ground beef, boiled egg, olives, raisins, and cumin. While these were baking, he put together two different salads: black-eyed peas with red peppers and pineapple, and a simple spinach salad that he would dress later. The sweet potato purses that Ivy wanted were already prepared, but he would boil and cool them at her place, so they turned out right. The fruit and cheese plate was done, as were about a hundred petit fours that had taken him the better part of his downtime over the past two days.

Jeremy had decided not to mention anything about the cost of all this to Ivy. He assumed she would pay him, but it sullied the experience to discuss money with her; he'd been mortified yesterday when she brought up paying extra for the menus.

At Ivy's house, he was greeted at the door by a man he'd never seen before, a pretty-boy type, with wavy brown hair and very bright blue eyes.

"I'm Adam," the man said, carefully relieving Jeremy of two of his larger trays. "Jane's husband."

"Oh, hey, great to meet you," Jeremy said, surprised. Jane had always gravitated to alternative types or strange-looking guys, like the white-haired man he'd met on Ivy's doorstep yesterday afternoon.

Ivy was in the kitchen, mixing a pitcher of sangria—she'd wanted to take care of the drinks herself—and Jeremy set down his supplies and, on impulse, kissed her on the cheek, which made her blush and turn away.

"What was that for?" she asked and nudged him with an elbow.

She seemed embarrassed but not angry, and Jeremy took this as a good sign.

"It was a 'Happy birthday to Lucky' greeting."

"He's asleep."

"Which is why I kissed you instead."

She smiled at him, a warm, easy smile, and Jeremy felt everything he'd liked today about Gretchen turning sour in his stomach. Her good traits, as solid as they may be, weren't enough to hold him. Every time he saw Ivy, he had to learn this as if for the first time.

Adam was arranging Jeremy's trays on the counter, and he was either ignoring this exchange or not paying attention.

Frank walked in and slapped Jeremy on the back. "The chef has arrived," he proclaimed. "Where's the cake? Can I check it out?"

Jeremy's eyes met Ivy's, and he felt a shimmer of worry move through him. "Oh, there's no cake, only petit fours." He popped open one of the containers and showed Frank the row of tiny cakes, iced with pale blue and decorated with white frosting ribbons. A Tupperware packed with miniature presents. "I have a tiered tray to set them on, so it will sort of look like a wedding cake when they're all arranged. I made a hundred."

"A wedding cake?" Frank said. "Sort of strange for a one-year-old's birthday, isn't it?"

"It won't actually *be* a wedding cake," Ivy said.

"Where are we going to stick a candle?" Frank wanted to know, peering at the petit fours with a frown.

"In one of those," Ivy told him, then turned to Jeremy and said, "They're really beautiful. Thank you."

"Those are cool," Adam added, joining the circle.

Three against one, Jeremy thought, waiting for Frank to say more, but he merely nodded, then moved to pour himself a glass of water from the tap.

JANE

Jane managed to avoid Adam until guests began arriving for the party. When she got home this morning, he was asleep. Then she took a nap, and when she awoke he was in the shower, then she was in the shower, and before she knew it, it was two o'clock and guests were knocking on the front door in a steady flow, as if they'd decided to walk in procession up the sidewalk and then into Ivy's house in two-minute intervals. Most of the people were friends Ivy had made at baby yoga and the library or teachers and administrators from Frank's school, but Jane recognized a few women from high school, a girl named Naomi who'd been on the volleyball team with Ivy, Patricia from the quad, Delilah from the apartment complex.

There were more babies than Jane had expected, at least five or six who were the same age as or a little older than Lucky, but so far they were all on good behavior, looking sweet-faced and complacent in the arms of a parent. Ivy was holding Lucky by the front door, bouncing him lightly and smiling as she greeted guests. She wore a bright green wraparound dress and her hair hung loose down her back. Lucky's T-shirt was a matching green. Jane watched her friend and felt an unfamiliar anger building. If Ivy hadn't let Adam in, if she hadn't welcomed him with wine and open arms, then Jane wouldn't be forced to go and talk to him right now, as she knew she had to do.

She found him in the kitchen, leaning against the sink, drinking a beer. Jeremy was fussing with a tray of food beside him, arranging it just so, and Adam was watching him and talking softly, telling him, Jane realized, about their kitchen in Wisconsin, the way it always smelled of barbecue, no matter how much they scrubbed it down. "It's like it used to be a rib joint or something. I can't figure it out."

"There are worse smells than barbecued ribs," Jeremy mused.

"True," Adam agreed. "But I'm a vegetarian."

"Oh, well, then that's rough," Jeremy agreed.

The two men had never met before, but they seemed a perfect set, with their ruffled hair and laid-back postures, and Jane was caught off-guard by how at home Adam looked in this kitchen. That was one of his talents, she understood: slipping into any environment with perfect ease.

"Hey," Jane said, forcing herself to step closer to Adam than she wished to be.

He turned and his face brightened, then clouded briefly before he smiled and said, "Jane."

Her name came out coated in kindness, even love, but he made no move to approach her, and she felt relieved, not wanting just now to be wrapped in his ambiguous embrace. She ladled out a cup of sangria from the punch bowl on the counter, sliced rounds of orange floating on the liquid's rosy surface like mini-inner tubes. "Would you like one?" she asked Adam.

"Please," he said, and accepted a glass with his free hand. He took a sip of the sangria, then a long pull from his bottle of beer.

"What about me?" Jeremy asked. "Am I just the hired help now?"

Jane had forgotten his presence, he'd been so silent fussing over his tray of food, and she wordlessly ladled out another cup and handed it over.

"Cheers," Jeremy said, lifting his glass.

Jane and Adam clinked cups, then looked uncomfortably at each other, both acutely aware this was no occasion for a toast.

There was a building pressure between them, and when Jeremy turned and left them alone in the kitchen, she felt the pressure become denser, viscous, and yellow. "The kids should be here any minute," she told Adam. "We all stayed at my parents' last night, but I came over early to help with the party."

"I didn't see you help with anything." He smiled, but the words were meant to rile her; she could feel this in his tone, in the relentless arrow of his gaze. So he'd flown all this way to start a fight. She guessed it was about time.

"You're right," she agreed. "I didn't do much to help out."

"So what have you been doing here?"

"Swimming with the kids," Jane said quickly. "Hanging out."

He nodded and took a swallow of beer. His eyes were tired, shadowed underneath, and Jane wondered if he felt as exhausted as she did.

"What exactly are *you* doing here?" Jane asked.

He shifted against the sink and sipped his beer, then took a swallow of sangria. Sun burned through the window behind him and rode his shoulders, lit the wavy top of his hair. "I wanted to see you. That's all."

"I'll be home in two days."

"I thought you might decide to stay." He said this calmly, as if extending her vacation would be an acceptable decision, not a threat to everything in his life.

Jane was considering how to respond, thinking again of the open house, that empty, white-walled living room looking out on the pool, when two women holding babies swept into the kitchen.

"Ivy said there's some baby food in the cupboard?" The one with short red hair directed this to Jane.

"Sure," Jane said, moving to stand beside Adam and reach into the cupboard to his right. There was a row of Gerber jars on the second shelf, and Jane read the flavors out to the women—"banana, sweet potato, harvest vegetables, pears"—while taking note of the heat that rose from Adam's body, thinking she might be repelled by his proximity but feeling instead a familiar pull.

"Pears," the redhead requested.

"Sweet potato for me, please," the other mother said.

Jane swiveled and held out the jars, then noticed that the second mother was Delilah, from Ivy's old apartment building. The woman recognized Jane at the same moment and smiled, revealing overlapping front teeth. "I hear Ivy's mother's coming to the party," she said. "Is that true?"

Jane shook her head. "I don't think so."

"Jeremy mentioned it was a possibility, but he's not the most trustworthy person I know." She laughed.

"Exactly," Jane agreed, though it didn't feel right to talk badly to this person about Jeremy, so she added, "His food is wonderful. Have you tried any yet?"

"Busy trying to feed this monster first." She kissed the top of her child's head, a dark-haired boy wearing a skull T-shirt. "This is Spencer."

Adam leaned in before Jane did, smiling at the boy. "Nice work," he told Delilah. "He's pretty cute."

"This is my husband, Adam," Jane told Delilah and the redhead beside her. The word *husband* felt rusty from disuse, but what else could she call him? *My husband for now? My husband until I figure out what the fuck I'm doing with my life?*

When the women were gone, Jane leaned against the counter beside Adam with a sigh. "This sucks," she told him.

"Yep."

His instant understanding of what she meant—the strange sound of the word *husband* and how she longed for it to sound normal again, to have never sounded strange in the first place—cheered her up a bit. It was not a small thing to be understood.

"C'mon," he said, placing a hand at the small of her back. "Let's go outside and get some food."

The party was centered around the pool. Jeremy's table of hors d'oeuvres was set up nearby, and people milled about holding blue paper plates, talking and laughing. Frank had set up the speakers outside, so that beachy pop music looped through the crowd, and a few couples were already dancing on the covered patio, twirling their children around between them. Jane stood beside Adam on the edge of the pool deck, wishing she were still sitting alone on the side of the Black Mountains, looking out over the city.

Later, Adam would likely talk her into joining those people on the dance floor, spinning Fern and Rocky between them like tops, and how would she possibly be able to refuse? Then he would pull her close, into their own separate dance, and the decade they had shared would flare into something bright and intangible, hovering around their swaying forms, and then all thoughts of leaving might just dissipate into the evening air, absorbed by other partygoers, other couples who would later sour and curdle, turning away from each other in bed.

Adam excused himself to the bathroom, and his absence made her even more uncomfortable than his presence. It was useful to have a husband at a party, she understood, another person to ease you into the unfamiliar crowd. Then she spotted Ivy and Ramona sitting together under the umbrella, and relief swept through her as she crossed the deck and perched on the arm of Ramona's chair.

"How's it going?" Ramona asked her.

"Not great," Jane said.

"He told me this morning," Ivy said in a low voice, "that you might be angry with him for coming here."

"Actually," Jane said, "I'm angrier with you."

"With me? What was I supposed to do? Turn him away?"

"No, but you didn't have to pal around with him."

"Well, he's a friend. We've known each other a long time. I'm not going to act like a total bitch to him."

"But you have no problem acting like one to me?" Jane had not come over here with the intention of starting a fight, but she felt an inevitable momentum now.

"What's that supposed to mean? We've been having a good time. At least that was my impression."

"A good time," Jane said in a sarcastic whisper. "My marriage is disintegrating. Ramona's off searching for her son. And you're just serving up cocktails, flirting with your ex-boyfriend, and preaching to me how to live my life."

Ivy stood up abruptly, knocking her knee against the edge of the table and sending splashes of red sangria all over the white cloth so that it looked as if a bloody scuffle had taken place. "I wouldn't be preaching if you weren't screwing everything up. Your life has been too easy, that's what I think. You've always had so much love that you can't even imagine what your life might feel like without it. Well, let me tell you something: It feels awful. Ramona knows, just ask her. We both know what it's like."

Ramona finally spoke then. "Sit down, Ivy," she said softly, reaching to touch her arm.

Ivy looked down at her, as if considering, then obeyed. She lifted her empty sangria glass off the table and peered into its depths, then set it back on the stained cloth and raised her gaze to meet Jane's. "I'm sorry," she said.

"No, you're right," Jane told her. "I don't know what it's like."

"Jane," Ramona began. "We just want to make sure you've thought this through. I mean, what are you going to do if you move out? You don't even have a job."

Jane nodded. "I have connections. I should be able to find something fairly quickly." In fact, a friend from the paper had sent her a link to a university job this morning, but she didn't want to get into the specifics. Thinking about the practical aspects of a separation held little appeal right now, sitting beside this swimming pool in a faraway state.

"I'm not worried about a job," Ivy said. "I'm worried about her heart."

"My heart is just fine," Jane told her, but even as she said the words she felt a contracting pressure in her chest as Adam stepped back onto the patio and scanned the crowd. Watching him, she felt the inevitable link between them, pulling her back to what was familiar. "I need a refill," she said and stood, then slipped around the edge of the tables and through the side door so as to avoid her husband.

Inside, she wound her way back to the empty kitchen where she refilled her glass with sangria, then leaned against the sink. Through the dining room's sliding glass doors, she had a partial view of the party outside. A group of women had gathered around Jeremy's table, where he was holding up a petit four, and it looked as if he were giving a lecture on how to create one. Frank stood close to the pool, holding Lucky and talking to his father. Her own parents would be here soon, along with her children, and seeing Adam would create a feeling of mutual delight and tension in all of them that Jane didn't think she could bear.

As if conjured by her thoughts, Rocky ran into the kitchen and clung to her legs with such force Jane staggered back, then crouched down to give him a proper hug. "When did you get here?" she asked him.

"Right now," he told her, then said with unblemished excitement, "Daddy's here! Out front helping Grandma."

"I know. I guess I should go help out too," she told him, but instead stayed where she was, pulling Rocky against her and kissing the warm top of his head. She'd missed seeing him this morning, she realized, missed eating breakfast with him and Fern the way she did every morning at home. Was that all it took, she wondered, just a few mornings off and she was ready for her routines again?

He fidgeted in her arms, then pulled away and ran outside toward the party. Jane watched him go, then went out front with the intention of finding her parents and Adam, wanting to get any strangeness out of the way and move forward with the day the best she could, but the walkway and lawn were empty, and she was turning to go back inside when she heard someone call her name.

It was Rex, striding up the sidewalk, waving his long arm and smiling. This was bad, Jane knew, very bad that he was here, but she couldn't help the sudden thrumming of her heart, the light-headed feeling of pleasure evoked by the sight of him. She met him on the sidewalk, looking over her shoulder for Adam or Ivy, her children and parents, but for the moment, no one was in sight.

"I never got your phone number," he said, by way of greeting. "And I wanted to ask you to dinner, tonight, or maybe tomorrow?"

"I can't," she told him quickly.

"Oh, okay." He twisted the small bun at the nape of his neck and looked to the side.

"There's just a lot going on here. That's all."

"Just a drink then?" He reached out and ran his palm down the length of her arm, then caught her hand in his.

The coolness of his skin calmed her, and she wanted him to pull her along the sidewalk, to lead her back to his house until this party was over. "It's good to see you," she told him, wanting to offer something. "Really good."

"Jane," Ramona called to her from the front step.

She took her hand away from Rex as swiftly as she could and turned toward her friend.

"Adam's trying to find you. Sorry to interrupt."

"Okay, just a minute," she told her, then turned back to Rex. In the glare of sunlight, the few lines on his face disappeared completely, and for a second, she could see his younger self, the one she faintly recalled. "I think I do remember you," she told him. "The palm tree at lunch? You always sat by yourself?"

He nodded. "That was me."

"I admired the way you managed to sit there alone every day without looking lonely or like some sort of outcast. You seemed, I don't know, happy."

"I was happy." He laughed and shrugged. "I didn't know any better yet."

"Neither did I."

"So who's Adam?"

"My husband. He just showed up last night, out of the blue."

"Oh." He frowned and rubbed his hands together. "All right. I know how that goes."

She wanted to ask him what to do, how to navigate the terrain, but his circumstances were not quite the same as her own. For one thing, he was the one who had been left, and Jane was the one trying to do the leaving. But she knew he felt the same deep ache she did, had the same cavernous hole caused by love's removal. "Maybe I'll stop by later?" she said.

"Whatever you think." He nodded once, firmly, and turned to go.

She watched his tall, sharp-angled form retreat down the walk, then he rounded the corner and disappeared from view.

Back by the pool, the party had grown more festive. The patio was packed with dancers now, and the music had grown louder. The sun began to lower and turn golden, casting everyone in a hazy glow that evoked the past, a memory of a party rather than an ongoing event.

Jane found Adam at the food table, sampling Jeremy's various offerings and drinking another beer. He knocked a stack of blue napkins on the ground and looked unsteady as he bent to retrieve them. Jane wondered how much he'd had to drink, then decided it was no longer her concern.

"Here I am," Jane said. She plucked an empanada off the half-empty plate and took a bite. It was colder than it was supposed to be, but delicious nonetheless. "Yum," she told Jeremy, who smiled.

"Oh, hi." Adam straightened up, then wiped away the salsa on his lip with a blue napkin. "I wanted to dance to this one song you like—I can't remember the name—but it's over now, so . . ." He shrugged and popped a grape in his mouth. "Next time."

"Next time," she agreed. "Where are the kids?"

He turned toward the pool and shrugged again. "Playing somewhere."

Jane searched the crowd, thinking someone should be paying attention to Fern and Rocky's whereabouts. The pool was empty, reflecting the peachy blue light of the sky. A hearty peal of laughter rose up from a group of teachers from Frank's school, and Jane watched as they toasted, sangria spilling down their arms. Two women nursed babies on the chaise longues under the palm tree. Ivy was leaning into Frank on the dance floor. Jane's parents were on the dance floor too, their jaunty, swinging step taking them around the edges of the crowd. They were deft together, as they had always been.

Ramona sat in a chair near the dancers, tuning her guitar, and then Jane saw Rocky and Fern emerge from behind the palm trees and run over to Ramona, where they leaned their heads to listen intently as she plucked each string. Jane's muscles relaxed at the sight of them, then tensed again as Adam leaned toward her and said, "I'm going to ask if I can give a toast."

The song ended, and the dancers scattered to reveal her husband, holding a microphone that belonged to a karaoke machine. Ivy whispered something to Adam, then nodded and stepped away. He tapped the microphone with his hand. "Excuse me, everyone, I'd like to make a toast."

The crowd took a while to quiet, but Adam made the request again, looking somber, and soon all eyes were turned on him, standing alone on the square of deck that had just recently been filled with people. He appeared thinner than usual, his blue T-shirt drifting in a breeze against his narrow chest. His cheeks were hollow, his sleepy eyes shadowed and grave so that he looked frail and exhausted, on the verge of collapse.

Then he stepped forward, onto a carpet of sun, and the light shifted, erasing the impression and returning him to his usual vigorous self. He smiled at the silent crowd, and Jane could feel people leaning in, wanting to hear what this handsome stranger had to tell them.

"First things first: Happy birthday to Lucky. You are very lucky, indeed." He raised his beer, and everyone raised glasses to toast Lucky's birthday. "Now, on a less festive note, I'm here to apologize," he announced, and his voice came out louder than necessary for the size of the crowd, so he pulled the microphone further away from his face. "I want to apologize to my wife, Jane, for being such a screw-up, such a poor excuse for a husband."

He swung his arm out and the crowd turned in her direction, the expectant faces observing her with curiosity or maybe pity.

"We've had a rough year," Adam continued. "Jane lost her job, and she may have even had an affair, but I'm not sure about that. It might just be that she doesn't love me anymore. It might just be as simple as that. She doesn't love me. Anymore."

Jane shook her head, meaning to convey that he should stop. Her mother gathered up Fern and Rocky and hurried them through the crowd and back into the house, her head bent toward them, whispering. Jane wanted to walk over to Adam, to take the microphone out of his hands and shuttle him away where they could be alone, but her feet were glued to the pool deck, immovable. Her limbs had gone cold, and she felt as if she were freezing from the inside out: first the stomach, then the heart, the brain, face, arms, torso, legs. She had a fleeting image of frost dripping from her fingertips when they dug her up in this very spot, centuries from now.

"And I can't really blame her, for any of it," he continued, "but I do want to apologize." Adam turned to Ramona then, who sat off to the side holding her guitar, watching him with wide eyes. "Ramona, play that one slow song of yours, won't you? 'One Night' I think it's called? Jane—" He turned back and held out his hand. "Please come and dance with me."

Jane and Ramona locked eyes, and Jane shook her head no again. The crowd was watching Jane, and she guessed they were waiting for her to run to the stage and embrace her husband, to provide them all with a moment of absolution.

"Ramona, c'mon," Adam said, turning back to her. "Please play it for us."

Jane could hear the alcohol in his voice now, the way it was wearing him down and revving him up at the same time, forcing him to plead for a song in front of thirty strangers. He must have begun drinking long before the party started, Jane realized now, because it would take a large quantity to bring him to this point.

Something seemed to unlock in Ramona then, and she set her guitar on the ground, then stood, took the microphone out of Adam's hands, and turned the music back on. Jane watched, still unmoving, as her friend put a hand on Adam's back and led him away to a table apart from the crowd. It took a few beats, but then people began talking again, and drinking and eating, even laughing, while a buttery rock song floated over the crowd. The mood was muted, yet the strangers also looked exhilarated, Jane decided, as if witnessing the crumbling of someone else's marriage had filled them with strange relief.

A hand touched her elbow, and she turned to find Ivy. "What do you want to do?" she asked.

Jane shook her head again, thinking about what a pure gesture it was, so simple yet so potent. It relieved her of the need to speak.

Ivy took Jane's hand and she felt herself begin to thaw at the touch, then allowed herself to be led inside to a back bedroom, away from everything.

RAMONA

She needed to leave. It was too much now, being here surrounded by all these people she didn't know, pregnant, unable to even have a drink in her hand. Then there were the babies, seven in all—she'd counted twice—bouncing on hips, nursing on lounge chairs, pulling at their mothers' hair. Reminders of the one inside her right now, and reminders too of the other one, the one from long ago.

She'd comforted Adam as best she could, reassured him that things would be fine, even though it was obvious things would not be fine at all, might never be fine again. She'd left him with Jeremy, both of them sitting at a table eating tiny cakes, then gone inside and retrieved a juice box from the fridge, which she drained and crushed in her hand, making her feel ridiculous. It was her duty to find Jane right now, but she couldn't bring herself to do it. She wanted simply to be free of this party, so she grabbed her keys from the bowl on the table and left.

Outside, she found a woman peering through the front window, hands cupped around her eyes as she pressed her face to the glass.

"Can I help you with something?" Ramona asked, crossing over to the woman, who startled at the sound of Ramona's voice and quickly stepped away from her position at the window.

The woman was older than most of the partygoers, small and plump with blonde hair turning white and overly large gray eyes with hooded lids. She was familiar, but also not familiar at all. Ramona knew her, but she couldn't remember why.

"Sorry," the woman said. "Just trying to decide whether or not I'd be welcome."

"Are you a friend of Ivy's?" Ramona asked.

"Ramona, it's me. Astrid." She smiled slightly, not a full smile, and Ramona noted the deep wrinkles around her mouth and the small, childlike teeth. Her face contained sadness but something else too, a neediness that made Ramona uncomfortable. Her eyes had a catlike quality. They were shaped like almonds and had probably once been very beautiful, a lovely centerpiece for her small face. She could not recall anyone she'd ever known named Astrid.

"Ivy's mother," the woman added, almost as an afterthought.

The information absorbed into her bloodstream quickly, and she could feel it bring her senses back to life, clicking every detail into place. Of course, this was Ivy's mother. "Hello," Ramona said and smiled. She was uncertain how to react. Was she supposed to be angry with this woman who had deserted her best friend? Or welcoming? Her instinct was to offer kindness, so she crossed the short space between them and shook the woman's hand, then changed her mind and moved into a quick embrace. "Have you seen Ivy yet?" Ramona asked. "Does she know you're out here?"

Astrid shook her head and turned to glance toward the red door. "I can't bring myself to knock."

"Come with me," Ramona said, taking her arm, but Astrid slipped out of her grasp and stepped back.

"I'm not ready."

"It's perfect timing," Ramona told her, knowing even as she spoke the words that it was not good timing at all, and likely never would be. "Lucas turned one today. We're having a party. You should come in."

"Lucas." The name rolled out slowly. Astrid appeared to savor the sound of the two syllables, then she said, "So that's his name. I didn't know. It was my father's name."

"Really? Ivy never mentioned that." Once it was out, Ramona realized how rude this sounded and tried to amend. "Well, maybe she did. I'm not very good at keeping track of those things."

"Those things?"

"Kid things," Ramona explained.

"Oh, of course," Astrid said and nodded. "You gave your baby away. That was you, right?"

Ramona stepped back, feeling as if she'd been physically struck. "I put him up for adoption, if that's what you mean. It's not the same as abandoning your child."

"You're right," Astrid said quickly. "Of course. Adoption. I didn't mean . . ." She didn't finish the sentence, merely showed Ramona her palms and shrugged.

Silence unrolled between them and wavered in the air. Here we are, thought Ramona, two mothers who deserted their children, with nothing to say. "I have to go," Ramona told her, then walked over to her car and got inside without looking back.

Driving away, her hands began to shake on the steering wheel. Astrid had left Ivy without a word during high school, which was entirely different than giving up an infant for adoption. The judgment that had risen out of Astrid's words—*You gave your baby away*—stung her skin, clung to the back of her throat, and she rolled the windows down and took long gulps of the warm air.

It was then that the correct question came to her. It was so obvious she didn't understand how she'd overlooked it before. She would drive over to the café, find the boy with the black glasses, and simply ask what year he was born. This wouldn't offer absolute proof, but it was a start.

Eastern Avenue seemed to stretch on forever, but the new freeways were foreign to her, so she stuck to the surface streets. Still, every road she crossed was new: Serene Avenue, Pebble Road, Wigwam Parkway, Windmill Parkway. There was no sense of order or any pattern to the names as far as she could tell, and so many homes and storefronts looked the same—beige stucco walls, red tile roof—that she began to regret the drive, her plan, her life, everything.

Sunset Road revived her. Here was a street from her youth, typically the farthest point they would ever travel south on a given day, then she reached Tropicana, and it was time to turn left, and all was familiar again, if slightly more packed with restaurants and strip malls and people. The sun was lowering over the Sheep Mountains, turning the sky its usual pink and orange. Soon it would be dark, and the party at Ivy's house would be done, and Ramona may or may not know if the boy working at the coffee shop was her son.

The early evening crowd at the café was decidedly different. Everyone was college age, possibly even high school, and black was the predominant clothing color. Silver jewelry glinted. Lips were painted almost purple. Ramona felt immediately out of place in her blue T-shirt and faded skirt, the braids trailing down her back like symbols of a lost era. A table of kids turned to watch her as she stepped inside, and Ramona lifted a hand and said, "Hey, what's up?" which made them immediately turn around and begin talking as if she'd never appeared in their midst.

She sat at a table for two in the corner and searched the counter for her son but didn't see him. There was an older guy with a Mohawk now, making a latte, and a black-haired girl with a pierced eyebrow. No sign of the woman with the bowler hat or the boy with caramel-colored hair and black glasses. Ramona sighed and closed her eyes, then leaned back in her seat, feeling as if she might just lay her head against the cool marble of the tabletop and pass out, into a dreamless sleep, but she kept her head upright, and when she opened her eyes again the place seemed brighter than it had been a moment ago, and louder, filled with laughter and shouting and the kind of wordless, pounding music that she hated.

She watched the counter for a few long minutes, willing the boy to emerge from the back room, wanting to get it over with now that she was here, but no one else appeared, so she rose and left without looking back, feeling the eyes of everyone on her as she disappeared up the stairwell.

The next step was to return to his apartment around the corner. It was quicker to walk, and the air felt good, cooling with the approaching dark. She undid her braids as she walked, thinking that it was time to give up this childish style if she was going to be a mother. Lights were on in the building, and she crossed the courtyard and sat on the same bench where she and Jane had sat together only yesterday afternoon. The windows of her son's unit were dark, but it was not quite black enough outside to require interior light, so she decided to wait. He may be home and just prefer dim natural light, the same way she did. This idea lifted her spirits. What if another person existed, right behind that door, with her own preferences, her own dislikes and fears? Strange things could be passed down. Rocky frowned exactly as Jane did, and Fern liked the same foods, dill pickles and liverwurst, weird things a kid shouldn't like. Lucky already smiled exactly like Ivy.

What if this boy were inside his apartment right now, enjoying the low light until the last possible second, drinking black coffee, and eating sourdough toast? Granted, it was a long shot, but it struck her as possible now, sitting out here in the satiny dusk watching his door. Many things seemed possible.

When the light outside deepened to a rich blue-black, a light came on inside his apartment, and Ramona felt vindicated. He was home, and he was just like her. The light propelled her up and over to the door, where she knocked lightly, then waited, hoping for a moment that he hadn't heard the knock and she could turn around and leave. Wasn't this already enough? Seeing his light come on as the sky turned dark?

The door opened, and Ramona's heart began to beat very fast as she waited for his face to appear, but it was the girl they'd seen earlier on the bike. "Can I help you?" she asked, her eyes taking in

Ramona, then looking quickly past her into the night, searching for someone familiar.

"Oh, hello," Ramona said. She was caught off-guard now and wondered why she hadn't considered this possibility. Up close, the girl was older than she'd thought, at least twenty, and not as pretty as she'd appeared from a distance. Her hair was amazing, long and silvery blonde, but her skin was marred with acne scars and her eyebrows were so pale they looked nonexistent, giving her a startled appearance.

"Is James here?" Ramona asked.

"Just a minute," the girl told her, then called his name out over her shoulder.

Through the half-open door, Ramona took in the apartment, which was neat and modern with a low, Swedish-looking gray couch and red leather chairs. The standing lamp by the couch was the one that had been turned on, and a yellow hardback book was splayed out in the circle of light hitting a cushion. So it was the girl who'd left the light out until the last possible second, caught up in her reading.

Ramona was waiting for the boy to appear from the hallway beyond the living room, but he surprised her by coming around from the other direction, wiping his hands off on an apron. "Yes?" he asked, pleasant but slightly wary, dark eyebrows lifted above his glasses.

She hadn't been this close to him yesterday, or heard his voice, and she waited, now, for a rush of recognition—it seemed she'd been waiting for this for a very long time—but nothing arrived. There was no inner feeling to indicate she'd created this person. He had nice skin with a warm, almost golden tone, and green eyes with an appraising gaze. His voice was low and even, calm but strong, the voice of someone who would succeed in the world, who would draw an audience.

"Hi," Ramona began. "This is going to sound strange, but I just have a quick question for you. I was wondering what year you were born."

He frowned at this and rubbed his chin, then placed one hand on the open door and the other against the frame as if bracing himself, or shielding the girl behind him from this odd woman. "Is this a survey or something? Because I really don't like to participate in anything like that."

She shook her head. "No, I just . . ." she trailed off. Why hadn't she planned some type of explanation? No innocuous reasons arrived, so she said, "I thought I might know you, but that depends on how old you are."

He took a step back and looked as if he were deciding whether or not to shut the door. "I don't understand," he said.

"I know," she said, trying to sound reassuring, to sound sane, and smiled at him, not wanting to mention the word *adoption* unless she had to, but this wasn't going well. He wasn't going to give up his date of birth to a stranger for no reason. "Could I come inside for a second?" she asked. "It's kind of a long and complicated story."

"Wait a minute," he said. "Haven't I seen you before? Yesterday, at the café? You were with that blonde woman?"

"That's right. I meant to talk to you then, but . . ." she trailed off and shrugged, not wanting to mention that she'd been practically sealed to her seat with nervousness. "You were busy working."

"Okay," he said, sounding slightly irritated, but resigned. "Come in."

Ramona walked in slowly, and perched on the edge of a red leather chair. It was a very spare room with gleaming wood floors and not a single piece of clutter, nicer than her own place by far. James sat down on the gray couch, and the girl sat beside him and took his hand. Ramona wished the girl would leave them alone, but felt she had no right to ask her to go, no right to be here at all really, so she just cleared her throat and smoothed out her skirt, then said, "Nineteen years ago, I gave up a baby for adoption, and it turns out the adoptive parents' names were Celeste and James Dillman. I thought you might be James Jr."

The boy nodded, and it reminded Ramona of the way Mark used to nod after absorbing information, a movement she'd forgotten about long ago. "Well," he began, "my name is James Dillman, that's true, but my father's name isn't James, and I'm not adopted, definitely not. Also, I'm twenty-two."

His words, delivered kindly in that low, even voice, sucked all the air from her lungs, and Ramona closed her eyes and leaned back in her chair. She shouldn't have come. She shouldn't have come. Because now that she'd visited every name on her list without success, she could feel herself sinking into empty space, into a future suddenly drained of color or texture, of any light at all.

"Hey, are you all right?" James asked. "Get her some water, Lila, or that iced coffee."

Ramona shook her head, her eyes still closed, wanting to tell him she was fine, not to bother, but she couldn't find the energy to speak. She managed to open her eyes and push herself upright. She accepted the glass of cold, milky coffee from Lila and took a sip.

Her last day in the hospital. She'd forgotten it for years, pressed it down somewhere out of sight, but it surfaced now, bobbed up into the room and held her in its grip. The baby in her arms, reddish pink, pale blue eyes, so much black hair everyone had to make a comment—the nurses, doctors, even her own mother. The couple was waiting down the hall—she didn't have to meet them if she didn't want to, and she didn't, not exactly, but she wanted to see them, to know they had kind faces, gentle hands—so she walked her baby down to them, along with the nurse, changing the plan at the last minute.

They stood beside a couch, talking softly with the woman from the adoption agency, but immediately turned when she came in.

They looked very old to Ramona, though she guessed they were only thirty, with lines around their eyes and baggy, comfortable clothes. Both of them brown-haired and brown-eyed, with the same nervous smile. They looked more like a sister and brother than husband and wife, a pair of sparrows.

"She changed her mind about meeting you," the nurse told them.

"Oh, of course," the woman said, stepping closer and looking down at the baby, who was beginning to mewl softly as if he knew what was going to happen next.

"Remember," the woman from the agency told them. "No last names."

"He's beautiful," the adoptive mother whispered. "Thank you so much."

Ramona recalled the soft curve of the woman's cheek, the tiny gold hoops in her ears, the tilt of her head as she looked at the baby. The father stepped over and nodded to Ramona as he slipped an arm around his wife's waist and leaned to look at his adopted child. He didn't speak at all, and the wife didn't say much either. They all just gazed at the baby, waiting for Ramona to hand him over.

That was the part she still couldn't pry loose from memory, the actual moment of handing over her child to those virtual strangers. It was better this way, she guessed, not being able to access that part of the day.

She took another sip of the cold coffee, set it on the low glass table beside her, then rose from her chair. "Thanks for letting me in," she told James.

"Good luck finding him," he said, standing up.

"I'm not going to," she told him. "This was my last stop."

"Oh." He glanced at Lila, then back to Ramona, obviously confused. "Well, take care, then." They shook hands, and she stepped outside.

Ramona walked quickly away from the apartment building, down the street, and around the corner to where she'd parked on Maryland Parkway a couple of hours earlier. The air in the car was warm and stale, no longer lemony, and she cracked her window, then lay her cheek on the steering wheel and looked out at the passing traffic, the rush of lights and noise moving by her in the night.

She sat like that for a long time, not quite thinking, just untangling her mind from the day. A desire rose up to see Mark, to tell him that she'd failed. Again. He had never agreed with her adoption plan, not really. She had no one to blame but herself.

Of course, there was also no one else to thank, if things had indeed turned out well. Her son's life might just possibly be a good one. This was her hope; this had always been her hope. She saw her baby again—all that dark hair, those pale eyes. It had been years since she'd been able to recall his face, the weight of him in her arms.

Her trance was finally broken by the insistent buzzing of her phone. Ramona fished it out of her purse, expecting Ivy and her questions, but the caller was Nash. She answered and the phone was warm against her ear, its hum comforting on her skin.

"When are you coming home again?" he asked. "I thought it was tonight, so I went to your place and was so mortally bummed out when you weren't there, I can't even tell you."

She smiled at the sound of his voice and pictured his face, its tanned, craggy contours, the sunburst of lines around his blue eyes. Maybe he was older than she thought, possibly forty-five. That was good, she decided. An older father might be more patient. "Tomorrow," she said, then took a deep breath. "And, there's something else you should know."

IVY

She kept expecting her mother to appear, to step through the sliding glass doors holding a glass of sangria, but the party was winding down, and she had not yet shown up. Frank had left to take his father home. Adam and Jane were off talking. Ramona had disappeared a while ago, who knew where. Now there were just a few stragglers, three teacher friends of Frank's who liked to drink, laughing together on lounge chairs, and Jeremy.

He was removing the uneaten petit fours from the tray, and she walked over to help him. "These were a hit," she said.

He smiled. "I thought it went really well, didn't you?"

"Perfect."

"I'll leave these for you in a Tupperware. I promised Fern."

"Oh, that's nice." She watched him lay each cake inside the container. "Is a check okay?"

He cleared his throat, not meeting her eyes. "Frank already paid me."

She nodded, feeling awkward and wishing Frank had told her, saved her this small embarrassment.

"Here," he said, passing her a silver tray scattered with empanada crumbs.

She followed him to the kitchen, where he started the warm water and tested it with his hand, then let it run while he stuck the Tupperware in the fridge and set the remaining trays beside the sink. He began to wash the first tray, steam rising around him as he scrubbed intently with a blue sponge.

Ivy moved to stand beside him. "I'll dry."

"Thanks."

Laughter reached them from outside, but it felt faraway, the sounds of a separate party, and Ivy accepted the first tray and set about drying it, recalling standing exactly this way with her mother, so many years ago. The steam, the warm towel in her hands. The silence was the same too, but this silence had a nice fullness; she didn't feel the absence of sound acutely, as she had back then. "I thought my mom would show up," Ivy said. "I guess I was actually hoping she would."

"She will," he told her. "Just give her time."

Ivy turned to watch Jeremy. His face was serious and intent as he washed the final tray. "Thanks for doing this today," she told him. "And thanks for helping with Adam. He was a wreck."

He smiled. "He just needed coffee and water."

"Other than that fiasco, I think the party went well, don't you?"

"Yeah, it was great. I booked a couple of other gigs with some of the teachers." He handed her the last tray to dry. "I wish I'd started cooking like this before my parents died, so they could see I wasn't a complete fuckup, but at least I could show you."

"I'm very proud," she told him, patting his shoulder, trying to put a bit of jokiness in her voice, but also the sincerity she felt.

"Where's your father today, by the way?" he asked.

"Not sure. His affections are still sporadic, even without the drinking." She shrugged. "It's all right. It would seem strange if he suddenly became a doting father and grandfather. It wouldn't seem like him."

The three teachers filed through just as she finished up the last tray. "Thanks, Ivy," the one with long red hair told her. Jessica, that was her name. "Really fun party."

The other two women thanked her, and she kissed each one on the cheek, then walked the trio to the door and saw them out.

After the trays were all dried and stored away, she and Jeremy sat by the pool, legs swinging slowly in the water, and finished the sangria.

Jeremy's black pants were rolled up, and his calves were startlingly white, his feet long and thin in the blue pool. It was almost dark outside, but still warm, still light enough to see Jeremy's profile clearly, its pointed nose and chin, those straight dark lashes.

"Lucky will probably wake up soon," Ivy said, idly, not really worrying about it.

He'd been tired when she laid him down, completely worn out from the day. She was worn out too, especially after her late night with Adam, but she felt alert and watchful.

"I always thought it would be me with the kids," Jeremy said. "A big brood of accidents that I would love like crazy anyway." He grinned. "Romantic, eh?"

"You could still have kids," Ivy told him. "You're only thirty-six."

"I guess I haven't found the right person to have them with yet."

"You will."

He took a deep breath, then a long swallow of sangria. "I never felt like *we* were completely finished with each other."

"Finished with each other. That's a weird way of putting it."

"You know what I mean. I can't even remember how or why we broke up."

She smiled to herself and shook her head. "Well, let's see. We were sitting by the fountain, and you said something like 'I want to be able to see other people without you getting so fucking pissed off.'"

"Ouch. I said that?" He shook his head. "Never mind, don't answer. That sounds like something I would have said."

"Then you immediately started driving around with that girl Sharon, with the spiral perm and those blinking lips earrings."

"Oh, right. I forgot about her." He shook his head again, as if amazed by his own idiocy. "Wow."

"It doesn't matter anymore," Ivy told him.

He rubbed his face with his hands, then held them cupped over his eyes for a long moment. She had thought this reminder of

Sharon would allow them both to laugh, but Ivy sensed he was on the cusp of crying. Was he really that pained by his old behavior? She put a hand on his back, his black T-shirt still warm from the sun, and sat there, waiting for him to be okay. A breeze lifted the hair on his neck and murmured through the palm trees across the pool.

When he moved his hands away from his face, he turned to her and smiled, his eyes dry. She couldn't recall ever having seen him weep, but she knew the signs of his sadness. They returned to her now: the covered eyes, the forced smile to show he'd gathered himself. She hadn't seen anyone cry in a long time, except for Lucky, and wondered if she would even know what to do.

"By the way," she said, hoping to distract him. "Thanks for the piggy bank."

"Piggy bank?" He raised his eyebrows. "What are you talking about?"

Then she understood: the piggy bank had been a gift from her mother. Ivy had collected them once, long ago, but she'd forgotten all about that. "Never mind," she told him. "I meant, thanks for the socks. I'm constantly losing Lucky's socks, so those are actually a useful gift."

She could explain to Jeremy about the piggy bank—it was a story he would enjoy—but she didn't feel like telling anyone that she'd figured out this small mystery. It was enough just to hold the knowledge on her own, to mull over this minor act of kindness. It was something, she decided. It was better than nothing at all.

"It's been nice having you around," she told Jeremy, finishing her last sip of sangria. "I thought it was a big mistake to hire you for this thing today, but I was wrong."

"Thanks," he said. "I'm glad you moved back."

"Well, it's not really permanent."

"No?"

Even as she nodded, she understood she was wrong. Frank loved his job here. He loved being near his father. Her own father was an off-and-on presence, but he lived here too, and he was Lucky's grandfather. And what if her mother was back for good? That would be something else to consider. She was so lost in this train of thought that she didn't see Jeremy leaning toward her until it was too late.

Ivy decided to accept his kiss, thinking he would try to pry open her lips and ruin this temporary peace between them, but he didn't. Their mouths pressed together briefly, and his hand reached up to touch her cheek. She expected the kiss to be familiar, even after all these years, but it wasn't at all. It felt completely new. She detected his kindness in the kiss, his wish to make her happy, and she understood they had become friends, or at least some strange semblance of friends.

Then they were separate again, and Ivy knew that he wouldn't try to do anything else. That was all he seemed to want, that brief physical connection that had been a little more than friendly, but not too much more. It did not cause her guilt or alarm, only a contented warmth.

He smiled at her, green eyes crackling, then swung his legs out of the pool. "I'd better get going," he said. "You don't need to walk me out."

Ivy sat by the pool for a while longer, then rose and began picking up the cups and plates strewn around the pool deck. Every few minutes she stopped to scan the backyard and sliding glass doors, as if her mother might be hiding somewhere nearby, waiting for the perfect moment to step out from behind the palm trees and make herself known. "She's not coming." Ivy said the words out loud even though she was alone. "She doesn't care about you."

"Who doesn't care?"

She turned quickly to find Frank walking toward her across the pool deck, holding Lucky in his arms.

"I didn't hear him cry," she said. "I've been listening."

"He wasn't crying. Just lying there cooing to himself."

Ivy nodded, taking him from Frank and swaying back and forth. She waited for her husband to ask what it was she'd been talking about again, but he didn't, and she guessed that was because he already knew.

REX

He thought he'd likely never see Jane again, but then there she was, walking by the window with a strange man who must be her husband. She glanced toward his house, and he raised a hand in greeting from his spot inside on the white couch, but she must not have been able to see him behind the window's glare because she turned away and kept going.

The man beside her looked concerned, with his furrowed brow, hands shoved deep into the pockets of his worn jeans. He had lots of brown wavy hair and a frat-boy handsomeness that struck Rex as all wrong for Jane. They were a couple that did not physically match—Jane was not as conventionally attractive as this man, or as ordinary—but Rex and Kristina didn't match either and had still managed many good years together. You could never tell what combination might work.

When they disappeared from view, Rex rose and went outside. Jane and her husband were walking past the old neighbor's house now, dusk darkening the air around them. Rex considered calling out to Jane, asking them both inside for a beer or lemonade, but decided against it and simply watched them walking, unobserved. They didn't touch or even appear to be on the verge of touching, and this struck Rex as a good sign, but they were exactly the same height, and for some reason, this fact disturbed him.

He crossed the lawn and got into his car, then sat in the driveway with the windows rolled down, thinking where he could go. Kristina had the girls until tomorrow evening, and he had not made a single plan. He considered calling Jessica for a second date, but her number was somewhere inside the house, and he didn't want to leave the car just yet. Besides, Jane said she might come by later, and it would be best if he were waiting alone.

First he drove over to the church and parked at the curb across the street. It was almost dark now, and he had expected the same empty structure from the night before, but there were lights on inside, and several people milling about on the front porch, talking and sipping from plastic cups. He watched these people for a while from inside his car. To his relief, no one seemed to notice his presence. It occurred to him that he'd entered a strange, ghostlike state, since Jane hadn't seen him either, and he decided the idea of disappearing altogether had a definite appeal.

His physical appearance had always been a burden, especially once he began to grow and didn't stop. People stared. They made odd, not exactly unfriendly, comments. *How's the weather up there? You're too young for such white hair.* And, more recently: *are you some kind of vampire?*

He knew that keeping his white hair long and wild didn't help him to blend in, but he'd decided long ago to embrace his strange looks, to make them more outlandish. This decision now felt childish and unwise. Why would he want to be more noticeable than he already was? If he were to step out of his car and cross the street to join the others right now, they would be disturbed by his appearance. They would try to hide their discomfort, like good churchgoers, but Rex had become adept at sensing aversion over the years. Maybe tomorrow he would cut his hair, possibly even dye it brown.

The breeze through his open windows felt soft and cool as he left the church and drove away. He headed his car in the direction of Kristina's new place, just planning to park across the street as he had at the church, and observe. He still hadn't seen this rented house of hers. She always wanted to come and get the girls, and always wanted to drop them off, as if she were hiding something.

The house was easy enough to find. He knew the address, and he knew this part of the city from past construction gigs. The street was quiet and a little older than his block, with bigger trees, elms and King Palms, and more variety in house color and shape.

Kristina's house was a pale pink with white trim and a carport. The grass was green, and bright geraniums flowered in a pot on the front step. It should have been cheerful, but it felt melancholy. Despite the bright flowers, it struck him as a lonely place.

A light was on in the front room and there was a large picture window facing out, but the blinds were closed, so all Rex could see were two forms moving back and forth. He rolled his window down further and heard the faint, living hum of music. The forms were dancing, he realized, as the shadows linked hands and spun. It was his daughters, dancing. The realization filled him with unspeakable sadness. They were just fine here, after all. Better than fine.

A car pulled up and parked directly in front of him. It was a dark blue sedan with tinted windows, so that Rex couldn't see who was inside. He guessed it was Peter and steeled himself for the moment when he'd step out of the car, but then a woman emerged, an old friend of Kristina's from the early days of their marriage. Ginger. Ginger Gonzalez. He and Kristina had always teased her about her name, because she looked nothing like a Ginger, with her long black hair and wide face. Her body was stocky and strong and Rex had always liked her, though he hadn't seen her in a very long time.

She reached back inside her car and pulled out a brown grocery bag, hefted it onto her hip then tucked her long hair behind her ears as she glanced up and down the street. Rex held his breath, not wanting to be caught, and thought he was home free when her eyes barely touched his car, but then she turned toward it again and leaned her head forward, trying for a better look. So he wasn't invisible after all.

He waved, not wanting his presence to frighten her, and she walked over to his open window and said, "Is it really you sitting there stalking Kristina or am I having a hallucination?" Her tone was not unkind, but it wasn't friendly either. It was obvious she'd chosen a side.

"I wouldn't call it stalking," he told her and shrugged. "I've only been here for a few minutes."

"Sitting in the dark outside your ex-wife's house. That's a pretty classic example, if you ask me."

"Ginger." He thought saying her name would help somehow. "Ginger, look. I was just taking a drive and decided to go and see the place where my daughters live half the time, all right? Take it easy."

She nodded and turned to look at the pink house, then back at him. "All right. Sorry." She reached into her grocery bag and pulled out an apple. "Want one? We're going to make a pie with the girls."

"Thanks." He accepted the apple and bit into it. It was on the mealy side, the skin thick and flavorless. "Kristina doesn't bake. You know that, right?"

"Polly wants to try it. I'm coming to the rescue." She shrugged and stepped closer to his car. Her face looked exactly the same as it had when he'd seen her last, still smooth and untroubled. As far as he knew, she had never married, never had kids of her own.

"Polly should have asked me. I'm good with cookies, at least."

They were both quiet for a minute, watching each other, then looking together toward the house with its lit windows. He was hoping, he realized, to be invited inside. Ginger had liked him once, and he was still basically the same person after all. Why couldn't the five of them sit at the kitchen table and peel apples? He pictured the surprise on Kristina's face when he walked inside, then the frown as she shook her head, disappointed by his pushiness.

"You should leave, Rex," Ginger said, turning back to him. "Don't worry. I won't tell Kristina you were here."

"Maybe I want you to tell her."

"No, you don't. Trust me, you don't."

He could feel a yearning building inside him, a desire to be behind the pink walls of that house. It felt urgent now, a basic need rather than an inclination. His face was hot. Sweat gathered on his lower back, and he shifted in his seat. "I don't understand why this happened," he said, his voice hoarse. "I don't see why we can't just get back together. Have you met that guy, Peter? He's such a jerk. How could she like him better than me?" He'd said too much—he could tell by the tight set of Ginger's lips—but it had felt good. His breathing was suddenly simpler, his thoughts in a straight, obvious line.

"She doesn't like him better than you."

"Then why?"

"I can't answer that. Only you two know the real answer to that one."

"But I don't know. That's the whole point. That's why I'm sitting here like an idiot stalker. I don't understand why we're doing this. Why we've *done* this."

Ginger shrugged and looked down at the ground, toeing the asphalt. "It was good to see you," she said. "I need to get this stuff inside."

"Okay," he said. "Okay, whatever. Have fun. Have a fucking wonderful time with my family."

She didn't say more, only turned and crossed the street, walked to the front door, and rang the bell. Rex watched the door open, and saw the pale oval of Kristina's face, her welcoming smile. He considered calling out to her, stepping out of his car and making a run for the door, but before he could move, Ginger ducked inside and the door closed behind them, intensifying the surrounding black of the night.

JANE

When they stepped outside, the sky was a ceiling of blues and purples, the color of a bruise. Jane turned back to look at the red door, wishing she could stay behind, but here was Adam, shoving his hands into the pockets of his jeans and hunching his shoulders against the lukewarm wind, and she had to walk beside him. It was the least she could do.

"The kids seem like they're having fun here," Adam said.

"They are."

"You look good too."

"Thanks."

"I like your hair. The stripe." He pulled on his own hair as if to illustrate.

"I did that a month ago."

"Oh." He looked down and shoved his hands into the pockets of his jeans again. "Well, it's nice. Different."

"Thanks," she said. It struck her that they could just go on like this indefinitely, talking but not really talking. She guessed that marriages had subsisted on far less. He was sober now and smelled of coffee and soap.

They ambled for a long while in silence, circling the neighborhood, passing the pocket park, then stopping at the low wall by the Black Mountains. It struck Jane that her walk this morning had been a practice for this one, that the route was almost identical but in reverse. She should have been running through her lines during that walk, because now she had no idea what to say.

At last Adam took a breath. "So I've decided to finish the dissertation by June and then really look for a good teaching position.

It might not be in Madison, but I can't just tend bar forever. Or maybe I could work for the city, some type of environmental position. I don't know."

She nodded. "All right."

"You don't sound impressed by my plan."

"No, it's good. That's a good plan." How could she tell him that she didn't care about his dissertation, or his job, his long nights away from home? She no longer cared about any of it.

"So I'd like it if you would come home tomorrow, and we could just forget about this separation thing, for a while at least."

Somehow, they'd arrived on Rex's street, and Jane realized she should have been paying attention to their path, that she should have steered clear of this block, but then they were in front of his house, and she glanced toward it but saw nothing. If Rex were to step outside right now, it might make this conversation easier. She could use him as an easy excuse—*look, I've met someone new and I'm not ready to come back*—but Rex wasn't the reason she wanted to leave Adam, and neither was the editor. They were both symptoms but neither was the cure. "I don't think I can forget about the separation," she told him.

"But why not? What have I done that's so awful?" He stopped on the sidewalk and made her face him. It was almost dark now, but light from a nearby street lamp revealed his pained expression. He had such a nice face, with clean lines and bright, trusting eyes. Jane tried to remember the first time she'd seen him, what she'd thought of him then, but couldn't. They'd met at a party, she knew that much, but the details of the night were hazy now, shrouded in dim, smoky air.

"You haven't done anything awful," she told him. *I'm the one*, she thought to say. *I'm the one who's done the awful things*. But the details of her transgressions did not need to be revealed. They would only cause him pain.

She took his hand and pulled him along the sidewalk, willing his feet to move with hers, to set them back in motion. It was easier this way. Moving helped her to feel as if this problem could actually be solved. And maybe it could, she thought again as they began walking. Surely they could think of something to fix this.

They'd traveled back to the Black Mountains and Jane paused to gaze up at their dark, eerie forms. Lights were beginning to come on in the houses up and down the street, and Jane thought about her own home in Wisconsin. Had Adam left lights on inside to ward off burglars? It was not something he would remember to do, and Jane imagined returning to ransacked rooms and broken windows, the cold spring wind winding through the front room and kitchen. Maybe there would be more snow—it was not out of the question in early May—and mice and squirrels would be nesting in their cupboards, protected from the elements.

"I'll keep sleeping in the front room," Adam said now. "But you can't move out. Think of Fern and Rocky. It'll be awful for them."

"Lots of people do it. It's not the end of the world." Even as she said this, she felt ashamed. She was always telling Rocky that something was not okay just because lots of people did it.

Adam sighed and trudged forward, rubbing his arms as if he were chilled, though it was still nice outside, not warm exactly, but far from cold. Jane jogged to catch up with him, then wished she'd stayed behind. What she wanted to do was turn around and climb the mountain in darkness, much the way she'd done this morning. Her rock would be waiting in the same place and she could simply sit and watch the city until she knew what to do.

"You're being so selfish," Adam hissed at her now. His voice had hardened, grown sharp with anger.

"I know," she admitted, "but you've been selfish for years. All those days and nights you did exactly what you wanted to do, as if you didn't even have a family. Staying out late after work, camping with your friends, taking trips to the Rockies when you really didn't need to go, sleeping in late while I got up with the kids and did five million things before we even saw you. I thought the idea was to raise our children together, but it doesn't feel like much of a joint effort."

"That's such bullshit. I got up with them so many times at night. I picked them up from school while you were at work. I fed them and dressed them and read them books. I don't even know what you're talking about!" He stopped his fast pace and slowed to glare at her. "This is what you're upset about? Taking care of the kids?"

Jane stopped and crossed her arms over her chest, looking back toward the mountains, then down the street, anywhere but into Adam's face. "No, not exactly. I don't know. My life just seems so dull. I can't stand it anymore."

"Your life. Is dull." He said it slowly, ladling the words with sarcasm.

She nodded, already regretting having told the truth—it sounded so petty, so shameful—but now that it was out she kept going. "Maybe it's just marriage that's dull, and it has nothing to do with you and me in particular."

"This feels very particular to me."

She looked at him then and saw that he was in pain. It would be so easy just to let all of this go, just to continue living her life in a state of depressed irritation. It was likely the kids would be better off with an unhappy mother who was present rather than happy and absent. That would be her own mother's advice: *Stay for the children; do everything for them. It was your choice to have them, after all.*

Jane looked away and started walking again. This fight was going nowhere. Somehow she'd gotten on the wrong track. The detour she'd taken to list Adam's faults had not helped matters. People had flaws—she had thousands of them herself—but this wasn't about Adam's errant ways, it was about something deeper. The word *dull* didn't do the feeling justice. It had to do with restlessness, with the notion or hope that her life should be larger than it actually was. She could almost see the shape of this other life, taking up more space than she'd ever taken up before. This bigger life still included Fern and Rocky, but she wasn't sure whether not it contained Adam.

Of course, it was not possible to put this into words without sounding ridiculous. How would she ever explain this feeling to Adam?

She turned and saw that he'd stopped walking and sat down on someone's lawn, so she backtracked, stepping slowly up the sidewalk until she was hovering over his stretched-out form. His eyes were closed and his hands were laced behind his head, as if he were enjoying a summer's day rather than lying in the dark on a stranger's lawn, the light from their porch engraving his face with shadows.

She nudged his tennis shoe with her toe, and he opened his eyes. "I'm so tired," he told her.

Jane sat down on the grass beside him and pulled her knees to her chest. "Me too."

They sat like that for a while, not speaking. Eleven years. She had spent eleven years with this person—more when you included courtship—and now she couldn't think of a single way to explain why she was leaving.

A teenage boy rode down the street on a skateboard, and the sound was startling after the long stretch of quiet. If the boy noticed her and Adam, he made no sign, simply curved a pattern down the asphalt then disappeared around a corner. But his presence had broken the spell; she was able to turn and look down at her husband.

His eyes were closed again, and Jane thought he might be asleep. He had a talent for being able to sleep just about anywhere. Then she remembered the first time she'd seen him. He'd been sitting in a chair in the backyard of a friend's house, the party churning loudly around him, sound asleep. Jane had gone over and lightly touched his cheek, for no other reason than she was a little drunk and he was so beautiful, she just wanted to place a palm against his skin. He'd woken easily, then looked up and smiled at her.

"Dull isn't the right word," Jane said softly. "My life feels too small. I know that sounds stupid, but that's about the best I can do. And I'm not saying it's your fault. That's just how I feel, and I have this notion that I won't feel that way so much if I leave."

Adam opened his eyes now and sat up, but remained silent, staring out into the street.

"Ivy says I've had too much love in my life and that I don't know how awful it feels not to have any, but I don't think that's my problem, or at least not the main one. That's her version of the world, not mine."

"So what is your problem?" he asked.

"I'm not sure. I guess that's what I need to figure out."

He glanced over at her now. All traces of anger had left his face, but he looked drained again, ghostly in the shadows. "When my parents got divorced, I promised myself I would never let that happen to me, but this is my fault really. I wasn't paying enough attention to my life. I haven't been, I guess, for a long time."

She thought to deny this, to tell him it wasn't his fault, but there was truth to what he said, enough for her to keep quiet, so she only offered, "Don't talk about divorce yet. Let's just try this first, and see what happens." The word *separation* suddenly felt too clinical, too heavy and glacial to say aloud.

"I guess I'll just get a good sleep tonight at Ivy's and then leave first thing tomorrow," Adam said, lying back on the grass.

"Okay," she agreed.

"Will you tell the kids I'm sorry I didn't say good-bye?"

"Of course." She shook her head and lay back beside him. "We'll be home tomorrow night."

"But then you're going to leave again."

"In a week or so," she said. She would have to find a small apartment and a job, but both of those tasks seemed possible. It didn't have to be a perfect apartment or a perfect job. For a while, everything would be temporary.

Adam turned on his side and propped himself up on an elbow to look down at her. "I'm going to miss you. A lot."

"Me too."

He reached to brush her hair away from her face. It was as if they were back home, lying together on their bed rather than on this cooling grass. "Maybe you'll decide to come back?"

"Maybe," she told him. "I hope so."

SUNDAY

JEREMY

The next morning Jeremy woke early, curled around Gretchen's thin form. Light poured across them, warming the bed and turning the room a milky gold. They'd gone to sleep early, soon after he got home from Ivy's house, and he felt thoroughly refreshed and content, the smooth expanse of Gretchen's back fitted neatly to his chest. He kissed her coconut neck, willing her to wake up, and she did, stretching against him, then turning so they faced each other.

"Let's go back to my place and I'll make us omelets," he suggested.

Outside, he enjoyed the muted, powdery blue of the sky, the absence of sound as they drove his Subaru through the quiet streets. It was Sunday, before 7:00 a.m., and the entire neighborhood seemed to be fast asleep. "This sort of reminds me of the old days," he told her, "when I used to come home from a show right before dawn, and the world seemed paused. But this is the opposite of that, I guess. This is the other side of the night. It feels different. Better."

"I know what you mean. I used to get up really early and go bird-watching with my dad when I was little. We'd drive out to the desert before sunrise and then spend the whole morning sneaking around with binoculars. I loved it. I think I used to be a morning person, then I started working late, and I got out of whack." She swung her loose hair over one shoulder and fiddled with the ends.

"I was never a morning person," Jeremy said. "But I feel good today. I like this."

"So how was the party yesterday?" she asked.

"It went really well," he told her. "A few of the mothers want to book me for their kids' parties. Maybe I'll have a new niche."

"Great," she told him, putting her hand on his leg. "Babies are being born every day. It's the perfect market."

This struck them both as funny, and they laughed. It occurred to him for the very first time that he could have a child with this woman if he wanted. They had never discussed marriage or kids or anything that serious, but these were the types of things most people desired—family, love, stability—why not him and Gretchen?

He thought again about kissing Ivy by the pool. It was bizarre, but something about that kiss had released him. There was a lightness in him today that hadn't been present in a very long time. The lack of passion he'd felt in that moment surprised him. There had been love, plenty of stored-up love spreading out through his limbs, but it had been a different kind of love than he'd anticipated. When he separated from her and leaned back, he understood that she felt it too: they were friends.

He wanted to tell this to Gretchen now, that he was finally over Ivy, but that would entail an admission of how in love he'd formerly believed himself to be, and he suspected Gretchen wasn't up for that part of the story.

At his apartment, Gretchen told him to relax, that she would make the omelets. He obeyed, grinding coffee beans instead and boiling water for the French press. He sat at the kitchen table, waiting for the teapot's whistle and watched Gretchen move around his tiny kitchen. She'd swept her hair up into a bun and was wearing his white chef's apron, the laces looped twice around her small waist. He watched as she cracked eggs into a silver bowl and grated cheese. She found a green pepper and onion, which she chopped quickly on his cutting board.

Gretchen had never cooked for him before, even at her place, and while he didn't expect the food to be much good, Jeremy felt more cared for than he had in a long time.

The whistle sang, and he rose and poured the water over the grounds, then put his arms around Gretchen's waist as she worked over the skillet and kissed her ear.

When she placed the omelet before him, it was messy looking around the edges but smelled wonderful. He took a bite and was surprised by how good it was. He was going to make a joke about cooking being his thing, or tease her about hiding her chef skills, but instead he just took another bite as she sat down across from him.

Gretchen took a sip of coffee, then undid her hair, and it fell around her shoulders. Jeremy felt an ache in his chest, watching her. He recalled all of the cruel thoughts he'd had about her, the way he'd dismissed her, both in his mind and to Ivy, many times. Now he wanted to apologize, to pull her onto his lap and hold on to her before she noticed what an asshole he'd been. If he could hide his face in her hair, maybe she wouldn't see him for what he was.

"Do you like it?" she asked, smiling.

"Yes, it's perfect," he said.

A million questions were stacking up inside him right now. He'd been so uncurious about her, so oblivious to who she was. He hoped there would be time to ask her everything he wanted to, but instead of starting now, he just said, "Thank you."

JANE

When Jane woke up in the morning, Adam was already gone. He'd slept on the couch, his black duffel bag packed and waiting on the ground beside him, but when she wandered out to the living room there was no sign that he'd ever been here at all. She sat down on the couch, almost expecting the cushion to still be warm, but it was cool and anonymous, and she felt an incredible sadness invade her, a feeling that seemed to drain the blood from her veins, leaving her weak and pale.

Fern and Rocky had spent last night at her parents' house. Her mother was dropping them off this afternoon, but Jane wished they were here right now, sitting beside her. Their busy noise would be a welcome distraction today, and Jane considered going to pick them up early, but she needed to go see Rex and knew she should do that alone.

It was almost 8:00 a.m., but everyone was still asleep, so Jane ate a strawberry yogurt in the kitchen as quietly as possible. Mourning doves sat on the wall outside the window, purring their content-ment, and Jane watched them as she ate, admiring their creamy nutmeg color, their bright eyes and delicate beaks. It occurred to her that this was the first time she'd eaten breakfast by herself in years, and even though she was standing at the sink and it was only yogurt, a peace settled over her watching those birds. She always planned to get up earlier than her children so she could sort out her thoughts and prepare herself for the day ahead, but this required rising before 6:00 a.m., and she'd never been able to do it. Now she saw that it would have been worth the effort. Her thoughts floated slowly through her mind and then organized into recognizable tasks: walk to Rex's and say good-bye, pack your suitcase, hold Ivy and Ramona close, be as kind as possible to your children.

Outside, she walked slowly up the sidewalk, feeling the blood begin to pour back into her limbs as she moved. The sadness was still there, but the hard top of it had lifted off and she felt stronger now, almost calm. Air moved over her bare arms. Sun pushed against her back. The sky was a rich, glittering blue.

Rex's house was familiar to her now, and she crossed the lawn and knocked lightly on the door, then stood waiting. The skateboards had been leaned neatly against the garage door and the lawn was freshly mowed; the concrete steps beneath her feet were scattered with bright grass clippings.

Rex answered the door tying a navy bathrobe at his waist, and Jane felt a flush of embarrassment. "Did I wake you?" she asked.

"No. Just took a shower after I mowed the lawn."

She noticed that his hair was wet, combed back into grooves against his skull. "I just came to say good-bye. My flight leaves tonight."

"Oh," he said, looking down at his bare feet, the palest feet Jane had ever seen. "Well, come in. I just made some coffee."

Sitting at the kitchen table, she sipped coffee from a chipped green mug and looked out the window at the telescope. The beer bottles had been cleared away, and it looked as if the backyard had been newly mowed as well. "You've been busy this morning," she said.

He slid into the chair across from her and followed her gaze. "I couldn't sleep."

They had sat in these exact positions two days ago, but Jane felt even more uncomfortable now than she had then. She wanted to follow him to his bedroom again and crawl beneath those dark blue sheets, but it struck her as a bad idea to push this any further. Tonight, she would fly across the country and, most likely, never see this man again.

"I saw you last night, walking with your husband," he said.

"Oh," she said, keeping her eyes on her hands. "I don't know how we ended up on your street. That was so stupid of me. I'm sorry." She looked up and tried to read his expression but couldn't. He did not seem upset, but possibly quieter than usual, though she wasn't sure. Maybe quiet was his set point, and she hadn't figured that out yet.

"No big deal," he told her.

His steady gaze unnerved her. Flutters of blood moved beneath her skin. The kitchen ticked slowly around them. He reached over and took her hand, and the warmth of his white skin surprised her as it had the first time. She wondered how long she would have to know him before his touch would seem ordinary. A year? Two years?

Jane released his hand, stood up, then walked around the edge of the table and sat down on Rex's lap. He looked surprised, but when she looped her arms around his neck, he circled her waist and pulled her against him. They didn't speak or move for several long minutes, and Jane could feel her body tightening into a single, expectant string. It was true that she may never see this person again, but that didn't really matter. She wanted to have sex with him one more time, to feel that lightness in her body, because it would likely be a long while before she'd feel that light again. She turned her face to kiss him, but he pulled away and gave her a tight-lipped smile.

"I don't think this is a good idea," he said.

"It is. It's a great idea." She smiled, trying to ease him back toward good humor.

He shook his head, then pushed her gently off his lap. Jane stood, looking down at him, deeply embarrassed. "I should go," she said.

"No, I'm sorry." He rose to stand beside her. "It's just . . . I'm sort of a mess still, about Kristina, and sleeping with you is not going to help matters, especially since you're leaving."

"Okay," she said, looking past him to the backyard. She had come to simply say good-bye but now felt as if she might cry. There was a building pressure in her chest, and her throat was raw. She thought of Adam, on the plane right now flying over the desert, then the mountains, then the long, rolling farmlands. The earth beneath his window would be bleak, still mostly hard, vacant soil. The house would be cold when he stepped inside. What kind of person was she to have sent him away with such ease? "I don't know what I'm doing," she told Rex, shaking her head. "I really just came over to say good-bye. And thank you."

"Thank you? For what?"

"Your kindness," she said. "Saturn."

He laughed, then slipped a hand around her waist, tapping his fingers against her lower back. He leaned to kiss her, just once, lightly, then pulled her against him. Jane felt his hard collarbone beneath her cheek. He still smelled of cut grass, despite his shower, and she breathed him in, committing the shape and scent of him to memory. She wondered if she would think of him at all once she was settled into her new apartment back in Madison.

At the door, she told him, "I hope you and Kristina work things out."

He shook his head. "I don't think that's going to happen, but thanks."

"Oh, well." She looked at the ground. "You never know."

Walking across the grass, Jane could feel him watching her from the front step, and she resisted the urge to turn around and wave good-bye one more time. She felt light and heavy at once now, as if her head and torso might float away while her legs trudged, leaden, up the sidewalk. She passed the dull brown homes, cactus gardens, pebbled ground, yellow grass, a lustrous blue birdbath, three tricycles scattered in a driveway. Every detail felt particular to this city, this moment in time. She could no longer recall what the streets looked like in Madison. That life seemed very far away, but she would arrive there tonight and find her car in the airport lot, then drive her children home and tuck them into their beds. Adam would or wouldn't be there, depending on his schedule at work, and she would or wouldn't be happy to see him.

IVY

Ivy was still in her robe when the doorbell rang. Frank was already off playing basketball, Jane had disappeared again, and Ramona had spent the night at the Golden Nugget. Lucky had just been fed and was now asleep in her arms, so Ivy set him gently in his crib, then went to get the door.

Her mother stood on the front step, looking much older, but still essentially the same. Those eyes of hers, usually hidden behind sunglasses, were heavy-lidded now, but still gray-blue, still slightly mournful. She was wearing an olive green blouse tucked into a black skirt, black hose, low heels, and Ivy thought she looked as if she were here for a job interview instead of a reunion.

"Ivy," her mother said, and her voice was exactly as Ivy remembered it, airy and tender. The sound made her recoil. It was too familiar, and this somehow made it worse.

Ivy didn't speak, but nodded a somber greeting, and they stood staring at each other until Ivy gestured for her to come inside.

Her mother wandered slowly through the front room, touching objects—an open book on the table, the back cushions of the couch, the rim of a lamp. The origami bird that had been thrown over the wall on Tuesday—a decade ago it now seemed—sat on the coffee table, and her mother picked it up and smiled. "Oh, I'm so glad you got this. I learned how to make these at the senior center in Phoenix."

So the bird was from her mother too. Ivy hadn't considered that possibility and this new information caught her off-guard, making her feel even stranger than she already did. "Senior center?" Ivy asked.

"I work at one, as an activities coordinator, but I guess I'm old enough now just to hang out there," she laughed and set the bird back on the table.

"And the New York piggy bank? That was you too, right?"

She nodded. "For Lucas."

So she did know about Lucky, and she somehow knew his name. "He's asleep," Ivy said.

"Can I just take a peek?"

Ivy considered this, then shook her head. She had thought she'd want to show him off, but now her main instinct was to protect him, to shield him from this woman who could not truly be trusted.

Her mother's face fell. Then she brightened, brushing off her skirt and smiling. "I lived in New York for a couple of years. Everyone says you have to live there at least once if you're an artist, but it's so dirty. And expensive. I didn't really see the point. Phoenix suits me much better."

Ivy wanted to ask where else she had been all these years but couldn't bring herself to do it. In fact, she didn't really want to know. She had expected something to open up inside at the sight of her mother, for forgiveness to move through her. Instead, each detail of her mother's years away etched a new groove into Ivy's skin, leaving her raw and wounded. "I think you should leave," she said. "I shouldn't have let you in at all."

Her mother turned quickly toward her. "Leave?"

Ivy nodded. "I don't need a mother anymore, but thanks for coming." She walked to the front door and opened it, then stood waiting for her to follow. She felt surprisingly calm, though a throbbing was beginning in her head, right at the base of her skull.

"Oh, Ivy," her mother said, rushing over to her. "I should have come sooner, I know that. I've been here all week just spying on you really, too afraid to say anything. I'm such a coward." A deep crease formed between her brows, and she reached out and lay a hand on Ivy's arm.

"I don't care about this week, or about any of it. I just want you out of here."

"Don't say that. It's not true. I know it's not true." Her mother's voice rose and faltered.

Ivy kept her eyes focused on the wall behind her mother's head. She wouldn't look at her face again, not ever. "It is true," Ivy told her.

Ivy felt a squeeze on her forearm, pleading, then her mother released her arm and and walked over to sit down on the couch.

For some reason, Ivy hadn't expected resistance, and she found she wasn't prepared to physically remove her mother from the house. She considered leaving, just getting in the car and driving far away while her mother sat there, but the notion of dragging Lucky from sleep to escape his grandmother struck her as a bad plan. Instead, she walked through the room and outside, then sat under the umbrella by the pool.

Her mother, to Ivy's surprise, did not follow her. Turning, she could just make out her form, still on the couch in the living room. Soon, somebody else would come home and find her sitting there and Ivy sitting out here, but she didn't care. It was peaceful beside the pool. A cool breeze ruffled the turquoise water. A pair of hummingbirds swung past on a current of air, then hovered in front of the trumpet flowers to drink. She would just wait this out; it would be simple.

The remains of yesterday's party were still in evidence around her, so Ivy rose and started cleaning up. She may as well do something while she waited for her mother to leave. There were plastic cups on the ground and empty plates covered with the empanada crumbs. Ivy gathered these items slowly, one at a time, and threw them in the trash can under the overhang. The job would go much faster with a garbage bag, but she wasn't going back inside unless she absolutely had to.

She listened for Lucky as she worked, willing him to stay asleep until her mother was gone. The idea of her mother holding on to

her son filled Ivy with dread. She imagined a strange poison seeping out of her arms and into Lucky, whole decades of stored-up love
that would have turned sour, curdled with age—the dark underside
of love, which Ivy knew to be black and sticky with despair. She
glanced toward the living room to make sure her mother hadn't left
her spot to wander the house and was relieved to see her still sitting
on the couch.

A petit four gleamed beneath one of the palm trees, and Ivy
retrieved it and tossed it in the trash. There were two more intact
cakes behind the other palm, and she wondered if one of the kids
had flung them here. She was tossing away the last one when she
heard a voice behind her. "Let me help you."

Her mother had already started gathering cups from beneath
a chair. The sight filled Ivy with unexpected rage. "Please go away,
Astrid." She hoped using her name would snap her into self-
awareness, make her understand she wasn't welcome.

But she turned to Ivy with a smile and said. "I'll just help you
with this, then be on my way. I promise."

"I don't want your help." Ivy stepped closer. Her anger must
have been evident, because Astrid backed away, no longer smiling.
Ivy moved toward her again, and again her mother backed up.

They were right next to the pool now, and Astrid turned and
looked down into its clear depths. "You always wanted a pool. I'm
so glad you have one, finally."

Her casual tone enraged Ivy further. "You don't know anything
about what I did or didn't want."

"Yes, I remember distinctly your saying how much you'd love
a pool. You were always such a good little swimmer. You always
begged me to jump in that awful fountain at our building, and I
had to hold you back."

She laughed lightly, as if this was a fond memory, and Ivy could
no longer contain herself. Without thinking, she stepped closer
and pressed both palms against Astrid's chest. It was soft beneath

her hands, the blouse silky and fine. Ivy took notice of these details as if from a great distance, then gathered her strength and shoved her mother into the pool.

The look of shock on her face as she hit the water cut a hole inside of Ivy, and into that hole poured all the worry she'd kept at bay for the last twenty years, the years during which she'd thought her mother must be dead. The different methods of her death—all vividly imagined—seemed to destroy a part of Ivy each time she considered what might have happened. She had never stayed away or silent for so long. If only she had sent a postcard, or called just once, Ivy might have made it through intact, but now she was walled up, too rigid to accept anything resembling kindness. She had to protect her son. That was the main thing. She must protect her son from this person flailing in the water at her feet.

"Ivy," another voice called to her from the doorway. She turned and found Jane, running toward the pool. "Ivy, what happened?"

The presence of her friend brought her back to herself, slowly at first as the colors of the trees and sky shifted into focus—everything was so bright—then with a rush of horror. Her mother couldn't swim.

Jane jumped into the water, fully clothed, then began dragging Astrid, flailing and frantic, back to the edge. Ivy got down on her knees and reached for her mother's hands. Somehow she found them, then pulled as hard as she could to get her safely back up onto the deck.

Jane lifted herself out easily and knelt beside Ivy. Astrid was sitting up with her knees to her chest, sputtering and coughing, but she seemed to be fine. How long had she floundered in the deep end before Jane broke Ivy's trance? It couldn't have been more than thirty seconds. Astrid's green blouse was suctioned to her body with water, and Ivy took in the dark shape of her bra beneath it, the rolls of fat at her waist. Her shoes had come off in the water, and through the dark hose Ivy noticed that her toes were gnarled and bumpy, an old woman's toes. Ivy tried to absorb every detail of her aging body, hoping it would help her to find an ounce of compassion, enough to allow her to apologize for pushing her into the pool at least, but nothing came. This woman felt like a stranger to her now, worse than a stranger—she would feel compassion for a person she'd never met—she was an enemy.

"I'll get some towels," Jane said, rising.

"Okay," Ivy said, still kneeling close to her mother. She searched her face, absorbing the lines and hollows, the age spots and smudged eye makeup. Her blonde hair was sealed tightly to her skull now, two strands striping her forehead. Her eyes were closed, and Ivy watched the twitching of her thin lids, spanned with fine blue veins. When she opened them, Ivy flinched back, as if she'd been struck.

"I know you don't understand why I left, and I can't really explain it, but I don't blame you for hating me. I deserve it."

Ivy nodded, unable to speak. It was true. She hated this woman.

Jane appeared and crouched down to hand Astrid a large, yellow towel. "I took some clothes out of your bedroom, Ivy," she said. "I hope that's all right." She passed Astrid a pair of gray sweatpants and a pink T-shirt.

"I don't care," Ivy said.

Astrid accepted the clothes then pushed herself up to standing. "I'll wash them and get them back to you tomorrow. I promise."

Ivy shook her head. "I don't want them back."

"It's no problem, really."

"Please," Ivy said. "Keep them."

"I'll just change in the bathroom," she said, then walked across the pool deck and disappeared through the sliding glass doors.

Jane retrieved the pool net and worked for several long minutes to get Astrid's shoes back on dry land, plunking one black heel beside Ivy, then another. "I guess those are ruined," Jane said. Her clothes were sealed to her skin with water too, but she looked agile and lean, as if her black tank top and denim shorts were part of her skin.

"C'mon," Jane said, taking Ivy's arm. They went inside and sat down on the couch, waiting for Astrid to finish and leave. Ivy expected some sort of admonishment from Jane for pushing her own mother into the pool, but they sat in companionable silence, Jane's damp arm linked through hers.

When Astrid returned from the bathroom, she looked better. Her thin hair had already begun to dry, and Ivy's clothes fit her just right. Her old clothes were in a plastic bag at her side. "I guess I'll be going," she said.

Jane stood and walked to the door, and Ivy stayed on the couch for a long moment, then rose and joined them. Astrid tried to hand Ivy a card, but Ivy wouldn't hold out her hand to receive it. She understood she was being childish, but she was using all her strength to simply stand here, and accepting what looked like a business card was more than she could handle just now.

"It's where I work, in Phoenix. In case you ever want to get in touch. I plan on staying there for as long as they'll have me." She smiled weakly and shrugged, but Ivy just shook her head.

Jane reached out and took the card, and Astrid looked extremely grateful. "Thank you, dear," she said softly.

"Oh, wait, your shoes," Jane said, and raced outside.

"You know, being a mother isn't easy," she told Ivy softly. "You'll understand one day."

Ivy just shook her head. "I'll never understand."

Then Jane was beside them with the shoes, which she passed over to Astrid. She looked at them for a second, then slipped them into the plastic bag with her clothes, and turned to go. "Good-bye," she told Ivy, then stood searching her face, waiting, Ivy knew, for an offering.

"Good-bye," Ivy said.

Her mother shrugged, then walked out the door, and Jane closed it behind her.

REX

Even though he knew he'd done the right thing by not sleeping with Jane, he now deeply regretted it. The house gaped empty around him, echoing, cluttered. His unmade bed was piled with sheets and last night's clothes. He sat on the edge and pulled the clothes back on over his newly washed body, not caring that they smelled of cut grass and sweat.

Kristina would be here in an hour or so with the girls, but until then he needed to occupy himself or else he'd find an excuse to run around the corner and talk Jane into coming back, which he didn't think would be very difficult since he was the one who had rejected her.

He fished his baseball mitt and ball out of the hall closet then went out on the front lawn and tossed the ball in the air as high as he could, catching it neatly on its way back to earth. The sound of the ball hitting his mitt had its usual soothing power, and soon he began to feel at ease in his own body. He should really start playing again, just for fun. It wouldn't be that difficult to find a team. It would likely work better to mend his fractured soul than any church, though he was still considering that too. Baseball. Church. Nursing school. These were definitely the building blocks of one possible life.

His neighbor's door opened, and Rosemary wandered out onto her lawn and stood watching him, her arms crossed over her chest. He could see from her expression that she wanted to say something, and he steeled himself for some criticism that hadn't yet occurred to him: the ball hitting his mitt was too loud, he'd done a poor job mowing his lawn, his daughters made too much of a ruckus playing in the driveway.

She walked slowly to the edge of her own grass then stood watching him. She wasn't smiling, but her expression was not unfriendly, so he decided to stop tossing the ball and see what she had to say. It was the polite thing to do.

Up close she smelled flowery, and her skin was thickly powdered. "How's your daughter's finger?"

"Fine. Almost healed. Thanks again for helping me out."

She waved a hand through the air, dismissing her role. "So how are you holding up anyway?"

The question was so unexpected that he laughed. "Me? I'm all right, I guess. I've had better years."

"My husband and I divorced a long time ago," she told him. "Before you moved in. It was one of the most awful years of my life, but better than the two years before that when all we did was scream at each other." She tucked a strand of gray hair behind her ear, revealing a silver hoop. "He lives nearby, and I still see him at the grocery store once in a while, or sometimes I have to go to a big event with him like our daughter's wedding, and every time I'm surprised that we were married for so many years. Now, he just seems like any other kindly older gentleman I'd meet. There's nothing special about him anymore." She shrugged and looked up at him. "Maybe there never was."

He nodded, aware that she was trying to help Rex by telling him this story, but it only saddened him further. In twenty years, at Polly's wedding, would Kristina just be another face in the crowd? "How long were you married?"

"Let's see. Twenty-two years. Funny, I've been divorced now the same number of years we were married. I hadn't realized that." She laughed and the sound was surprisingly girlish. "I've had a few boyfriends since then, but no one who really stuck. But you're younger than I was, and you're a man. You'll find someone, like that." She snapped her fingers.

"I don't think so," he told her. "Actually, I'm not sure if I want to. I really loved Kristina. Still do, I guess."

"I know," she said softly.

Her words seemed to touch his skin, to open a panel in his chest. Breathing was difficult for a minute, and then easier, as air flowed into his lungs in a rush. "Do you want to toss the ball?" he asked her.

She laughed again and shrugged. "Sure, why not? Just don't break *my* finger."

He handed her his mitt, then backed across his lawn to the driveway. She looked funny wearing a baseball mitt with her flowered housedress and white cardigan, but she was smiling gamely, her mitt lifted to her chest. Rex tossed a ball to her underhand and she caught it, then flung it back. It curved out to the side and then into his waiting hands, hitting his palms with more force than he'd anticipated. The slight stinging felt good, just right, and he tossed it back again and she caught it.

The skin on his cheeks and forehead was beginning to burn, but he didn't want to quit the game for sunscreen. Rosemary dropped a couple of balls, and he did too, but for the most part they kept a steady rhythm. She seemed to be enjoying herself and paused the game to remove her sweater and toss it on the grass. "You're good," he called over to her.

"Thank you," she trilled back. "It's been a long time."

Kristina would be here soon with Polly and Callie, and Rex wondered how she would react to this strange game of catch on her old front lawn. Likely, it would irritate her. She'd never much cared for Rosemary's nosiness, even before their fights and the woman's subsequent admonishments had begun. He guessed she may still be mad about the way he'd talked to Peter the other night, or the fact that he'd been sitting across from her house last night watching the windows—he was sure Ginger had told her, despite her promise not to—and he decided he would apologize for whatever he'd done wrong, if need be. There was no use in causing more discord. It would not make anything better.

He saw Kristina's car round the corner at the far end of the street, her small face above the steering wheel. As she drew closer, he could make out his daughters in the backseat, both of their blonde heads bobbing to music. He would pitch the tent in the backyard tonight, he decided, and they could grill steaks and roast marshmallows, then curl up together under the tent's orange dome and tell ghost stories. He would tell them about the time he took their mother down into the cave, deep beneath the shell shop, and how he was certain he'd seen a dark shape lurking beneath the water.

RAMONA

"So I told Nash about the baby, and he was actually pretty excited." They were poolside, sipping iced tea under the yellow umbrella. Rocky and Fern were having one last swim before the drive to the airport.

"You told him before you told *me?*" Ivy asked.

"You already knew," Ramona said.

"That's true. I did." She smiled and leaned back, crossing her legs.

"And he *is* the father," Jane added.

"Okay, okay, I forgive you," Ivy said with a laugh. "I'm happy for you both."

Water sprayed over the edge and hit Ramona's bare legs. "Sorry, Aunt Ramona," Rocky called to her. He'd just begun calling her that, an hour ago, and now he was leaving. She waved and smiled to show him it was fine, then watched as he paddled over to the steps where Fern was playing in a pink inner tube.

Ramona had slept at the Golden Nugget last night, going over everything in her mind. Before falling asleep, she'd begun to write a song in her head that she managed to remember this morning. It was about the drive home she would make today, that long road through the desert, the miles of empty land flanking Interstate 15, which were too harsh to support much life. The words weren't exactly right yet, but the image was there: her car cleaving a line through that still and barren land, while a new life grew inside her. It would be difficult to craft without sounding too sentimental, but she would try. It was something to work on.

"Why aren't we swimming?" she asked her friends. "It's getting hot."

"Jane has to leave in half an hour," Ivy said.

"My suit's packed," Jane added with a shrug. "Besides, I've already been in once today."

"I still can't believe you pushed her in the pool," Ramona said, trying to suppress a laugh.

"It isn't funny," Ivy said, setting her lips in a tight line. "She could have drowned."

Jane nodded, as if agreeing, then broke into a grin. "It's a little bit funny."

"You would have pulled her out if Jane hadn't been there," Ramona told Ivy. "She would not have drowned."

"You don't know that," Ivy said.

"Yes," Ramona said firmly. "I do."

Ivy shook her head, then pressed her lips together. Ramona could tell that she was trying not to smile. "It was an awful thing to do," Ivy said.

"Well, she sort of deserved it. One shove in the pool for twenty years of absence? That seems more than fair," Jane said, nudging Ivy with an elbow.

Finally, Ivy allowed a laugh. "Well, when you put it that way."

"Do you think you'll ever call her?" Jane asked.

"I don't think so," Ivy said. "But maybe. You never know. I do like knowing where she is, for some reason, even if I never speak to her again. At least I know she's okay."

"Let's at least put our feet in," Ramona said, rising from her chair and walking to the water's edge. Frank had cleaned the pool half an hour ago, and its blue depths were pristine and inviting. Ivy appeared at her elbow and looked down into the water too. "You should stay another night, with us," Ivy said.

"I can't," Ramona said. "I've got a show tomorrow night. Besides, I'm sort of homesick."

Lucky cried out then, from the bedroom, and Jane leapt up. "I'll get him."

Ramona and Ivy watched her disappear through the sliding glass doors, then sat down on the edge and dropped their feet in the cool water.

"Do you think she's okay?" Ivy asked.

"I think so," Ramona said. "She looks happy."

"She does, doesn't she?" Ivy mused.

Jane appeared in the doorway, holding Lucky in her arms, then walked over and handed him to Ivy before settling down beside Ramona and dipping her own feet into the water. Ramona thought about how long she'd known Jane and Ivy and how much longer she hoped to know them. Once her son or daughter was born, she would travel to see each of them more often; maybe she'd bring Nash along next time too.

"Come in," Fern called to them now, waving from the circle of her inner tube.

"Yeah, come in," Rocky added, sending a splash toward their shins that fell short of hitting their skin.

Ivy looked at Ramona, then Jane, before she shrugged and slipped into the waist-deep water. She was wearing a blue sundress, and the skirt floated out around her in the pool, its color darkening to a deep lapis. Lucky was cradled against her chest, his feet submerged, and he squirmed in her arms until she lifted him up and around so that he was facing everyone. This seemed to make him happy.

Jane went next, slipping in up to her middle then diving forward, all the way under, before surfacing with a grin. "It feels great. Your turn, Ramona."

Ramona shook her head. It had been her suggestion that they swim, and now she couldn't bring herself to join them. She was wearing the shorts and tank top she'd planned to wear driving home, but her clothes would dry quickly. It wasn't that.

She placed her hands on her stomach, watching her friends and their children circle around her. There seemed to be an invisible line between her and the people in the pool, and once she crossed it, there would be no going back. She saw herself driving home again, her car the only one on that long stretch of desert. There was a certain insulated comfort in the image.

"C'mon," Jane said, waving her in. "What's the holdup?"

"I think I'll just sit this one out," she said.

"Ramona," Ivy scolded. "It's your last day here. Play along."

She was beginning to straighten her spine at their urging, preparing to lift her legs out of the water and go sit at the table alone. It would be easier to return with a baby she decided. A child could be a shield, a buffer of sorts.

Ramona had one leg out of the water when she felt small slippery hands wrap around her other calf. It was Rocky, attempting to pull her in. His touch was so unexpected, so different from the touch of a grown person, that she relaxed for a moment. Then there was a yank of unexpected strength, and she was in the water, completely submerged.

She stayed under for a long second, looking up at the quivering surface of blue layered with the drifting shapes of palm trees, the sky behind them, slightly lighter than the water. It was warmer in the pool than she'd realized and peaceful. The silence of the water was thick, the voices of Jane and Ivy moving on top of it. Rocky's legs kicked beside her as he treaded water, most likely worried that she would be angry with him for pulling her in, but she wasn't. She wasn't angry at all.

Ramona touched her stomach again, then pushed up and surfaced beside her friends.

Acknowledgments

Thank you to my father, Paul, and my mother, Juliet, who have always been encouraging about my writing, even when it manifested itself as tawdry teenage poetry.

Much praise and gratefulness is due to several of my writing friends who helped me in the early or late stages of this manuscript—and believe me, there were many stages: Michelle Wildgen, Guy Thorvaldsen, Ron Kuka, Heather Lee Schroeder, Andrew McCuaig, and Tenaya Darlington.

Many thanks to my wise and tireless agent, Rayhané Sanders, and to my editor at Skyhorse, Maxim Brown, for believing in this book.

Finally, thank you to my husband, John; my son, Malcolm; and my daughter, Lux. I'm so lucky that you're my family.